LOVE IN BLOOM

Everywhere you go it seems that love is in the air. Outside, the temperature might be cold, but some of Arabesque's most popular authors are ready to warm your heart with tales of lost love, passion, and happily ever after.

LOVE IN BLOOM

FRANCINE CRAFT

LINDA HUDSON-SMITH

JANICE SIMS

ARABESQUE
BOOKS

BET Publications, LLC
http://www.bet.com
http://www.arabesquebooks.com

ARABESQUE BOOKS are published by

BET Publications, LLC
c/o BET BOOKS
One BET Plaza
1900 W Place NE
Washington, DC 20018-1211

All Kensington Titles, Imprints, and Distributed Lines are available at special quantity discounts for bulk purchases for sales promotions, premiums, fund-raising, and educational or institutional use. Special book excerpts or customized printings can also be created to fit specific needs. For details, write or phone the office of the Kensington special sales manager: Kensington Publishing Corp., 850 Third Avenue, New York, NY 10022, attn: Special Sales Department, Phone: 1-800-221-2647.

First Printing: January 2002
10 9 8 7 6 5 4 3 2 1

Printed in the United States of America

CONTENTS

LOVE'S MASQUERADE

Francine Craft

To Myles—a very sweet man.
To June M. Bennett, Mary Brown,
and Delores Sumbler—great friends.

AUTHOR'S NOTE

Celebration of Valentine's Day began in the early fifteenth century. It was connected to several priests with the surname of Valentine. Early legend states that February fourteenth was held to be the first day that birds mated. In the early stages it was a religious affair, but it quickly evolved into a day for romantics. Valentine's Day is now celebrated all over the world with exchanges of gifts and much love and merriment.

ONE

It was cool for mid-October, but Maya Williams was fast getting hot under the collar. Standing at the counter of Personal Printers in Washington, D.C.'s L'Enfant Plaza, her annoyance was growing.

The young male clerk argued with her in a supercilious way. "Ma'am, I think you're going to have crowded copy. A lot of this could be left off—and should be."

Maya sighed with exasperation. "That's why I asked for help. I'd like to see the whole range of copy laid out."

"Well, I don't know," the young man insisted. "If you ask me—"

He was cut short by a sinewy man at least six foot two who came to them. "Let me handle this, Mac," he said smoothly. He smiled at Maya with big, perfect, white teeth, and pointed at a wall plaque behind him. "We mean this, you know. We *do* aim to please.

She felt a surge of electricity pass between them, and for a moment Maya couldn't get her breath. He was something short of a god, more deeply attractive than handsome, with close-cropped, curly jet-black hair, a long face, and humorous dark black eyes. He raised heavy, smooth black eyebrows at her.

"Now, ma'am, let me ask you to start over. My young assistant is a brilliant guy, but he sometimes thinks he knows best." He was trying not to stare at her, but her healthy black hair done in three lengths of braids ending in black beads fascinated him. The round face with its brown eyes and sculpted mouth and naturally arched eyebrows over long, soot-black lashes gave her a piquant look. Her lissome body in its heather-lavender coat dress was a dancer's body. He was thirty-four; he'd place her at about thirty-one. She was cool, with banked fires; yeah, he'd bet on it.

Maya flushed, her dark honey skin growing warm. She wanted to say something, but her stomach was fluttering and his eyes were magnetizing her.

He stuck out his hand. "Chris St. John, owner of Personal Printers. We aim to please, like the sign says."

Her hand clung to his a little too long and his eyes narrowed.

"You've changed," she managed to get out. "Remember high school? Dunbar? Are you *that* Chris St. John?"

"One and the same. You've changed, but I'd know you anywhere, Maya Williams. You moved away in your sophomore year, left a lot of guys heartbroken."

"I don't think so, and how would you have time to know?" She chuckled. "As I remember, you were one of the players, girls coming out of your ears."

"And you were a tease. I let others believe I was a player. I had a lot of other things on my mind."

She remembered. He had been a senior when she moved with her parents to New Orleans. He was friendly with her, pleasant, but that was all.

He grinned. "I gave myself one more year back then. When you were a senior, I'd be in college, and I planned to make my moves on you."

They each searched the other's hand for wedding rings. Neither wore one.

"Nice shop you've got here," she said. "The printer I've been using didn't seem capable of handling an invitational brochure for our Sweetheart's Ball on Valentine's Day and some brochures for my shop."

Chris glanced at the shop copy. "So you own a health food store."

She nodded. Healing Hands. It was her pride and joy.

"Let's sit and talk about this," he said. Damn it, something about her turned him on, sky-high. He led her to a nest of ivory leather chairs and a big glass cocktail table. They sat side by side. As his hand brushed hers, she felt another jolt of electricity and caught her breath. He looked at her levelly, denying nothing.

"Are you married?" he asked suddenly, not meaning to ask it. Some women didn't wear their wedding rings.

She shook her head. Having known him gave her license. "Are you married?"

"Not anymore."

Long fall afternoon rays of sunshine came through the plate-glass windows as they talked about the copy.

"You've already got the shop brochure copy laid out very well. True, the ball copy is a bit jumbled. What do you want to accomplish here?"

She marshaled her thoughts for a few minutes, more aware of him than ever. Finally she said slowly, "Two friends and I, well, all of us own shops. Lillian has a flower shop over in Georgetown. Dosha has a scarf and leather shop on K Street and my shop is on Connecticut Avenue just beyond Dupont Circle.

"We've given this ball for three years and it has been a great success. This year, the *Post* and the *Washington Informer* want to cover it and we want something special. Our theme is the Wondrous World of Love."

"Sounds very interesting. Go on."

She spread her hands. "Valentine's Day is celebrated the world over, pretty much the same, with flowers, candy, gifts, dances." She glanced over to him. His eyes on her were warm, beguiling. She crossed her ankles in her flattering backless tan suede shoes. "Want to hear more?"

"I do."

"Well, Valentine's Day's been around since the beginning of the fifteenth century. From what we find now, there was a priest and a bishop, both named Valentine, and seven or eight or more others with the same last name. At first, there were religious overtones to overcome the pagan side. All manner of customs grew up. If you dreamed of your opposite sex the night before Valentine's Day, that would be your husband or wife. Also, the first person you saw that Valentine's Day morning might be your mate. And . . ." She looked down quickly.

"And?" he asked supportively.

"Well, from the beginning it was held that February fourteenth was selected because that was the day birds began to mate each season."

His blood was racing now. What in the hell was going on with him and this woman?

She laughed then, her crystal-clear voice tinkling. "That's when the old priests demanded that young people choose a saint to be close to on Valentine's Day, and not a sweetheart."

"Spoilsports. How long did that last?"

"Not very long. We've had what we have today for a very long time."

"Valentine's Day is my birthday," he said softly.

"Oh!" she exclaimed. "What a wonderful day to be born on. Mine's January the twenty-eighth. We're both Aquarians."

"A good sign." His eyes twinkled.

He wanted to ask her questions about herself. He wanted to tell her what his life had been like, and sadness closed in on him like a vise. She saw the look and her heart went out to him.

A leggy young girl of ten or so came in shyly. "Excuse me," she said, "but, Dad, I need the purple marker in your shirt pocket."

He introduced them and as the pair shook hands, the child's boneless flesh seemed to melt into Maya's. She was a lovely child with almond-colored skin and thick black braids.

"Janna," Maya said. "What a lovely name."

"Thank you. I'm busy drawing. I'm going to go now."

Maya's eyes followed her across the gleaming hardwood floor until she was out of sight.

"What a lovely child," she said.

"Do you have children?"

"No." He noted the shadow that passed over her face. "No. I have no children. Is she your only child?"

"Yes." His voice grew cool. "Now, back to business. I'm going to spend a while with your ball copy and come up with ways to give us space, beauty *and* information. I guarantee you I'll make this a special invitation package, something your guests will all remember. Already, I see separating the invitation itself from the information you have here and using that information wisely. You've got a great idea. I think we can do business. I'd certainly like to try."

Maya stuck out her hand. He was such a smooth operator, and yet it went deeper than that. As a man, he was no flash in the pan, but he was sophisticated. Was he a player? He was attractive enough. This time, *his* hand lingered, clasping hers.

"Why don't I give you a call tomorrow?" he asked. "I've added two new hires, one of whom is the young man you first talked with. Training can be hell. Do you have that problem in your shop?"

"Oh, yes, in the past, but now . . ." Her eyes sparkled. "I've got a manager anybody else would kill for and a crackerjack clerk and gofer. But I'll tell you, it hasn't always been that way."

"Hmmm. A couple of my people are very good. We've landed a big government contract and it's running me ragged."

Maya drew a swift breath. "Then you're probably cutting back on other work. You've got a long time with this, but it's an ornery task. I'd understand if you couldn't put much time on this project."

He rocked a moment or two. "Nothing doing. I need something that touches my soul, and this does. You're going to have masks and a ballroom? Beautiful decorations? That kind of thing? I love pomp and circumstance."

"You're right on the mark. The ball is from ten to two in the morning. We unmask at midnight. This year we have a huge champagne bowl." She paused. He certainly had gotten into the spirit of things. "You're welcome to come, and bring a guest."

He started to explain that there was no guest he wanted to bring. Stella, his ex-wife, would have been delighted to go, but Stella lived on Diamond Point Island in the Caribbean and he didn't intend to find someone new for a very long time.

"That's kind of you," he said. "I'll consider it."

She felt a little nonplussed now. Was she coming on to him? Did he *think* she was coming on to him? *Coming on to him,* she chided herself. She was swallowing him whole.

She laughed nervously. "I don't want to seem too forward, but I feel I know you."

"I don't think you could be too forward," he said gallantly. "You're a warm, giving woman, and I wish I'd met someone like you years ago, before it was too late."

Alarm bells went off in her head. What was he talking about? Well, she wouldn't find out today anyway. She was going to get out of here before she made a fool of herself flirting with this man.

TWO

After Maya left, Chris paced the length of his customer area. Her light, spicy, floral scent stayed with him. It had been ages since he'd particularly noticed a woman's perfume, and he felt both happy and deeply bothered. He knew he wanted to see her again and he wished he didn't. His heart had been ripped out with his divorce two years ago and he wondered if he would ever be ready for love again.

Maya. Sure, he'd thought her pretty in high school, although he was three years her senior. She'd sure developed into a sterling woman. Now he cautioned himself. Maybe she was a heller. Looks could be deceiving; Stella, his ex-wife's looks certainly had been. Stella had turned out to be a regular ballcrusher.

"Dad, you look happy and sad. How d'you *do* that?"

Chris laughed at his little girl and pinched her cheek as she ran up to him. "You'll find out when you grow up, munchkin."

"Okay. That lady you were talking to had pretty braids. She's nice."

"Just like you've got pretty braids, lovely brown skin, and you're nice.

The little girl giggled. "You're sweet, Daddy."

As the bells to the shop tinkled to let employees know they had a customer, Chris sat down, then got up again.

"Hey, buddy," a deep bass voice said. "Where's my welcome wagon?"

"I need something to drive you away," Chris teased.

Chris exchanged high-fives with a medium-height, very dark-skinned, handsome man in a police uniform. A sergeant. Walter Hampton.

"I'm glad you're back in town, Hamp. I missed you."

"Yeah, I missed you and the kid, too. Job's been running me ragged. I sure wish the perps would declare a field day."

Janna frowned, tossing her black braids. "You're talking funny, Uncle Hamp. What's a perp?"

Hamp's laughter rumbled in his chest. "You're not old enough to understand. That's shorthand for *perpetrator*, someone who does wrong things and hurts people, or steals their property."

Janna nodded. Hamp watched the little girl leave and fondly wished he were her real uncle. He had come to love the child.

"How's business?" Hamp asked as they sat down.

"It couldn't be better," Chris declared. "Tell me all you know about Valentine's Day.

"Valentine's Day? Buddy, I've been a lonely man since my divorce three years ago. I've wined them and dined them. . . . He shrugged. "A couple of women have sent me valentines, but I didn't send them one because I didn't want them getting the wrong idea."

"I know what you mean." Chris reflected that in the coming years he would be like Hamp, alone, except that he had Janna to raise, and that tickled his very heart.

"You should have come a little earlier," Chris said. "A woman came by with shop copy and Valentine's Day copy she wants run. Did you know February fourteenth is the first day birds mate for a given year?"

"Say *what?* Man, what are you on these days?"

Chris laughed. "It's thought to be true. Celebration goes all the way back to the fifteenth century. I knew this woman in high school. She moved away."

Hamp narrowed his eyes and looked at his buddy. "She's affecting you, partner. You're kind of lit up."

"You're imagining things."

But Hamp didn't think he was imagining things and he hurt for his friend. He had been the one who'd seen Chris sick with grief day after day, night after night, the one who'd nursed him out of drinking binges when he'd almost lost his shop. A fitness buff, Chris had slacked off and lost much of his zest for living. Stella had meant everything to him. Losing her had nearly taken him under. But his love for his little girl had helped. It was a solace, too, that the judge had ruled that he keep Janna during the school year and she went to stay with Stella during the summer.

Now things were so different. In a little less than two years, the drinking was well under control and he was running again. Chris was beginning to laugh again, and business at the print shop was going over the top.

Chris's thoughts were remarkably like Hamp's. Every time he got close to a woman, alarm bells went off. And yes, he, too, had sent no valentines since his divorce from Stella.

The two men went out to the printing plant where machines hummed busily. Employees moved briskly. Chris laughed, about nothing. He felt happy. Printer's ink was in his blood. He'd earned a master printer's certificate and a business degree at Tuskegee and picked up an MBA at the University of Alabama. He liked working with print, liked the way raw thoughts and dreams became reality on paper. Now he shrugged. Stella had wanted something better, higher for herself. He made a good living; she had wanted a grand one.

She'd found the kind of man she wanted when she went on vacation without him to Diamond Point, an island in the Caribbean. The man still hadn't married her, but she hung on.

He remembered those tormented nights after she had told him it was over. She hadn't even tried to be kind. "He's a once-in-a-lifetime find for me," she'd said. "Maybe one day you'll find someone to take my place."

Chris kept glancing at the telephone and touched the wireless phone in his green smock pocket.

"Why don't you let me take you and Janna out to dinner?" Hamp said. "Since it's Mrs. Nickens's night off, you won't want to cook."

Chris shook his head. "No. She's taking a different night off this week. Give me a rain check."

"Sure. The way you're cleaning up here, government contracts and all, you can buy me a month of dinners."

"Police pay isn't lagging behind much these days."

"It ain't in your class."

"You'd never swap, would you now?"

Hamp laughed. "No. At least we've both got work we love. That's something."

Yeah, Chris thought, it was something, but not enough. He pushed a stray thought of Stella from his mind and brought in thoughts of Maya. Meeting her again was like finding a part of him he'd liked very much and lost.

On Connecticut Avenue near Dupont Circle, Maya walked into her health food store, Healing Hands. She always felt a burst of pride at the interior that was pine paneled and done in shades of ivory and deep blue. She had had counters installed with high-backed stools where people could sit and decide what they wanted. Several deep blue cushioned plastic chairs were placed about, inviting comfort.

It was late afternoon and just now the well-stocked store was empty of customers. There would be an after-work rush because she carried ready-to-cook health food dinners and some other foods. A devotee of her own health foods, her sparkling health proclaimed that she practiced what she preached.

Clara Jakes, a superbly groomed, middle-aged woman came from the stockroom. She put her head to one side.

"How'd the visit to the printer's go? Do we have Valentine's Day wrapped up for our ball?"

Maya found herself flushing. "Well," she said quickly, "if the printer's cooperation has anything to do with it, we'll make out like gangsters. He's not just going to cooperate, he's *collaborating* with me. Oh, Clara, this is the first time we've had the ball at Wilson's. I'm excited."

"You're excited, all right. Did some hunk whistle at you?"

Maya threw back her head, laughing. "No such luck." Then she sobered a bit. "Actually, the printer turns out to be someone I knew at Dunbar when I lived here as a girl."

"Tied up, no doubt. Aren't all the men in D.C. taken?"

"Seems like it. That's all right with me. I'm not looking. It was just nice to run into a man who seems truly friendly."

Her voice had gone wistful and Clara glanced at her sharply.

Clara laughed hollowly. "I'm looking and I've been looking for some time. I'm fifty-four and I may throw in the towel after this season."

"You have several male friends."

"Who borrow money, eat my cooking, don't take me out, whistle long and low at jailbait teenagers on sitcoms, and other things I'm tired of. Take my advice. Rope this guy, tie him up tight, and lock him in if he's all you say he is."

"You're not talking like a feminist."

"I'm talking like a *feeling* feminist. Listen, love, I'm putting money into a ball gown you wouldn't believe. I've read that material you've gathered for the brochures that go with the invitations and I'm real hopeful."

Clara's hair was curly black and her eyes in her cinnamon-colored face were green and brown. From the beginning she had been Maya's treasured right arm. Clara had one son she doted on and who had been in trouble more than once.

Peetie, an older teenage boy, and Jackie, a teenage girl,

came in from the stockroom and began to wait on customers who were filing in.

"What about soy nuts?" a blond woman asked. "Did they come in?"

"I'll get a few cans," Peetie said. The woman looked around, then smiled at Maya. "You've got a store after my own heart here. Great stock, up-to-the-minute, first-rate customer service. I could spend my whole paycheck here."

Maya thanked her, smiling.

A dour older man came up. "You the owner?"

"I am. How can I help you?"

"By staying the way you've got it running now. Sometimes I think I come here just to get a smile and a pleasant interchange. Not that I'm always pleasant. My arthritis doesn't let me be. I need to see a doctor. It's driving me crazy." He touched his gnarled right hand.

"Sir," Maya told him, "do see a doctor, but others are having wonderful results with food supplements called glucosamine sulfate and chondroitin sulfate. I've taken it with good results when I've had a twinge of arthritis. My doctor recommends it."

"*You* got it? You look like you're just out of your teens."

"I'm thirty-one."

"I'll be darned. Who's your doctor?"

Maya told him and took one of her calling cards and wrote her doctor's name and number on it.

"Thanks. I'm Ken Lewis. I like your shop and maybe you can help me with my damned arthritis. You carry that stuff you told me about?"

"I sure do. I'll give you the smaller bottles to try, and don't forget to see your doctor."

"You better believe I won't." He flashed her a grateful smile.

An hour later when the crowd had thinned out to a trickle, Maya drew a deep breath. She had a chance now to reflect on her meeting with Chris St. John. Other than that great printing shop, what had he done with his life? His little girl was a love for certain, but did he date, have a steady, or play the field? He had said he wasn't a player, but did that mean anything? Players weren't likely to tell you they were players.

When the last customer had gone, Maya, Clara, Peetie, and Jackie went through the cash registers and locked them, drew the vertical blinds, and closed up. Peetie, with his gangling teenage limbs, swiftly put fresh wares on the shelves. A cleanup crew would come in a little later.

"Why don't you leave early?" Clara said. "I can handle it."

When her cell phone rang, Maya didn't answer it at first. *What now?* she thought grumpily, then answered.

"I hope you don't mind my calling you so soon," she heard.

Chris! Her heart jumped.

"I'm pleased."

"I think I'm losing my mind, but I wonder if you'd like to have dinner with me this evening. I won't keep you out late."

Yes, she thought, do *keep me out late.* "You know," she said, "I think you're reading my mind. If you'd be willing, I'd like to take you out to Wilson's in Crystal Lake. That's where the ball will be held. It can give us both ideas."

"Ideas of all kinds," he murmured.

"I'm sorry. Your voice went low and I couldn't hear you." He laughed. "Nothing really. I was teasing you."

"As I remember, you always were a big tease."

"Trust me," he said. "I tease far less often now."

THREE

Maya was keyed up as she drove her dark red BMW along Connecticut Avenue on her way home. Traffic was snarled and she was glad she didn't have too far to go. Her mind was very much on what she would wear. She had a date! Since her divorce she had seldom dated and had been attracted to no one. A delicious shiver shook the length of her body.

Friday night wasn't a good night to be up late. Customers usually thronged the shop on Saturdays. Clara ran the shop on Sundays from one to five and chose to take off only on Mondays.

A car horn beeped and a woman's shrill voice cut the air. "Idiot!" Maya glanced ahead to a red-faced woman whose angry face spewed invectives to a man on her left who had cut too close to her. Fortunately, he didn't retaliate.

Traffic cleared somewhat after Connecticut Avenue and she went onto and down Seventeenth Street to Pennsylvania Avenue. The BMW purred like a big cat. She always enjoyed driving it, but she needed to take it in for a tune-up.

Her apartment was a three-bedroom on the waterfront. Now as she pulled into the yard of her redbrick building, she looked at the sparkling Potomac River glittering in the streetlights. Good restaurants lined the waterfront. She checked in with the guard, drove into her parking space in the subbasement of her building, and got out of the car.

Once inside her apartment, she drew a deep breath and kicked off her shoes. Chuckling, she remembered that she had been aware of Chris's eyes on her legs. They weren't the greatest, but they were long and shapely, with beautifully turned ankles. She glanced at her watch. He had said he'd pick her up around eight.

In her bedroom removing her clothes, she stacked her braids on top of her head and looked in the mirror. She looked happy, she reflected, and she hadn't looked particularly happy for some time. *Oh, hell's bells,* she thought. She had forgotten to pick up the mail. A friend in New Orleans had promised to send her more information on Valentine's Day. She hoped Chris wouldn't mind sandwiching in more material. This ball was going to be something!

She got into the big oval, coral-colored tub before much water had run in, pulled powdered oatmeal from a metal shelf beside the tub, and sprinkled it onto her skin and into the water. She took a big, plastic bottle from the shelf and dribbled lily-of-the-valley bath oil onto herself and into the tub. Light floral scents always smelled so good in fall and winter.

In the quiet room she lay back soaking, humming a Mariah Carey tune about butterflies. She grew somber then. It hadn't been two years since Les and she had split up; she had had all she could take of his verbal abuse. To her surprise he hadn't contested her suit.

"Women come and women go, babe." He had been jovial. "Eight women to every man in this town. Maybe next time I'll get me two women and a couple of concubines."

To her protest that there were *not* that many women to every man in D.C., he'd shrugged. "Maybe there're not eight, but there're more than I need. I've got my mind on other things."

Les was a lawyer, a damned good one. His father was a lawyer. His grandfather had been a lawyer. The Townsends were very wealthy from legal work and real estate. Criminal lawyers, they handled some of the topflight cases in D.C., Maryland, and Virginia. Les had gone to prison for appropriating a mentally ill patient's money. Fed up with his verbal sadism, Maya had already filed for divorce by that time.

Out of the tub, Maya wrapped herself in a huge pink towel and rubbed herself down, tapping more bath oil onto her body.

She was picking up weight. Les liked his women thin, nearly emaciated. She had been much thinner when they married. Stress and a deep love of good food had taken care of that. He had nicknamed her "Fatstuff," explaining that while she wasn't exactly fat, she was getting there and his calling her that would help her ward off getting any bigger. Oh, no, she wasn't going to spoil a perfectly good evening thinking about Les.

She was dressed in record time in cream velvet pajamas with a leopard-print silk sash. She flipped her gold hoop earrings and chose a long twenty-two-inch gold rope that she knotted. She undid the pins that anchored her braids and thought she had made a good choice of hairstyles. Long bangs cut just above her eyebrows, side braids cut to the shoulder, longer braids in the back. The small jet-black beads at the end of the braids added a special touch. They glittered just a little. Next time she would try obsidian beads.

She got nervous when the building's concierge called to announce Chris, and she stood near the door to let him in. He held an armful of flowers.

"Oh, Chris, you shouldn't have," she protested as he thrust the blossoms at her.

"I'd like to have brought twice this," he said, grinning, "but I didn't want you to think I was overdoing it. Besides, I don't even know if you like flowers."

"I love them." They stood a little apart, glancing shyly at each other. He wore a deep brown, beautifully tailored suit with a pale blue shirt and a diagonally striped blue, tan, and brown silk rep tie.

"You look good," she complimented.

"Not handsome?" he said, laughing. "Not like a Greek

or African god? Well, I tried." His eyes twinkled, looking at her.

"Okay," she said, "I didn't want to overdo it, either. You've always known you were handsome. You're an African god, all right. I'm sure the women don't let you forget it."

"You sound a bit bitter," he said easily. "The aggressive members of your gender got you down?"

"I'm getting over it. This is about the fifth or sixth date I've had in two years. I'll manage."

He came closer and touched her face. "I tease a lot, but I try to be gentle with it. If I say something that hurts you, just kick me." He glanced down. "You should wear skirts more often, as much as I like your outfit tonight. Your legs are something to look at."

"Thank you, I think. Would you like something to drink? Look around. Would you like the cook's tour of my place?"

"Love it," he said, "but we need to get a head start. I've got a hard day tomorrow and I'm sure you have, too." That didn't keep him from taking in the very large living-dining area with its heavy glass, beveled-edge, and marble-topped tables. Orchid, lavender, and beige with touches of scarlet and aquamarine was the color scheme and he thought he had seldom seen a room better put together.

"My compliments to your decorator," he said.

"Which was largely me. My shop just really started showing a profit two years ago. I splurged on this. I couldn't help myself. If I have to go into bankruptcy because of it, I'll get a studio. Living here has been worth it."

She took time to put the flowers into four vases.

"I'll arrange them tomorrow," she said, admiring the red roses and the peonies, the broadleaf fern, the baby's breath, and the multicolored, spicy-scented carnations.

"They're beautiful," she told him. "Thank you."

"You're welcome."

She sparkled and he wanted to kiss her, nibble on that satiny, honey skin. But he wouldn't kiss her—not for a long time, maybe not ever.

* * *

Out at Crystal Lake, Wilson Cartwright met them at the door of his restaurant and bowed low.

"Welcome to my humble place. I love that coat."

Maya looked down at her beautiful autumn haze mink coat.

"I'll take it for you," Wilson said.

Seated in a cozy corner table near a bay window that let them look out on the extensive yards of Wilson's at the big pond and bare-branched weeping willow trees, Maya felt excitement coursing through her.

"That's a beautiful coat. You've got great taste, lady," Chris said as they waited for a server.

"In case you're wondering if I'm rich, I'm not. One of my friends owns a scarf and leather shop and has ties to New York's garment district. I got this coat for a song."

"Good for you for being smart as well as beautiful."

"Thank you. You certainly know how to pay a compliment and I'm not going to demur."

The waiter, a smiling middle-aged man, came to them. "My boss tells me to pull out all the stops. We both recommend our prime rib roast."

"Sounds good to me," Chris announced. "Agreed?"

Maya nodded.

When the waiter left, Chris turned to Maya. "Is this place going to be big enough for your event?"

Maya nodded. "That wall over there opens out into a much larger room. Many, many D.C. clubs are giving their balls here now. Wilson's a cultivated hustler."

"Yeah. I heard about this place, but just never came out. I generally choose somewhere in Maryland. This won't be my last time coming here, and. . . ."

"And?" she questioned gently.

He shook his head. "Nothing." There was a finality in his voice that she wondered at. And he sat musing that he had been going to say he hoped he could bring her here often. *Whoa!* he cautioned himself. Two years without a woman hadn't done him any harm. Sure, he'd had a few light dates and never gone back for a second try. At the rate he was going, he thought, he would heal enough to start a new relationship in about twenty years.

"You're awfully quiet. Is anything wrong?" Maya asked.

"I get that way sometimes. Tell me more about this ball, how it came about."

Maya thought about it a minute. "Well, we're a small group of shop owners, doing well, and we wanted to have a good time as well as raise enough money to award a few college scholarships. We give bake sales and garage sales all year. And there's this annual masked ball, the Sweetheart's Ball that we dote on."

His eyes admired her. "I read your copy after you left. I think I can do a helluva job on this for you."

"I hope you can. I'm really wrapped up in this. We all are."

He leaned back, a sense of relaxation beginning, then a sharp tension struck that almost made him swear.

"Think you've gotten over your divorce?" he asked. "Because I seem to be having a rough time with getting over mine."

She felt caught up. "I'm sorry. No, I haven't gotten over it completely, but I feel better about it. It was the right thing for me to do."

"You took back your maiden name."

"Yes."

"Who was the lucky guy?"

"Les Townsend."

"*The* sole scion of *the* Townsend family?"

"One and the same. You seem surprised."

Chris shrugged. "He screwed over a friend of mine pretty badly, a CPA he owed over 20K for setting up a company and handling his books. The guy asked Townsend for payment and Townsend asked for a week longer, which he gave him. Your guy took this time to plead bankruptcy, Chapter 7. He refused to talk with him. My friend lost his head and attacked Townsend, tried to choke him. My friend had a baby about to be born. He spent ninety-one days in jail."

"I'm sorry. It's the kind of thing Les did often. And don't call him 'my guy.' He's messed over a lot of people, including me.

"What did he do to you? No, don't answer. That's too personal."

"It's okay. Les wouldn't think of hitting a woman, but his tongue scorched my very soul. He's a verbal sadist, a smiling verbal sadist."

"Didn't you see it coming? When you were courting, I mean."

Maya shook her head.

Tense now and feeling her pain, he half closed his eyes, wanting to comfort her.

"He always pleaded innocence," she said softly. " 'I'm a verbal klutz,' he'd say. 'My mother was always too busy with her club work to properly raise me, and my father just doesn't give a damn, never has. Great lawyer. Poor father. He used to call me his demon seed. I guess I've just tried to live up to it.' Then Les would go on his knees, begging me to forgive him for his verbal drudging."

Her voice grew thoughtful. "When we were divorcing, I used to say I'd never go to hell when I died; I'd had my share here on earth. He set me up in business to keep me from being interested in his work. He backed me to the hilt. He was great that way, but when I began to be very successful, he started pulling me apart. Do you know what he went to prison for?"

"Just what I read in the papers."

"He's gutted clients' accounts from time to time and gotten away with it. He had a client at St. Elizabeth's whose account he robbed. Her son brought suit, and after quite a time his lawyer was able to get a conviction. Les has been at Lorton for two years now. He was sent up before our divorce became final."

Chris leaned over and lifted her soft, slender hand. "No rings, then?"

She held up her right hand. "A birthstone. Garnet."

His hand had one fraternity ring on it. He wanted to stroke her all over. She was making him feel spontaneous. Making him feel things he couldn't remember ever feeling before. Richer. Deeper. His heart felt expansive and he was scared.

"Let's dance before the food is served."

She nodded and rose, coming around to his side. The dance floor was at the other end of the room and they walked slowly until she turned to him, fitting into his arms as if she belonged there. *Love 'n Us,* a hot new group, was playing tonight.

Her perfume was getting to him. He pressed her soft, yielding body closer and put his mouth close to her ear.

He seemed bashful. She thought about the pleasant, caring things he said. But right now actions were speaking louder than words. Unwillingly, she drew away a little. The man didn't know his own power. His fit, rock-hard body drew her like a magnet. A faint odor of some really good man's cologne emanated from him. She smiled. He smelled a bit like expensive tobacco.

"Are you still smoking?" she asked him.

"I was never a smoker. Oh, I toyed with a pipe a while back. I decided I like life and my health too much to go on. That's a sore point between my ex-wife and me. She smokes like a chimney, and inhales deeply. What you're smelling is a tobacco-scented cologne I get from a Baltimore chemist."

She laughed. "I wanted to be sophisticated when I was in college, so I smoked. I could never get into the habit. Food is my weakness. Rich food."

"You mean you don't eat the rabbit food you sell?"

Her warm breath fanned his face, giving him the aroma of mint. He drew her closer. He was gliding along emotionally and he didn't know where he was going.

Suddenly aware of her breasts pressing against his chest, he asked, "Would you think I was crazy if I said I wanted to make love to you?"

A surprised chuckle came from Maya. "We met today, if you remember."

"We met *again* today. We've got years behind us. We spent a year in high school together."

"We didn't date."

"I was a coward."

"No. You were on to Stella Rice like a husk on wheat. Later, you married."

"I like the analogy. I was young and you didn't seem all that interested in boys even though they were crazy about you. I used to wonder if boys made fools of themselves over you because you didn't care, or if you didn't care because they made fools of themselves."

"I don't remember all that attention."

"You got it. How do you feel about getting our coats and stepping outside on the terrace?"

"Are you that crazy about the cold?"

"It's my favorite time of year."

"Okay. Let's."

She was a good sport, he thought. Something else in her favor. She'd be an easy woman to get along with, unlike Stella who was spiteful, always wanting her way.

FOUR

On the terrace, looking out on the star-patinated water of the big pond Wilson had had put in, Maya shivered a bit, although she was warm. So many spangly stars. One ripe, full moon.

They were silent until she said, "You're a nature lover."

"Definitely."

Where was this leading? she wondered. And he wondered, too, where they were going.

Their overcoats were unbuttoned and his big hands reached inside and spanned her waist, then drew her close to his unbuttoned suit coat as thrills shot through her.

"I want to make love to you."

His words were simple, artless; his voice was hoarse, breathless. She was so intense, tears started in her eyes. She wanted this man, wanted him as she could remember wanting nothing else before. He took her face in his hands and pressed the sides gently. His mouth closed on her soft, luscious, open lips. The fierce fires of wanting swept through both of them and she gasped a little for breath, unwilling to come away.

There were kisses in this world, she thought, but she had known none like this. His tongue probed hers, gently, tenderly, then roughly as if he would bend her to his will.

Her tongue did its own probing. Tongues of fire seeking to erase a painful past and garner a more loving present.

His tongue darted into the corners of her mouth and lingered there. Then with silken darts her tongue traced his jaw-bone with little thrusts. His breath came hard as he pulled her to him more tightly. She could feel him against her, wild with wanting as she whimpered.

With a groan, he released her. "I'm not going to apologize," he said. "I want you too much for that."

She was trembling now. "*Don't* apologize. That kiss was one of the best things in my life. I've dreamed about being kissed like that, but I told myself it only happened in romance novels."

He laughed then.

"I'm not an easy lay, though," she said staunchly.

"I never thought you were. We're both lonely. We're drawn the way few people are. You don't mind my telling you I want to make love to you?"

"Mind? I love it. I'm hurting with wanting you, but it won't happen soon—*if* it happens at all."

"You're right. *If* it happens. We go back a while, Maya, even if we didn't click back then. So I want to be careful." He took her hand and squeezed it. "I'm in one hell of a bind. I took it hard when my ex, Stella, left me for another man. She was pretty flagrant. I haven't gotten over it."

He hated talking about it, hated thinking about it. He always wanted to tear up the world when it crossed his mind. He and Janna had been like nothing to Stella; his little girl had suffered, too.

Maya put her hand to his jawline again. "The more deeply hurt we are, the longer we take to heal. Do you believe in prayer?"

"I'd be dead if I didn't."

The force of his words shook her. She wished she could see his face more clearly; trees on the terrace threw their shadows. Maya hunched her shoulders a bit. She wished she could stay out here all night long.

"I guess the waiter thinks we've slipped out on him. I'm going to take you in. We're working together now so we have to see each other, but if I seem to hold back, please try to understand why."

She wanted to be clear about it. "Because you're afraid of being hurt again."

"Yes. Aren't you?"

"A little. But Les and I were never in love the way I suspect you and Stella were and maybe still are. I know now that Les was getting back at a woman who'd ditched him when he married me. My mother, who's dead now, felt that any woman who didn't marry by twenty-two was wasting her life. She adored Les. My father, who's also dead, saw through him. I loved Les at first, but it didn't take him long to kill that love."

Love'n Us was playing their newest tune, "Shake It Like That," a song with a double meaning. Younger couples were on the dance floor, making the most of it. Rafe Sampson, the elderly man who sang with the band and played a wicked harmonica, had taken over, his gravelly voice delighting his listeners.

"I love you when you
    shake it like that.
I was leaving, I was
    gettin' my hat.

Then you began to dance
    up and down.
Your rhythm, it just
    turned me around.

I'm your film
    and you're my photomat.
We make perfect pictures
    when you shake it like that!"

Maya and Chris were hardly seated, the cold air they'd just come through making them shiver in spite of their heavy coats, when Wilson came with their food.

"I want this to be special," he said, "for two special people."

Prime ribs, scalloped cheese potatoes, green peas and baby onions, acorn squash, and a big salad of greens and myriad colorful raw vegetables, all beautifully served on gold-edged china, along with heavy Waterford crystal glasses.

The food looked superb. "I took the liberty of also preparing you a special dessert," Wilson said. "Chocolate cheesecake with raspberry topping, drenched with the best brandy you've ever tasted, which'll come later. Enjoy!"

They ate in near silence then, each keenly aware of the other, tense one moment, comfortable the next. They talked only about the food, nothing else.

When they were through with the main course, a waiter cleared the table and the cheesecake was served with Dom Perignon champagne. They ate the delicious dessert and drank heartily.

"I'm roping you two in," Wilson said as he inquired about their meal. "Don't be strangers again."

Maya ran her tongue across her bottom lip. "I can't wait to come back."

"And I can't wait to bring you," Chris said, "unless you have other plans."

He raised his brows and she was somber. "I have no other plans."

Wilson nodded, glancing from one to the other. Were they new lovers? About to become lovers? Wilson adored romance and did whatever he could to hurry it along.

When they had finished their meal, Wilson came back, his eyes sparkling. "I want you to see a little addition I've made," he said.

He led them past the many diners and to a fairly large, empty room that was glass enclosed. Ficus trees and other plants were set about. The gleaming hardwood floors were bare.

"Like it?" Wilson asked.

"Love it," they both said as Wilson grinned.

"This is a special room," he said, and led them to a smaller glass-enclosed room. "Lovers can come out here and watch the galaxy and not be cold in winter nor hot in summer. I'm all for love. I can never believe what my wife and I have got."

"You're a lucky man," Chris said wistfully.

Sighing, Maya didn't comment. She was too full. The midnight-blue skies with the hanging moon and brilliant stars brought on romantic feelings, but Maya thought that with this man at her side she didn't need the moon and the stars.

The larger glass-enclosed room was well lit, but the smaller one was lit only by the galaxy.

"I'll leave you two alone to enjoy it for a little while," Wilson said. "By the time of your Sweetheart's Ball, this space will be in full operation as a ballroom. I've had so many requests for it. D.C.'s discovered me in a big way."

They were out longer than they'd expected to be, but they were finally back at Maya's door.

"Would you like a nightcap? A glass of wine?"

Chris shook his head. "I need to turn in early. I promised I'd be up early to take Janna to soccer practice."

"I had a wonderful time," she said.

"So did I." His gaze on her was narrow, thoughtful. She reached out and touched the scar on the side of his face near his left eye.

"How did this happen?"

He shrugged. "I fell onto a rock when I was a rollicking kid, hell-bent for leather."

"I'll bet you were a good kid."

"Don't bet on it. I got into my share of trouble."

They were so close. *Please come in,* Maya wanted to say. *I want to go into your arms and stay there for a lovely while."*

She was certain he bent to kiss her, but he stiffened as

she swayed toward him. Instead he softly touched the side of her face.

"Good night," he told her, and said nothing about calling her or seeing her again.

Inside her apartment, she sat on the sofa, reliving the night. She began undressing in the living room and looked at herself in the full-length mirrors. She looked happy, keyed up. The disappointment that he hadn't stayed didn't show.

Going into the kitchen, she made herself a cup of the hot chocolate that always made her sleep better. She turned out the lights, opened her vertical blinds, and stood looking out at the lights sparkling on the waters of the Potomac. It was a scene that never failed to make her catch her breath. Standing there, she slowly sipped the hot chocolate and re-lived her just-passed hours. She didn't kid herself. She always enjoyed herself when she went out. It was the kiss that lingered in her mind. His mouth on hers had been heaven. In a wild rush she felt ecstasy cover her with its warmth. She had to have more kisses like that. He had been about to kiss her again. What had stopped him?

At his house on Upper Sixteenth Street, Chris sat in his garage in his black Infiniti. He had made quite a bit of money now, but material things meant less to him than they did to others. He smiled wryly. He'd always wanted love, and he'd felt he had it when he'd married Stella. Beautiful Stella. It hadn't taken more than a year for that to go bad, but the marriage had lasted eight years because he didn't want to give up on it. His own parents had been divorced and he knew how it hurt a child. So he'd put up with her drinking too much, her affairs, and her growing coldness. But after all his reticence to end their masquerade, she had asked for a divorce. She'd fallen in love with a very wealthy diamond merchant who lived on Diamond Point, an island in the Caribbean.

His daughter, Janna, had been no obstacle to Stella. The

child had always adored her mother, but Stella had paid little attention to her from the beginning.

Unsmiling, Stella had told Chris, "I made a mistake. I was never in love with you. I always wanted to be rich. Now I've got my chance. Duncan is the man I mistakenly thought you were going to be. I'm sorry it had to end this way. God knows I've tried and so have you."

He'd cried raging, hot tears and begged her to reconsider. There was nothing he wouldn't do for her, but she had been adamant. If Stella had been beautiful before, she was goddesslike in her newfound happiness. Day after day, night after night, he was ragged with pain.

Duncan Majors, Stella's new man, had come to D.C. and he and she had painted D.C. red—all while she was still married to and living with Chris. He had known what it felt like to want to kill then, hearing her constant laughter in her happiness.

"I can take it if I have to," he'd told her, "but consider your daughter. Children can be cruel and women get called names for less than what you're doing."

But Duncan had stayed two weeks and Stella had seen him every night and most days. Duncan paid little or no attention to Janna.

"What happens to her when you get married?" Chris had asked.

"He'll take her because he wants me."

"I won't give you trouble with the divorce if that's what you want, but let me have full custody of Janna."

She'd shaken her head. "No, but I will let you keep her for the school year and I'll take her summers. Chris, she'll have a ball with me. Duncan has a *palace* on Diamond Point."

She'd hugged herself then, laughter spilling from her Cupid's bow mouth.

Nothing dissuaded her. She and Chris were divorced, but in over two years, she and Duncan still hadn't married. Night after night, Chris had come awake with cold sweats, feeling his heart was stopping. Surges of fury had filled him and he'd wanted to find Stella after she'd moved out, put his hands around that swanlike throat, and keep squeezing. Only God and Janna had saved him.

He left his garage by the front entrance where he usually came in through the kitchen. He wanted to see the stars and the moon he'd watched with Maya. It always gave him pleasure, too, to look at his Tudor-style house that was atop a round hill. Lush plantings that he'd had a hand in set it off and he was very fond of it. Stella had never liked it. Now, he thought wryly, why should she? It wasn't a castle. Women like Stella were meant to live in castles.

Reluctantly he went inside. He felt a little dizzy and he knew from past experience what was wrong. He really liked Maya Williams, could love her, but bitterness had coated his heart like steel when Stella left. He had once thought love was lasting, love was Stella. His love for Janna and hers for him was real, but *romantic* love, that was love's *masquerade.* Fickle and all too often destructive. Despoiling. Making him play the fool.

Softly opening Janna's door, he looked in. She was on her back, her arms flung out. She woke, stirred a bit. "Dad?"

"Yes, sweetheart. Go back to sleep. I'm sorry I woke you up."

"That's okay. I wanted you to wake me up. Did you have a good time?"

"Yeah. I'll tell you all about it in the morning."

Her eyelids were so heavy she could barely stay awake. "Good night," she told him as he bent to kiss her cheek.

Janna was a great kid, full of warmth and feeling. Loving. He felt largely responsible for that. Stella let her do whatever she wanted to do, spoiled her outrageously, yet was never really there for her. One thing he swore was that his daughter was going to be able to love if he had anything to say about it. She knew real love with him and would know it with others.

Mrs. Nickens, the woman who took care of Janna and stayed there nights when he was going to be late, slept down the hall. She loved her little charge. Janna's teacher adored her. Yeah, in spite of his busted heart, his little girl was going to love and be loved. There was going to be much more for her than love's masquerade. The problem was that when he was interested in someone else, the night sweats began again and he was rocked with the searing pain of memory for what he and Stella had gone through.

Going up the hall to his own master bedroom he looked around him. The house had been completely renovated since the divorce; it had made living there easier.

In bed, no sooner had he switched off his lights than thoughts of Maya's voluptuous body in his arms tonight, her floral perfume, and the yielding softness of her body came to him. Her fantasy nearness made him rise and harden as he had seldom risen in his life and her soft, clear laughter filled his ears. He'd probably come to love her if he could still love. But he saw his life ahead. Not even deep friendship with a woman for a very long time. He dated seldom and he would continue to date seldom. When a woman got too close, he simply walked away. He didn't want to be cruel, but he felt he could die if he knew another siege of torment like what he had gone through two years ago.

He fell asleep quickly and Maya's arms were around him again. She was naked now and he was groaning with desire. This was a dream and nothing stopped him as he entered her. Nothing stopped him. He was ecstatic. Nothing stopped him, and he was grateful for dreams.

FIVE

The next morning, Maya came awake feeling chipper, yet she didn't want to get up. She stretched languidly and desire coursed through her veins as she remembered Chris's kiss from the night before. With a sigh, she thought about her full day ahead. It was still early. She grew somber thinking of the way Chris had stiffened when she would have drawn him closer. Sighing again, she reflected that she had too much to do to brood.

The scent of the flowers still filled the rooms. With all his money, Les had not been a man to send flowers. Instead, he had given her expensive presents she'd never particularly liked.

Getting up, she showered and found better containers for the masses of flowers. One particularly dainty tea rose caught her eye and she took a knife and cut the stem shorter, then found a bud vase. It would go nicely with her breakfast.

Later, outside in front of her shop, Healing Hands, Maya smiled. Connecticut Avenue was a great place to do business. Expensive, but well worth it. She held a bouquet of some of the many flowers Chris had brought, then went in and put the flowers on the counter.

Clara, Peetie and Jackie were all busily waiting on customers. The middle-aged blond woman who came in two or three times weekly smiled and spoke to her.

"I guess you can't help but notice how often I'm in here," she said. "I'm Wanda King and I'm interested in the really great books you carry. In just a little over a month, I'm feeling much livelier. And your stock is great, too."

Maya smiled. "I'm glad you think so. Don't forget we're happy to order what we don't have here."

"You're an herbalist, aren't you?"

"Yes, I am. I never stop studying. The field fascinates me."

"Those flowers are beautiful, but to get back to books, everything you've told me about has helped. I've been coming in a little over a month and I guess I want to talk because that echinacea you told me about stopped my cold in its tracks. You told me to get it early and I did. About this time every fall I'm in bed with a two-week cold, but not this year."

An older male customer, Ken Lewis, cleared his throat. "Ladies, I couldn't help overhearing what you were talking about. I tried echinacea and it worked for me. Ek-in-a-sha." He said the word slowly, then turned to Maya. "Any time you want a testimonial, I'm willing to speak up."

"Thank you. I'll probably take you up on that."

"Who'd you study with?" he asked.

"Dr. Byron Turner in San Francisco. I was just telling Ms. King I never stop studying."

"A woman after my own heart."

The man and the blond woman smiled at each other.

"Help yourself to refreshments," Maya told them, indicating the counter with a very large coffee urn, tea bags, and chocolate packets. There was also a giant bowl of mixed nuts and small wheat and rye squares.

"It's so nice in here," the blonde said. "I come here when I'm blue."

The older man looked her over, liked what he saw, and told her, "A woman looks like you's got no business being blue. Shucks, you oughta have the whole world at your feet."

The blonde threw back her head, laughing. "That's the best compliment I've had in a long time."

The woman and the man moved on toward the counter with the refreshments. They smiled at someone behind Maya, and as she began to turn, two very soft hands shielded her eyes.

"Guess who!"

"A woman. I can tell by these hands."

"Two small thirty-five-year-old hands." Dosha Sears chuckled fondly. She removed her hands from Maya's eyes, and the two women hugged.

"Oh, love, I wasn't expecting you so early," Maya said.

"You know who gets the worm." Dosha was the essence of femininity—all soft curves, softspoken, a woman known for her sweetness.

As the two women chatted, another woman came in with a few customers.

"Lillian! You're both early," Maya exclaimed.

"Let's get the ball business over and get back to work. I thought for a little while I wasn't going to be able to make it."

Lillian Moon was model thin, model tall, and a dish. A successful, stylish woman, she lived for her career, but she longed for a man. She was sharply envious of Dosha's marriage and of Maya's golden life with Les when they'd been together. She shrugged now and sighed deeply.

The three women chatted with Clara for a little while, then went into Maya's office. On a big white sheet on her desk, Maya drew up added plans for the ball as they talked. They all got a chuckle discussing the birds mating and the fact's relevance to Valentine's Day.

"I've got a love of a printer for us," Maya told them.

"You're lighting up when you say that," Lillian teased. "New printer? Or new man in your life?"

"Mind your own business," Maya retorted happily. "He took me out to dinner last night."

Lillian arched her brows and continued teasing. "I thought you never mixed business with pleasure."

"I'm allowed one exception to the rule."

"Well," Dosha said pertly, "we're waiting for the details."

Maya threw her head back, laughing. "You'll never hear them from me."

"Ha," Lillian said. "This from a woman who lives and breathes romance."

Maya looked from one to the other of her beloved friends. "Maybe it's over before it begins. He hasn't called."

"You're not giving him much time. What's his name?"

"Christopher St. John."

Dosha's head went up. "Owns a printing shop in L'Enfant Plaza? A hunk?"

Lillian's eyes were fixed on Maya. "You've got the expectations of a teenager, my dear. Men these days are playing hard to get."

Maya shrugged. "He may be a player for all I know."

"I don't think so," Dosha said slowly. "I met him at a party a few months back. I just took it for granted he was married. He seemed settled."

Maya shook her head. "He's been divorced for a couple of years. His ex lives on an island in the Caribbean. He has a lovely little girl who was in his shop when I went by yesterday."

Lillian chewed her bottom lip. "Girlfriend, you've come half a lifetime in a day's space. Now, if this hunk is single, maybe you and I are going to be *ex*-girlfriends. Give me a break, ladies. I've been single all my life and looking. Maya made a bad choice. I'm willing to take that chance. Clara and I aren't bad on the eyes, yet we've never been married. How old is this dude?"

"Thirty-four," Maya said. "We were in high school together. He cooled down in a hurry when I was getting too close last night. Maybe he's taken, even if he's not married."

"Yeah," Lillian said. "That's a good reason not to call."

"Let's talk about our Sweetheart's Ball," Maya cut in.

"Yeah, let's. Lover Boy's too young for me. I like them

older, but if he's got a friend . . ." Lillian hunched her shoulders. She was thirty-nine.

"I'll ask, if I ever hear from him again."

"Impatience, thy name is Maya," Dosha chided. "If he calls within a week, it's good. He's probably a busy man."

Lillian pursed her lips, then said somberly, "Spoken like a truly married woman. Settled and profoundly contented."

Dosha shook her head. "I don't know how contented I am these days. I want a baby and I don't get pregnant."

"Have you tried in vitro?" Lillian asked.

"We've tried that, too."

Maya nodded. She knew the feeling. Sometimes her arms seemed so empty without a child, yet she was glad there had been none with Les, her ex. That had made it much easier.

Lillian and Dosha finished up their business with Maya and left. As they walked out, Maya reflected on them. Both were sterling friends. All three women were doing extremely well, except that Dosha didn't have the baby she wanted so much. Lillian was without the man she wanted. Maya felt she could wait; she wasn't anxious to get involved again, although Chris St. John made her think of changing her mind.

Midafternoon, alone in her office, Maya found herself staring at the phone. She shrugged. Was she waiting for Chris St. John to call? Looking down at her deep pink desk pad, she sketched a heart and put arrows through it, labeled it Sweetheart's Ball. She just had a hunch that having the ball at Wilson's was going to ensure that it was a stellar affair. Come January, everything concerning the ball would begin to roll. Mating birds were seldom far from her mind these days, ever since she'd come across that bit of information in a book on major holidays. Her eyes crinkled as she smiled widely. She was kidding herself, she chided. The birds got locked in her mind only after dinner with Chris.

Looking glum, Clara stuck her head into the room, then thoughtfully came in and closed the door behind her.

"What's wrong, Clara?"

The middle-aged woman leaned against the door. "You're not going to believe this."

"What is it?"

"Les is here. He wants to see you."

"Les?"

"Yes. Same old, same old. I told him I'd see if you were too busy to see him, said you had a meeting in an hour or so across town. I tried to buy you some time."

Maya's heart plummeted. "So he's out of prison?"

"That surely isn't his ghost. He's out there, all right, and as smirky as ever."

Maya bit her bottom lip. "Send him in, Clara. I want to get this over with."

"I can say you're gone and we didn't realize it."

"No, I want this over with. I won't run and I won't try to hide."

"Okay. If he tries to pull anything, remember we're right outside."

Maya got up and went to her manager. "I can handle this, Clara. Trust me."

Reluctantly Clara went out as Maya stood at the corner of her handsome curved oak desk. In a few minutes Les Townsend stood in the doorway, his red-brown hair and skin, his medium height, stocky body immaculate in carefully blended, expensively tailored dark and light gray.

"Hey, babe!" He came to her swiftly, his arms held out from the time he entered.

"No, Les. Don't touch me. I don't want you to."

Glowering, Clara stood in the doorway.

"It's all *right,* Clara. I'll be fine."

Closing the door behind her, Clara left them alone.

"Have a seat, Les." Damn it, she thought, her voice was quavering. She had nothing to fear; Les wasn't a violent man, except verbally. Angry, and sometimes not so angry, he could verbally flay and had nearly verbally assassinated her. All the ugly names you heard so often, and a few foreign ones, filled his vocabulary. He had books on insults and put his knowledge to use.

"Sit down, Les," she repeated.

"You first."

"No, *you* first. This is my office."

She had expected him to wrangle. Instead she was surprised to see him nod and sit down. She wasn't going to offer him refreshments.

"You're looking great," he complimented. She sat across from him, determined to get a grip on herself. She wasn't going to respond to that.

"Why are you here?" she asked him. "When did you get out?"

He grinned. "Day before yesterday. I had to check in with my parole officer and I had a few loose ends to tie up." He stroked his chin. "My first free moments, I headed straight for you. Aren't you happy to see me?"

"Why should I be?"

"You may be when I tell you what I've got on my mind."

"Spill it, because I've got a lot to do the rest of the afternoon. It's getting crowded out there and I'm needed on the floor."

"They'll manage without you. You always believed in getting good people."

Bitterly she thought, *Except for a husband.*

He was silent and she didn't push him. Instead she looked at him and quickly remembered a little. Les Townsend, son of Mack Townsend, millionaire criminal lawyer, just as his only son, Les was a wealthy criminal lawyer. Their marriage had grown to be hell with his verbal sadism, his drinking, and his flaunted mistresses.

Les had gone to prison for gutting the assets of a St. Elizabeth's Mental Hospital female patient who had trusted him implicitly; she had called him her son when she was coherent. His father's money and political clout hadn't been able to save him. Her real son had been adamant in fighting

with some money of his own, and Les had been out of luck
with the judge assigned to the case.

These thoughts had flashed across her mind. Now she
faced him, her chin lifted. "Well, Les?"

His head tilted, eyes narrowed. "Lord, you're looking
great. I wasn't always exactly faithful to you, but I damned
sure was faithful in my fashion. I still love you."

"Let's not discuss us and the past. You don't love me. I
don't think you ever did."

"You're wrong. I had a good time married to you. Okay,
no past. Would you like to know how Lorton was? I got
out way early for good behavior."

"I don't need to know about Lorton *prison*." She delib-
erately brought in the word.

Les threw back his head, laughing. "I didn't think of it
as a prison," he said, "but as another kind of *gated community*."

Maya couldn't help smiling a bit. Trust Les to make the
sublime ridiculous and the ridiculous sublime. He preened
himself over having made her at least smile. His next question was harder.

"Are you tied up with someone?"

"Why would you need to know that?"

"I'm interested."

"Don't be."

"I can't help it. Our divorce was a mistake."

"You're a smart guy. You've always been able to do what
you wanted to do."

"Up to now. I'm not going to beat around the bush.
Looks like your business is doing fine."

"It is."

"Remember who set you up, who backed you all the
way?"

"Yes, Les, I *do* remember. I'm grateful, but I don't owe
you my life. I was married to you at the time you staked
me. Now I do not feel I've got to pay you back."

Les looked pleased.

"A lot of money went into this place. It would have taken

you a long time to get that kind of money together. You'd have to live poor to do it."

"I don't mind living poor. My parents weren't wealthy and we were happy."

Les licked his lips. She always could get to him. "Listen," he said softly, "I've got a proposition for you. In . . . *Lorton*"—he hesitated a bit—"I spent my time planning. Now I need your help."

"Oh?"

Maya leaned on her elbows. "Same old Les, intent on making a fast buck. I'm in it to help people, Les. If I make money, so much the better. In so large a part, herbs are me and I'm them. They do wonders for the people in this world."

"To each his own. I believe in making money—a lot of it."

"Being a criminal lawyer didn't leave you poor."

"Well, you know, it's bandied about that Rockefeller said, 'How much is enough? A little bit more.' "

"Some would call that greed."

"Reality, babe. Man's—and woman's—cupidity has been uppermost since the beginning of time."

"Exactly what is it you want from me?"

"Basically everything. I want us back together. In business together. Herbs via mail order is big business now, and I want us in together. I've changed. I know what I lost. Things will be different this time."

"No, Les," Maya said quickly. "Strike me off your list. We're through."

"You owe me and I'm going to keep begging.

"I don't owe you messing up my life. If you keep asking, I'll keep saying no."

"You won't be sorry."

"I'm already sorry that you asked."

"I think you're leaning that way. How long do you need to think it over? We were always a pair."

"You're wasting your time."

"I won't stop."

She wanted him to leave now, but he crossed his legs and took out a cigarette holder.

"Mind if I smoke?" The lighter was in his hands, lighting the cigarette as he spoke. How like Les.

"Would it matter if I said I minded?"

He grinned broadly. "Be kind to me. I'm turning over a new leaf. Hell, I'm turning over a new big *stone*." Maya grimaced. She could just imagine the worms under that stone he was turning over.

SIX

Maya went out of her office with Les. As they rounded the corner, Chris came in as Les followed close behind Maya. When she saw him, her face was wreathed with smiles that Chris returned.

"I got some great new ideas I thought you'd like to see," Chris said. "Study them and call me about them."

"Don't rush. We've got plenty of time to get the invitations out and the brochures run. Chris, I'd like you to meet Les Townsend."

Chris shifted the flat package he was carrying to his left hand and extended his right.

"I'm the ex," Les said jovially. "The bad egg you've surely heard about."

Chris didn't respond to that, but little demons were dancing in his brain. Townsend was a good-looking guy. Smooth. Rich. He seemed to have charisma. These days, many important men had gone to prison and come out ahead. Had Maya completely gotten over him? That was all that mattered.

"I've got to get back," Chris said to Maya. "I came out to pick up a couple of articles, which is why I brought the copy."

Maya gave him her best smile. "I thank you, but I wish you wouldn't rush."

Les looked from one to the other, his eyes half-closed.

"Don't let me drive you away. I'm told I'm history, but I don't believe everything I hear."

"Les, really," Maya said with disgust. Les was a trouble-maker, never happier than when he was causing discord.

Chris turned to Maya, saying, "I'll call, or call me."

Maya touched his arm. "Either way is fine. Please don't work too hard."

Chris's glance swept her body, claiming her although he didn't know it.

Les and Maya were silent until Chris was nearly out the door, then Les put his hand on her arm, never seeming to notice when she brushed it aside. He put an arm around her waist and she fastened her hand around his wrist and loosened his hold.

"Les, don't!" she said sharply.

He laughed, pleased to get a rise out of her. "Don't play little Miss Goody Two-Shoes with me, kid. I knew you when. I always could light your fire. Maya, we've got to get together soon."

Maya breathed harshly. He hadn't lost the power to make her boil.

"How far has it gone with you and Lover Boy?"

"I'm not going to answer questions about my personal life."

"Egotistical bastard, leaving me alone with you. I'd have hung around to see what's going on.

"He's a gentleman—class to the bone—that sort of thing. You wouldn't understand people like Chris."

Les laughed gleefully. He had put her on the defensive. "I'm a Townsend, love, of *the* Townsends. My family could buy and sell St. John."

Maya looked at him levelly. "That's the whole of your life, Les. Money. Money. Who's got the money?"

"You liked it well enough when we were together."

"Never as much as you thought I did." He had stolen from a client, a woman confined to St. Elizabeth's, a mental institution, gone to prison, and still money was his god.

Looking at her, Les reflected that she was shapelier than he remembered, more sensual. He wanted to see her again.

"We'll be seeing quite a bit of each other. I'll enjoy that."

Maya shook her head quickly. "No, Les. We're not going to be seeing each other."

Les's face fell. "I didn't set up negative conditions when I set you up in this business. Okay, okay. I'll give you a chance to get used to my being around. I learned a lot in prison, like biding my time and taking my chances."

"I'm glad you learned something."

"Do I dare kiss your cheek?" He smiled maliciously. Maya knew her employees were watching, but that wasn't why she said it.

"Not unless you want me to slap you."

"Feisty wench. I hope you remember what that used to bring on in me."

Maya remembered. Her feistiness had always turned him on; her anger based on hurt. At first, they had had a fairly good sexual relationship, based on all the wrong things. Fighting and making up. Quarreling and making up. She had been young, anxious. Les was ten years older. She had soon been turned off by his verbal sadism. With Chris she felt calm, relaxed, blissful.

"Hey, you left me," Les reminded her. Her skin grew warm and she thought of Chris's kiss the night before, almost like an incantation for protection against Les.

Les touched her arm briefly and walked away, but not before he came closer and said in a stage whisper, "I'll call you."

The next ten days or so passed pleasantly. Chris was very busy, but he took time to call and they had lunch a couple of times. She was busy, too. She didn't hear from Les and she considered that a blessing.

* * *

It was a dreary day when Maya picked up the phone in her office and her face lit up.

"Rainy weather always makes me wish for you," Chris said.

"But not sunny weather?" she retorted.

"Any weather. Who am I kidding? Maya, I need a favor."

"Name it."

"I've got to fly up to New York tonight to be sure I'm there for a meeting tomorrow morning. We've got a hot contract for a college yearbook. It's a plum. Lots more work attached to that."

"Congratulations!"

"Thank you. The favor is I need to leave my daughter with you. Her nanny, Mrs. Nickens, has to stay with her own sick daughter. . . ."

"She's more than welcome. Is she willing?"

"Yeah. She's a great kid. And, Maya, she admires you so much."

Very late that afternoon at her apartment with Janna, Maya waited for a seafood platter delivery from a nearby restaurant. The platter was of Janna's choosing. Maya had asked if she wanted to go out to dinner and she had said no.

"I'd like to stay in with you, if you don't mind."

"Why, no, my little darling. I love being here with you."

The child seemed to be older than her years. Maya had asked her to bring some lounging pajamas if she had them and she did. Now each showered and slipped into the pajamas. Maya's were orchid-colored silk jersey with a sheer orchid coindot silk-print sash. Janna's were blue and white flowered crepe.

"You look like a doll," Maya complimented her.

The child looked down. "Thank you. When I grow up, I'd like to be as pretty as you are. I think you're nice."

"Why, thank you. You're a love."

"I brought my mom's picture. Would you like to see it?"

"Yes, I would."

Janna went out and returned with a large photograph in a gold-painted frame. Stunning. Red-gold hair, alabaster skin, emerald eyes. Not many movie stars were as lucky.

"Isn't my mom beautiful?" Janna asked.

"She certainly is."

Suddenly the child's face crumpled and she looked sad. "I don't look like her; I wish I did. I'm not going to be beautiful."

They sat on the sofa and Maya reached out and drew the girl to her. "You're already beautiful," Maya said staunchly, "and give yourself time. You'll be a knockout."

"But not like Mom."

"Janna, listen to me. Each person, each human, is special, altogether special. You're graceful. Beautiful skin and eyes, a lovely slender face. But always remember, it's what's inside that matters. You're warm and kind. Smart. You've got a father who loves you, and that love will pay off in spades. . . ."

Janna threw her arms around Maya's neck and hugged her tightly. She looked happy now.

Finally she began to talk. "I get to spend summers with Mom and Duncan. One day they'll probably get married. I was so hurt when she and Daddy broke up, but in the summer she lets me do whatever I want to, and Duncan buys me everything I want. He's neat."

"I'm glad you get along so well with them. I'm sure they love you."

"Yes. I can't wait to see them next summer. Duncan is having a boat made with my name on it. He's rich."

"I see. And that makes you happy."

Janna smiled widely. "It's like being in fairyland or Disney World." She raised her thin arms above her head and clasped her fingers. "Oh, I can't wait!"

The takeout food came then and Maya set the table as if for another grown-up. Pink damask, silver, and crystal.

"Gee, you're a sweet lady," Janna said as they sat down. "This table looks great."

"Would you like to say blessings?"

"Yes." And the child offered a lovely blessing.

"Who taught you to give thanks for the food so well?"

"Dad. Mom thinks it's silly."

"I see," Maya said thoughtfully. "I've always liked saying them. And as I said, you do them beautifully."

The child ate with exquisite manners. Maya smiled inside. *Not going to be beautiful? Not on your life, kid. You're going to be one of the best and the brightest.*

As she was taking food to her mouth, Janna put her fork down, with the food still on it, back on the plate.

"Mrs. Nickens is nice," she said, "but I'm having fun with you; it's better than with anyone except Mom and Dad. Are you always so much fun?"

"I hope so. Would you like to hear some music?"

"No. I'm just enjoying being quiet and talking with you. Miss Williams, may I ask you a question?"

"Darling, call me Maya if you're comfortable with it. And yes, ask me any question. I'll answer if I can."

Janna fidgeted a bit. "Well, you and Dad haven't been seeing each other for too long, but he talks about you all the time, asks me how I like you. He says you're a peach. Do you like him a lot?"

"I do. A whole lot, and I think he's the peach."

"I asked him the question and he looked sad. Now I'm asking you. Will you two be getting married?"

Janna looked at Maya quizzically. "I can't answer that, sweetheart."

"Do you even want to? Get married, I mean. I think Daddy does."

With her heart fluttering, her eyes misting, Maya answered, "After all, that would be a long time down the road."

"If he loves you and you love him, grown-ups get married when they fall in love."

"Oh, my dear," Maya said slowly. "If only it were that simple."

SEVEN

Early January of the following year

Everything was going along splendidly, Maya thought as she stood at the front of Helping Hands, surveying the scene. Satisfied customers milled about, waited on by Clara, Peetie, and Jackie. It was late afternoon and she had just come in from outside. She pulled on a dusty blue smock that matched the shop's decor and went back to her office.

A big box of ivory-and-gold invitations sat on the desk, with one displayed. She picked it up; Chris had done a great job. Another box held the colorful brochure that would go with the invitations, information about the origin of Valentine's Day. She never failed to smile when she thought about the annual first day of the birds' mating.

She and Chris were closer. They were both very busy and didn't see each other too often, but they had occasional lunches, a dinner or two. She had visited his home. She knew he was running scared and she didn't push it.

They had had a good time at Christmas at her apartment. She had invited him, Janna, and Mrs. Nickens to a dinner she cooked and they had enjoyed it.

She smiled, thinking about Chris. He had held back from passion. Their kisses were warm, sweet.

"So we're friends," she'd said to him Christmas night

when Mrs. Nickens had taken Janna to her house to spend the night.

He had been somber, had taken her face in his hands. "Maya, I'm not going to lie. What I feel for you goes far beyond friendship, but I can't go through what I went through before in my divorce. Help me and maybe I'll get over it, but maybe I won't. It's still strong. It eats at my very soul. Be patient, if you can. If you don't want to, I understand."

"Do you want to go on with me?" she had asked him, her voice trembling.

"More than anything."

"Then I'll keep on seeing you. We have to keep it tucked in, though. I'm a passionate woman and you're a passionate man. We strike sparks. We have to be careful."

"I'll be careful with you. We won't kiss again the way we did that first night."

But Maya had stood thinking then that she *wanted* him to kiss her again and again, and to never stop, the way he had that night. He had been true to his word. Sweet, soft kisses in reality; blazing kisses that seared them both in fantasy.

That weekend they'd all addressed the invitations. Clara and Jackie had the best handwriting. Mrs. Nickens had asked if she could help. Including herself, she had rounded up ten people.

She had her back to the door when Les came in and walked over to her. "I've kept my word not to hassle you," he said at her elbow. "I told you I'm learning fast."

It wasn't fast enough, Maya thought grimly. She was suddenly angry with him. Yes, he'd kept his word, coming by only when he needed or said he needed to buy something.

"Les," she said suddenly.

"Yeah."

She was going to say it; she should have said it long ago. "Do you ever think about your client who died of a broken heart because you'd gutted her estate?"

"Whoa, babe! We don't know that Essie Moore died because of the stupid thing I did. She wasn't a happy camper.

I had the world in a jug with the stopper in my hand and I pulled a fool trick like that. I had plenty of money. Why'd I do it? You tell me."

"I don't think you've ever been really remorseful."

"Don't say that. Sure I have. We all make mistakes. My old man is not exactly a shining angel."

"You're old enough not to be blaming him. You've got a good mind. You just like living on the edge."

He grinned and shrugged. "And that's a fact. That's me. I don't try to explain myself, babe. I just try to live with the cards I've been dealt."

"And the cards you pull out of your sleeve."

Les laughed. "That's my girl, always telling it like it is."

When he left a few minutes later without any more talk about the two of them, she thought she might have bothered him a little. She hoped he continued to keep his word about not coming by often.

"Telephone, Maya," Peetie called.

"I'll take it in my office."

Maya walked in and sat on the edge of her desk. She said "hello" softly into the receiver and her heart jumped. "Chris!"

"What're your plans for the weekend?"

"Just addressing the invitations. Janna is going to make enough cookies and sandwiches to keep us in refreshments."

"Guess who *taught* her to make several kinds of cookies?"

"Not you?"

"Uh-huh. I've got to display my culinary talents to you. What's your favorite meal?"

"I have several favorites. High on the list is shrimp-and-crab gumbo over brown rice. A great big greens, avocado, and tomato salad. Start the whole thing with gazpacho and I'm happy."

"I'm writing that down. How about dessert?"

"Oh, Lord, I never met a dessert I didn't like."

"Be specific."

"Okay, any flavor of ice cream, although my favorite is vanilla. I like chocolate-to-the-bone cake and I like coconut pineapple cake. Why are you asking all these questions?"

"You'll find out. Are you free next weekend? Saturday evening and night?"

"I am. Hey, that's seven days away."

"Good things take time."

Maya hung up and went back outside, beaming. "The sun certainly is shining on you," Clara told her. "Or is it Mr. St. John?"

"I'll never tell." Maya chuckled softly. She wondered just what Chris had in mind.

Later that afternoon a young man came in with a messenger envelope addressed to Maya. "No tip," he said. "I'm from Mr. St. John's shop, so I've been tipped."

Maya opened the brown messenger envelope and took an invitation from a big white envelope. It read that Christopher St. John requested her presence at an elegant dinner at his house a week from this Saturday night. She couldn't help passing it around for her coworkers to see.

"Congratulations," Clara said. "From where I stand it looks like you've made a conquest."

Maya blushed. "I never turn down a dinner invitation."

It was four o'clock and things were beginning to slow down. Shortly after five it would bustle again. Maya thought again about the just-passed Christmas. Chris had given her a stunning large sunburst twenty-two-carat gold pin. She had given him twenty-two-carat gold nugget cuff links, and she thought of all those flowers he had bought for her in the beginning, and still did on occasion. He was a generous man.

She had to do something special for his birthday on Valentine's Day and she had been thinking hard.

When the phone rang, Maya picked it up. Janna's sweet voice sounded excited.

"I thought you'd want to know," she said. "Dad's going to teach me to make double raisin-apple oatmeal cookies. I only know how to make the regular kind. Ten people are going to be happy. And I've got great fillings for the sandwiches, plus Mrs. Nickens and I baked a ham. We're all set. Dad and I are going to bring the stuff over to your apartment early Sunday morning."

"You're a big help to me, honey," Maya told her. "Thank you so much."

EIGHT

The next week fairly flew by. The Sweetheart's Ball invitations had been mailed and some people had already responded. Walking the length of her store, Maya reflected that the only fly in the ointment was that Les had begun to come in to the shop more often. When she pointedly asked him why, he swore that he was there for herbs, beginning to believe in their usefulness. He had always derided herbs, calling them "witches' brew." She couldn't help but wonder what he was up to.

Today was Saturday, late afternoon. She had to go home and dress to go to Chris's. He was picking her up and he had never seemed so dear as when he turned down her offer to drive herself over.

"No way," he'd said. "I'm an old-fashioned guy. I pick up my woman and I take her back home." He'd flushed then. "Do you mind my calling you 'my woman'?"

"Frankly, no," she'd replied. "It sounds good."

Chris had been uncomfortable thinking about the tightrope he walked with Maya. He wanted her, needed, craved melding with her, but the marrow of his bones hurt when he thought about loving again. Maya was nothing like Stella, but the best of people fell out of love, came to prefer others. He damned himself for a coward, but he knew all too well the hell Stella had put him through.

* * *

That night, seated at Chris's house before a roaring fire in the big fieldstone fireplace, Maya felt happy. The house was quiet with Janna away. "I'm going to be thinking about you and Dad," the young girl had said, "but Mrs. Nickens is showing me how to play chess and we're going to have fun. You have fun, too. I helped with the chocolate cake."

They had hugged each other. "I haven't lost the taste of the cookies you made for us. You're such a love."

Janna had blushed. "Mom's coming in a week or so."

Maya felt a twinge of what she wasn't sure.

"Oh, really? I'll bet you're happy."

Janna had hugged herself. "We're going to lay out plans for the three of us for this summer. It's going to be fun."

Chris had looked concerned. Now he came to her with a tray of drinks. She chose sangria.

"My little girl is all excited," he said as he put the tray on the coffee table and sat down. "She really loves Stella and is very fond of her fiancé. I just hope Stella doesn't disappoint her."

"She's a rare child. You must be very proud of her."

"She's not the only one I'm proud of." Maya blushed as he studied her intently.

"Are you talking about me?"

"I am."

"Then let me say I'm just as—or more—proud of you. You'll get through it, Chris. Just have faith. Trust yourself." He looked strained and her heart went out to him.

"It's been over two years. A lot of the time it seems better, then when I want to move on, I suddenly feel yanked back and it's hell again."

"Have you thought of seeing a therapist?"

"I've thought of everything. I did see one for a brief while, but he thought time might work for me. I'm thinking of going back."

Maya's heart leapt then fell. Therapy didn't work for everyone.

His living room was large, comfortable with the field-stone fireplace covering a good part of one side. The sleek, mahogany furniture blended nicely with dark blue sofas, needlepoint chairs and small touches of dark red and ivory. Chris had brought her here on brief visits, but they usually met at her apartment. She was a queen, he thought, with her beautiful braids. Dressed in a cream cashmere sweater with oval cutouts along her shoulder line that displayed the tempting brown flesh, she was a luscious star. Sitting there, he couldn't keep his eyes from the cream cashmere flannel skirt she wore with the slits high up her thighs. Hell, he grumbled to himself, dinner sure wasn't what he wanted now.

"Let's talk about something else," he said. "The food is simmering. I promise you a feast."

"All done by you. Janna said she helped with the cake."

"Yeah. She's going to make a first-rate cook. You know it's a miracle the way that kid's warmed up to you. Other women have come and gone and she was always cool, distant. I never pushed it. I thought perhaps she just didn't want to share me, but with you . . ."

"Ah, we're a mutual admiration society."

"Do you want kids?" Chris asked as Maya felt a pleasant jolt go through her.

"Yes, I've always wanted them. Les didn't, so he had a vasectomy."

"That must have hurt."

"Yes, but we try to get over things. Do you want more children?"

"I'd like at least a couple. Janna frequently talks about having a brother or a sister." His eyes roved her body relentlessly. God, but he'd like to plant his seed in her loving womb and have it flower with his child. Stella had given birth to Janna unexpectedly in New York when she was visiting. He had missed out on that.

With the talk of children, they grew quiet. "Music?" he asked her.

"No, I'm happy just sitting here talking with you."

"Same here."

"Hungry?"

"A little."

"We could eat now. Dance, talk later. I like to linger over dinner."

She smiled. "So do I. We like a lot of the same things."

He got up and pulled her to her feet. "Let's make this a collaborative affair."

In his stainless-steel kitchen, she breathed in deeply the wonderful aromas coming from the pots. He stepped into a pantry and came back out carrying a spray of gardenias in a crystal vase.

"I thought you'd like these."

"Thank you. I love them. They smell so good."

With a pair of kitchen shears, he clipped a blossom, leaving some stem, and put it behind her ear. "We need a hair clamp to hold it."

"We're in luck. I have a packet of hair clamps Dosha asked me to get." She went to her purse and got the clamp, fastened the flower more securely. He kissed her softly by the flower.

Sitting down to dinner, Chris smiled. "You have no idea how hard we worked on this—Janna even more than I."

The food was scrumptious with the promised shrimp-and-crab gumbo over brown rice. A big tomato, greens, and avocado salad sat in a crystal bowl. Soft French bread was cut in slanted slices. Maya didn't think she had ever tasted anything so good.

"Wine?" he asked.

"I'm going to stick with sangria. Usually I like white wine with seafood, but I'm getting besotted by sangria. Did you make the dressing? It's delicious."

"No. Mrs. Nickens gets credit for that."

Suddenly music came on. "The Andante Cantabile" from Tchaikovsky's *First String Quartet*.

"That was on time set?" she asked.

"Yes. Do you like what I selected?"

"It's one of my favorites. I could listen to it all day. Your music sounds wonderful."

"Yeah. I've got a newly engineered radio and it's quite remarkable. Radio and CD player in one."

"I haven't heard anything better, ever."

They ate slowly, savoring their food, making small talk. When they had finished, Maya got up, picked up the plates and salad dishes and took them to the kitchen. Chris came into the kitchen and in a few minutes had prepared on plates big slices of solid chocolate cake and mounds of homemade vanilla ice cream.

"Let's take this into the living room," Chris suggested. "Just a minute. I forgot something." He got a decanter of brandy from the wet bar and sprinkled it over the ice cream. Then, pouring some of the brandy over the cake, lit it with a cigarette lighter he got from a nearby drawer. The flames flared and their eyes met, held.

"You think of everything," she said. "I'm impressed."

"Not as much as I am."

Finished with their dessert, dishes stacked in the dishwasher, Chris and Maya lounged in the living room. She thought he looked so handsome in his tan tweed jacket, dark brown trousers, and cream-colored woolen gabardine shirt.

"We need to go jogging to work off all that food," Chris said.

"It's so cold out there. We could dance."

Chris laughed. "I anticipated that." He went to the CD player and soon Marvin Gaye's melodious voice filled the room with a dreamy, sensual song. She went into Chris's arms as if she belonged there.

And, she thought, *we danced at Wilson's the first night we met after so long a time of not seeing each other. He kissed me with a magician's touch. When will it happen again? Will it happen again?*

As if in answer, Chris's lips found hers. At first his kiss

was playful, warm, nibbling. Then his tongue darted into the corners of her mouth and she opened to him. Groaning, he held her tightly against him and his tongue sweetly savaged her waiting, responsive mouth.

Her breath was mint and honey. His big hands cupped her bottom in the soft cashmere skirt and he was nearly panicked with feelings deeper than any he had ever known.

Giddily Maya leaned heavily against him. As a Teddy Pendergrass CD switched on, she laughed a little. "See what a simple dance lets us in for?"

He shook his head. "It's not the dance. It's you. Us."

He drew away then, releasing her so abruptly, she almost fell.

"I'm sorry," he murmured. "Other things come before this."

Nonplussed, she frowned. "We can stay in control."

"Can we?" He sounded anxious. Bitter.

"Oh, Chris," she said softly. "Don't be afraid. If you don't want this to go any further, it's all right. I understand."

"Do you? Because I sure as hell don't. Come into the bedroom with me, love."

"Bedroom? But I thought . . ."

He placed a finger over her mouth. "Don't talk. Just come with me."

NINE

With a sense of wonder, she let him lead her to his bedroom. He bowed and gestured for her to sit on the king-size bed that was covered in a deep blue quilted satin spread.

"No peeping," he said. She glanced up at him to find his face somber as he left her. Walking over, he took something from a bureau drawer and held it behind his back.

"What is it?" she asked him. He sat on the bed beside her and held out a midnight-blue velvet ring box, then snapped it open. Three brilliant white diamonds winked at them. Her heart nearly stopped.

"How utterly beautiful," she breathed.

"The ring," he said, "was my mother's engagement ring. She didn't want Stella to have it." The ring was princess-style, flanked by two smaller diamonds. All together, the ring bore at least four diamond carats. Exquisite.

Chris looked sober, caring. "On her deathbed my mother told me when I found a woman worthy of my love, she wanted her ring on that woman's finger. It was not to go to anyone else."

"Oh, Chris." Warm tears came to her eyes. "I don't know what to say."

"I won't ask you to wear it now because I can't ask you to marry me, but I want you to keep it."

"Are you sure? I know you're still hurting."

"Yeah, I'm hurting, but it's gotten better since I've been

with you. Honey, you don't know how much you mean to me. I'm trying to get past this, but I'm not there yet."

He took the ring from the box and put it on her left ring finger, kissed her hand, his hot mouth on her hand thrilling her. Floodgates of desire opened in her then and she flung her arms around him fiercely. "Even if you're never able to come to me, I love you. I want you to know that."

She expected him to shy away, but instead he pressed her closer, so close her ribs hurt, but she did not cry out. It was an exquisite pain. He leaned back with her and rolled her on top of him as he kissed her with passion born of desire.

Then of one mind they struggled up, each disrobing, leaving clothes in a heap on the floor. Standing beside the bed, shuddering, for long moments Chris gazed at her silken, naked brown body. She closed her eyes against his sinewy frame with its rippling muscles and the brown wonder of him. He was so beautiful, she thought.

Standing near the bed, caught in a frenzy of passion, they spent a long moment getting their breath, then he caught and crushed her to him and lifted her. He held her tightly against him, glorying in the softness of her body against the rock hardness of his own. He rose against her like a mighty oak and she nearly fainted with desire. Still holding her, he bent and threw back the covers of the bed, then easily picked her up and laid her down.

She laughed shakily to steady herself. "Coming up, one broken back."

"Oh, I can handle you," he said huskily.

In a moment they were a tangle of hands and arms, then Maya relaxed, weak with wanting him. He intended to wait, caress her, kiss her all over, go slowly, but they were no match for the fires inside them raging out of control.

He got a thin latex shield from his nightstand. Rolling slowly under him, she pulled him in, and fighting to steady himself he entered the nectar-laden passage of her body and went deep. She cried out his name and he answered her.

Then he groaned as he felt the tremor of his loins and she moaned softly as she trembled in ecstasy.

He was wet with perspiration as they lay side by side. He leaned down and pulled the covers over them. "There is sex," he said softly, "and there is ecstasy sex which you get with love."

"Yes. Chris, you were so good."

She looked then at the ring that flashed fire on her finger.

"I want to be good for you and to you. Don't give up on me. If only you knew how I'm trying."

"I do know. You'll always have every ounce of patience I have."

He kissed the palms of her hands, tongued them softly. He asked, but he knew. He'd felt her.

"That was too fast. Did you climax?"

"Yes. I didn't need more time."

He held himself on his elbow and looked down at her. Slowly she stroked his still-moist flesh.

"What do you say about a shower with me?" he asked.

"I'd say by all means."

He got up, pulled on his robe, and went out to the kitchen. Going to the table, he selected several gardenias and took them back to the bedroom where Maya lay with the covers pulled up to her chin.

"What on earth . . . ?" she began.

"I brought them in for a reason," he said, placing them on the night table.

She was disappointed. Was he finished for now? This had been so good; she wanted more, much more.

"Rise and shine," he said lazily.

In the shower with its frosted sides, they let warm water splash over them and soaped each other lightly.

"Do you always shower when you make love?" she teased him.

"No. I'm just preparing for the long haul."

"The long haul?"

He laughed and rubbed his hairy chest against her breasts, causing her to shiver with joy.

"Yeah. That was a brief version of act one. Now we'll have act two and maybe act three."

"You're a greedy man."

"You're going to tell me you'd be satisfied with what we just got?"

"I could get by on it. It was that good." He slid his hand between her thighs and stroked her and she felt heat like a scorching late July day take her. He grinned, thinking he knew what she felt. Taking a condom from a shelf, he began to slip it on with her slender fingers helping him.

"Think you can stand it standing up?" he asked.

"Ah," she murmured. "This is no time for a play on words. This is serious stuff we've got here."

"Maya," he said softly.

"Yes, love."

"I love you more than anything in the world."

"And I love you the same way."

He opened a bottle of bath oil and spread a little on her, then himself. The aroma of sandalwood filled her nostrils as she closed her eyes.

He watched her long black lashes close against her cheeks. He entered her then with the warm water splashing over them.

"I said it was good," she said, "but this is glorious."

"Don't talk," he murmured. "Move, woman, *move!*"

And she obeyed his command, her healthy body working concentric circles as they stood there. They were silent then, building emotional bridges, each going deeper into the life of the other.

The house was silent, humming only with the electrical appliances. They got out of the shower and dried off with huge bath sheets. He had found that she had a personal odor beyond the bath oil on her now. Beyond perfume and cologne. Going into the bedroom, he switched on the CD player and reloaded it, set it to repeat. Marvin Gaye's "Sexual Healing" rolled into the room and Maya's heart lurched. The smooth baritone voice was luring them on. Chris. This man, this time.

They danced a little while, naked bodies feeding on each other. Then he lifted her and put her on the bed. This time he turned out the major lights and put a rose light from the night table into the lamp socket. Rose light covered them, making her radiate an unearthly beauty.

"Now," he said.

He stripped the petals from the gardenias on the night table and held some in the palm of his hand. The other petals lay on the table.

She didn't ask what he was doing. Whatever it was would be no different from everything he'd done this night—wonderful. Slowly he crushed the petals and rubbed them over the front of her body, then he turned her over and crushed more petals. She touched the gardenia in her hair.

"We're really on some island," she said. "Tahiti. The Caribbean. Hawaii."

"I don't need to pretend as long as I've got you."

Getting on the bed with her, he besieged her with kisses, his tongue darting relentlessly over her with wet kisses. His mouth lingered on her breasts, sucking the honey from each as if he were famished for sweetness. And, he thought, in fact he was.

Her nipples hardened as she stroked his flat nipples and she felt him tremble.

He cupped her face in his hands. "Okay," he said. "Let's get this show on the *road.*"

"You're greedy," she teased him again.

"You don't know the half of it."

He sheathed himself, then entered her slowly, his hands beneath her bottom, pulling her hard against him.

"I want to know all about you," she gasped.

"Just know I love you, and don't talk. I'm going to concentrate on what we're doing to each other. We'll talk later."

She smiled a bit wanly. She had been talking to keep from melding into him. Fusing with him. She bucked wildly then as she felt him inside her, thrumming.

After a short while, withdrawing, he began to kiss her all over again and this time he lingered in the core of her, kissing every bit of her and staying there as she cried out. He was wild with loving this woman, far beyond mere desire. He thought then that he was headed for trouble because he was going to have to have her now. There could be no going back.

And the thought of all that ragged, raw, ugly pain returning if she hurt him, made him wince. For a brief moment, he felt the old hurt, then he came back to the present. Maybe it didn't have to be that way. He could damned sure try.

This time as he entered her again, he slid into a deeper spot and she breathed a sigh of ecstasy and hugged him tightly. Again, her tongue played with his nipple and he braced himself to wait for her climax, but he didn't need to. She was streaking past stars in the firmament. Reaching out, she caught two stars, then laughing, realized that what she saw was the light in Chris's eyes. Her body shook then with climax and release and she loved him more than she had ever thought she could love anyone.

Chris gave one more deep thrust and he was over the edge, exploding in wonder like rockets shooting into space. He was here in this wondrous place, deep in the body of this beloved woman, surrounded by nectar sweeter than honey. He was warm and wanted, even as he wanted her. He felt the hard throbs of his shaft as he kept exploding, then he was rife with peace and ecstasy.

TEN

Maya woke early in Chris's bed. Sunday. Six-thirty. Chris slept soundly and Maya looked at his precious face. Reaching out, she touched the scar beside his eye, then leaned over and kissed it. He stirred and reached out for her, bringing her down to him.

"When will Janna and Mrs. Nickens be back?" she asked.

"Not until around twelve. They're going to church from her house."

"We should go to church."

"Believe me, I'll be taking you many Sundays. I want you to meet my pastor and his wife. But today I want to ride down to Hains Point."

"Oh? That's like going home—it's so close to where I live."

"I'm aware. We'll see the Roosevelt Memorial, Jefferson and Lincoln Memorials and look at the bare-branched cherry trees."

"And the Potomac."

"And the Potomac," he echoed. Then out of the blue he asked, "Why are you such an exquisite piece of work?"

"It doesn't seem to take much for you to think so."

"That's only where you're concerned."

"You're sure that's not just because you're a man?"

"I'm positive. I'm *feeling,* love, things I haven't felt in a very long time, and maybe never."

"So am I."

Chris looked thoughtful, sniffed a bit. "I keep inhaling a fragrance that's bewitching. It certainly doesn't smell like any perfume I've smelled."

Maya smiled lazily. "Voilà!"

"Okay, what is it?"

"You'd never guess. An Indian friend tipped me on taking a vanilla pod, steeping it in a little plain oil. It's wonderful for some foods and has a knockout fragrance. I put some in vials, and that's what's driving you mad."

He sniffed again. "No, sweetheart, it isn't the perfume. As much as I like it, *you're* what's driving me crazy."

She smiled her pixie smile. "Every day is Valentine's Day with you, huh?"

"Since you came along."

He traced her jawline with the tip of his index finger.

"God, I wish I weren't such a mess emotionally."

"You'll get over it one day."

"I sure hope so."

"Let's rise and shine. I want an early start," Chris said.

"On going to Hains Point?"

"On many things."

Something was happening to him, he thought. This woman's eyes on him were like stars and his heart lurched about, as if it would come out of his chest and join with her if he held back.

"Okay! Okay!" he murmured to his heart. "I'll hold her close."

" 'Her?' Are you talking to me?"

Chris gave her a fake leer. "Yeah, I'm talking to you. My own body is threatening to betray me if I don't squeeze you right now."

He pressed her sweet softness close to his own rock-hard body and she grew faint with wanting him again. She was melting with desire for him as he held her tightly enfolded in his arms.

"We're a couple of greedies," she murmured as he kissed her throat and stroked her body: the full hips, her pert, saucy breasts that seemed to be reaching out to him with their taut brown-tipped nipples.

Smiling, she searched his face and found it raw with wanting her. "What can I do for you, sir?" she murmured.

Without hesitation, he answered, "You can keep on doing what you're doing." Then his face got somber. "Maya, do you have any idea what you mean to me?"

She pulled away and propped herself up on her elbow.

"I know you like me, have some love for me, but I also know you're afraid, and I know why. We'll take it one step at a time."

"You're wonderful. I don't deserve you."

"Hush. You deserve everything that's good."

Each had gotten up and gone to the bathroom earlier, so there was nothing to stop their blossoming. In his arms, she looked at the crushed gardenia petals on the bed, at the leaves and stems on the night table. "Why are you smiling so?" he asked her.

Her skin grew very warm as she answered, "I'm thinking about last night." Her throat half closed with the rapture of his embrace.

"There's more where that came from."

"Like the sign in your shop says, you aim to please."

"And that goes double for you."

They moved in slow motion this time, intent on giving each other and themselves pleasure. She bent and lightly took his flat nipples in her teeth and he thrummed with joy.

"I've got your tender spot," she told him.

"Hell, I've got a *lot* of tender spots where you're concerned."

"Do men have a G-spot?" she asked him.

"We're an all over G-spot."

Making a loose fist, he tapped on her body just beside her core and at first she didn't get it. Then, laughing, she said, "Come in! Please come in." He smoothed on a sheath.

"We understand each other," he told her. "There's nothing we can't do together."

But no sooner had he said the words than a mild sadness filled his heart. She was giving him everything. What was he giving her?

He cupped her face in his big hands. "I never want to hurt you," he said fiercely.

"Please don't worry so, sweetheart. I know this isn't an ideal situation, but I love you and you love me. Things aren't perfect between us, but we have so much. Knock again and forget everything else." Her vision was misting as she pressed closer still.

And he did knock again and she opened to him. Relaxed, yet mildly tension-driven to a goal, they moved rhythmically and easily. Banked fires exploded to a conflagration, and in the hot, wet sheath of her body, he felt joy that only she had brought him. Throwing all else aside, he lived in this moment, with this woman, in this time.

Later he showered, then went into the kitchen to prepare breakfast, refusing to let her help him.

"Spoilsport," she told him between kisses. "I'm going to shower."

"Yeah. Don't need anything while you're in there. If I see your wet, naked body, I'm *lost*. Sweetheart, just exactly what in hell do you do to me? I've never felt this way before."

Maya grinned. "I'm your special gift, love, and you're mine. We're nature's gift to each other. Let's make the most of it."

When he came back a half hour later, she had showered and was in bed with her favorite cream lace nightgown with the very low V that showed most of her cleavage. He came in and set the tray on the nightstand. The gardenia he'd put in a bud vase reminded him of last night.

He stood looking down at her propped up in the bed pillows. "You're trying to drive me mad with lust," he told her. "You should be wearing something fastened up to your chin."

She raised her head, laughing. "I *like* turning you on. You turn me on. Oh, how you turn me on! I'll never need damiana, or Yohimbe, or any other lust-raising herb as long as I've got you. No more now. I'm starved."

Breakfast was out-of-season cantaloupe, shipped from Peru, a tall glass of freshly squeezed orange juice, scrambled egg with cheese, sourdough pancakes with blueberry syrup, and sausage, bacon, and ham.

Just looking at the luscious breakfast, Maya groaned. "Now, you know every time I look at food, my hips grow another inch. . . ."

"Shut up, woman, and eat. I will glory in your hips, even if they get ten more inches around. I've got big hands."

"I think you're lying, but I'm going to make myself believe you."

He got his tray from the kitchen and sat beside the bed.

"I've never been served breakfast in bed before," she said, "but I've often dreamed of it. Thank you."

"And I've never served anyone breakfast in bed. You're welcome. Something tells me that if I can ever get my act together, we'll make a lot of firsts."

Late morning found Maya and Chris on Hains Point by the Tidal Basin. Warmly dressed in a woolen dress and a camel-colored cashmere overcoat, Maya studied Chris in his camel-hair overcoat. His profile was to her as they stood at the railing watching the Potomac sweep by. A high wind rippled the Potomac River's waves in fanciful patterns. Suddenly he turned to her, put his hands around the sides of her shoulders.

"Maya," he said softly, "if I die tonight, I would say I've gotten a lot of the best the world has to offer, and do you know why?"

She shook her head slowly. "No."

"Because you've brought me everything I ever wanted, but I—"

"It's all right, love," she told him. "I can and will wait."

He crushed her bundled form to him and hugged her tightly. "I love you," he said. "I'll always love you."

"That makes two of us," she said quietly. "Just hang in there, tiger. Come hell or high water, we're taking our show on the road."

He laughed heartily then, but looking deep into his eyes, she saw sorrow deeper than any she had witnessed. Les had covered his feelings or felt little. Life was a game to him, based on wealth and success; humans were expendable. Chris was tender, seductive, rich with feeling.

He was everything she had ever wanted in this world.

They walked around, looking at the monuments they had seen so many times before. The bare capillary-vein-arterial limbs of the cherry trees stood in naked splendor, awaiting the millions of blossoms and leaves that would clothe them in spring's thaw in a couple of months.

They walked back to the Hains Point railing. "I can't forget last night," Chris finally said. "Being inside you was like some kind of magic. The way you welcomed me, held me, was so wonderful. I'm sorry I have no words to tell you what it meant to me."

"Ah, yes, last night," she told him. And because she felt bashful, Maya asked him, "What about this morning? Short, but very, very sweet."

"Oh, God, Maya, *all* of it." He took her gloved hand and kissed it. "You're the woman I've got to have, honey. I would take a chance, even if it tears me up, but I'm trying to protect you."

She thought about the ring in her purse and a few tears came to the corner of her eyes. "You're my best protection," she said. "I feel secure with you, Chris. I always have. I always will. If you hurt me, I'll know you couldn't help it and I'll understand. Believe in us. Believe in yourself."

ELEVEN

Early Monday morning, as she talked with Clara, Walt Hampton, Chris's best friend, came by Maya's store.

"Hey, Wonder Woman," he said cheerfully.

"Sounds good," Maya said, "and I thank you, but why do you call me that?"

"You've got my buddy hitting on all his cylinders."

Maya's skin warmed. "If that's true, I'm glad. He's certainly set me rolling."

They beamed at each other, all over the absent Chris.

Clara came up with a question. "Isn't horsetail one of the herbs we have to be careful about? I can look it up, of course, but I need the info quickly."

"It certainly is," Maya told her. "It's one of several that we have to look out for."

"Thanks. I thought so." Clara told Walter, "Anything you want to know about herbs, just ask the chief here."

Maya's attention piqued. These two were looking at one another in a special way. "Can I help you with anything?" Clara asked Walter.

"Believe me, I'll think of something. Are you free for lunch?"

Clara looked startled. "I think so."

"Good. I'll pick you up at one. Is that a good time?"

"It's perfect," Maya cut in. "And don't hurry back."

Clara laughed. "Thanks, boss. Now if we can go to some

place in his district, he can take as long as he wants. My
brother is a Memphis cop. I'm on to their ruses."

"Jeez, I try to make a simple date and I'm categorized,"
Walter said, laughing.

Maya had her back to the door, so she didn't see Les
until he was at her elbow. He put his hands on the side of
her shoulders and turned her to him.

"Angel face," he said tenderly.

"Don't *do* that," she said sharply, and he chuckled, proud
of himself, and moved away to pore over stacked boxes of
herbs on the shelf.

The phone rang and it was Chris. "How about going with
me to Mimi's tonight" she said, "to help me select a ball
gown?"

"I'm game. What time?"

"I'll meet you there around seven-thirty. I've got things
to finish here."

"Done. I'm still walking on cloud nine. What about
you?"

"Same cloud. Chris, we can make it."

She thought better of it no sooner had she said it. No
one could feel someone else's pain; they could only imagine
it.

She quickly said, "I'm sorry, honey. That was a thought-
less remark. Forgive me. I only meant I'll stick with you."

"Don't apologize," he said gravely. "I know you're on
my side and I couldn't be happier about that. One day . . ."

He didn't finish his sentence and she went on to talk of
other things.

That evening at Mimi Rogers's dress shop on Connecticut
Avenue, Maya felt more than a little tense. What could she
do to make Les keep his hands off her?

She rang the bell, and Mimi, a roly-poly, beaming woman
with pale skin and black hair, greeted her at the locked door.
No sooner had she settled inside than Mimi let Chris in.

As Mimi went to the back to get the dress rack, Chris kissed her quickly.

"Shouldn't we have had dinner first?" he asked.

Maya shook her head. "I was in the pizza mood at lunch and I overdid it. Meloy's has fabulous pizzas and I ate late. All that pepperoni is still hitting home runs in my stomach."

Chris laughed. Narrowing his eyes, he reflected that he couldn't look at her without reliving the past Saturday night and Sunday morning. Why in hell couldn't things be different? He *had* to fight free of his fear.

Seeing that something was on his mind, Maya wisely kept silent.

Coming back, Mimi gave Chris a wide, benevolent smile. "You're going to have a treat to watch. As a dressmaker, damn, I'm good."

"You're the best," Maya praised her.

Taking a long time, Maya selected five dresses and Mimi took them to the dressing room.

"I'm so excited, I'm forgetting my manners," Mimi said. "I've got fabulous frosted raspberry tarts and almost any kind of liquor you choose, plus coffee, tea, et cetera, et cetera. I'm not going to watch my weight while it's what it is. If I gain any, I'll be more careful."

"I'll watch Maya's weight," Chris said as they disappeared into the fitting room.

Then Mimi left Maya in the fitting room and went back to Chris. "You've just got to try a tart. You've got that lean, hungry look."

Chris laughed. "You don't have to ask me twice."

"What're you drinking?"

"Coffee, please. Cream, no sugar."

He glanced around him at the magazine rack, got up, and selected an *Ebony* and an *Esquire,* then also decided on a *Black Enterprise.* "I missed last month's issue of *Enterprise,*" he said. "I get a world of help from it."

"So do I," Mimi said, going back to her kitchenette.

She served the raspberry tart on a lovely flowered china plate. "I made these, so you see I'm not a one-talent woman. Relax. You two are my last customers. I'm closed for the night to everyone else. Maya is a favorite."

"Great. She's my favorite, too." They smiled at each other.

Mimi went back then to help Maya with the gowns.

Maya chose a fitted yellow silk jersey shot through with silver spangles. It displayed her figure to marked advantages. She looked at herself in the mirrored fitting room and sighed. How was she ever going to make up her mind? Well, that was why she had asked Chris to come.

At the fitting room door, she saw that he was deep into a magazine.

"All clear?" she called.

He put the magazine aside. "As clear as I can get when a beautiful woman is displaying it all for my benefit."

"Just stick to the subject."

"I am. Model it for me."

"What do you think I'm doing?"

"Well, give it the model spunk, more pizzazz, lady."

"Well," she retorted. "You try working all day in a shop and having any pizzazz left over."

"You've got it. You just don't like flaunting it."

Holding her head high, Maya modeled the gown in front of him, turning, half turning as he looked on, pleased.

"I like," he said. "How many are you going to try?"

"Mimi knows how important this is to me, so I'd guess all five. It has to be perfect, Chris. It really does. This masked ball means so much to all of us. What do you think about you and me going as Freda Erzulie and Damballah, the voodoo god and goddess of love?"

"Sounds good to me. Where do we get the masks?"

"At a shop over in Georgetown. Enough of this dress. Let's see what you think of the others."

She was soon back out in a pale blue chiffon, draped and flowing. She came to him and he got up, kissed her on the lips. "The show's getting better and better."

His enthusiasm fed her happiness. He sat down and she made a few more turns for him, then popped back into the dressing room, where Mimi came to her. "I've got one here I had forgotten. I put it away as a must-have to show you. I warn you, you're going to faint with pleasure."

Mimi unzipped the white dress bag and drew out a soft rose-red silk, peau de soie gown. Maya gasped. Mimi had outdone herself. The skirt was half-full, its silken fabric falling in soft folds. The bodice was stunning. Maya slipped into the dress with Mimi's help. Cut low and nearly backless, it was draped in blossom fashion into two folds that stood away from the breasts with an inner curved portion that displayed cleavage, but hid what needed to be hidden. Spaghetti halter straps wound around her neck.

In the salon, Chris put the magazine aside, making a mental note to read a certain article the next day. "Hello," Maya called, softly, standing at his chair. She walked away from him then, to the center of the room and she jolted him. He whistled loudly, long and low.

"Really," she teased him, "you're going to run out of compliments before we're done."

Chris half rose, then sat back down. "That's *it,* sweetheart. That dress is for a queen and that's you. *Take it!*"

"If she doesn't, I'll take it and make her wear it."

Maya looked at herself dreamily. "It is lovely, isn't it?"

"Magnifique!" Chris said, wondering what was happening to him. He was thirty-four, and not even in his teens had he been so turned on. What was this woman doing to him?

"Well, I guess that's it, then," Maya said. "I'll look at the others, but I don't know when I've liked a dress this much. Don't bill me for this one. I'm sure it's very expensive. I'll write you a check now."

"Mimi," Chris said, "may I speak with you a moment?"

"Of course."

Maya looked at him with surprise. "I'll go into the fitting room and look at the other gowns. Give you two some privacy."

Maya separated the several gowns on the dress rack and looked at each one. The woman was a designer from the heart, but she had seen Chris's eyes flash fire as he looked at her in this particular gown.

Back in the salon, Maya got her purse. Mimi shook her head, "No."

Maya looked at her, then at Chris. What had they talked about?

"The gentleman is taking care of the bill," Mimi said.

"Oh, Chris, you can't. This is so expensive."

Chris grinned, then was sober. "I'm doing well, so I'm not exactly a pauper. What good is money if I can't buy something for a special woman?"

When she still looked uncertain, Mimi went back to the fitting room and Chris continued. "You wouldn't let me give you anything expensive for Christmas or for your birthday. Now, let's add it up. This is for Christmas, your birthday, and yes, Valentine's Day to come. I'm going to be the proudest man at the Sweetheart's Ball. Don't spoil my pleasure. Please."

She hugged him, leaned against him. "When you put it that way. You gave me the ring."

"That was a gift of love from my mother, who would have loved you."

"Thank you."

"Besides, right now I'm withholding the most precious gift of all—myself complete, free. Or is that putting myself too high on the totem pole?"

"No. That's exactly right."

She felt misery sweep her then because his words were a reminder. She was in the ball game, but she was a long way from being home free.

Driving down northwest Seventh Street, Chris slowed at the MCI Center.

Maya said thoughtfully, "Someone coming back would never recognize the East End. No wonder they call the AARP Building D.C.'s Taj Mahal. All these splendid apartment buildings, museums.

"If you ever get a chance, go into a building to your left three blocks down. There's a room in that old building shaped like an egg and an atrium you wouldn't believe."

"Yeah," Chris mumbled, and was silent.

"My dress is really beautiful."

"Stunning."

Maya put her hand on his thigh. "Cat got your tongue? You haven't said ten words since we left Mimi's."

Chris expelled a harsh breath. "Stella called shortly before I came to pick you up."

"Oh?"

"They're—she and Duncan—coming in day after tomorrow. She wants to talk with me about some things. I couldn't get her to say what."

"And, of course, Duncan's been here before. They painted the town red when you were still married."

"So true." Her saying it brought a sharp pain in his chest.

"Chris, I'm sorry. It's plain you're not feeling good about this visit."

"I couldn't get a damned thing out of her. I just can't imagine what's going on. When I last saw her, six months ago, she came alone and said she was thinking of moving back to D.C. . . ."

"Maybe she was putting out feelers for going back to you."

"I never knew. I gave her short shrift."

"Chris?"

"Yeah."

"Maybe I have no right to ask this, but don't you think in some small part of you, you're still in love with Stella? She's a beautiful woman."

"No," he said tightly. "Stella is stunning, gorgeous physically. Poised. Well-spoken. *You're* beautiful. You radiate care and concern for others and your world. Stella's selfish to the bone. . . . Look, I'm sorry, but I don't want to talk about it.

"But I'll tell you this. I want you to go with me when I talk with her. I was still just mulling it over."

"But isn't that going to be awkward?"

"I shouldn't think so. Duncan will be there. When he's around, he shadows her."

"Yet he's not ready to get married?"

"Something like that. Will you go with me?"

"Yes," she answered without hesitation.

"She's asked that I bring Janna. . . . You never know with Stella."

He sounded bitter and more than a little angry, and she cooperated with the silence he seemed to need.

Chris didn't come in, but he parked and walked her to her lobby. He kissed her gently. "Don't mind me. You were a knockout in that dress. You're the one who's beautiful, Maya, all the way through."

TWELVE

Maya was a little nervous about meeting Stella and Duncan when Chris and Janna picked her up from her apartment. Dressed in a heather-lavender silk-and-wool wraparound dress, with an amethyst pendant and matching drop earrings, she looked radiant, but felt she was no match for the beauteous Stella.

At her apartment door, Chris whistled the way he had two days earlier when she was trying on her ball gown.

Janna's face lit up. "Gee, you look pretty, Maya."

"Thank you, love. You both look spiffy."

"Mom bought me this coat. She sends me a lot of things."

"As for me," Chris said, "I'm glad if I appeal to the lady."

Maya smiled. "I give it way past mere appeal." She hugged them both then and went to get her wrap, noting that both father and daughter wore tan cashmere coats. She had been going to wear her navy princess line overcoat with the fox fur collar, but chose instead a plain cashmere coat that nearly matched theirs.

"Oh, great," Janna said, laughing. "We're Papa Bear, Mama Bear and Baby Bear."

Chris smiled at her fondly. "You're a mighty happy kid."

And Janna glowed, moving ahead of them as they set out.

* * *

Stella and Duncan had chosen the Four Seasons hotel in Georgetown, one of the city's poshest. Stella answered the door to their room and Janna made a beeline for her mother, crying, "Mom! You look so beautiful."

"Why, thank you, little one."

Chris introduced Maya as his fiancée. Stella smiled thinly and shook hands.

Janna threw her thin arms around her mother, but Stella took a deep breath and disengaged the child's hands and arms.

"Now, sweetie, you don't want to spoil Mommy's sparkling white clothes." She'd preened for their benefit in her winter-white wool suit and emerald-green lace blouse that showed her red-gold hair and emerald eyes to great advantage. Perfect grooming gave her the illusion of even greater beauty.

"My hands are clean. See? I washed them before I left the house."

"Oh, there now. Be a good girl, will you?"

"Okay, Mom." Janna's voice sounded so resigned, and a look of hurt passed over her face. "Where's Duncan?" she asked.

"Here's Duncan." A medium tall, beige-skinned man with light brown hair came into the living room from the bedroom. Janna started toward him, but he stiffened, held out his hand. "How are you, kid?"

"Fine," Janna mumbled.

"Nice suite they gave us," Duncan said, smiling.

"Yes," Chris said, looking a little grim.

"I'm going to order room service," Stella said. "Of course, help yourself to the hors d'oeuvres and whatever is in the bar. We have plenty."

Chris spoke up. "We won't be staying long. You wanted Janna to come by."

"Yes, she's the reason we're here. Tell me what you'd like and I'll order it."

"Nothing for me," Maya said, thinking they were milling about like people at a boring cocktail party.

"Janna and I have eaten," Chris said, thinking it was okay to lie under the circumstances.

"I don't want anything, thank you," Janna said in a small voice.

"What? No sodas, no strawberry tarts for you?" Duncan tweaked Janna's ear and she flinched.

Then the child's appetite got the best of her. "I don't see any tarts."

"They're in that basket under the white cloth. Go ahead. Eat one, or a couple."

"Dad? Maya?"

"You go ahead. We may want one later," Chris told her.

Stella's smile was dazzling. "I'm your mother and I always think of what's best for you."

"Can we sit down?" Duncan asked.

Stella and Duncan sat close together on the sofa. Maya and Chris sat on a sofa, with Janna in a straight-back chair.

When they'd entered the suite, Maya had noticed that Stella seemed to be wearing a wedding band. Now she turned it around, displaying a big white diamond.

"Beautiful," Maya said. "Congratulations."

"I'll say," Duncan interjected. "That bauble set me back a pretty penny. Next comes the plain, gold band and that's why we're here."

"We're leaving early in the morning." Duncan pursed his lips. He might have been a handsome man, Maya thought, if his presence didn't seem so devoid of deep feeling.

Janna dropped her tart on the deep beige rug.

"Oh, really," Stella scolded her. "You're too big a girl to be spilling and messing up things. Now, that's enough. Forget what I said about another one."

Chris got up, went to his daughter. He took her napkin and put the crumbled tart on it and threw it into the wastebasket.

Without saying anything, Maya poured a little water from a pitcher on the table into a handkerchief from her purse and wiped up the small amount of strawberry stain. Chris gave her a grateful glance. "It's okay, honey," he said to Janna. "Don't feel bad. More than one time when I was a kid I spilled spaghetti, chocolate ice cream. You name it. Being a klutz makes a kid seem more like a kid."

Janna giggled with relief and turned to her mother. "I'm sorry. You look real pretty, Mom."

Stella lifted her chin, posing. "You're *so* good for my ego. Come here."

Janna rose from her chair and stood by her mother who touched the child's hair. "Who's taking care of your locks these days? I'd like to give them a few whacks. Smooth hair looks best on you—not braids, for heaven's sake."

"But my hair's not naturally smooth—like yours," the child protested. Stella's bejewelled hand went to her own silken hair.

"I think her hair is lovely that way," Maya broke in. "It's all a matter of choice." Her hand went to her own braids.

"Yes, I guess it is," Stella replied. "Ah, well, when I tell you why we're here, I don't think this will be so important. Sit down, Janna."

Dutifully the child sat back down. Then Stella said again, "Come here. Sit beside me, but please don't touch my nice white suit. Can you do that?"

"Sure," Janna assured her mother.

Maya frowned. Was the child breathing faster? Or did she imagine it?

Stella sat between Duncan and Janna, with her hand in Duncan's. "Do you want to tell them, or shall I?" Stella asked him.

"Maybe I'd better. I can be more realistic about it."

"Tell us what?" Chris looked at the pair levelly.

"I'm marrying Stella, at long last," Duncan said evenly. Then he thought a moment. "Maybe you'd better tell her the rest. She's your kid."

Stella's alabaster skin paled. "Well, here goes," she muttered. She put a perfectly manicured hand behind Janna's back. "We made a lot of plans for the summer, remember?"

"Oh, yes," Janna breathed. "Duncan's buying me a boat to sail on Diamond Point. And we're going to Africa and Europe. All summer. The whole works." Her little face suddenly glowed.

"Well, I'm afraid you're going to be a little disappointed. . . ." Stella said.

"Disappointed?" Chris asked harshly. "What is it?"

Stella plunged in. "Duncan and I are getting married in early summer and we are, indeed, touring a number of countries on our honeymoon. . . . I'm sorry, little one, newlyweds really don't need company."

Janna reacted as though she'd been slapped across her face. "But, Mom, Duncan, I wouldn't be in the way. There're people who would watch me for you. You *promised*. . . ." She couldn't keep the hot gush of tears away.

"That's enough, Janna," Stella exploded. "I didn't raise you to be a spoiled brat."

Chris got up, went to Janna, and pulled her up from between Stella and Duncan. "She's not a spoiled brat, Stella, and I won't have you calling her one. She's disappointed and disappointment *hurts*. Not that you'd know much about that."

"I was disappointed enough in *you*," Stella said coldly.

"Let this be about Janna."

"I'm sorry," Duncan cut in. "Maybe I should have handled it, but it's one of my failings. I'm not all that fond of kids. No patience. We've got little to say to each other."

Janna looked stricken as she glared at Duncan. "But I thought you liked me. *You* were the one who said you'd buy me a boat. I didn't ask you for one."

For a moment, Chris began to shush her, but decided to let her have her say. Then he pulled the child up and hugged her. "It's all right, love. It's all *right*. Maya, you, and I will go away on a great trip to New York."

The sobs slackened then and Chris pulled a big white handkerchief from his pocket and dried Janna's tears.

"I said I'm sorry"—Stella thrust her chin out—"and I am, but things happen to us we don't always like." She threw out her arms theatrically. "Be happy for me, all of you," she trilled. "I'm so happy for myself."

She and Duncan hugged and kissed and nuzzled as if they were alone. "Forgive us," Stella said. "We're in love." She studied her ring again. And Maya's eyes nearly closed, thinking of Chris's mother's ring, now hers. *That* ring was far more beautiful than any she had ever seen.

"I guess we'd better go," Chris said finally. "I hope you two find the happiness you look for."

"Speaking of happiness," Stella purred, "you two seem close, yet I see no engagement ring. What's going on?"

Chris smiled grimly, his eyes narrowed. "It's a private matter, but these days I don't envy anyone."

Out on the street in front of the hotel, the parking lot attendant went to bring Chris's car around. As they stood waiting, Maya stroked Janna's shoulder in her heavy coat.

"Okay, dollface?" she asked the child.

A wild sob suddenly took Janna. "I'm no dollface," she grated. "I'm *ugly*. Mom's the dollface and you're a dollface, too. I'm always going to be ugly. . . ."

Maya pulled the child to her. "No, sweetheart. Listen to me. We all go through trying times when we're growing up. You *are* beautiful, but the way a child is beautiful. And I promise you when you're grown up you'll be even more beautiful."

The child was not to be consoled.

"Mom promised me the trip and Duncan promised me the boat. I *hate* promises. Don't promise me anything."

Ruefully, Maya thought Janna was always so sedate and placid, that one forgot she was only ten, until times like this.

"I know you're hurt and you're disappointed," Chris said, "but Maya is trying to help. And she's right. You're my little beauty queen."

But the child's body stiffened in Maya's arms after a moment of relaxing and Maya bent down to look at her. Her forehead was cold when she touched it. "Janna!" Maya cried. "What *is* it?"

"I—I can't breathe," Janna wheezed.

Chris turned to the doorman. "Please call an ambulance," he ordered.

THIRTEEN

Later that night, Janna was hospitalized at George Washington University Hospital. Chris and Maya were beside themselves with anxiety.

As Chris and Maya stood near her, Janna twitched spasmodically, and cried out in her sleep, "No, please. I want to go with you."

A blond young man with spiky hair came in. "I'm Dr. Mark Hudgspeth," he told them. "I'm an ear, nose and throat specialist, and I checked Janna when she first came in."

The doctor called Janna's name, but she slept, snoring lightly.

A black-haired, tan-skinned young woman paused on the doorsill and came in with her hand extended.

"I'm Dr. Annice Steele. I'm a resident, and child psychology is my specialty. How is my patient? Has she been asleep long?"

"Yes," the other doctor answered. "She's been asleep about an hour or a little more."

Chris introduced Maya and himself.

"Thank you both for getting to my daughter right away."

Annice shrugged. "We do our best, and sometimes that's very good. Could we sit and talk about this?"

Chris nodded and they walked over to a bank of four plastic cushioned chairs and sat down. "Some background will be helpful." Dr. Steele's voice was soft, soothing. She liked this young couple and ruefully thought she would kill for Maya's hairdo.

"If I seem to stare," Dr. Steele said, "it's only because I'm admiring your beautiful hair."

"Why, thank you," Maya responded. She had felt the sting of Stella's criticism about *smooth* hair, which probably meant straight hair. She had nothing against that, either. She wore her hair in many arrangements.

Chris gave Dr. Steele the background of Janna's asthmatic attack. When he finished, the doctor nodded. "I'm glad you didn't take this lightly. Asthma can be very dangerous. Her breathing isn't all I want it to be, so I won't talk long. Dr. Hudgspeth and I are working together on this. For the moment, she's okay, but I don't want her to weather another attack until she's strong enough."

Chris gave the doctor a brief background of the night's events.

"Children are so easily disappointed," Dr. Steele said. "They take separations hard."

"Janna's always been good about that," Chris told her. She has seemed to shuttle between her mother and me nicely. She's always been an outgoing child."

"You noticed no change after the divorce?"

Chris thought a long moment. "A little. I expected some. I may have closed my eyes to it. She had violent spells of asthma when she was a child, but lately she's had no attacks at all."

"What span of time do you cover with *lately?*"

"I'd say three years or so. I expected her to fall apart with the divorce. She didn't. She said she wanted to stay with me winters because she liked her classmates and friends. She was delighted to go summers to Diamond Point to be with her mother."

"Is she close to her mother?"

Chris thought a long moment. "I'd say she's always been closer to me. Her mother is very active socially and didn't spend a lot of time with her when she was younger. Beginning at about age nine, it seemed to me she began to worship at her mother's shrine."

"Her mother's a beautiful woman," Maya added.

"I think it goes beyond that," Chris said. "I think she was and is beginning to feel rejected and this is her way of playing up to get the attention she needs from her mother."

"I think you're right," Dr. Steele said. "Now you're free to wander around a bit while I talk with Dr. Hudgspeth."

"Dad!" Janna's plaintive voice called.

Chris quickly went to the bed and hugged the girl.

"I passed out."

"Yes, you passed out."

The ENT doctor came to Janna's bed. "You're looking a whole lot healthier," he said, grinning. The young man turned to Chris and Maya. "She gave me quite a scare. Now my hope is unlimited."

"Maya," Janna said.

"Yes, love."

"You're so good to me. I love you. I love Dad. But, please, could Mother come to see me here? Dad, if you talk to her, I'm sure she'll change her mind and I could ask again, too."

Fantasies of fabled trips through Africa and Europe had filled Janna's head for many months and she felt a stake through her heart to give them up.

Chris glanced at his watch. It was six minutes past midnight. Stella and Duncan were late-nighters. He thought she'd come to her child's side.

"Sure, baby," he said gently. "I'll call now."

Reluctantly he left the room. He had no wish to speak with Stella. Damn her selfishness.

At the pay phone in the hall, he called information for the hotel number. It seemed to take forever to reach them. The voice was clipped, efficient. "I'm sorry, sir. Those parties have checked out."

"Checked out? But I was by there several hours ago."

"I'm sorry, sir, but while we were talking, I checked again. They've signed out."

"Thank you," Chris said tightly.

Checked out. He doubted Stella gave a thought to the disappointment she must have caused Janna. He could have cheerfully strangled Duncan and Stella.

Chris felt his step lagging as he went back to Janna's side. The doctor was tapping and probing her skinny little chest.

"Well, Dad, what did she say?"

Chris felt his throat constrict. "I'm sorry, sweetheart," he told her gravely. "They've checked out. Stella said earlier they were going to New York from here." He put a hand on her cheek and stroked it, as one lone tear trickled down.

"If you feel like crying, cry. Let it all hang out," Dr. Steele told Janna.

"That's for sure." Dr. Hudgspeth seconded the advice.

"Now," Dr. Hudgspeth said to them, "I think she's rallying, but did you bring her bad news?"

"Yes. It couldn't be helped."

"Too bad. I think she's over the worst part, and I have truly good inhalers that will handle whatever comes up." He turned to Dr. Steele. "You talked with her?"

"A little. She was groggy. You had given her a mild sedative."

"When she's fully awake around morning, could you question her about anything that might help me treat her? I'm going to hold her for at least a day. I think we can be on top of this."

"Good," Dr. Steele responded. "Why don't you two go and get some rest and come back around eight in the morning?"

"I'd just as soon stay," Chris said.

Dr. Steele shook her head. "No. I want you both to get some rest. And I want to talk with you, Mr. St. John. I think this child is in a mild state of shock. We call it post-traumatic stress disorder. It's more difficult to treat in children. They don't understand as well. Will you follow my suggestions?"

"Yes," Chris said. "But I won't be able to sleep."

"Then rest, as best you can. I know what you're up against."

At the pay phone, Chris called Mrs. Nickens and told her what had happened.

"Can I help in any way? Oh, the poor darling."

"I'm sorry we didn't call you earlier. Everything's just been so helter-skelter. I thought it was a minor episode and we'd be bringing her by. No. There's little any of us can do, but you know how much I appreciate your asking. I'm going to spend the night at Maya's and we're coming back here in the morning."

"I'll go and pray for the little darling, and don't you forget to pray, too."

"You have no idea how many times I've prayed. She's got to be all right."

He didn't tell her what had happened with Stella, just that Janna's mother had given her bad news. But Mrs. Nickens clenched her fists. She had *never* liked the vainglorious Stella. One day she should have to pay for all the damage she had done.

At home Maya prepared grilled-cheese sandwiches and hot chocolate. Both Chris and Maya took only a few bites of the sandwiches and could eat no more, but they drank the soothing chocolate.

In the living room Chris sat on the sofa. "My poor Janna," he said sadly. "To have this hell come back on her when I thought it was gone for good."

In the bedroom they slept fitfully in each other's arms. Maya hugged him tightly in the glow from the night-light and her heart was heavy when she saw a tear trickle down his cheek just as one had trickled down Janna's.

FOURTEEN

Janna went home two days later and Maya kept tabs on her by visits and by phone, but she didn't seem to recover. In spite of talking to Dr. Steele, the psychologist, the child was depressed, fearful.

Chris came over late three nights after Janna had been discharged.

At Maya's door, they went into each other's arms. "There is something I have to talk with you about," he said.

"Okay."

"This isn't going to be easy." He looked deep into her eyes, then kissed her long and hard as if he couldn't stop.

"Let's sit down." He ran a finger inside his collar.

He led her to a love seat and sat beside her.

He cleared his throat. "I don't know how to say this."

"Just start at the beginning."

"I talked with Stella, chased them down. They're back on Diamond Point."

"Oh?"

"I'm going to Diamond Point and I'm taking Janna. I'm going to try to make Stella change her mind. I don't think she's thinking clearly."

Maya nodded. "It may not be a bad idea."

"I thought you'd see it that way. Now please understand what else I have to tell you. . . ."

A quick shiver raced along her skin. He looked so tense.

"I'm cutting you loose. Maya, I love you more than I ever thought it possible for me to love, and I know you love me."

"Yes. You're breaking up with me?"

"For *your* good, my darling. I've had a chance to think long and hard. You deserve so much better than the tattered heart I can offer you. One way or the other, I'm going to beat this thing, my terror of just coming apart. When I care, it goes so deep.

"My little girl is like me. She's taking her cue from me, I've come to believe. She's in pain because I've been in so much pain. Can you understand that?"

"Yes, I think I understand. When do you plan to leave?"

"Tomorrow morning."

She reflected dully that this time he had not asked her to go with him—as a buffer—to Stella.

He pulled back his jacket and got a pen and pad from an inner pocket. "You can always reach me at this number. Give me a chance to get it together without your warmth and your tenderness. I can't lean on you and pull myself together."

"Don't I help you?"

"Of course you do. But you make me think of what could happen if you should decide to pull out."

"I wouldn't—"

He pressed his hand against her mouth. "Hush, sweetheart. We never know when we'll get tired, fall in love with someone else, move on. None of us can really know our hearts completely."

He looked so strained, she was alarmed for him. He had to let her help him, but he didn't want her help.

Losing his grip on the pen he wrote with, he watched it fall to the rug and bent over to retrieve it. Without thinking, he went on his knees to her. Putting his arms around her waist from where he knelt, he buried the side of his face in her lap.

"My God," he said. "My little girl's heart is broken, and

I can do nothing to help her. Damn Stella! Damn her to hell!"

She stroked his hair and the side of his face as her tears fell on him.

"I want to help you," she told him. "There is a bond between Janna and me."

"I know. There's a strong bond between me and her, but the strongest bond she seems to feel these days is with Stella. Dr. Steele said children change allegiances at certain ages, but she's worried about Janna, too."

"Does she feel going to Diamond Point is a good idea?"

"She thinks it could help. Stella may not be thinking clearly, and I'm sure she doesn't realize the severity of Janna's illness. I'll keep in touch."

"I know you will."

"Check on Janna, sure, but know that I'm breaking away in order to come back stronger, if I feel I can. I won't ask you to wait. You've got too much going to be linked to the emotional cripple I am."

"No," she said. "I refuse to believe that. You're a deeply hurt man, not an emotional cripple."

"It's true. I'm going to leave now while I can. I want to hold you, make love to you from the depths of my heart, but I won't. In some future, if you haven't found someone else, perhaps we can be together again. . . ."

"I won't find somebody else."

"I hope you can if I can never heal from this."

He got up then, and she rose with him, put her arms around his neck. He gently disengaged them.

"I'm not going to kiss you again, or make love to you. I love you more than life itself, and loving means protecting the one you love. You deserve far more than I have to give right now."

She had to ask it. "Are you still in love with Stella?"

He shook his head slowly. "I've asked myself that same question. And I don't think so. But the feelings of rage are still there, so there must be something. I only know that I love *you,* Maya, more than I've ever loved anyone. But I've said it before—I've got to free myself."

She placed a slender hand on each side of his face.

"I believe," she said, "I really believe that new love can heal the hurt that old love has dealt us."

He smiled sadly and said nothing.

He left then and she wandered about the apartment like a ghost. She felt weightless, as if she didn't exist.

She went to her wall safe, slid back a panel, and watched it come open. She got the diamond and sat on the bed with it in the soft light from a bedside lamp.

Had he held her the night he gave her the ring? In agony, she felt every stroke, every nuance of his body interlocked with hers. Felt him deep inside her, throbbing with love and desire.

"Stop it," she whispered. "He's gone, and no matter how much it hurts, my love couldn't stop him."

FIFTEEN

Next morning at Healing Hands, business was slow. Rain drizzled drearily outside and the sky was overcast. Maya stood near the big plate-glass windows as Clara waited on the store's one customer.

Reluctantly she thought about Chris and the night before. No kid should have to suffer what Janna was going through now. Was the trip to Diamond Point going to be a wise one? she wondered. Then she thought, only time would tell.

She had eaten a diet bar and drunk a big mug of very strong black coffee after she got to Healing Hands. Racing to get out of the apartment, she had felt overwhelmed by her visions of Chris in torment. She didn't think he still loved his ex-wife, but the chains of emotional slavery still seemed to partially bind him. And he had asked her to call only to check on Janna. *He'd said he had to free himself.*

Chris had also said that many emotions masquerade under the mask of love. Fondness. Caring. Affection. But *was* it a masquerade? Didn't love, in fact, *incorporate* all these emotions? They served as the lagniappe—an extra particle—of love.

She had been looking down when she was aware of the door opening, water being shaken from an umbrella, and a loud cough. She looked into Les's merry eyes. "Hey, don't let me wake you up," he chortled. "How's it going?"

Maya shrugged. "Well enough," she began, but things

were not going well enough. She shook her head and didn't say more. Her three coworkers had been solicitous, kind, but hadn't pried. Her face, in the mirrors she had encountered at home and here, was bereft of joy.

"Hey," Les offered, "you don't look so hot. Need a shoulder to cry on?"

"No. But thanks for offering."

He cocked his head to one side. "Something tells me this is about man and woman stuff. St. John let you down?"

"Les," she protested. "You always were too inquisitive. It's none of your business."

Les laughed. "I'm a lawyer, sweetie, in case you'd forgotten. I'm one of the best, and nosiness goes hand in hand with it."

"If you say so."

A raincoat-clad figure came in the door. Lillian. She made a beeline to Maya, pausing between Les and her. Even in her misery, Maya noted the silent interchange between these two, and she had some questions of her own.

Lillian kissed her cheek. "Here I am, a long way from my shop in Georgetown. I'd have brought you some flowers, but I came from home. I need to get a copy of the invitation list. Don't ask what for."

"Clara knows where it is. She can make you a copy or you can make your own."

"Hey! You look kind of beat," Lillian exclaimed. "Has that gorgeous St. John been keeping you up late hours?"

Maya bit her lip. "Let's not talk about anything personal."

"Sure," Lillian said, looking at her friend closely. "One more week and it's Sweetheart's Ball time. I, for one, can't wait."

Maya could think of nothing that interested her less at the moment. Was she the same joyous woman she'd been a few days ago?

Lillian turned to Les. "Keep me company. Give me someone to flirt with while I make copies."

"You got a taker," Les said jovially. "I'm your man."

They went off, giggling like two schoolkids and Maya decided she wouldn't brood; she'd keep busy.

She saw Walt Hampton in his policeman blues reached the shop, and she met him at the door.

"You picked a nasty enough morning to be out in," she told him, trying to hide how upset she was.

"Hell," he said, "for a policeman or woman, *any* morning is liable to turn into a nasty one."

"You wouldn't give it up for anything."

"Never said I would. Look, can we talk a minute?"

"Someone's making copies in my office. Is out here good enough to start?"

"Yeah. I'm not going to say much. My buddy told me what happened at your apartment last night. Of course, I know about his kid and Stella's disappointing her. Chris is fit to kill. I know you've never seen him torn up like this."

"I can take it. I only want to help, and I think I can."

The dark brown man with his clear mahogany-colored eyes looked at her and sighed. "Let him go for a little while. Let him find himself again. Stella's doing what she did opens the old wounds and he's bleeding badly. I predict he'll come back to you, but I sure don't know when. He really loves you and that's a fact."

Clara passed and he grabbed her hand. "A quick good morning," he said.

"Good morning to you," Clara greeted him, smiled deeply, and passed on.

Walt bit his bottom lip. "You've been as good as gold for my buddy and I want everything good for you two, but I know him. He bucks when someone doesn't believe in him, let him have his way. . . ."

"How am I doing that?"

"He thinks you might not understand how he can hold on to his pain so long. I tell you, the guy feels guilty about still being angry at his ex-wife. He's scared it might mean he still cares about her. Now, my take is he completely loves you and is over Stella. I'm no psychiatrist, but I know it sometimes takes a helluva long time for some things to sink in. Give it time, Maya. Sure, check on Janna while they're on Diamond Point. He told me he told you to. But let *him* go for the moment. See what happens."

He stopped and took her hand, squeezed it. "Well, I've got to go courting. Give Miss Clara a few minutes off, will you? And, Maya, I'm really looking forward to that masked ball." Then he grew sober. "I'm just sorry it can't be a happier time for you."

"I'll manage. You go ahead and court. And yes, Walt, I'll take your advice." She paused a moment. "Do you think their going to Diamond Point was a good idea?"

"I do. This way Janna can't help but know her dad's on her side, pleading her case." He grinned impishly. "I predict that the three of you will one day be a happy family."

Maya tried to smile, but it fell flat. Hamp walked away to join Clara. *One day,* Maya thought forlornly, *but* when?

Lillian left with her copies, but Les stayed on.

"Looks like you and Hampton had a lot to talk about. I haven't run into him in quite a while."

"Nosy bug's got you again."

"You tickle the hell out of me when you say that."

"Because it's true?"

"I guess. Now, I don't want to take up all your time, but can I ask you some trenchant questions?"

"If you'll stop being a lawyer for a few minutes and spare me such terms as *trenchant.*"

"No problem. Maya?" He seemed to fumble for words, unlike the Les she thought she knew.

Quite wistfully, he said, "You used to tell me I needed to change, that some parts of me were decent, good. Do you still believe that?"

"Yes, I do."

"In spite of my taking my client's money?"

"Those were the bad parts of you."

She would have sworn she saw tears in his eyes, but they didn't fall.

"In prison and now, I dream about my dead client. She haunts me, and I tell you I'd pay her back twice or more over, if I could. I may have caused her death. I know that now."

Maya looked up, surprised. "When you came by here when you got out of prison, you didn't seem penitent to me. Were you?"

"Yes, I was penitent. My father taught me to be as hard as nails. He thinks you're not a man unless you are. But I'm not going to blame him. *I* did what I did. I've been changing and didn't realize it or fought it. Now I can accept that I want to change. I've *got* to change."

"Now it's my turn to be nosy," Maya said.

"Shoot."

"Why is it so much more important now? I assume it is."

"Yeah, you assume right. I can't talk about it yet, but I will soon. And, Maya?"

She looked at him levelly as he touched her cheek. "Thank you for always being honest with me, for telling me like it is. I hope everything goes well with you and St. John, if he's what you want."

Maya only nodded, not trusting herself to speak.

Business picked up and Maya found that getting involved in running her store kept her from thinking of Chris and Janna.

She sat at her desk looking at planning photos for the ball. They had enough pledges to give four one-year scholarships to Howard University. But Maya, Dosha, and Lillian wanted to do much more and had set up for it. She had no doubt that their ball would be gorgeous this year.

Her heart hurt when she reflected that this year was to have been her greatest masked love ball. She had all of the emotions that added up to love in Chris, she was sure, but would he ever be free to completely love her?

The phone rang and she answered on the first ring. A soft little voice said, "Maya?"

"Janna!"

"I won't talk long. I still don't feel so good, and I've got a bad cold."

"I'm sorry, sweetheart."

"Do you miss me?"

"Oh, how I miss you, and you know what, I miss those delicious cookies you make and I hope I'll be getting more soon."

"Do you really?"

"Yes, really and truly. I really look forward to eating them with you and Chris and Mrs. Nickens again."

Maya heard a quick sob from Janna and her heart constricted.

"Bye, Maya," the girl said. "Good-bye."

Maya held the line open for a moment. It had been so eerie, like a fairy voice. She wanted to go to Janna, sweep her into her arms, and comfort her, make everything all right. But at the moment, she was unable to bring comfort to herself. Clasping her hands under her chin, she prayed as she always prayed that God would assuage the child's, Chris's, and her own suffering and their pain.

When she got home that night, Maya found two gray-and-white doves on a perch in a cage. Her cleaning lady left a note saying they had been delivered late that afternoon. There was a card saying simply, "Chris." Nothing about love.

The birds came with enough food for a month and detailed instructions on their care and feeding. She broke down and cried then.

She slept fitfully and got up twice to check on the birds. Without clearly thinking it, she told herself, "You need a baby to check on." Her body hurt with craving Chris.

On Diamond Point Island in the Caribbean, Chris walked slowly along the beach near his hotel. It was evening and he thought the heavens surrounding him had never been more beautiful.

He had just been to talk with Stella and Duncan. Janna

had a heavy cold and was in bed. Who was it who said that the germs of *heartbreak* and *disappointment* were what caused colds? He had thought Stella was relenting and would go through with the plans she and Duncan had initially made to buy Janna a boat and take her with them on major trips.

Duncan had shrugged. "Why, sure, I can buy her the boat. That's little enough, but try to see my side of it, St. John. Not everybody loves kids, and I'm one who doesn't. Stella understands. Don't you, babe?"

Duncan and Stella had kissed then, long and ardently, and Chris had left, crestfallen. As he walked away, Stella had gone with him to the door. "It'll work, Chris. You'll see. She's just a child, and I think we've all spoiled her. Time for her to grow up."

But, he thought now, Janna wasn't just a child. She was one of the lights of his life; the other was Maya.

Walking on the powder-soft white beach, watching the star-spangled sky and the nearly full moon, Chris closed his eyes. What was he going to do about Janna? His heart hurt for her disappointment. Some people took things harder.

The moon seemed to come closer, shedding its pale light. "Okay, Mr. Moon," he said with bluff heartiness, "you're the keeper of hearts, god of Valentine's Day. Tell me what I do now."

And what was he going to do about Maya? As he said her name aloud, he *felt* her presence, smelled her vanilla fragrance. Vanilla. Trust Maya to know the little known. He was sick with the memory of her naked body under and over his, her silken skin and fragrant hair. The beautiful black braids he loved to play with. He reached out to touch her softness. The air was empty, and he nearly cried aloud.

In two days he and Janna were due to go back. All his pleading was for naught. What in hell was he going to do?

Treading sand, he walked to a gift shop just off the beach and selected a huge black-and-white stuffed panda. Kids liked stuffed animals. It sure as hell wasn't what his kid needed or wanted, but it might help a little.

Mirthlessly he chuckled to himself. Two days and it would be Valentine's Day. The first day of birds' mating season. He envied them. He would send Maya flowers and candy, had sent a pair of doves, but he would not be at the Sweetheart's Ball. He had to stay a while longer, talk some sense into Stella. Make her see what she was doing to Janna.

He remembered Maya in the rose-red dress he'd bought her, her eyes sparkling and her long, black lashes sweeping her cheeks.

Where did they go from here?

SIXTEEN

The night of the Sweetheart's Ball was clear and starry. Maya, Dosha, and Lillian all arrived at Wilson's early and found themselves ecstatic over the decorations. As sad as she felt, Maya felt her spirits lift.

Dosha caught her hand. "It's going to be all right," Dosha said, stroking her friend's hand. "And maybe you can be happy for me, even if you are unhappy."

"What's going on with you?"

Dosha's face was immediately wreathed in smiles. "I'm pregnant," she said, and Maya hugged her.

"That's wonderful. I'm delighted for you."

"I wanted to call you last night. I just found out yesterday, but I wanted to see you when I told you."

"Oh, this is just the best of news. Was it in vitro, or is that none of my business?"

"My life is your business, sweetie. You're my best friend. No, it was not in vitro. It was in snuggle-up-to-each-other and let nature take its course. I recommend it."

A shadow fell across Maya's face. She wasn't getting any younger. "Does Lillian know?" she asked.

"No. I wanted to tell you first. I'll tell her sometime during the ball. We're so busy talking babies, I haven't had a chance to tell you how magnificent you look. That's some gown."

"This is the present from Chris I told you about. I haven't had a chance to show you."

"He really loves you, and I know you love him."

"Yes, on both counts. I adore your dress." Dosha preened a bit in her empire-style cream silk jersey that flattered her slightly thickened form.

Maya looked at her friend through half-closed eyes. She had noticed a burgeoning of Dosha's figure but had absent-mindedly thought she was gaining weight. Dosha loved sweets.

The friends all knew which mask they would be wearing. Dosha touched Maya's mask. "You found a good replication for Freda Erzulie, voodoo goddess of love."

"I think so. And you're no slouch with your tigress mask."

"Ladies." Rip, Dosha's husband, came over to them. "Gorgeous gown, Maya."

She thanked him and he asked her, "Has my wife told you her news?"

"She has, and congratulations."

"I'm a happy man."

"I know Wilson is the best when it comes to entertainment," Dosha said, "but he's outdone himself."

A pat on her back caused Maya to look around and into a dove mask which hid Lillian, resplendent in burgundy-draped satin.

"Tweet-tweet," Dosha teased. "Where is your escort?"

"He'll be along shortly."

The four walked over to Wilson Cartwright and his crew of servers dressed in red-and-gold jackets and black trousers. Wilson wore a tuxedo as did all the men who were guests.

Wilson quickly thrust champagne glasses from a tray into the hands of the four. "I promise you the evening and night of your lives," he said. "Four hours of joy and bliss."

"It's already started," Dosha said, "but then I've had a ball just planning this and working with you." Dosha looked at Maya a bit apprehensively. She wished her friend could be happy, too.

The dance floors were highly polished. Palm trees were set about. A huge banner proclaimed the theme of the ball: THE WONDROUS WORLD OF LOVE. In one section of the room, depictions of famous couples lined the walls, with captions underneath. Romeo and Juliet, Damballah, the great snake god, and Freda Erzulie, the voodoo goddess of love. Maya, Dosha, and Lillian had drawn from the world in selecting their tribute to lovers.

"I can feel it in the air," Wilson said. "This is a success before it even begins." He glanced at his watch. "Ten o'clock." He went to a nearby microphone and announced, "Ladies and gentlemen, *ball time!*"

The band was Love'n Us, led by Rich Curry and his wife, Ellen, featuring Rafe Sampson who tore up a harmonica, had a husky voice and had a large following of fans. In his sixties, he had long mastered his art and had done himself the favor of coming out of the alcoholic shadows.

Rip and Dosha danced off, but not before Dosha had given Maya's hand another little squeeze. It was good to have friends, Maya thought. They helped when your world turned upside down.

She thought Lillian looked splendid and told her so. Looking at her dove mask, she smiled behind her own mask. "You couldn't have picked a more appropriate thing to be," Maya said.

"It wasn't altogether my idea. I'm just beginning to date a sort of vain man. He likens us to two doves." Maya smiled sadly as she thought of the two doves Chris had sent her.

Maya chuckled. "I think I see your mate coming over."

"Ladies," the tall man said as he reached them, "the masks are great. The gowns are splendid." He kissed Lillian's hand first, then Maya's.

"I'd know that gesture anywhere," Maya told him. "Les, you and Lillian make a great pair."

"How'd you guess?" he teased.

"She was your wife for these many years," Lillian told him, "and anyone knows your voice. It's quite distinctive."

"Guilty as charged. Dance, babe?"

"Are you going to be all right?" Lillian asked. "I mean, we're leaving you alone."

"Feel free. I like my own company." She walked over to where Wilson stood alone, surveying his wonderland. Long-stemmed red roses lay in a heap on a long table and ball-goers were claiming them.

"If I had a fortune, I'd share it with you," Mimi the dressmaker said as she came up to Maya. "Isn't she a fabulous ad for me?" she asked Wilson.

"I'll say," he answered. "All the masks are stunning. Good thing I have a list of the masks I need to talk with."

"Sometimes we have more than one mask of the same character," Maya said. "If necessary, I just have to ask."

Mimi's husband claimed her and they danced off.

With a start, Maya saw a man in a Damballah mask, and her heart leapt, but as he danced closer, she saw the man was far shorter than Chris. She nearly wept with disappointment.

Someone in an elegantly draped black ball gown came up to Wilson. Her mask was of a female lioness; her partner had a really stunning male lion's head. Maya almost expected him to roar any minute, and wondered who they were.

"Wilson, you've set the ball world on fire this time. I'm going to make sure my fraternity uses Wilson's for our spring ball from now on."

His companion added, "A number of my sorority sisters went wild when they saw this place tonight."

By eleven, Rafe Sampson and Love'n Us had hit a high stride and dancers were lively one set, then close and swaying the next.

Ellen's sweet soprano voice caressed them:

"Like a season of the year
    you changed and left me.

After you wooed and won
  my lonely heart.

Like all nature we went through
  a birth and dying.
Now like nature, can't we make
  another start?"

That was the chorus and Maya listed carefully. But it was
the last verse that caught and held her.

"It is winter now, and
  I sit thinking.
  I believe, I just believe
  that I can make you know
That I'm still here, and I still wait
  and, oh, my darling,
We can be hurt, but heal with
new love, and so."

She barely heard the chorus as she thought about the
verse as Ellen sang it. *I believe, I just believe. . . . We can
be hurt, but heal with new love.*

"I'm your new love, Chris," she whispered. "I'm your
new love who can heal your broken heart."

The food was superb. Baked hams and turkeys, sushi,
roast beef and roast pork, fried fish, candied yams, a variety
of carved raw vegetables and green salads.

A huge bowl of pineapple-rum punch sat on a table by
itself. Another of eggnog, thick and velvety, sat a little ways
away. A stunning, huge heart-shaped cake sat on a table on
a wooden wedge slanted for better display. Numerous
smaller cakes sat on nearby tables.

Pies and tarts, and bowls of mixed nuts were set about.
Wilson brought Maya a sampling of a lot of the food.

"You've got to taste this apricot-stuffed pork roast," he
said. "My chef is a master at everything he touches."

Maya didn't feel very hungry, but she accepted the food and bit into it.

"Best pork I've eaten," she said after a minute. "I've never ordered your pork. I'm always busy getting stuffed on the sushi and your fried turkey."

"Come more often. Try everything. What do you think of my doves. I mean, the *real* birds. I think that was quite an idea."

"Oh, Wilson, you're chock-full of ideas. This one is especially close to my heart."

"Well, what else could I do? After you told me it's thought Valentine's Day is the first day the birds mate, my mind got to humming."

Maya looked again at the large section enclosed with wire mesh, painted white. Behind the wire were fifty pigeons flying about and resting on swing pedestals. A sight to behold. Maya reached out and pressed his hand. "Only you would think of this."

"Maya, let me ask you a question I perhaps shouldn't ask."

"Feel free."

"Is something heavy on your mind?"

"Yes. You're very perceptive. But I just can't talk about it."

"If there's anything I can do . . ."

Maya's coworkers, Jackie and Peetie, then Clara and Hamp, came by. "We've really got this cooking," Clara said.

"I'll say," Maya replied.

"Are you enjoying yourselves?" Maya asked Jackie and Peetie.

"If it gets no better, it's already been about the most fun I've ever had. That band is hot!" Peetie exclaimed.

"Thank you so much for making us a part of this. I'm loving it," Jackie assured her.

Maya looked at Hamp and Clara and smiled. "I'm going to be nosy," she said. "I think you two have gone beyond the lunch stage, even dinner. Would you say you're a couple?"

Hamp's eyes nearly closed as he laughed delightedly. "I'd

never deny it." He looked drolly at Clara. "Let's dance, woman. Show me love!" Then he looked at Maya and rubbed his chin.

"You're going to dance at least twice," he said. "There'll be no turning down invitations to dance. As soon as I get Clara's heart to jumping, I'm coming back to get you."

Maya couldn't help laughing at his zaniness. "All right," she said. "I'll dance with you."

Both Hamp's and Clara's eyes on Maya were sympathetic.

"You circulate, you hear?" Hamp said. "My buddy wouldn't want you to brood."

Maya reflected that the masks went the gamut. Animal masks. Birds. Famous lovers. She and her friends had done a marvelous job and a helpful one with the scholarships.

Wilson announced it was time for the scholarship awards. Initially, it was to have been Maya's job to announce winners, but she asked Dosha to do it. Now Dosha was onstage proclaiming the winners.

Two young girls and two males, all four of whom would graduate from high school this spring, were the happy recipients. One girl cried and Dosha soothed her. The girl hugged her tightly, as did the other three students.

"This," the girl said into the microphone, "is the most wonderful night of my life!"

Maya wandered out to the glass-enclosed annex where one could see the stars and to the smaller annex that would only hold a few couples. She remembered when Wilson had laughed and said, "This is my special place for special lovers."

She had been ripe with laughter then; now she felt so sad. Janna's little voice came back to her saying, "Goodbye." For a moment, she felt a blazing hatred for Stella. How was this going to end?

Going back to the eggnog bowl, she ladled herself a half cup and sipped it. She had eaten little since Chris left. She hadn't asked him when he'd return. He needed time away from her. Suddenly, surrounded by all the merriment, she felt a small pain in her chest and tears filled her eyes.

This was to have been a night of nights. She looked down at the beautiful rose-red silk peau de soie dress and thought about the diamond in her wall safe. She looked up at the starlit night and wondered: *My love, what are you doing now?*

Unmasking would take place shortly before twelve and the ball would last two more hours. At twenty of twelve, four people who were willing to give up their claim to the prize were selected to judge the best masks.

Maya touched her own papier-mâché mask. Freda Erzulie. Goddess of love. Earth Mother. What irony. Tonight, Maya was a waif and alone.

Dosha came to her again. "Are you okay, love?"

"I'll survive. I know you're having a baby, but what gives? You're more than ecstatic."

"I guess I am. Bear with me."

Maya's laughter was a little choked. "Chris always asked me to bear with him."

"Have faith," Dosha said. "Trust."

The loudspeakers were busy announcing that the judges were ready with their decision on the best masks, and the room buzzed, then grew quiet.

Wilson did the honors. The superb lion and lioness masks took first prize, a peacock and his hen took second. Then human replica masks took over. Third prize was for a farmer and his mate. Honorable mention was a crowned king and his queen, parading in fake ermine capes.

A woman near Maya, giggly with champagne and having a good time, told Maya, "I want to link hands with your group. You've got the world on a string."

Maya smiled and thanked her. More and more her heart weighed heavily in her chest, then for a stunning moment, she *felt* Chris's presence as if he stood beside her. She gave a little gasp of surprise and looked around her. The masks were all off now. In a few minutes it would be midnight and he was not here. A sob rose in her throat and she choked it back.

"Maya, please come with me," Dosha said. "I want to

show you a certain star that's out tonight. Maybe it will bring you luck."

On the way out to the glassed-in connection, Maya stumbled and Dosha caught her. The clock struck midnight and joyous cries sounded from behind them. A man in a tuxedo in a Damballah mask stood with his back to them.

Dosha called. "Turn around," and he did, taking the mask off. Maya's feet had wings as she went to him, crying, "Chris, oh, Chris! You're here!"

Holding her so tightly, she thought her ribs would break, he whispered, "I have so much to tell you."

"Don't talk," she said. "Just hold me."

Dosha slipped away quietly and they were alone.

Through tears, she told him, "I just *felt* you with me a few minutes ago. Can you understand that?"

He nodded and, between kisses, told her about the time on the beach in Diamond Point when he had *felt* her presence.

"We have to be together. We're for each other."

"I wasn't sure when you were coming back. I only had faith that someday you would."

He held her face in his hands as he talked, as if he could never tire of looking at her. "I thought Janna was getting worse; she was so disappointed in her mother and Duncan. They refused to change their mind. I left her in the hotel room with a baby-sitter, dozing and I walked on the beach. That's when I felt you with me. When I came back, she was sitting up, looking far less ill.

"She told me she had called you, that you two didn't talk long, but you told her you missed her cookies. Her face was beatific when she said it. Then she grinned impishly at me and asked, " 'Dad, why don't we go back and marry Maya?' "

Maya's laughter pealed in the cool room. "Is this a proposal?"

"You're damned right it's a proposal, wedding to take place as quickly as possible."

He thought her eyes were like stars as she told him, "I think that can be arranged."

He squeezed her tightly again, then relaxed a bit.

"We should go in," she said. "We have almost two hours to dance and make merry. The setting is beautiful."

"We'll stay fifteen to twenty minutes," he demanded, "then we're going home."

"I want to dance with you." She pretended to pout.

"We can dance at your place. You got the doves?"

"Yes, and they're billing and cooing up a storm. It eased the pain . . . a little."

Looking earnestly into her eyes, he said, "I never want to hurt you again. My love for you is no masquerade. It's as real as anything can be." His kiss then was long and ardent and they both wished it never had to end.

In Maya's apartment that night, they stood at the windows looking out on the Potomac River as it swirled sharply in the wind, sparkling like diamonds.

Maya pulled away a little. "Happy birthday, love. I have something for you. I was going to send it by messenger."

She went to the night table, picked up a gold foil-wrapped package, and took it to him. He unwrapped it carefully and smiled beatifically at the gift. A black leather-bound special edition of the *Holy Bible*. Still holding it, his arms encircled her and he could not seem to hold her tightly enough.

"My love," he said huskily. "My precious love."

Her eyes were like stars as she told him, "You once told me that if you hadn't prayed when you and Stella broke up, you wouldn't have made it. Always pray, Chris. It's the kindest thing we can do for ourselves."

Chris walked with her by the birdcage, reached in, and smoothed one bird's feathers, which caused the bird to ruffle.

"The birds kept you company when I couldn't be here."

"Ah, no one keeps me company the way you do. You

didn't eat any of that splendid food at Wilson's. What can I get for you now?"

"I'm not hungry for food," he said with a fake leer. "I just want my fill of you."

"What am I going to do with you, greedy man?"

"Fill me to the brim with your sweetness."

"We were going to dance here. Remember?"

"Later."

In the dimmed rose light, he unzipped her dress and helped her out of her clothes until she stood before him naked. Then she helped him disrobe. His tongue probed the hollows of her throat and breasts as they lingered on the cusp of ecstasy. He watched her long black lashes and her closed eyes. It was time. He lifted her then and carried her to the bed, where he gently lay her down.

In the midst of the most passion she had ever felt, she asked softly, "How's your back holding up?"

"I can handle you," he replied. "I promise."

Wild with desire, his big hands stroked her as she trembled beneath him.

Laughing, she whispered, "Don't take all night. I want you now."

He laughed explosively, ready and willing to do her bidding.

"At your service, ma'am. The first possible moment, I want a baby with you, on your beautiful body. Are you game?"

"I'm game and more. We have a few sets of twins in our family."

Torpor overtook her then and a splendid surge of passion. Deep inside her, he felt the tremors of his turgid proof of love.

"The birds know what it's all about," he murmured. "Happy Valentine's Day, my love."

ABOUT THE AUTHOR

A Mississippi native, Francine Craft has lived both in Washington, DC, and in New Orleans. She has pursued a lifelong interest in writing, including magazine and newspaper articles and songwriting. She is also keenly interested in photography. A retired government legal secretary, Francine has been an elementary school teacher, a business school instructor, and a research assistant for a large nonprofit organization.

Francine lives with a family of friends: a dozen big, lively goldfish; a parrot; and a very large Siamese cat that likes to jump from high furniture onto her lap.

Francine would love to hear from you and will answer all correspondence. You can write to her at: P.O. Box 44204, Washington, DC 20026.

FORBIDDEN FANTASY

Linda Hudson-Smith

To Rudy—my beloved husband, my forever
valentine . . .

In loving memory of Mary Edna Cook

Sunrise: August 9, 1926
Sunset: August 12, 2001

ONE

The powerful propellers of the magnificent cruise ship *Forever Fantasy* sliced through the crystal waters with ease. Leaving a frothy whiteness in its wake, the large ship sailed from San Juan, Puerto Rico, destined to make port in five captivating islands of the Southern Caribbean: St. Thomas, St. Maarten, Dominica, Martinique, and Barbados.

Excitedly animated over the prospect of spending fourteen wonderful days at sea, and lazing on the sunny beaches of the Caribbean, the passengers crowded at the railings of each deck, releasing colorful streamers into the air, waving farewells to friends and family members who stood ashore shouting enthusiastic "Bon voyages."

The spiraling winds gushed through Ashleigh Ayers's long, cascading copper-brown ringlets as she watched the shoreline rapidly grow distant. Flushed from the stinging, cool winds, her healthy champagne-gold complexion had begun to take on a windblown appearance. Using her delicate hands to shield her luminous topaz eyes from the sun, Ashleigh turned her face away from the menacing elements.

With no one on shore to bid her farewell, Ashleigh felt overwhelmingly sad and all alone. All through her childhood it seemed as though no one had been there for her, that no one had ever really cared about her. Though she was traveling with her dear friend Lanier Watson, loneliness was never very far away.

Abandoned at birth, she often felt all alone in the world. A Catholic orphanage had been Ashleigh's home from the time she'd been born until she'd turned six. She knew very little of her background, but she was aware of how she ended up living at the Angels of Mercy Orphanage.

Many years later she'd learned that her sixteen-year-old mother, whose name she'd only recently discovered, had left her at the orphanage located on Galveston Island, Texas, in the care of Sisters Theresa and Alberta. All she'd ever been told was that her mother had no means to care for her after her teenage father had been accidentally killed while working to repair a Texas storm-damaged highway. He had been hit by an intoxicated, speeding motorist. Her parents were to marry on the very day his funeral had taken place. If they'd been married at the time of his death, her mother, who committed suicide the day after she placed Ashleigh at the orphanage, could've raised her child on the widow's benefits she would've been eligible for.

Wiping the falling tears from her eyes, Ashleigh forced a bright smile to her generous lips. She hadn't come on this cruise to throw a pity-party, she reminded herself. She was sailing away with the hopes of achieving a sense of closure regarding the two sets of parents she'd lost a long time ago. Her natural parents and her foster family, the only ones who'd ever really loved her. She also needed to bring closure to a fantasy relationship she'd been dreaming about for the past twelve years, a relationship that was obviously never meant to be.

A romantic Valentine's Day cruise was the perfect place to start looking for a real, flesh-and-blood soul mate. A soul mate that would love her the same way she loved him would be a dream come true. Even though a lot of couples would be on the ship, Ashleigh was told by her travel agent that many single men had also booked through her agency for another special event. But the only dream come true for Ashleigh was Austin Carrington. He was the only man she'd ever desired, but his heart belonged to another.

Now that the handsome African-American NFL quarterback, Austin Carrington, often referred to as A.C. by his Texas Wranglers teammates, was engaged to be married, Ashleigh knew her fantasies had to come to a screeching halt. Besides, she hadn't seen Austin face-to-face since she was twelve years old, but she never forgot the intense promise he'd made back then.

He'd even made a promise to keep his promise.

Mindless to the spraying mist assaulting her delicate skin, Ashleigh closed her eyes, turning her face back toward the swirling sea air. Sighing deeply, Ashleigh traveled back in time, allowing her mind to go adrift. She then conjured up the sweet memory of a special place in time, a time when she had been referred to as Sariah, her actual middle name.

It was a fine spring day as twelve-year-old Sariah sat on the front stoop of the Carrington home, the foster home she'd resided in for four years. Birds chirped sweetly, flowers tossed out heady scents, and the family dog, Tyler, was busy chasing a darting butterfly through the crisp green grass.

Ashleigh recalled how she had smiled so beautifully when Austin's tall, lanky frame settled on the step below the stoop where she sat. Austin had always been shy and kind of unsure of himself, but right after he'd turned sixteen his confidence began to skyrocket. Besides being the most popular guy at Jefferson Memorial High School, his heralded position as the starting varsity quarterback had become an even greater boost for his confidence.

As Austin made himself comfortable on the lower step, he took Sariah's small, fair hand and placed it in his large, toffee-brown one. Quickly, he withdrew his hand when two exact replicas of him came from around the side of the house. The Carrington triplets were dead ringers for one another, but Sariah always could tell Austin apart from Dallas and Houston.

Austin Carrington was the only triplet that brought the sunshine into her smile. . . .

"Come on, Austin," Dallas drawled in a heavy Texas accent. "The other guys are all waiting for us at the baseball diamond. We're going to be late for practice if we don't hurry up and get across town."

Austin rapidly got to his feet. "Go ahead and get in the car," he told his two siblings. "I'll be right there."

Smiling tenderly, he turned back to Sariah, reaching for her hand again. "I've got to go, little one, but I'll be back. I love you, Sariah, and I'm always going to take care of you. You and I will always be together. That's a promise. And I even promise to keep that promise!"

Although Austin had looked upon Sariah as his little sister, it hadn't stopped her twelve-year-old mind from fantasizing about him and hoping that she'd one day grow into a beautiful woman, a woman that he would fall hopelessly in love with and one day marry. Sariah lived and breathed life into that fantasy for the next twelve years. As Ashleigh, she still held on to that pseudopromise of long ago.

Even as Ashleigh opened her topaz eyes, Austin's final words still rang in her ears. She'd never seen him face-to-face since that fateful day. That very same afternoon, and for a reason that was still unbeknownst to her, she had been removed from the Carrington residence and placed in yet another foster home. Though she'd survived her horrendous situations, they were experiences she'd never, ever forget.

Although twenty-four years had come and gone since the day she'd been abandoned, the painful memories of yester-years were always fresh in Ashleigh's mind. The scars weren't visible, but they were there, running very, very deep. Those horrible memories would forever reside inside of her damaged soul. . . .

A light touch on her shoulder grasped her attention, launching her back into the present.

"I've been looking for you," whined the five-foot-eight siren, Lanier Watson, Ashleigh's closest friend. "Where the heck have you been?"

Ashleigh brushed loose strands of copper hair from her face. "I've been somewhere between now and the past twenty-four years." She scowled at the rapid beat of her heart. "I'm sorry. I know I promised not to do this, but I can't seem to help myself."

A sympathetic smiled played around the corners of Lanier's full mouth. "It's okay, Ash. I know exactly how you feel. I've also been fighting my own demons of the past." Lanier wiped a single tear from her own mahogany-brown face. "We might have been mistreated orphans, but we turned out to be pretty darn good women despite our unfortunate circumstances. Once we get back home to Galveston Island and start fixing up that large old house we've just purchased, we're going to help as many abandoned and abused kids as we can take on. That is, without allowing the quality of their care to be compromised."

"I second that emotion." Ashleigh felt her melancholy mood lifting. "That's a pretty big house we've bet most of our savings on. Six bedrooms can hold a lot of kids even if it is going to take us a while before we'll be ready to fill them all up. There's a lot of work to be done on that old place."

"I know." Lanier shook her shiny black curls. "We should get to our cabin. I still can't believe your Mr. Early bestowed this wonderful trip on us. He is some kind of man, Ash!"

Taking one last look toward the barely visible port, Ashleigh blinked hard. Leaving one island for another island paradise seemed so surreal to her. She'd never been to another state and here she was in another world. Yes, old Mr. Early was some kind of man. A very dear, wealthy man, Ashleigh mused with warm sentiment. He also was a man who thought of Ashleigh as his very own daughter, treating her as such. He loved to shower Ashleigh with lavish gifts because he thought she'd already lived a lifetime of misery for one so young.

Thomas Early had become Ashleigh's mentor and her saving grace. With more money than he could spend in one lifetime, he was known for donating large amounts of cash to black colleges so that underprivileged African-American students could get a quality education. As an honor student,

Ashleigh had been one of the lucky recipients of the Thomas Early Scholarship Fund. Her counselor had given her the good news.

Although Mr. Early often visited the inner-city high schools, he rarely got personally involved with the students who were to benefit from his altruistic spirit. But when he'd heard about the poor honor student, Ashleigh Reed, who hadn't even been recommended by her teachers to receive a scholarship, he had taken matters into his own hands. He'd only met with Ashleigh briefly, but it was only after he'd heard from someone else about how hard her life had been that he took a very special interest in her future. The cruise was just another way for Mr. Early to show Ashleigh how very proud he was of her glowing academic accomplishments and for the loving, compassionate woman she'd turned out to be.

Ashleigh sighed as she gathered her copper ringlets to one side and twisted them around her fingers. "He *is* something else. And that's why we're not going to turn this trip into our usual pity-party session." Ashleigh laughed. "By the time we get back to Galveston, our troubles and my Austin Carrington will be but distant memories."

Rolling her eyes, Lanier snorted. "And a married man, I'm sure! However, we've had enough sadness for right now. Let's go below and get ready for the evening."

As her mind turned over three of the words Lanier had so innocently spoken, Ashleigh followed alongside her friend quietly, feeling the sickening impact of her comments.

A married man . . . she echoed silently. Just the thought of Austin marrying anyone but her made her want to scream out loud her vehement disapproval of his upcoming nuptials.

Ashleigh stopped to take one last glance at the rolling sea. It was so beautiful. It was a perfect day, a perfect time of year, a perfect time to get on with the rest of her life.

Looking annoyed and puzzled at the same time, Lanier nudged her traveling companion in the ribs. "Are you coming to the cabin or not? I've been trying to get your attention for the past few minutes. Are you zoned out or what?"

Ashleigh swallowed hard. Although Galveston Island, Ashleigh's home for the past two years, was also a serene paradise, she couldn't wait to make port in some of the Caribbean's most famous paradise resorts.

Located on the Gulf of Mexico, Ashleigh loved everything about Galveston Island. Boasting quaint residential areas, office buildings, and timeless shopping venues, the small island was steeped in rich history. Considered a quick getaway for those who lived in the larger Texas cities, Galveston's beaches were pristine for the most part. Tourism was a large part of the beautiful island's financial success.

The fact that Galveston was so close to Houston, Austin's hometown—and the place where he was employed—was an extra-added bonus for her. Reading about Austin in the newspapers was a favorite pastime of hers. Houston was also close enough for her to attend all of the Texas Wranglers' home games. As a football fanatic and a number-one Wrangler fan, she made it a point to tune her television in to all the away games. Austin, always so near, yet so far away, was the reality that Ashleigh had thus far rejected. Austin's ritzy world, a world she was sure she could never fit into, was so far removed from her own, it wasn't even funny.

While Ashleigh stood brooding over Austin, Lanier had made the acquaintance of a group of single women who were all traveling together. The irony of the situation was that they were all in the same field of work: social services.

Lanier told Ashleigh that the group of women worked in the same county but different field offices from where she and Ashleigh were employed as social workers. Lanier then introduced Ashleigh to the five women—Denise, Beverly, Marion, Brenda, and Judyann—all of whom seemed to be very pleasant and cordial. Like Ashleigh and Lanier, they had all graduated from Texas Southern University with bachelor degrees in social science. But they hadn't met one another until they found themselves working in the very same social services office.

With all their assigned cabins located on the same deck, the women separated, promising to see one another throughout the cruise and, hopefully, while hitting the trendy tourist spots. Everyone had confessed to being maniacal shoppers.

The category-eight, ocean-view stateroom was more spacious than either Ashleigh or Lanier had expected. Flowered wallpaper done in various shades of mauve and blue gave a serene feel to the room. Mauve wall-to-wall carpeting covered the floor. Cheerful, indirect lighting brought a subtle brightness to the cabin. Twin-size beds, stationed on opposite walls, faced the floor-to-ceiling balcony door, which offered a full ocean view. A compact mirrored vanity rested along another wall.

A beautiful arrangement of fresh wildflowers sat atop the slender six-drawer dresser, along with a chilled bottle of champagne. Gaily wrapped baskets of fresh fruit had been deposited on each of the twin beds.

To say the least, Ashleigh thought with amusement, the one small bathroom was going to be an interesting ordeal for the two women who loved to indulge themselves in long, luxurious toiletries. Lanier had already made a mad dash for the shower.

Lanier unzipped her garment bag and pulled out a skimpy black dress that looked as though very little material had been used to fashion it. "What do you think of this one, Ash?"

Ashleigh looked at the fashionable dress and laughed. "Well, for sure, it will earn you a lot of male attention. Can you really fit your voluptuous curves into that wisp of a dress?"

Lanier scowled. "It certainly fit when I tried it on at the store. It's spandex, so it should give quite a bit. At any rate, this is the dress I'm wearing. If you're embarrassed by it, just act like you don't know me." Lanier laughed in the throaty way that men thought was sweetly seductive.

Ashleigh scoffed. "I haven't been embarrassed by your apparel yet. If I were, I'd never act like I didn't know you. Our friendship has always been unconditional."

Looking at her questioningly, Lanier saw that Ashleigh wasn't making any attempt to unpack her clothing. "Aren't you going to get dressed for the evening, Ash?"

Rubbing her hand across her forehead, Ashleigh sighed. "I think I'm going to pass. I'm really tired. It took loads of time and a lot of work just to get ready to travel on this floating hotel."

Studying Ashleigh with concern, Lanier sucked in a deep breath. "I can't believe you're going to lock yourself away in this cabin," Lanier scolded gently. "When are you going to get over that man? It's not like you two were ever involved in a burning love affair. Besides, you were only twelve when you last saw Austin—and only eight when you went to live in their house. What did you know about love at that age, anyway?"

Ashleigh walked over to the bed and dropped down on top of the spread. She then looked at Lanier with an almost tangible sadness. Gathering her heavy hair to one side, she twisted a few ringlets around her fingers, a nervous habit. "I don't expect you to fully understand my feelings, Lanier, especially when I don't understand them myself. But Austin was the only one of the brothers who showed any genuine interest in me."

She tugged nervously at the corners of the freshly scented bedspread. "The other two boys were nice enough to me, but Austin was the one who made me feel special. When you're starving for love and affection . . . and someone seems to be giving you exactly what you need, I guess you can make more of it than it really is. I know I was young, but I've never stopped thinking about Austin Carrington. I just can't seem to get out of my mind the kind, loving look he always had in his eyes. But I'm on this cruise to do just that. By the time we arrive back in Galveston, Austin will be out of my system once and for all."

Noticing the glistening tears in Ashleigh's eyes, Lanier walked over to the bed and hugged her. "I'm sorry. I didn't mean to upset you. Listen, I'll go ahead up to the Flamingo Lounge. Once you've pulled yourself together and rested a bit, perhaps you can join me for a drink. Okay?"

Ashleigh smiled generously. "Okay. I'll rush through my shower and then I'll make an appearance. You look absolutely gorgeous in that dress. It fits perfectly and I don't imagine that you'll ever get a chance to be lonely on this cruise. Go out and knock them boys dead!"

Lanier gave a warm, reassuring squeeze to Ashleigh's hand before she headed out the cabin door.

Intending to keep her word, Ashleigh rose from her comfortable spot, grabbed her suitcase, and hoisted it onto the bed. Thinking about being all by herself, something she was used to, Ashleigh knew she could be in a crowd of millions and still feel lonely.

Looking down at the bed, Ashleigh yawned. A short nap would do her tired body justice, but Lanier would be sorely disappointed if she didn't show up. They had vowed to dance and party away the next fourteen days. Sleep was only a small part of their agenda. Meeting men, men, and more men was high on their list of priorities. Reciting their intended agenda out loud, she stepped into the bathroom to prepare herself for a shower.

Though Ashleigh had teased Lanier about her minuscule dress, the one she'd chosen for the evening wasn't any less revealing. Every sensuous curve on her body was delicately outlined through the clingy material. Though cleverly designed to offer a hint of discretion, a thigh-high slit up the right side revealed just enough creamy skin to ardently arouse any hot-blooded male, deviously taxing his imagination at the same time.

Ashleigh brushed her long, copper curls until the golden bronze highlights sparkled and shimmered through. She then placed dainty teardrop garnet earrings, her birthstone, in her pierced ears. Turning around and around in front of the mirror, she smiled when the satisfactory image of herself reflected in her topaz eyes stared softly back at her.

Although she was an elegant young woman, her delicate features made her seem almost childlike. Emotionally, she sometimes felt like a child. Her champagne-gold complexion, soft and tender as a newborn's bottom, carried a healthy glow. Large, deeply set topaz eyes complemented her lovely face dramatically.

After splashing on a grossly expensive fragrance, compliments of Thomas Early, she grabbed her small purse off the dresser and made a beeline for the door.

With Lanier having told her which lounge she'd pop into before going to the dining room, Ashleigh wandered into the room where lively music boomed rather annoyingly from the numerous built-in speakers.

Finding Lanier seated close to the bandstand, with the other women they'd met earlier sitting close by, Ashleigh approached the table and pulled out the chair directly across from her friend. A smiling waiter was there before she had a chance to seat herself.

"Good evening, señoritas!" His eyes zeroed in on Lanier's tiny black dress, her ample cleavage loudly summoning his unwanted attention.

Not wanting to encourage him, Lanier totally ignored the waiter's flirtatious jet-black eyes as she politely gave him her drink order.

"One Hurricane coming right up." He turned his attention to Ashleigh. "And you, señorita. What is your pleasure?"

"An original frozen margarita. I prefer the glass to be lightly salted, please." The waiter grinned widely as he moved away from the table.

Lanier chatted on above the loud music. Ashleigh carefully surveyed the lounge, discreetly checking out all the men who appeared unescorted. While some of the men were dangerously gorgeous and others were beyond description, she was surprised to see so many black men on board the ship. She had expected to see a few, but to see so many brothers in one place was truly amazing, certainly delightful.

Lanier poked Ashleigh's shoulder, her eyes directing Ashleigh's attention toward the two men standing at the bar. "Look at the bodies on those hunks, Ash," Lanier whispered.

As though they'd heard Lanier, both men turned around and smiled in their direction. "Oh, no, I hope they didn't hear me! Oh, my God, they're coming over here. And they're twins!"

Ashleigh didn't respond. She couldn't. Nearly choking on her own tongue, which felt like a chunk of lead in her mouth, her topaz eyes filled with a quiet terror. The men coming toward their table were two of the Carrington triplets. She would've recognized them even if they'd been in drag. But which two of the three brothers were they? Dallas and Austin? Dallas and Houston? Or Austin and Houston? Ashleigh finally released the choke hold she had on her breath when the two men nodded politely but kept on past their table.

Lanier was rather disappointed, though she kept quiet about it. Ashleigh's sparkling topaz eyes had grown as big as saucers. A fluid sadness appeared to float about her pupils.

Deeply concerned for her friend, Lanier covered Ashleigh's hand with her own. "You look as though you've seen a ghost. Oh, dear." Lanier suddenly realized that one of the two men was none other than the famous quarterback for the Texas Wranglers. Ashleigh's Austin Carrington.

"You never told me Austin was a twin. I'm surprised I've never read it in any of the newspapers." Lanier was unable to believe her own eyes.

Shaking her head, Ashleigh gulped thirstily at her drink, trying to ease the dryness in her throat. The salt certainly wasn't helping matters. The icy liquid made her teeth chatter, but it was the Carrington men that made her knees knock uncontrollably.

"I don't know which one was Austin, if either, which is surprising. I thought I'd recognize him anywhere—without any difficulty whatsoever."

Lanier frowned. "What do you mean by that? It has to be one or the other, unless . . ."

Ashleigh nodded. "Triplets, indeed! And all of them have been mentioned in the newspaper at one time or another. All of them are highly successful professional sports figures. Of course, I know more about Austin than the other two even though they all perform before the hometown crowd. Dallas plays professional baseball and Houston plays pro basketball."

Lanier couldn't contain her laughter. "Austin, Dallas and Houston? What's up with the very patriotic names? I'm not sure I want to know their father's name. Does this family love Texas, or do they love Texas?"

Ashleigh grinned. "Beaumont Carrington III is a very loyal native Texan. Mr. Carrington eats, drinks, and sleeps Texas. The man would die for Texas—would kill to preserve its honor. Being a true Texan, he did everything in a big way." A shadow of pain flickered across Ashleigh's features. "He and Angelica Carrington, his wife, were so generous, which is why I can't understand . . ." Her voice trailed off as she purposely left her sentence unfinished.

Ashleigh and Lanier were good friends, but they hadn't known each other long enough for Ashleigh to spill her guts about all the misery she'd experienced after being snatched from the Carrington home. Long enough to become business partners, but not nearly long enough to confide in each other some of their darkest, innermost secrets. They had touched on a lot of their past pain, but each of them seemed unprepared to share their most soul-damaging hurts, the ones that had taken the worst toll on their still-fragile emotions.

Ashleigh couldn't bring herself to tell anybody how the very people who had professed to love her so much had

abandoned her. On many occasions she'd been told how
happy they were to have her as a part of their close-knit
family. Besides their very own triplets, the Carringtons had
been foster parents to many other children, but Ashleigh
had been the only female. That alone had made her very
special.

Angelica had doted on her "little lamb," the pet name
she'd lovingly given Ashleigh. Much to Ashleigh's shock
and displeasure, Angelica had put her so-called "little
lamb" out to pasture without so much as a wailing bleat of
dismay. As she was doing this very moment, Ashleigh often
wondered why.

"What can't you understand?" Lanier hoped Ashleigh
wasn't going to fall victim to a fit of depression. But it
looked as if one was coming on.

Waving Lanier's question off with her tiny hand, Ashleigh
wished Lanier wouldn't press her any further. "It's nothing,
Lanier." Though she sounded calm, she was unable to hide
the awfully injured look that had crept into her eyes.

Deciding that it was best to drop the whole thing, Lanier
focused her attention on the interesting-looking folks who
had taken to the crowded dance floor. Everyone appeared
to be enjoying themselves as they rocked back and forth to
the rhythm of the lively, compelling-you-from-your-seat
music.

Still thinking about the Carringtons, Ashleigh imagined
that they wouldn't even recognize her as she was now. She
didn't look at all like she had back then. Her hair was longer
and much healthier, the braces on her teeth had long been
removed, and the skinny body of a preadolescent had mi-
raculously blossomed in all the right places. No. She shook
her head. They wouldn't recognize her original birth name
or her.

The nuns had thought her middle name was so much
prettier than her first name, so she had simply become
Sariah to all who'd known her back then. For whatever reason, her last name had been changed to Reed, which was
the surname of the first foster family she'd ever lived with.

She'd changed her name back to her legal one, Ashleigh Ayers, after she turned eighteen. She had done her level best, without much success, to bury Sariah alongside the painful memories that had been hers and hers alone to bear.

TWO

Surprised to see the Carrington brothers walking toward their table again, Ashleigh felt her breath catch. Quickly, she told Lanier that she didn't want them to know who she was, not unless they guessed that she was the little girl who had once shared their home. The drastic changes that had occurred in her should make it virtually impossible to uncover her true identity, she hoped feverishly.

How could they recognize her? There hadn't been a single thing about her that was noteworthy. In fact, nothing about her had been remotely attractive, so she thought. And she still hadn't discovered her own natural beauty, which was more than skin-deep. In the absence of love, Ashleigh often saw herself as the ugly duckling that would never turn into a beautiful swan. No, they wouldn't recognize her, she reassured herself once again. Not in a million years.

This time the Carrington brothers stopped at the table, smiling appreciatively at the two attractive women. "Hey, ladies!" Their greeting came simultaneously, as though they'd known exactly what the other one was going to say.

That often happened with the Carrington multiples, Ashleigh knew, firsthand.

One brother extended his hand and grasped Lanier's. "I'm Dallas Carrington. This here clone is my brother Houston. Are you ladies here alone this evening?" His attention was raptly focused on Lanier.

Lanier casually removed her hand from Dallas's seemingly possessive grip. "I, Lanier Watson, am alone." Lanier flirted openly with the strikingly handsome Dallas. "But I can't speak for my friend Ashleigh."

Wondering how she was going to extricate herself from this complicated situation, Ashleigh frowned. It was now confirmed that neither man was Austin, which she had immediately known once they'd drawn closer. Neither of them had the brain-numbing effect on her that Austin had. She had no desire to play games with Houston, especially when her heart belonged to the absent triplet.

Smiling, Ashleigh looked up at the two dangerously handsome men. "I'm here alone, but I'm afraid I'm not feeling very well. If you all will excuse me, I'm going to return to my cabin." Ashleigh practically leaped out of her seat.

Instead of returning to her cabin as she'd planned, Ashleigh wandered out onto the deck and stood at the railing. Sunset was close at hand. All about her she saw young lovers holding hands and sharing intimate kisses as they waited for the first stars to appear in the purple sky.

Shivering as a bout of loneliness struck a painful chord in her heart, Ashleigh slid her wrap around her slender shoulders. When it accidentally slipped to the deck, another pair of hands reached for the red wrap at the same time hers did. An electric shock shot through her entire anatomy as strong, toffee-brown hands grazed her own. Without looking into the face of the man whose gentle hands retrieved her wrap, she knew whom the hands belonged to. She would know even if she were blind.

Standing before her, touching her with his soul, burning her with his infectious sexuality, skyrocketing her heart toward heaven, was Austin Carrington, the man she loved with every breath in her. The same man who'd once promised to take care of her forever . . .

As she looked up into his dreamy ebony eyes, her heart skipped a beat. Undisguised embarrassment flashed in her topaz ones.

Austin appeared equally as affected by Ashleigh as she was by him. His eyes drank in her outward beauty.

"Have we met somewhere before?" Not so good with names and faces, he flipped recklessly through his mind's memory bank trying desperately to place her. In his profession he'd met scores of women, but there was something quite memorable about this one. Something that viciously tugged at his heartstrings in a strange sort of way.

The now-composed Ashleigh tossed him a heart-stopping smile, showcasing the dazzling even white teeth she took especially good care of. "Perhaps we have, especially if you believe in reincarnation," she taunted flirtatiously.

His own teeth, as even and dazzling white as her own, gleamed brightly as he grinned broadly. "I don't know about that, but there's something very familiar about you." Instantly, the topaz eyes that he was so sure he'd looked deeply into before mesmerized him. But if he recalled correctly, the topaz eyes that he keenly remembered had been lusterless with a deep, abiding pain, the kind of pain that lent their owner an unnatural maturity far beyond her actual years. These seductively dancing eyes held a mixture of childish joy, hypnotically cloaked in a daring streak of inculpable mischief.

His slightly amused expression suddenly changed into one of cheerless uncertainty. Then it dawned on him. He had seen those eyes before, but they hadn't belonged to the stunning woman that now stood before him. The topaz eyes in question had belonged to an angelic child whom he'd often fantasized about when imagining what she might look like as an adult. This arrestingly beautiful woman that now stood before him was the mirror image of the woman he'd created in his mind, in what seemed like aeons ago.

"Why don't you take a picture?" she harassed haughtily, fearing that her true identity could soon be compromised. "It will last a lot longer. Do you always stare so intently at people you don't even know?"

Shaking his head, Austin hunched his shoulders. "I'm sorry. I didn't mean to stare at you like that. It was rude of me. It's just that you remind me of someone I knew a long time ago." He tried hard to convince himself that she couldn't possibly be that someone, that special someone for whom he'd searched high and low for so many years. That special someone who had definitely been a forbidden fantasy . . .

At the age of sixteen, he'd been oddly attracted to a twelve-year-old girl, who had been strictly off-limits—legally and morally. Sariah, he thought wistfully. Angelic Sariah, with the luminous topaz eyes, the fiery copper hair, and a complexion that looked as though it had been lovingly kissed by the golden rays of a summer sun. The same golden champagne complexion as that of this stunning woman who did crazy things to his entire being despite the fact that he had just recently broken off his engagement to another.

Hoping to quash their discomfort, he laughed, wanting to lighten the tension that seemed to surround them. "Why aren't you inside enjoying all the exciting festivities?" He seemed quite curious about her.

"I guess for the same reasons you're not. I'm not much of a party animal. I love my solitude and my own company."

Admiring her knack for being direct, he laughed again. "In view of what you've just said, don't you think a cruise was hardly the wisest vacation choice? You won't find any solitude on this ship. It's definitely not a place where you can be alone with yourself, especially when celebrating Valentine's Day is one of the events. Tell me, why did you choose a vacation cruise?"

Tightly gripping the railing, Ashleigh looked out to sea. Quickly, she looked away as a wave of nausea washed through her finely sculpted, flat abdomen. Something had made her dizzy. She wasn't sure if it was Austin standing so close to her, or the symptoms of seasickness. Here in the flesh, out on the open seas, unwittingly, Austin caressed her with his ebony eyes, easily burning her skin with his devastating sexuality.

Seasickness or sick for Austin's love? She didn't know which.

"I didn't choose it," she finally responded. "It was chosen for me. Does that answer your burning question?"

Involuntarily, as though his hands had a will of their own, they brushed an unruly copper tendril away from her face. He knew his well-meaning gesture was improper, but the feel of her hair made him glad that he'd risked touching the copper-colored satin.

"You don't seem to be the sort of lady that would allow anyone to make choices for her. Must be someone special, huh? I guess by now he's wondering where you've run off to."

Her smile was smugly arrogant. "What makes you think it's a he? In fact, what makes you think I'm here with a man, period?"

Giving serious thought to her questions, he swept tapered fingers through his own mass of begging-to-be-crushed sable-brown curls. Possessing a flawless toffee-brown complexion, an angular jawline, and sporting the trendy, lightly unshaven look, Austin was as sexy as a century was long. His sparkling bedroom eyes kept themselves busy by keeping Ashleigh slightly off balance.

He had hardly aged at all, Ashleigh surmised. Still, he possessed that engaging, boyish appearance, a constant but welcoming haunting of Ashleigh's dreams, day and night. Austin was the sort of man every woman dreamed about. He had a way of possessing Ashleigh's very soul, without so much as the slightest touch of his hands to her heated flesh.

"Well," he began, "I can't imagine any man being stupid enough to let a beautiful woman like you come on a cruise unescorted. And by your own admission, you said your vacation was chosen for you. Where I come from, one and one always adds up to two. Am I even close to hitting the nail on the head?"

"Not even." She made another attempt at focusing on

the now-choppy seas. *Big mistake.* Her stomach lurched violently.

Valiantly, quelling the urge to toss her earlier meal out to sea, she hoped that she could make it to a chair before she fainted dead away at Austin's very athletic, oversize feet.

Gasping, Austin reached out to her when she nearly toppled over. "Steady, girl," he soothed, his sexy Texas drawl gently assailing her weakened senses. "Put your arms around my neck. I'm going to lift you and carry you over to one of the deck chairs. That's it," he said calmly, when she was nestled safely in his arms. "Just hold on tight."

Gladly, Ashleigh thought dizzily, laying her spinning head against his expansive chest. Unable to speak, she closed her eyes, inhaling deeply of Austin's compelling manly scent, with its outdoor freshness. She was on the other side of heaven.

Then she felt the chilly metal from the lounge chair beneath her. That brought her fully back into the here and now.

"Are you okay?" Concern laced his voice. Carefully, he removed his hands from around her slim waist.

How many times had his tender hands come into contact with her person? She could hardly remember all the times he'd touched her. His hands were callused back then—and still were. But they were the gentlest hands she'd ever had to caress her in such a tender, loving way. How could this insane crush have lasted for so long? And when had it turned into sweet love? As surely as she shared the same air with Austin Carrington, she was even surer that her feelings for him were tantamount to true love. Austin was the only man she'd ever truly loved, especially if she was correct in naming the wild, untamable emotions she still felt for him.

"Are you feeling better now?" His tone sounded even more anxious.

Ashleigh managed a laugh, but it was weak. It lacked its

normal melodious inflection. "I'm fine." She'd lied through her dazzling teeth. She felt as sick as a dog.

Confident that she'd told him a little white lie, Austin pulled up a chair, seating himself in front of her. "Why don't I believe you?" He cocked his head to the side.

Aware that she'd been caught telling an untruth, she looked slightly abashed. "I'm sorry, but I didn't want you to worry needlessly. I'll be just fine after a few minutes of rest."

Reluctantly, he stood. "In that case, I've got to run. Someone is waiting for me. Take care of yourself. And you might want to report to the ship's infirmary. Dramamine just might do the trick." He disappeared before she could come up with a suitable response, even before he'd found out if she was unescorted.

Sure that he was out of the line of her vision, he stopped and put his head in his hands. He hadn't wanted to leave her side, not for a second. If he'd stayed a moment longer, he knew there was no way he could've controlled his urge to take possession of her luscious mouth—passionately, hungrily, uncontrollably.

The woman with the topaz eyes, the fiery copper hair, and the champagne-gold skin was probably just another forbidden fantasy, just like the forbidden fantasy of long ago. Only this time it had nothing to do with age. It all had to do with the fact that he'd just escaped marriage to Sabrina Beaudreaux, the spoiled-rotten daughter of the head coach of the Texas Wranglers.

For more than a year Sabrina had chased him unmercifully, catching him between a rock and a hard place, when she'd asked her father to invite him to one of their high-class bashes. Wanting to please his one-and-only treasure—his daughter—Pete Beaudreaux had practically insisted that Austin act as Sabrina's date for the evening. After one thing led to another, six months later, Austin found himself engaged to the very woman he actually disliked.

* * *

Finding herself all alone, as she had so many times before—but not liking it one bit—Ashleigh lay her head on the arm of the deck chair and wept bitterly. For once, just once in her not-so-illustrious life she'd like to have an altogether different personality. Instead of the insecure, soft-spoken, scared-of-her-own-shadow woman she'd grown into, Ashleigh would like nothing better than to be transformed into a sultry seductress. A dangerously sexy siren, with a provocative way of talking and a traffic-stopping way of walking, a take-charge kind of woman, a woman who knew exactly what she wanted and how to get it.

It would be so utterly wonderful to be able to command attention, both male and female attention alike, just by walking into a crowded room, to have others look on in awe of the electric magnetism she'd so easily exude, to have heads turn, to hear whispers of envy from both genders. To possess worldly knowledge and a tangible power that reeked from every fiber of her being, to dazzle listeners with a soul-deep intellect—all this would fulfill a lifelong dream. But if she could have Austin's love and adoration she'd gladly forego all of her fanciful whims. Although she'd gladly give it all up for a life with Austin, she still couldn't help wondering what it would feel like to be in solid control of her own destiny.

With a half smile tugging at her lips, she indulged herself in a few more minutes of nonsensical reverie, imagining herself as the woman who simply had it all. *Hell,* she thought, *there's no reason why I can't act out my fantasy for the next fourteen days. Other than Lanier, no one else knows me.* Though they were unaware of it, the triplets knew her. But not as the woman she was today. The woman who was a far cry from the small girl they'd once claimed as their sister. If they did happen to learn her true identity, she wouldn't give them any reason to think she wasn't the very successful, confident character she was dying to portray.

Anyone could slip into a role for fourteen days, she told herself. When the cruise was over, no one would be the wiser. They'd all go their separate way. Then she'd easily step back into her old and very-worn-down shoes. And if she were lucky, maybe, just maybe, she'd be strong enough to throw the old shoes away and continue walking in the new ones until she truly became the woman she so desired.

The phrase, "Fake it until you make it," didn't seem such a bad way to effect the outcome she wanted. Yes, Ashleigh, a.k.a. Sariah, would give a command performance. She was almost certain that she could pull off a daily encore nicely.

Now that the waves of nausea had somewhat subsided, she carefully pulled herself up from the deck chair, hoping she wouldn't fall flat on her face. Slowly, she walked back to the cabin where she planned on falling right into bed.

Lying flat on her back, Ashleigh tiredly stripped out of her clothing, piece by piece. She then tossed them onto one of the comfort chairs facing the floor-to-ceiling windows. It wasn't all that late, but she had no desire to face the throngs of people who were probably having a wild and grand time in the ship's many entertainment venues.

Turning on her side, clad in only her underwear, Ashleigh pulled the blue spread over her body wondering if that someone waiting for Austin was his fiancée. Had they come on the cruise to celebrate their upcoming marriage? Maybe they'd decided to elope. Or could they be on their honeymoon? She paled at the thought. If so, why would Dallas and Houston accompany them on such an intimate occasion? Triplets or not, it was a ridiculous notion.

Remembering that the three boys had been extremely close, maybe it wasn't such a ridiculous notion, she surmised. There had often been talk, a lot of talk, of a triple ceremony when they were old enough to marry. But it appeared to her that Dallas and Houston were definitely loose and on the prowl. It was quite obvious that Austin's mirror images had been busy scoping out the cruise ship for unattached females.

Something rumbled loudly, grabbing Ashleigh's attention.

Recognizing that the sound came from her own stomach, she realized she hadn't eaten anything since lunch.

Glancing at the bedside clock, she saw that it was just a little after ten. Sure that there would be food available somewhere on the ship, Ashleigh got out of bed and dressed in haste.

She then stepped into the red-carpeted hallway. It was eerily quiet. Not a single soul lurked about the corridor. Having heard stories about ghosts taking up residence in the hulls of large ships, Ashleigh hurried through the long halls, quickly making her way to one of the lounges. While hoping to find something to snack on, she prayed she wouldn't have to wait for the midnight buffet to be served.

Looking around the gaily decorated lounge, she spotted Lanier. Smiling and looking as though she'd discovered the eighth wonder of the world, Lanier was surrounded by a large group of broad-shouldered males, none of whom appeared to be less than six feet tall.

Ignoring all the unwanted attention she'd drawn to herself by making such a late appearance, Ashleigh moved away from where Lanier held high court. Hoping she wouldn't be stuck with just her own company, she prayed that Lanier would be gracious enough to rescue her. But she doubted it. Lanier looked as contented as a well-fed, mud-bathing pig. Nothing short of a fire drill was going to make her move from her imperial position.

Feasting on plump, boiled shrimp and a variety of fresh-cut vegetables, Ashleigh thought about all the times she'd sat at the Carrington dinner table barely able to take her eyes off Austin. Despite the fact that two other people looked exactly like him, Ashleigh's heart would beat wildly for only one of the three young men. All the Carrington men had had healthy appetites, Ashleigh recalled. Angelica Carrington had spent a good deal of her time in the kitchen, but she never seemed to mind. It hadn't mattered how many extra mouths there were to feed; there had always been enough food for everyone. No one had ever gone to bed hungry or thirsty.

But it hadn't always been that way for Ashleigh. After she'd left the Carrington home, hunger at bedtime had become par for the course for her, she remembered painfully.

Applause suddenly thundered through the room. Ashleigh's attention was quickly drawn to the burly man who had just stepped onto the raised platform located near the center of the lounge. The music came to an abrupt halt as he lifted the microphone from its resting place. His baritone voice immediately infiltrated the lounge. He somehow looked familiar to her.

"I would like to welcome all of those who are here for the first reunion of the Jefferson Memorial High School Football Team. As the state champions for two years in a row, we were the only football team in the history of Jefferson High to win back-to-back championships. We would also like to welcome members of the NFL's Texas Wranglers. . . ."

Barry Atkins, a Carrington neighbor, Ashleigh mused. It all made sense now. The boys had played football for Jefferson, making them very much a part of those back-to-back championships. After all, Austin had been the quarterback then, which meant he was probably here for the reunion, not on his honeymoon. Ashleigh suddenly felt giddy with relief, sobering fully when she realized that his fiancée was more than likely on the cruise with him.

Risking a glance at the tables where all the jocks had gathered, Ashleigh could see that Lanier was still the only female in that particular area, which was puzzling. *Lucky imp,* Ashleigh thought, slightly amused. But she just couldn't imagine all these good-looking men attending a reunion and Valentine's Day cruise without bringing along the special women involved in their personal lives, especially on something as romantic as a Caribbean cruise. When Barry, who'd lost the starting quarterback position to Austin while injured, mentioned something about a double celebration, she could only guess that he was talking about a bachelor party for the incomparable Austin Carrington.

Before the next sentence tumbled from the speaker's lips,

Ashleigh gasped painfully. Unable to listen to anything that might have to do with Austin's upcoming nuptials, Ashleigh removed herself from the premises, without so much as a word to Lanier.

Being alone in the cabin was the last thing she wanted, so she opted for a moonlit stroll on the deck. That could be just as bad as being alone, especially when there was no one special to share the romantic atmosphere with. It was clear to her that Lanier had another agenda. But she couldn't blame her friend for her own miserable state of affairs. They had come on this cruise to live it up. It would be unfair of her to try and place any type of restrictions on Lanier.

Lanier had also suffered a broken heart. The difference was that Lanier's heart had healed and she was looking to give it away again. Only this time Lanier had vowed to give her heart to the right man, to a man who deserved all the love she had to give in return.

It couldn't have been a lovelier evening. Ashleigh could see that romance was alive and well as she looked all about her. She could actually feel the dizzying effects of the sweet love hanging gently in the air. Romantic music wafted across the deck. Looking upward, she saw that the stars appeared to dance in tune with the softly melodic sounds.

"Oh, if only," Ashleigh breathed. Looking forlorn, she rested her elbows on the ship's railing. Closing her eyes, she wished upon a star for Austin to appear.

"If only what?" came the lusty male voice from behind her.

Ashleigh didn't need to turn around to know who was behind the sexy voice. He always had that effect on her. She had already sensed his presence. Often delusional where Austin was concerned, she hadn't given any serious weight to one of her most basic instincts.

She turned to face him. "Just wishing upon a star. But I can't tell you my wish. Have you ever wished upon a star?" She already knew that he had. Would he remember those nights? Probably so. It had been on the eves of the most important football games of the season. Though he hadn't shared his wishes with her, she had known they had to do with winning. He always prayed before every game, too, she recalled, conjuring up the image of him on his knees inside the Carringtons' den.

He nodded. "Many times. In fact, I made a wish earlier, but the stars were still hiding out then. Yet it seems to have come true anyway." Smiling, he moved closer to her. Leaning against the railing, he crossed his arms. "My wish was that I'd get a chance to talk to you again. I didn't even introduce myself earlier, nor did you tell me your name." He bowed from his waist. "Austin Carrington at your service, my fair maiden. Do you mind if I walk the plank with you? It's a beautiful night out, but not as beautiful as the bright stars in your topaz eyes."

Ashleigh controlled her desire to laugh with glee. "As a matter of fact, I do mind. I've been taught never to walk the plank with strangers." Ashleigh found herself drowning in the mischievous glow in his bedroom eyes. She braced herself for another round of his witty foreplay. It was beginning to look like Austin really was on the cruise alone. It appeared to her that he was as much on the prowl as his two brothers were.

"I'm Ashleigh Ayers," she finally responded. "And I'm on the cruise with my best friend, Lanier, who just happens to be a lovely female. We came on the ship unescorted."

He grinned broadly. Her statement had nearly sent his mind over the top. "Well, in that case, Ashleigh Ayers, maybe we need to get a little better acquainted."

The innocent, airy kiss he placed on her mouth was as quick as lightning, but Ashleigh felt it down to the core of her soul. The bewildered way in which Austin looked at her suggested that it had had no lesser impact on him.

He grinned again. "Maybe that little display of gentle affection will help us get on our way to becoming fast friends. I already feel as though I know you. I guess it's because you remind me of someone I knew a long time ago. Your eyes and hair are the very same color of hers.

Much like yours, her skin also looked as if it had been kissed by the sun."

Ashleigh could barely breathe. Slowly, she tilted her chin upward. "Who is this person you're speaking of, might I ask? Was she someone special to you?" She couldn't help hoping that Austin just might be speaking of her as Sariah.

Placing his hands on either side of her, he gripped the railing, imprisoning her between his massive arms. "Someone very special, Ashleigh, but that was a long time ago. Nor was it what you're probably thinking." He fought with the tiny voice daring him to taste her again, to bury his nose in all the places she'd dabbed with the alluring scent she wore.

"Oh! And just what might I be thinking, Austin Carrington?" Lustfully, her eyes connected with his, wanting desperately for him to kiss her again.

He liked the sound of his name on her luscious lips. She'd said it as though it left her breathless, exactly the same way she made him feel. "That I'm speaking of a past lover. I'm not. We never even came close to being lovers," he said with what sounded like regret.

Again he imagined what young Sariah would look like as an adult. She had to be beautiful, as beautiful as the woman before him. The closer he studied Ashleigh, the more he decided she looked like the adult Sariah he'd created in his mind.

It hadn't been all that long ago since he'd given up on ever finding Sariah. He thought she deserved to know why she'd been taken from their home. It had had nothing to do with the Carringtons not wanting her. The entire Carrington family had loved her, still loved her.

Ashleigh had the urge to wrap her arms around his neck and draw his lips to her own, but she could never be that bold despite the fantasy role she'd vowed to play. Austin aroused primitive cravings in her that she hadn't known existed before now.

Quicker than he'd kissed her, she ducked down and out from under his arms, freeing herself from the prison of his sexually powerful physique. "Sorry, but I really don't like to be caught in tight spaces."

Neither did Sariah, he recalled.

Boldly, she asked, "Why didn't you ever take the woman you spoke about as your lover?" She didn't dare to look him right in the eye.

As though the very thought of Sariah as his lover was more than he could possibly bear to picture, he shuddered. "You wouldn't understand," he said softly. "Besides, it's something better left in the past." But he'd much rather have Sariah in his present and his future. Wishful thinking about Sariah wasn't going to help him, so he decided to change the subject. "Can I get you anything, Ashleigh?"

Staring at him incredulously, Ashleigh wondered why he'd decided to put the skids on their discussion. It seemed as though he needed to talk about his feelings. Perhaps she was mistaken. . . .

"No, thank you, Austin. I've already stuffed myself. Besides that, it's time I get back to my cabin. I'm starting to feel a little chilled." She then looked at him as though she were inviting him to share his warmth with her.

Missing the look she gave him, he felt deeply disappointed by her desire to leave. He pointed to the moon and the stars. "The night's still young. It'll be hours and hours before the dawn steals into the skies. Let me get you a hot drink to warm you so we can continue our walk. Perhaps we can even dance to the hypnotic music drifting about us. What do you say, Ash?"

That you're very much engaged, Mr. Carrington. She knew that she'd be a fool to get caught up in this tantalizing game of charades. But didn't everyone play the fool at one time or another? "I don't want anything to drink, Austin. But I would like to continue our walk." Smiling, she totally blocked his personal entanglements from her mind.

Feeling breathless, he closed his large hand around her small one. Smiling brightly, he gently squeezed her fingers. "Let's lose ourselves to the dazzling night."

Quietly, Austin led Ashleigh across the deck, turning

right as they reached the other side of the ship. After carefully guiding her through the maze of deck chairs and tables, he directed her toward a set of stairs. Holding her from behind, he allowed her to proceed him to the uppermost deck.

THREE

As they reached the top deck of the ship, Ashleigh gasped in astonishment. It was as if they were all alone, on top of the world. The darkened sea, lit only by the silvery moon, was breathtaking. It was a sight only true lovers would appreciate, yet she could do so, too.

Before she could express her utter joy to him, he swept her into his arms, dancing her all around the deck. The sea winds whispered intimately into her hair as Austin whirled her around and around. He drew her very close. Then, without warning, he spun her away from him. While teasing her, he laughed at all the wondrous expressions crossing her glowing, angelic face.

Startling her, he lifted her into his arms and carried her to the darkest corner of the deck. Standing her on her feet, he pulled her in close to his muscular body. His fierce ebony gaze pilfered what was left of her mental stability. "Oh, Ashleigh," he moaned against her sweet lips. "Another time, another place, I would've devoured you long before now. I would've promised you my heart and my soul," he rasped painfully. But he had just recently broken the promises he'd made to someone else. Feeling disheartened, he was nearly crazy with desire for the magnificent woman that he held in his arms. "Ashleigh, all I can promise you is tonight, maybe tomorrow, too. Or even the entire fourteen days of this cruise." He shrugged his broad shoulders. "I don't know what else to say. Beyond that, I can promise you nothing."

Closing her eyes, Ashleigh shut out the echo of his words, words that cut her to the quick, words confirming for her that his heart belonged to another. One night was better than having nothing at all. But did she dare sell her soul to this charming devil? Did she dare cavort about with a man whose heart she'd never possess?

His heart may belong to another, but her heart belonged to him, only him. Her soul was his, too, so why shouldn't she give him the rest of her? She felt bewildered at the prospect of having Austin to herself, for whatever amount of time he was willing to give her.

Because Ashleigh Sariah Ayers is not that sort of a woman, an intimidating voice echoed inside of her head. *Ashleigh Ayers wouldn't play those kinds of games with her own heart.*

Ashleigh shut out those words, as well. Austin Carrington, the man she'd yearned for forever, was here before her, offering himself to her, and she was going to take him up on it. She had a few offers of her own to make—kissing him would do for a start.

Touching her lips to his ear, she tenderly kissed his lobe. "Here's to tonight, Austin. Let tomorrow take care of itself," she whispered. She then opened up to him like a flower to morning dew. *All is fair in love and war.*

Taking her mouth, as though it were his and only his to claim, Austin's pulse raced full speed ahead. A drunken stupor came over him, intoxicating his mind, body, and soul. Sweet, so sweet. Feeling delirious, he relished her with a little more caution, as though she were forbidden fruit. The same fruit from his long-ago *forbidden fantasy.*

Pushing her hands through his sable-brown curls, Ashleigh pressed her body into him with an urgency that gripped his loins unmercifully. Grasping her waist, he molded her against him, darting his tongue in and out of her mouth. Sensation after indescribable sensation burned into the soft but firm flesh of her inner thighs. Feeling the lower portion of his anatomy hardening against her, she clenched her teeth together to keep from screaming out to him the pleasures he gave her. Neither Ashleigh nor Austin had ever felt so good. Neither of them wanted these wonderful feelings to ever cease.

Austin had been engaged to another woman, but Ashleigh was the only woman who'd ever made his heart sing, his mouth thirst, hunger and crave—all at the same time. She made his loins ache with an explosive yearning, a tortuously indefatigable yearning.

Sabrina had never made him feel like this. No, not at all, not even close. He somehow felt that without Ashleigh there to minister to his every physical, mental, and emotional need, he'd never, ever feel this good again.

Slowly, tediously, and oh so sadly, Ashleigh's sanity returned, trapping her uninhibited desires like an angry vise. Whirling away from Austin's sweetly devouring hands and mouth, she turned her back to him. Greedily, she drew the salty sea air into her burning lungs. Tears trickled down her face. The strong winds blew them out to sea as quickly as they fell.

Scared to touch her again, Austin watched her slender shoulders convulse, wishing he could take on the weight of whatever had disturbed her. He'd somehow hurt her, it seemed, which had not been his intention. Lowering his hands to his side, he clenched and unclenched tight fists, riding out the waves of his own emotions. Holding Ashleigh, comforting her, was what he needed to do, but he wasn't so sure she'd welcome his touch as eagerly as before. The urge to run his fingers through her windswept ringlets was unbearable.

No longer able to stand the distance between them, he circled her slight waist from behind. "I was out of line, Ash," he whispered. "I'm sorry." Moaning, he pressed his lips into her copper curls. "I'm not sorry for what we just shared. I'm just sorry that it seems so distressing to you. But I can't be sorry for something that felt so good, so right."

Staring into the blackened sea, Ashleigh tilted her head

back, resting it on his chest. "It's okay, Austin. I'm not sorry, either. But I do need to go now."

Ashleigh turned back around to face him. She could barely breathe as Austin brought his tender lips so close to hers. She nearly fainted from disappointment when he suddenly withdrew the very lips she'd longed to feel on hers, again and again.

"Why do you look at me that way, Ashleigh? You look as though you're scared to death. Who's responsible for the haunted look in those brilliant eyes of precious topaz?"

Ashleigh blinked back the bitter tears. *You are.* She moaned inwardly, recalling his twelve-year-old promise to her. *You're engaged to be married, yet your quivering lips seem to suggest that they're desperate for the taste of mine. It seems you're about to make another pseudopromise, Austin Carrington.* She freed her tears as her shattered heart careened recklessly from the impact of being near him yet unable to confess her interminable love for the man who'd forgotten his long-ago promise to her.

Looking deeply into his eyes, she kissed him as though it would be their last kiss.

Rapidly, almost recklessly, she crossed the deck and disappeared down the stairs, leaving behind the man she loved desperately.

He was a man who now had a gaping hole where his heart had once been. He felt as if his heart had somehow been removed from his chest and successfully transplanted between her delicate breasts.

For a man who rarely gave way to tears, Austin could not stop himself from doing so. How could a man with no heart still have such powerful emotions? What was he feeling with? His brain was numb, incapable of feeling, yet he felt every damnable emotion that could be named, and then some. As he thought of Sabrina, it stunned him that he couldn't even recall what she looked like. No matter how hard he tried, he just couldn't bring the image of Sabrina Beaudreaux to mind.

All he could see before him were the topaz eyes and the

angelic face of the woman who'd just run away from him, the woman who had escaped with his heart buried between her delicate breasts. There were only two other times in his life that he'd felt such hopelessness: the time he came home from baseball practice and learned that Sariah had been taken away, and the time when he'd realized that he'd never find her—which hadn't been all that long ago.

He had cried on both of those occasions, too. He'd cried for the little girl who'd known so much pain; he'd cried for the beautiful woman he'd known she'd one day grow into. He'd constantly yearned to find her and tell her the truth of why she was taken away from them.

He had been sure that once Sariah became an adult that the four year difference in their ages would no longer matter to anyone. For her to turn eighteen was the one day he'd eagerly looked forward to, only to find that she'd disappeared off the face of the earth.

But was he now trying to make Ashleigh a substitute for Sariah because they looked so much alike? Or had he fallen deeply for Ashleigh because of the way she made him feel inside?

Though extremely popular with the ladies, Austin had never let it go to his head. He knew that his position as the Wranglers' starting quarterback was behind his popularity. Half of the females that he encountered probably wouldn't give him a second look if he wasn't a member of the Texas Wranglers. Austin Carrington was well aware that he wasn't your normal athletic jock. He had a large ego, but it rarely surfaced off the football field. Even then, he simply played the game to win. He never allowed himself to think he was anything less than the best quarterback in the NFL. While he knew how to get down in the trenches, he never failed to remember that his team members were a large part of his success. If the offensive lineman didn't block effectively, he wouldn't have enough time to get a good pass off. If the wide receivers didn't catch the ball, his speeding projectilelike passes, on the numbers or not, would be nothing more than worthless.

Everyone on the team had a specific job to perform, but to be the leader of the team, one had to possess an extraordinary talent. He also had to earn his teammates' respect, which he'd earned in spades. There were precious few African-American quarterbacks in the NFL. Because of those numbers, Austin knew more was expected from him than most. He never came up short on his delivery and his amazing statistics spoke for themselves.

He thought Ashleigh might know about his profession, especially if she lived in Texas, but if she did, she didn't seem at all curious about it. That was one of the many things that had impressed him most about her. She hadn't asked what type of car he drove, nor had she asked if he owned real estate, stocks, and bonds, or any of that other superficial garbage that a lot of women seemed to care about. Those were the types of things that Sabrina would want to know before she'd even consider accepting a man's offer to take her out. Sabrina was the type of woman who wouldn't offer a man a mere smile, unless he made at least six figures.

How had he ever allowed himself to get involved with a rich, money-hungry, status-conscious, spoiled rotten brat? Sabrina was a daddy's girl. But in this instance, Daddy had not only been a great friend to him, Pete Beaudreaux was also Austin's boss.

Austin cringed when he thought of the conversation that he'd overheard Sabrina having with her best girlfriend. It was the very conversation that had given him his way out of their going-nowhere relationship with irrefutable justification.

Tired of thinking, tired of wondering, tired of asking himself questions he didn't know the answers to, he decided to turn in for the night. Maybe his dreams would take him back to the place he'd been earlier, the wonderful place he'd shared with Ashleigh. He could save the soul-searching for later, yet he knew he'd have to face all of his demons sooner or later.

While he knew for sure that he wasn't on the rebound, for Ashleigh's sake, he planned to take a snail's-pace ap-

166 *Linda Hudson-Smith*

proach toward their relationship. He didn't want to find himself in the same position with Ashleigh that he'd found himself in with Sabrina.

Ashleigh hadn't been in the cabin for more than five minutes when Lanier walked in the door looking like she'd just won the lottery. After retrieving her nightclothes, Ashleigh made herself comfortable in the center of the bed. She then peeled away her clothing, layer by layer.

"If it isn't the queen bee," Ashleigh jeered playfully, her eyes laughing gently. "The last time I saw you, you were holding court with a swarm of husky worker bees. Which one did you crown king? You know the one you mate with has to die afterward, don't you?" She continued to tease Lanier, laughing out loud.

Tugging her dress down over her curving hips, Lanier laughed, too. "You caught my act, huh? I haven't decided which one is worthy of me yet. Dallas is a sweetheart, but that boy has a serious roving eye. Where did you run off to?" In one quick motion, she removed her panty hose. "One minute you were there, then you were gone. You haven't been here in the cabin all this time, have you?"

Shaking her head, Ashleigh placed a pillow under her neck and lay back. "No, I had a date with destiny. You're not going to believe this, but Austin Carrington is on the cruise with his brothers. He and I have connected in a strange sort of way, twice already. Before you say it, I know he's engaged. But I think somebody forgot to tell him."

Lanier drew her lower lip between her teeth. "I learned that he was on the cruise from Dallas. But before I could get to you to warn you, you had disappeared."

Turning on her side, Ashleigh hugged the spare pillow to her abdomen. "He's as sweet as he always was. I want to be with him regardless of his present relationship. He wants the same, if only for the duration of the cruise. Should I give in to the madness? I could get hurt, you know."

Lanier looked worried. "I don't know, Ash. If you get all caught up in him now, what are you going to do when the cruise is over? I don't want to see you bear another ounce of pain."

Ashleigh punched the pillow. "I guess I'm going to be hurt no matter what. I've been hurting all my life. What else is new? If I don't take this opportunity to be with him, I know I'll regret it for the rest of my days. I feel no shame in wanting to give myself to Austin, but my conscience is not going to stay out of it. In fact, it's been on my case all evening."

"Looks like you've got a worthy wrestling partner, Ash. I'm not sure which one I'm rooting for to win."

"I know I'm playing Russian roulette. With only one bullet in the chamber, it'll be just my luck to get it, straight through the heart. We shared a very intimate encounter this evening and my libido is dying for more of the same. Making love to Austin would be the end to all ends!"

Lanier frowned. "Ash, I hope you make the right decision. I don't want to see you throw yourself overboard because you made the wrong one, which could mean the end of your life."

Ashleigh sucked her teeth. "Oh, save the drama. I haven't ever considered taking myself out, no matter how difficult things got. I have to learn to take more risks, Lani. I'm sick and tired of being afraid to go after what I want. And I want Austin Carrington. Desperately."

While slipping a lavender chemise over her head, Lanier studied Ashleigh closely. "The stubborn determination in your voice is unfamiliar, except when you talk about helping the children who have been treated as we have. But where your personal life is concerned, I've never known you to speak so aggressively. But I can certainly remember the aggression you displayed when we were making a bid on the house we purchased. You showed a lot of spunk and courage during that entire process. It seems that your determination only surfaces when you want something badly enough. You wanted that house for the kids . . . and now you want Austin. I'm forced to admit that I'm going to have to place my bet on you. Though the odds aren't in your favor, I'm convinced that you won't give up until you've won. I just hope that in your victory, you don't end up drowning in the spoils."

Already dressed in a white lacy nightgown, Ashleigh slipped under the covers. After making herself comfortable, she looked over at Lanier. "Was Houston upset when I ran off like that earlier? I hadn't meant to be rude, but I didn't want to play games with him."

Lanier sat down at the dressing table to remove her make-up. "I don't think so. However, Houston and Dallas won't be staying for the entire cruise. They'll be flying back home sometime before the completion of the trip. Dallas has to report back to camp to prepare for spring training. As we know, Houston's basketball team is in a great position to make the NBA play-offs. That's another reason I won't let myself get taken in by Dallas. I like him, but a professional athlete is not what I'm looking for. I want and need a man who's ready to settle down." Lanier frowned at the slight pimple above her right eye. "I don't want another broken heart."

"I know you don't." Ashleigh stretched out in the bed. "Are there any of those types left? It seems to me that if Austin is engaged, he should be acting a little more settled. Maybe he's really not ready to get married. Hopefully he'll find it out before it's too late."

"As long as women are willing to play men's silly games, why should they settle down? If Austin is coming on to you like you say he is, he's not in love with the woman he's planning on marrying. True love doesn't work that way. Love is not a warm, fuzzy feeling like most people believe. Those are just emotions at work. Love is an action that can be easily recognized. Actions will tell the real deal every time."

"Hmm." Ashleigh moaned. "I like that. But can't people treat their mates extremely well and still play around?"

"I guess. But there are still actions in there. If a person

is playing around, it will eventually show. In true love, you can't be all things to more than one person. When there're more than two people involved in a relationship, everyone gets cheated from Jump Street."

Feeling ashamed of herself, Ashleigh lowered her lashes. "I see what you're saying, Lani. So I guess I'm going to have to watch myself around Austin. I want him, but not at the expense of hurting someone else. I don't know what made me think I could do such a thing. I haven't been thinking straight since I first encountered Austin."

Lanier smiled sympathetically. "I do. It's your love for him. His fiancée is his responsibility, not yours. Only he can hurt her. Don't give up on your dreams where he's concerned. But please be very careful, my friend."

Feeling the lulling sensations of the sandman, Ashleigh turned on her stomach and placed her head back on the pillow. Lanier had given her some food for thought, but she was just too sleepy to digest it all. Hopefully the morning would bring her a fresh perspective. Then she could figure out what to do about Austin Carrington. She already knew what she wanted to do with him. Making wild, passionate love to him still remained at the very top of her list.

After terminable hours of chasing the elusive ghosts in her mind, just before the sun emitted its first rays to bring about the dawn, Ashleigh found herself climbing the stairs to the uppermost deck, hoping the fresh sea air would help make her drowsy enough to sleep.

Another deck might have been more suitable for ridding her head of all its hazardous debris, she mused. It was a mistake to have chosen the same deck where Austin had twirled her about like they were teenagers at the prom. She still felt his wet kisses on her mouth. She moaned, aching to have his lips and tongue flirting with her own again.

Clad in only sweats and a lightweight jacket, Ashleigh shivered at the raging sea winds whipping across the deck. Moving to the far corner, where Austin had taken her earlier, she dropped down in a lounge chair, sighing heavily. Her state of mind was nothing short of tumultuous, yet she felt a certain peace. Austin was the last person she'd expected to meet on this cruise, but she couldn't think of anything that could've brought her more pleasure. Learning that his fiancée wasn't on the cruise with him was even more pleasurable.

But his behavior in the absence of his bride-to-be puzzled her. In the absence of the woman he planned to marry, Austin seemed quite willing to share himself with the likes of her. Was it just her he wanted to be with? Or would he have latched on to some starstruck groupie who thought a night with a famous quarterback would be a rare feather in her fanciful headdress.

When a noise startled her, she peered into the hazy fog hanging over the deck like a smoky curtain. It only took her a minute to recognize the figure as Austin.

The hulking athletic figure outfitted in a navy blue jogger strutted across the deck and stopped right at her feet. Austin's boyish smile caused her heart to pump like a jackhammer breaking into cement. She saw that his curly hair was wildly tousled, looking as though it had never been introduced to a brush and comb. When his sexy ebony eyes bore into her own, she turned away to ward off the insanity his intense gaze brought to her entire being.

His sigh came long and hard. "Damn you," he said huskily. He pulled her up from the lounge, bringing her into his arms roughly. "Where are you hiding the magnets?"

She shot him a puzzled glance. "Excuse me?"

"Excuse me, hell. No, Ash, I'm sorry, I can't do that. What you're doing to me can't be excused." He nipped ravenously at her lower lip. "Are you going to tell me where you're hiding the magnets? Or am I going to have to frisk you?"

She smiled lazily. "Maybe you should just stick to throwing bulletlike passes and leave the frisking to the boys in blue."

"What's that supposed to mean?"

"I know your stats on completed passes. Very impressive, I might add. But with me as a rival member of the defense team, you're bound to throw a few interceptions."

He tilted her chin with his fist. "So you've been reading about me. And all this time I thought you liked me for me."

Her topaz eyes flashed a glint of anger. "I don't think I deserved that cutting remark. Why don't you think I could like you for you?"

He released her so quickly that she fell back toward the lounge. Disturbed at his juvenile action, he caught her before her body made contact with the chair.

Somewhat alarmed by his strange behavior, Ashleigh whirled away from him. "What's wrong with you? Is the motion of the ocean starting to get to you, too?"

His arms snaked around her again, bringing her in close to his heat. "What's happening to me has nothing to do with the movement of the ocean—and you damn well know it. I can deal with the ocean very easily, but the soul-stirring motion in your hips is an entirely different matter altogether. I don't know how you managed to draw me out of my cabin and out onto this windy deck, but I have every intention of rendering your magnetic powers useless against me."

Wrenching herself away from his rough but intimate grasp, Ashleigh attempted to storm off to her cabin. His reach was quicker than her feet. Austin was just plain dangerous. His being in such close proximity to her had precious little to do with it. He could be miles away from her and he'd still be dangerous, dangerously sexy.

With his tongue effortlessly pushing past her clenched teeth, Ashleigh realized his quickness wasn't limited to just his arms. Her mouth was utterly trapped beneath his. Against her will, her lips undulated traitorously with his. Knowing that fighting against him was only going to make him more determined to play the role of conqueror, she twisted her fingers in his curls. Hungry for the taste of his mouth, she kissed him back fiercely.

* * *

The ship's decks were awash with brilliant sunshine and sun-adoring women and men clad in the latest designer swimwear. In hopes of achieving the darkest tan possible, well-oiled bodies stretched out lazily on the colorful deck chairs and lounges, glistened like precious jewels beneath the blazing Caribbean rays. Throughout the ship there was no shortage of laughter or animated conversations.

As an aerobics class was held on one side of the uppermost deck, the moans and groans from all the professional couch potatoes were easy to discern. The lively exercise music roaring from the outdoor speakers could be heard on every deck.

Wearing a gold lamé bikini, which looked marvelous against her rich mahogany skin, Lanier floated on her back in the swimming pool. Happily, she entertained a few of the same jocks she'd held high court with from the previous evening.

Less than two hours of sunshine had turned Ashleigh's champagne-gold skin to a mesmerizing golden bronze. The bright yellow-and-white polka-dotted bikini she wore was the perfect complement to her slender, sun-caressed body. A simple pair of yellow sandals was stationed at her side and a pair of Ray-Ban sunglasses nestled in her copper curls.

As a featherweight breeze stroked the back of her neck, much different from the heavy sea breeze blowing in from the sea, she sucked in a deep breath. Knowing she'd find Austin behind her, she tried hard not to respond to his tantalizing way of getting her attention. It only became more difficult when his warm, sweet breath on her neck caused her insides to tremble.

Not to be ignored, he dropped down on the same lounge she occupied, forcing her to scoot over to make room for his powerful, athletic physique. "Were you trying to blow me off, Miss Ayers?" He frowned slightly.

Feigning total ignorance, Ashleigh looked over at him and shrugged her shoulders. "Why, I don't know what you're talking about, Mr. Carrington." She grinned mischievously. Although she would like to ignore him, she knew she could no more ignore the chivalrous Austin than she could successfully swim across the Caribbean Sea.

"In that case, I guess I have nothing to worry about."

He removed the suntan oil from the table next to the lounge. After pouring a generous amount of oil in his hands, he began to spread the sun-warmed oil over Ashleigh's back. Having expected him to rub the oil on his own body, Ashleigh gasped when his palpable fervor spread through her like the fiery flames from a major forest fire.

He abraded her neck with the same virile gentleness she'd had the pleasure of making the acquaintance of long ago. "Relax, Ash. That's it," he soothed. Placidly, she complied with his wishes. "Can you feel some of those contrary kinks in your neck melting away?"

"Yes." Her voice was hoarse with yearning.

He turned her over on her back. "Good. Now I'm going to work on winning your heart." He was well aware that she'd already hijacked his.

She gave him a bold, challenging look. "Win mine . . . or lose your own?"

"Acid tongue, huh?"

With his titillating laughter drifting across the deck, several smiling women waved at him. It was obvious that he'd been the target of their attention, Ashleigh noted.

Pangs of jealousy made Ashleigh feel ridiculously uncomfortable. Knowing that Austin could have his pick of any woman aboard the ship didn't make her feel any better. But Austin already had a woman, she reminded herself. A woman he loved enough to make his wife.

Using the tip of his nail, Austin outlined the area around her heart. "So, you think you're capable of making me lose my heart," he taunted. He smiled smugly. "What would you say if I told you I've already lost it?"

No, she thought painfully. *Don't tell me. I don't want to hear the truth. The truth is supposed to set you free.* But she couldn't bear to hear the truth from his very own lips, not about the woman he'd lost his heart to. She didn't want to be set free from him. Not now, not ever . . . *Please, Austin, spare me the heartbreak of the unmitigated truth.*

"I'd say that that someone is in for a serious letdown." Her tone was void of malicious intent. "Could we just change the subject?" She sounded almost desperate to do so. While Austin had no idea how strong her feelings were for him . . . she was so sure that he couldn't care less about hers.

The desperation in her request was not lost on him. He carefully studied her beautiful face. Then, out of his own desperate need to make physical contact with her, he bent his head and grazed her lips.

Seeing the hungry look in his eyes, Ashleigh backed away. It was too late. His arms had wrapped tightly around her before she could gulp in the next ragged breath. *Awesome* was an understated word for the way Austin made her feel.

His roving tongue met with her own. Knowing that his kisses were exactly what she'd been waiting for all her life, Ashleigh allowed him to sear her lips with the blistering heat from his engaging mouth.

When he finally released her, she was shaking all over. Her body simply craved him. To have him make love to her was the one and only way those cravings would ever be satisfied. Even then, she seriously doubted that her hunger for him would ever dissipate. Austin was in her head and inside her heart to stay.

Highly agitated with himself, Austin ran quaking fingers through his wind-tousled hair. This just wasn't fair to Ashleigh, he thought furiously. How could he have recently broken his engagement to one woman, yet want another one so desperately? He wanted Ashleigh more than he'd ever wanted anyone. But there wasn't anything he could do about it. That he couldn't give Ashleigh all that he wanted to frustrated him to no end.

Back off, he told himself. This was not the type of woman that men toyed with and just walked away from. No, not Ashleigh Ayers. She had a way of getting under a man's skin. Unwittingly, she was tearing away at his very flesh. She was irresistible. And she was also very vulnerable, he somehow knew. She wasn't fooling him one bit. Her saucy attitude was a cover-up for something buried so deep inside of her, it would take a steam shovel and an excavation team to unearth.

Wondering what he could possibly be thinking, Ashleigh shot him a worried glance. "Are you okay, Austin?"

Oh, God, he moaned inwardly, taking her in his arms again. No, he was not okay. He wasn't sure he'd ever be again. Even her sweet voice did wonderful, crazy things to him.

"Ash," he whispered, "there's something I have to tell you."

"No!" She pressed her fingers against his lips. "Whatever time we have left is ours. Exclusively ours. No promises. No regrets." She breathed in deeply, calmly.

Holding her away from him, Austin looked deeply into her topaz eyes. "Do you know what you're saying, Ashleigh? Are you really sure that you want what's been happening between us?"

His question was somewhat sobering for her. Blinking back her tears, Ashleigh's lips curved into a slight smile. "No promises. No regrets," she reiterated. "This doesn't have to be complicated. This doesn't have to be complicated at all."

Doesn't have to be complicated! This was the most complex situation he'd ever found himself in. What could be more convoluted than leaving behind one woman, only to find yourself lusting wildly after another just a short time later.

Well, maybe it wasn't the most perplexing situation he'd ever found himself in. Having found himself engaged to Sabrina in the first place was the epitome of complications. At least he was completely thrilled at the prospect of spending more time with Ashleigh. Whether it was for one night or an eternity of nights, he sensed that he'd never be disappointed in her . . . and he didn't think he'd ever tire of her refreshing personality.

Sabrina had already disappointed him more times than he cared to remember, just by being herself. She'd been so self-centered. Would she ever wake up and realize that the whole world didn't revolve around her? No matter how hard he tried, he just couldn't imagine that ever happening. Sabrina actually thought that she made the world rotate on its axis.

"No promises. No regrets," he finally said.

At that moment, he couldn't help recalling the sincere promise he'd once made to little Sariah, the only promise he hadn't been able to keep.

"I'm glad we have that settled. Now, will you bestow upon me the honor of escorting you to the captain's dinner this evening? I'm sure you already know it's a formal affair." He wanted to ask to escort her to the Valentine's celebration, but he would wait until later. He didn't want her to think that he was taking anything for granted.

Smiling blissfully, Ashleigh gently touched his cheek. "As you wish. If you look half as good in formal attire as you look in those royal blue swimming trunks, I'm going to be the envy of every woman on this cruise ship."

He kissed her forehead. "Just as I'm already the envy of every man!"

Smiling at his comment, she began to gather her things from the deck. "Talking about dinner has worked up my appetite. If you'll excuse me, I'm going to slip into something appropriate for the lunch setting."

Austin grabbed the towels and the suntan oil. "I'm going to escort you to the cabin. I'll be waiting for you at the entrance to the dining room. That's with your approval, of course."

The look she gave him said she wholeheartedly approved of his plans. As he eagerly fell into step with her, he slipped his hand possessively beneath her right elbow.

When they reached the cabin, he glanced at his watch. "Is twenty minutes enough time?"

"Make it thirty. Women have a little more to take care of than you men who can look good without even trying. See you soon."

The white backless sundress she wore was elegant and stylish, the seasonal dress a perfect fit on her slender figure. A gold-and-white headband kept Ashleigh's copper curls out of her face. The golden bronze lip shiner she wore on her mouth was a nice complement to her deep tan. On her small, slender feet she wore gold-braided sandals.

Austin looked like a walking advertisement for men's summer wear. Ashleigh smiled up at him, her eyes raking over his exquisite body with pleasure. His crisp white tennis shorts and salmon-colored polo shirt were simple enough for an informal lunch date. When you poured an amazing athletic body like Austin's into them, the total package was enough to leave a female's head spinning like a top.

His sable hair looked damp and shiny. Ashleigh had to fight the urge to push back an unruly curl that had fallen down onto his forehead. His ebony eyes, fringed with long, thick lashes, appeared as shiny as his hair.

Smiling at one another, Ashleigh and Austin strolled toward the dining room starving for more than just food.

Before the two could sit, the two other Carrington men approached the table. Houston had to laugh when he saw the woman his brother was with.

Ashleigh wasn't the first woman who had preferred Austin's company over his own, or Dallas's, for that matter. But the brothers were too close to one another to let any woman come between them. There was just something about Austin that women craved. But if you'd ask Austin, he would just blame it on his profession. The ruggedness of a football quarterback had always had it over basketball and baseball. Austin's extremely physical position was far more appealing to women than that of a basketball point guard or a shortstop in baseball.

The three brothers gave one another a high-five.

"Hello, Ashleigh Ayers. Nice to see you again," Dallas said.

Ashleigh's topaz eyes gently swept over both men. "It's nice to see both of you, too."

Remembering how she'd run out on the two men the previous evening, Ashleigh first extended her hand to Dallas and then to Houston. "I'm sorry about how I reacted the last time we met. I just wasn't myself. I hope no offense was taken."

"None was taken, Miss Ayers," Houston offered kindly.

Austin looked on with a perplexed expression.

Ashleigh lowered her lashes. "Please call me Ashleigh." Dallas and Houston nodded.

"Well," said Austin, "shall we all sit down and have some lunch? It looks like they have enough food to feed the entire NFL." He smiled at Ashleigh, as though he had no control over his facial muscles. Finding that he couldn't stop himself from smiling in her presence, he no longer tried to.

"I'm all for that," Houston agreed. "Big brother, why don't you go ahead and pass the blessing? Then we can make a few scoring passes at all that food you just spoke about."

His two siblings had always looked to him for leadership, Ashleigh recalled, although Austin was only minutes older than his two brothers were. Austin had great leadership qualities, which helped him to easily gain the reverence of his teammates. He had also become the big brother to many of them, as well. Ashleigh remembered reading that in the newspaper.

Houston took a long look at Ashleigh. "You really look familiar to me. And you're even more beautiful in the light of day. Brother," he said to Austin, "you are one lucky stiff."

"I was thinking the same thing," Dallas piped in. "You look like someone we know."

The two men studying her so closely as they went through the food line made Ashleigh terribly uncomfortable. Were they starting to recognize her? Fearing that her identity was once again at risk, she was nearly ready to take flight.

Austin sensed her discomfort. "Are you okay, Ash? You're starting to look a little pale again. You're not going to faint on me, are you?"

She shook her head. "I'm fine, Austin. Just hungry."

Back at the table, the triplets talked as they ate. Ashleigh remained silent. Every now and then Austin cast a concerned glance her way, but she would just smile and quickly look away. The moment Lanier and her high court joined the table, Ashleigh noticed how the conversations had instantly become livelier.

Lanier possessed a wonderful sense of humor and Ashleigh could see that she thoroughly enjoyed the laughing responses she received from the others. If she could only be that witty and charming. . . . At any rate, she wasn't the least bit envious of her friend's knack for doing so.

Though she didn't know it, to Austin, Ashleigh was every bit as witty and charming as her friend . . . and much, much more.

FOUR

Not long after taking the first few mouthfuls of food Ashleigh once again began to experience those not-so-subtle symptoms of seasickness. Suddenly, she felt as though tidal waves were washing up on the shores of her stomach. The dizzy feeling in her head had her seeing double.

After quickly excusing herself from the table, she made a mad dash for the nearest exit. Knowing she couldn't make it to the cabin in time, she rushed to a deserted corner of the ship and leaned over the railing. She just barely made it. In an anguished state, her insides heaved and wrenched wretchedly.

Just as the deck swayed crazily, rising up to meet her petite body, Austin reached out and pulled her into the safety of his strong arms. "Ash," he called out, his tone anxious. "Ash!" He looked around for a place to lay her.

Kneeling, he lifted her head and placed it on his knee. Stripping out of his polo shirt, he folded it into a makeshift pillow. Austin lowered her to the deck and nestled her head on his shirt. Ashleigh's eyes opened the second her head hit the soft pallet.

"Welcome back," he soothed. Obvious signs of relief were written on his face. "I'm going to assume that you didn't take my advice when this happened before. Am I right?"

Her mouth felt dry as cotton. "Yes," she managed weakly.

"I was . . . going . . . to go to . . . the infirmary, but I got sidetracked. Boy," she croaked, "I can't believe I went out like that."

Austin lifted her head and placed it against his chest. "Believe it, girl." He snapped his finger. "You went out just like that. I'm just glad I was here to break your fall. If your head had hit the deck, the medical staff would've had to have you airlifted to the nearest hospital. How do you feel now?"

Ashleigh closed her eyes as another wave of nausea spread through her, only this time she didn't have anything left in her stomach to heave up. "Not so good. I think I need to go to my cabin and rest. Will you help me get there?"

His smile was tender. "Of course I will, but not before we stop by the infirmary. The doctor will need to give you something to get this problem under control. Otherwise, you're going to be positively miserable until we make port. Up you go." He gently helped her to her feet and then quickly pulled his shirt back on. When Ashleigh looked as though she was about to faint again, he lifted her and carried her all the way to the infirmary. Inside the medical cabin, he laid Ashleigh down on a treatment table. He then explained the problem to the nursing attendant.

Within minutes she and Austin were on their way. When Ashleigh realized she'd left her waist pouch, which contained the key to her cabin, in the dining room, they were already at the door of her cabin.

"Oh, Austin, I left the key in the dining room. Will it be much of a bother for you to fetch it for me?"

He grinned like a schoolboy. "No, it won't be a bother, but I have a better idea. My cabin is only a couple of levels up. After I get you settled comfortably, then I can retrieve your bag. I promise not to seduce you."

"You can't do any more than I let you."

With the awesome strength Austin possessed, she knew that he could do anything he wanted to her. But she was confident that he would be a perfect gentleman. He was not the type of man that would force himself on a woman. If anything, he probably had to keep women from forcing themselves on him.

Her reply seemed consensual, exactly what he'd been hoping for. He didn't dare risk asking her again. Before she had a chance to change her mind, he swept her up into his arms and hurried along to his cabin.

The stateroom suite that Austin solely occupied was much, much larger than the cabin Ashleigh and Lanier shared. Done in soft peach and quiet hues of blue, the cabin contained a peach-and-blue sofa, two matching chairs, a dinette set, a desk, and a small refrigerator. A wet bar, stationed in one corner of the room, was stocked with a varied assortment of drinking glasses. The wallpaper was adorned with an array of dainty peach and blue blossoms, its borders boasting a collection of showy butterflies. The king-size bed, dressed in a solid powder-blue bedspread, looked reasonably comfortable. The all-glass balcony door allowed for a magnificent panoramic view of the never-ending blue waters.

She gave a thorough once-over of the entire suite from over Austin's broad shoulders. "Nice." The bathroom door was closed, but she wasn't at all interested in seeing it since she had a good idea that it was probably a lot bigger than the one she and Lanier shared.

He carefully deposited her petite body on one of the overstuffed chairs. "Comfortable?" She nodded. "Can I get you something before I run back to the dining room? The refrigerator is stocked with plenty of refreshing drinks."

"A cold glass of water will do nicely. My mouth is still very dry. I imagine that the medication the doctor gave me is only going to add to it."

Austin got the water and handed it to Ashleigh. He then relieved her feet of the gold sandals. "Would you like to lie on the bed, or do you just want to stay curled up in the chair?"

"I'm fine right here. This chair is very comfortable. I'll be okay until you return."

Without offering a response, Austin exited the cabin. He waved to her before gently closing the door behind him.

As he rushed to his destination, he thought about the captain's dinner, which Ashleigh had agreed to allow him to escort her to. He was somewhat disappointed that her illness would probably keep her from attending. If that were the case, there was no way he was going to let her spend the evening alone. In fact, he was going to enjoy looking after her, that is, if she would allow him to. There would be many other affairs on the ship for them to attend together. The Valentine's dance had suddenly become important to him. Before he'd met Ashleigh, he hadn't cared about it one way or the other.

When Austin returned to the cabin, he found Ashleigh fast asleep. She had moved over to the bed and her sundress was tangled up high around her tanned thighs. It was then that he saw the small birthmark, resembling a four-leaf clover, on her left upper thigh.

Dumbfounded, he dropped down in the chair. He stared at the small marking. This was no coincidence. What were the chances that two different females carried the very same birthmark, in the same spot? It has to be Sariah, he thought in utter amazement. Oh, God, how could this be? How had he missed the unusual birthmark when she'd been clad only in a skimpy bikini? And why hadn't she admitted to knowing who he was? She'd been acting as though he and his brothers were virtual strangers. There was no way she could've forgotten the four years they'd spent under the same roof. Unless . . . she had amnesia. . . .

This woman was not acting at all like the little girl who had been a part of their family. Sariah had loved being in the Carrington home. She'd constantly thanked them for making her feel like one of the family. He had been her hero. He was unable to keep himself from smiling at the memory of her adoration of him. Yet, here and now, she'd been carrying on as if she'd just met the Carrington triplets for the very first time in her life.

Why? He was powerless to tear his bewildered gaze from

her sleeping frame. Had she come on this cruise knowing he and his brothers would be aboard? Was she here for revenge? No, he thought, Ashleigh didn't have a vengeful bone in her entire body. She hadn't displayed any type of unusual behaviors toward him and his brothers. He couldn't even imagine her showing anger, let alone setting them up for something unpleasant.

Copper curls, topaz eyes, skin the color of champagne, now the unusual birthmark. It all added up. She was a dead ringer for the adult Sariah he'd created in his mind. He hadn't been substituting Ashleigh for Sariah at all. He'd been wildly attracted to her in the same way he'd been reservedly attracted to the adorable, much-too-mature little girl whom, oddly enough, he had ended up pining away for. He'd even fantasized about her as an adult, day in and day out.

His entire world had been turned upside down the day he'd returned from baseball practice and found out that she'd been taken away. He had demanded answers from his parents, but they just didn't have them. It seemed to be a total mystery as to why she was yanked from their home. Then, nearly eight years later, he learned the ugly truth. His parents had tried to spare him the pain, but nothing could've saved him from the anguish and disheartened feelings the so-called truth had visited on him. Still, he didn't know how the malicious rumors started.

Nothing or no one, other than the return of Sariah, could've brought him the slightest bit of consolation. He and Sariah had bonded in an unusual sort of way, which made him miss her like crazy. Sariah had been the one person who had filled his life with the joy of laughter.

What was he to do now? Did he confront her with what he knew? Or did he just sit back and participate in whatever game she was playing? Either way, the next several days were going to be very interesting. He couldn't help wondering what the final outcome was going to be. Silently, he prayed that neither of them would get hurt.

* * *

Despite Austin's loudly voiced objections Ashleigh had insisted on attending the captain's dinner. She felt much better and the prescribed medication had already begun to work wonders on her nausea and dizziness.

Ashleigh looked radiant in a backless, strapless ivory formal gown. A gold lamé scarf, draped loosely around her neck, flowed elegantly down her back. Along with the dainty gold satin pumps she wore on her feet, Ashleigh's entire outfit made her look ravishing.

No longer carrying the earlier pallid look, Ashleigh's complexion was now back to its normal, healthy color. In fact, it glowed. Her newly acquired tan was stunning against the cool ivory of her luxurious gown.

Having a hard time keeping her pulse under control, Ashleigh looked up at Austin and smiled brightly. He looked absolutely wonderful in his winter-white dinner jacket and black tuxedo pants. Making Ashleigh feel as though she floated on a cloud, he whirled her around the dance floor. Austin was quite the accomplished dancer. The music was slow and provocative and neither of them could deny the heady sensuality passing between them.

When the music turned funky and upbeat, Ashleigh and Austin let their hair down, gyrating and swinging wildly to the faster-paced tunes. Although Austin hadn't figured out Ashleigh's agenda where he and his brothers were concerned, he had already made up his mind to remain silent on his discovery of her true identity. At least for the time being. There had to be a darn good reason why she wanted to keep her true identity a secret. Until he could find out her reasons for wanting to do so, he was just going to participate in the game.

Grabbing her by the hand, he escorted her off the dance floor. "We need to sit out the next few songs. I don't want you to get tired. You're hardly fully recovered." He slid his arm around her slender waist.

Ashleigh would've objected, but she guessed that it wouldn't do any good. Austin had a determined look about him. It had already been hard enough to convince him that she felt well enough to make the dinner. Not wanting a repeat performance of yesterday's fiasco, she had eaten very little of her meal. Austin had grown very protective of her and she loved the constant fuss he'd been making over her. It seemed like old times.

"Okay, boss. However, I don't plan to stay seated for too long. The funky reggae rhythm just won't allow me to do so."

"Do you want a drink, Ash?" he asked, once they were back at the table and seated.

"Only water. No alcoholic drinks for this kid. You'll be picking me up off the floor again if I so much as take a sip of alcohol. Like you said, I'm not fully recovered. Oh, there's Dallas and Lanier out on the dance floor. They look really nice together." Austin nodded his agreement. She felt rather sorry that Dallas wasn't the man Lanier was looking for.

Lanier wore a magnificent sky-blue gown fashioned by House of Style. Like Ashleigh's gown, the dress was backless but it had spaghetti straps tailored in rhinestones. Both Dallas and Houston wore the same exact attire as Austin, which made everyone think they were seeing triple. No one but their parents, Ashleigh, and a handful of their high school classmates had ever really been able to tell the three dashing men apart.

Ashleigh waved at the group of women she and Lanier had become well acquainted with. Smiling, they all waved back. Beverly, who seemed to be the leader of the group, discreetly gave Ashleigh the thumbs-up sign. Ashleigh smiled, knowing Austin Carrington was often their main topic of conversation. They'd even told her, since it appeared that she had him snagged, they could only hope that Dallas and Houston might find time to give each of them a spin around the dance floor. Lanier had made it clear to everyone that she had no special designs on Dallas. As for Houston, it was obvious that he was footloose and fancy-free.

Austin stood and braced his hands on the back of

Ashleigh's chair. Leaning over, he brought his face intimately close to hers. "Care to get some fresh air?"

She eagerly pushed her chair back from the table. "Would love to. I imagine it's very beautiful outside this evening."

When Ashleigh removed the scarf from around her neck, Austin took it from her and draped it around her shoulders. He doubted that the sheer wrap would be enough to keep the sea winds from toying with her delicate skin. As he was a gracious man, he would have no qualms about giving up his dinner jacket. Several heads turned as they made their way to the exit. Slipping his arm around her waist, he pulled her close to his side. Austin knew he hadn't any right to feel so possessive of her, but he couldn't help himself.

Knowing who she really was made him more than a little overprotective of her, mainly because he knew of all the pain she'd once suffered. He didn't know all that had happened to her once she'd left the safety of their home, but he knew she hadn't had an easy time of it before her arrival. He'd seen the last hellhole she'd lived in. A few years back, when he'd visited the Macks, her former foster parents, they didn't know where she'd run off to. It had been obvious to Austin that they hadn't cared whether she was dead or alive.

Resting his back on the ship's railing, Austin drew Ashleigh into his arms. He searched the depth of her topaz eyes. "You really look radiant, Ash. You had me worried there for a minute. I was beginning to believe the rest of the cruise was going to be ruined for you. Seasickness is not something you can easily recover from. How are you feeling now?"

Ashleigh reached up and coiled one of his satiny curls around her forefinger. "Thank you for the compliment, Austin. I was a little worried myself. I guess you noticed that I ate very little. My stomach is still a little upset, but other than that, I feel just fine."

"We've hardly had the time to really get to know one another. Tell me about yourself, Ashleigh. I want to know all about where you came from and where you're going."

Ashleigh gulped hard. *I came from nowhere—it looks as though I'm going to the same place. Without you in my life, all roads will undoubtedly lead to nowhere. You belong to another. That's just the way it is.* She couldn't help wishing that he wasn't engaged, wishing that he was exclusively hers.

"I don't think it's a good idea for me to tell you all the details of my life. We only have a few days together. So where I came from and where I'm going really doesn't matter here. When the cruise is over, we'll undoubtedly have to part company."

She paused for a moment, looking pensive. "Austin, I've been thinking about us. And I've come to the conclusion that we can't allow our relationship to progress any further. As you yourself said, you can promise nothing beyond this cruise for us. And I said that our relationship didn't have to be complicated, but it's becoming just that. You see, I've fallen deeply for you. And you've made it clear that you're unavailable to me."

Austin's heart was so full, he thought it would burst right out of his chest. She had fallen for him. But what did that really mean? Was she trying to tell him that she'd fallen in love with him? While he hoped she had, he knew she was right about their relationship. It had become complicated, but it had nothing to do with his unavailability because his fiancée was his ex-fiancée. It had everything to do with the secrets Ashleigh held inside of her. It had everything to do with who she really was and why she wanted to hide it. He decided not to reveal his eligibility until the mystery was solved.

She was no longer Ashleigh Ayers to him. All grown up now, she was simply his precious, beloved Sariah. From the questions he'd been asked by his brothers, he sensed they were also suspicious of who Ashleigh claimed to be. They had asked him if she reminded him of anyone, which had suggested to him that they also questioned the resemblance between her and Sariah. Although they hadn't voiced their concerns aloud, he knew they were worried about his becoming entangled with someone who might not be exactly whom she said she was.

Suddenly fearful of their fantasy coming to an end, his arms tightened around her. "What made you change your mind? Weren't you the one who insisted on 'No promises. No regrets'?"

With tears in her eyes, she looked at him thoughtfully. "I wasn't being realistic, Austin. I was caught up in the romantic eroticism of it all. If we take this any further than we already have, when this cruise is over, there are going to be regrets. Deep regrets. And I'm afraid I won't be the only one who will feel the devastating impact. I came on this cruise for fun, not for heartbreak." Her lips tenderly grazed his cheek. "I think we should at least consider sparing one another all the grief."

Wishing they could've come together under different circumstances, he already felt deep regret—that of not being able to give her all she desired. His broken commitment to Sabrina had become an unwelcome weight on his broad shoulders. He felt horrible about it. Nonetheless, it had been a commitment he just couldn't keep. And he had to be careful not to make that same mistake with Ashleigh.

"I wouldn't think of not honoring your wishes, Ash, but I can't say I'm thrilled. Ashleigh, I *do* think we should continue to build a friendship. If we don't, we might suffer even deeper regrets. There's nothing wrong with us remaining friends, is there?"

Unable to stop herself from claiming his irresistible lips, Ashleigh urgently pressed her mouth against his. She immediately felt the warmth of his searching tongue slip past her teeth. *Damn it to hell,* she thought heatedly, encircling her arms around his neck.

The absorbing kiss was not the sort that "just friends" indulged in. It was the kind of torrid kiss that impassioned lovers yielded to. Both thinking it could be the last kiss they might ever share, neither of them tried to suppress their intense hunger for one another. The kiss deepened until near-bursting emotions filled their hearts.

As they moved apart, Austin quickly brought her back to him. "Let's forget everything and everyone while we slow dance under the illustrious illumination of the moon. The angels will be sorely disappointed if we don't. First, let's look up and make a wish on one of the thousands of stars gracing the heavens above. Close your eyes, my sweet-heart."

Ashleigh closed her eyes as she looked toward heaven. On the brightest star in the universe, she wished for her and Austin's hearts to melt together as one. Smiling, she buried her head against his chest. She would take all the magnificent memories of this evening to bed with her to-night—every night, for the rest of her life.

The cool sea air blew haughtily off the ocean, causing Ashleigh to draw even closer to Austin. High above the blackened seas the brilliant stars were like no others she'd ever seen. In their special corner of the ship's deck where Austin had first kissed her, Ashleigh and Austin felt as though they were the only two people on the planet.

As their eyes locked feverishly, Austin bent his head and claimed her lips ever so gently. She moaned against his mouth as she deepened the kiss, making Austin feel as though he floated on a cloud. The slightest touch from Ashleigh numbed his brain and turned the rest of his anat-omy into a trembling, throbbing mass of frenzied muscles.

He lifted his head and held Ashleigh at arm's length. "I know I've said this before, but you are so beautiful, Ash." He pointed up at the stars. "If it was within my power, I would purchase several stars from the sky and have a jew-eler fashion them in the most exquisite star-studded ring. Then I'd have him design a dazzling star pendant and a pair of matching earrings. What a rare sight you'd be—and you'd always have ample light to guide you on the darkened path," he whispered. He claimed her mouth once again.

Ashleigh tilted her head, dying to feel the electric touch of his moist lips against the base of her creamy throat. "Yes," she moaned huskily. As his lips gently grazed her soft skin, her legs grew weak. Then his lips moved from her throat to the luscious swelling of her breasts.

It was early morning when she finally slipped into her cabin. After she and Austin had slow danced in the moonlight, they'd slowly strolled the various decks beneath the illumination of the distant universe. While they had indulged in more kissing and intimate touching, it had been seriously hard for them not to give themselves over to the strong cravings stirring deep within their souls.

As she lay in bed thinking about their evening, Ashleigh was glad they'd decided to spend more time together to see just where the sunny days and balmy nights would take them.

For too long she'd dreamed about having Austin at her very fingertips. Now that he was within easy reach, no matter how temporary it might be, she had foolishly tried to keep him at bay. When her thoughts transferred to Dallas and Houston, she trembled slightly.

The two carbon copies had recently been eyeing her curiously. They seemed to be watching her every single move. In view of Austin's engagement, it wasn't at all odd that they might disapprove of him getting involved with someone on the cruise, especially if they were particularly fond of his bride-to-be. Yet it seemed to be something other than that. They'd been looking at her as if they were trying to place where they might have seen her before. Had she done or said something that had reminded them of Sariah? Had she said or done something that might have made them think she wasn't who she said she was?

Well, for sure, her name was Ashleigh Ayers. But the Sariah part of her identity, which she'd kept a secret, was what smacked of willful deceit. Earlier, when she'd thought about the birthmark on her upper thigh, it had been too late to do anything about it. It was then that she first began to realize that her birthmark was the one thing that could possibly give away her true identity.

Everyone in the Carrington home had at one time or another passed comment on the unusual marking. The family had used the swimming pool on a regular basis. It was when she wore a bathing suit or short-shorts that her birthmark was right out there in plain sight. For sure, there had been no way of concealing it in the skimpy bikini she'd chosen to wear. In fact, she'd completely forgotten about the small marking.

No sooner had Ashleigh finally managed to fall asleep, than she was awakened by a loud noise. Lanier had accidentally knocked over the telephone. Its crashing sound brought a startled Ashleigh straight to her feet. Wagging her finger playfully at Lanier, she lay back down.

"Oh, I'm sorry for waking you up, Ash. I know you couldn't have been asleep for too long. When I came in at five, you weren't here yet. You must have had one hell of a good time. How are you feeling?" Lanier gave Ashleigh a questioning look. "Did you stay in Austin's cabin?" A frown creased her brow.

Ashleigh grinned smugly. "I'm feeling just fine. And, no, Austin and I didn't make love. That's what you're really asking, isn't it?"

Lanier's eyes glittered with mischief. "I guess you could say that. Are you sorry it didn't happen, Miss Ash?"

Ashleigh pursed her lips. "Very sorry. But I know we made the right decision for now. Austin and I are still going to spend time together for the duration of this trip, but we're not going to become too hot and heavy with one another. After all, he's engaged to be married."

Lanier dropped down on the bed. "I'm not so sure about that anymore, Ashleigh."

"What! What are you talking about?"

Slowly, Lanier stretched out on the bed, driving Ashleigh crazy on purpose. Laughing inwardly at Ashleigh's impatient body language, she folded her fingers into her palms and studied her square-tipped nails.

"Lanier," Ashleigh screeched, "get on with it, will you? What did you mean?"

Lanier laughed. "Okay, already! I overheard a couple of the jocks talking this evening, but I'm not sure I got it exactly right. Hal, the big, burly one, told Jason, the thick-necked one, that he'd never seen Austin so happy. Then Jason said, 'He sure got over his broken engagement mighty fast.' And Hal replied, 'Hell, I'd be celebrating, too, if I just escaped from a fate worse than life in prison. He was never in love with Sabrina in the first place.' According to Hal, it seemed that Austin just didn't know how to tell his coach the truth about how he really felt about his beloved daughter."

Ashleigh whistled. "And?"

"That's all I heard. I'm not sure of everything that was said, but I did tell Dallas that I'd heard Austin was no longer engaged. Dallas's response was almost vehement when he told me that I shouldn't involve myself in listening to or spreading malicious rumors. He in no way confirmed for me that Austin had broken off his engagement. But I sensed from Dallas that something is definitely out of sync with Austin and his fiancée. He told me if I wanted to know anything about him or either of his brothers' private business that I should ask them myself. Of course, I felt horrible for having pried into Austin's private affairs."

"Of course." Ashleigh whistled again.

"I know you read it in the paper that Austin was engaged, but has he actually told you that himself, Ashleigh?"

"No, not exactly, but he's insinuated that he's unavailable. I thought the football players were here for a double cele-bration. I left the room because I didn't want to hear them announce Austin's engagement. You were there. Didn't you hear what the double celebration was all about?"

Lanier shook her head. "I must have missed it when I followed you out of the lounge that day. I was worried about you, but you had already disappeared by the time I reached the corridor. They might have been talking about celebrat-ing his return to bachelorhood."

Ashleigh smiled wryly. "I see that I'm not the only one who might have secrets. If what you overheard is true, Austin is free to pursue another relationship. But I have to wonder if he's emotionally free. Apparently this must have happened to him fairly recently."

Lanier shrugged her shoulders. "Why don't you just ask him?"

Ashleigh pulled a face. "Are you kidding? I'd never do that."

"Then what are you going to do?"

"Play it by ear, I guess. I'm curious to know where he really wants our relationship to go. I don't think just friendship is his ultimate goal, but I'll have to wait and see. This is really getting more and more complicated, but I have to admit that it's intriguing. If Austin's engagement is actually broken—and he's emotionally free, he won't be free for long. I'm going to reclaim that boy's heart if it's the last thing I ever do. He may not have known it back then, but my feelings for him were different from any sister-and-brother relationship. I used to think I saw his feelings there in his eyes. I only saw him every single day. But I was too young to fully understand things. A sixteen-year-old boy was more than off limits to a twelve-year-old girl, and vice versa. I constantly dreamed of growing up. I wonder if he might've dreamed the same dream."

Lanier moved over to Ashleigh's bed and sat down on the side of it. "I don't know exactly what you're feeling, but I do understand your need to find out if Austin could feel the same as you do. But, Ashleigh, I don't think you're going about this the right way. I think you should just tell him who you are and let come what may. When he does learn who you are, he may not like the fact that you attempted to fool him. He may also become suspicious of your motives. Is that how you want this to play out?"

Ashleigh dropped her chin to her chest. "I don't know what I want to do anymore. There are times when I think I should tell him the truth, but then the fear of it all sets in. But if he should just come to me and specifically ask me if I'm Sariah, I'm not sure I could deny it. He knows I remind him of someone, but I don't think he's really sure of who that someone is. I just hope he falls in love with me before he comes to the truth."

Lanier's mouth fell open. "That doesn't sound like you at all, Ash. You're playing with a raging fire, my friend. I just hope you can pull yourself away from the flames before you get third-degree burns."

Ashleigh sighed. "Since I'm no longer making any sense, I'm not going to talk about this anymore. We'll talk later on, after I've had a couple of hours of sleep. Pleasant dreams, Lanier."

"Same to you, Ash."

FIVE

The breakfast buffet tables were loaded with a variety of delicious-looking foods, hot and cold. The warm scent of freshly baked pastries filled the air. Fresh fruits, whole and cut, had been placed in oversize clear bowls. Miniature boxes of cereal, stacked on glass shelves, came in a large assortment. Fresh juices flowed from their chilling dispensers as passengers pressed colorful glasses to the release levers.

Austin, dressed in khaki shorts, a royal blue polo, and leather sandals, added a buttery croissant to the fresh fruit plate he was preparing for Ashleigh. After pouring two glasses of orange juice, he carried the tray out to the open deck, where Ashleigh sat quietly, looking out at the clear blue waters.

Boasting broad straps, crisscrossing in the back, Ashleigh looked darling in a royal blue polka-dot sundress. She would've preferred shorts, but the birthmark had become an issue for her. The wide band of the straw hat she wore on her head matched the dress. Her feet, propped on the lower railing, looked neat in the bright blue patent-leather sandals she wore. The golden highlights in her copper hair glistened beneath the bright yellow rays of sunshine.

Austin removed a plate from the tray and set it in front of Ashleigh. "I hope you can eat a substantial amount of food this morning. We've got to preserve your energy. You haven't eaten all that much over the past couple of days."

Ashleigh pulled out a chair for Austin. Using discretion, she moved it closer to her own. "I know my appetite hasn't been the best. I'm going to try real hard, but I don't want to risk eating too much and getting sick again. We've got far too many days to go out here on the sea."

Smiling at her discretionary gesture, he sat down and moved the chair even closer to hers. "Practically everyone on this cruise has seen us together at one time or another. You don't always have to be so discreet. I'm proud to be seen with you, Ashleigh. What we do on this cruise is nobody's business but ours. We've already discussed what we're about."

Ashleigh blushed. "Are you sure about that, Austin? Haven't your brothers and teammates made it their business to say something about us being together so much?"

Austin shrugged his broad shoulders. "What if they have? I'm a grown man, Ash. Are you concerned with what others might have to say about us? If so, why?"

Ashleigh studied him intently, wishing he had referred to himself as a "free man." She already knew he was grown. Although Lanier had told her what she'd overheard, she wanted to hear Austin declare himself single. She wanted to be sure of his heart's availability, without having to ask him herself.

While thinking about Austin's questions, she picked up a chunk of ripe cantaloupe and popped it into her mouth. With her eyes still trained on Austin, she chewed the juicy fruit slowly. "I'm not concerned, but I am curious about what the people in your circle have been saying about us. What *are* they saying, Austin?"

Austin grinned. "Other than them telling me how beautiful and sexy you are, they haven't said much else. You remind my brothers of someone, but they haven't yet figured out who." Having baited her purposely, he watched closely for any overreaction to his statement. When she swallowed hard, Austin knew his statement had caused her a bit of discomfort.

Trying to come off unaffected, Ashleigh speared another piece of melon with her fork and bit off a tiny piece. "I remind everyone of someone, but no one can ever figure out who it is I remind them of. I just have one of those everyday kind of faces."

Austin chuckled. "There's nothing everyday about your beautiful face. You have the kind of face photographers dream about and would kill for a chance to shoot. Along with your gorgeous face, you also possess the type of body that appears in every man's fantasy."

Smiling, she waved off his flattering comments. "Can I have a teeny bite of your egg?"

He lifted her hand and kissed her wrist. "You can have all of my egg, beautiful."

When Austin stuck his fork into the scrambled egg and brought it to Ashleigh's mouth, she opened to receive it. He repeated the gesture several times before she pushed his hand away.

"Had enough?"

Licking her lips, she nodded. "I'm full. Now I'm ready to do some serious shopping. Are you still coming with me?"

Kissing a spot of butter away from the corner of her mouth, he picked up a napkin. After dabbing the paper all around her lips, he kissed her full on the mouth. "That's sweet." He kissed her again, allowing his tongue to mingle with hers. "That was even sweeter, baby. You sure you want to go shopping? I can think of a few other tantalizing ways for us to spend our afternoon. We can start by booking ourselves one of the Jacuzzis up in the health club. I hear the water jets have quite a stimulating kick to them."

Ashleigh laughed at the way Austin wiggled his eyebrows in a suggestive manner. "We can start our afternoon by disembarking from this ship. I hear that St. Thomas is a must for gold and precious gems. We can do the Jacuzzi later on."

"Promise?"

Boldly, she pressed her lips into his hair. "Promise."

At the ship's disembarkation ramp, Austin kept his arm possessively around Ashleigh's waist. One of the ship's many photographers took their picture in front of the life preserver boasting the ship's name. With her hands clasped together around Austin's waist, Ashleigh looked up into his eyes, smiling brilliantly as the shutter clicked.

Within easy walking distance, an abundance of local shops were located just a few short yards from the dock. Side by side, with their arms touching, Ashleigh and Austin strolled toward the center of the busy shopping district.

"We can get a cab and go into downtown if you'd like," Austin offered. "We don't have to be back on board until five o'clock." He glanced at his wristwatch. "It's just a little before eleven now. The ship won't set sail until five-thirty."

Having removed her hat, Ashleigh shaded her eyes from the sun with her hands, looking ahead to the dozens and dozens of quaint little shops. "Let's check out these shops first. There may be no need to go any farther into town. I really want to get back to the ship so I can lie in the sun before our dinner seating, but I don't want to interfere with your plans."

Smiling gently, he took her hat from her hand and put it back on her head. "My plans are all designed around yours. Look, Ash." He pointed at the water lapping against the shore. "See how transparent this water is. It's so blue."

Ashleigh gasped with delight. "I've never seen water so blue. Actually, it looks turquoise to me. It's magnificent. You can see straight to the bottom. Look at all the colorful fish down there. This is awesome. I wish I knew how to snorkel or scuba dive."

Ashleigh laughed when Austin had to duck his head down to enter a doorway. Enchanted by her laugher, he grasped her hand and directed her away from the entry to the jewelry shop.

He brought her hand to his lips. "My height tickles you, doesn't it?"

She shook her head. "Not at all. I'm mesmerized by your height. I love tall men."

His eyes growing solemn, he drew her down on a nearby bench facing the water's edge. "Is there a tall man waiting for you at home? By the way, where is home for you?"

Ashleigh pressed her lips together. "I'll take the Fifth on the first question. As for the second, I live in an apartment on Galveston Island, Texas. But I'll be moving in a couple of weeks." Just to annoy him, she removed her hat and placed it on the other side of her. The truth of matter was that she didn't want anything between her and Austin.

Another piece of the puzzle had fallen into place for him. Austin frowned. "Not out of Texas, I hope."

She grinned. "Not a chance. We're moving into a great big house on the island. We just purchased it. We're going to take in lots and lots of foster kids."

Austin's breath caught. He gulped at the lump in his throat. Another possible clue to her true identity? Sariah had often talked about helping kids like herself when she got older and made lots of money. In fact, she had taken an oath to do so. Even in her budding youth she had talked of serious plans to help other unfortunate kids.

" 'We' equals two or more. Who's the other part of we? Or are you going to plead the Fifth on that one also?"

Though flattered by it, she laughed at the jealous streak flashing in his eyes. "My friend Lanier, Austin. We bought the house together."

He eyed her intently. "Foster kids, huh? What makes you think you're equipped to deal with those types of kids? They need special care because they come from sensitive situations."

Ashleigh smiled gently. Her eyes teared up.

Besides the fact that I am one? In many ways, I'm still one of them. Will always be one of them, emotionally.

"I'm a social worker, Austin. A well-trained professional. The depth of my compassion is another reason I'm qualified. Lanier's a social worker, too. She and I are going to make this work if it kills us. We're terribly passionate about Haven House, which is the name we've chosen for our home." Frowning, Ashleigh suddenly realized she had probably revealed way too much about herself. But she loved talking about her plans for Haven House.

Austin couldn't stop himself from touching Ashleigh's face with the back of his hand. Her compassion filled him up. *My beautiful Sariah,* he empathized in silence. *Your heart is opened wide right now.* Much like he'd vowed long ago, he made an oath to protect her heart from ever being broken again. This time he would keep his promise. Now that he'd found her, he couldn't imagine ever letting her go. First, he had to uncover her hidden agenda.

"Haven House," he reiterated softly. "I like the name. Any child that gets the opportunity to come live there will be richly blessed. How many rooms?"

"Thirteen rooms all together. Six bedrooms, three bathrooms, a huge family room and dining area combination, with a large country kitchen. The private upstairs loft is what I'm going to take as my bedroom. In time, we hope to expand the place. There's lots of land to do so. We hope for Haven House to one day become a fortress where love and compassion freely abide. There's much work to be done on that old place before we can begin to fill it to capacity."

Austin caught a few of her curls between the soft pads of his fingers. "Are you saying the house is not ready to be occupied?"

"Hardly. We have to paint, new carpet has to be installed, and we need new plumbing. We've got a big job on our hands, but Lanier and I are up to the challenge. Lanier and I make a good team because we have a lot in common and we share like goals. However, we're going to need to come up with some surefire techniques to raise money for Haven House. We've about exhausted our savings."

Austin got to his feet. "I'd like to hear more about Haven House later. In the meantime, I'll try to think of ways for us to get the money you need. Let's go into the jewelry store we were about to go in when I dragged you over here to sit down."

She stood and dropped her hands to her side. "I may have already mentioned this, but I hear you can find great bargains on jewelry here on St. Thomas."

"In my opinion, St. Thomas *is* one of the best islands for buying diamonds and gold."

"Are you looking to purchase a diamond?" She had a look of innocence on her lovely, darkly tanned face.

The way in which she'd asked the question made Austin wonder if she'd heard about his engagement. The announcement of his impending nuptials had been in all the major newspapers, but he was sure the press hadn't gotten wind of their breakup since it wasn't plastered all over the tabloids. At least not yet.

At the entry to the shop, he turned to face her. "No, I'm not looking for a diamond." He kissed her forehead. "I'm simply looking for a friend. Will you be my friend, Ashleigh Ayers?"

Smiling, Ashleigh laid her head against his chest. "I'd be honored to have you call me friend, Austin Carrington. I don't have many."

He tamped down his need to kiss her in the way only friends that were also lovers kissed. Yet he wanted to lose his heart to hers and have her lose hers to his, for all eternity.

As soon as Ashleigh and Austin entered the jewelry store, a smiling saleswoman immediately came to their aid.

"We just want to browse." Austin didn't want them to be followed around the store.

"I'll be close by should you need me. Just wave and I'll come running."

Austin laughed. "I bet you will. Thank you."

Ashleigh cooed and awed her way through the first few showcases. Then she appeared to have been struck dumb. Her mouth moved but no sound came from within. All she could do was point at the most marvelous trillion-cut diamond ring that she'd ever seen—at least five carats. She was in total awe of the flawless gem. She was sure that the ring cost a small fortune, which would probably be enough money to run Haven House for a couple of years or more.

When Austin summoned the saleswoman, she nearly fell over herself getting to them.

"May we see this ring?" He pointed at the very diamond that Ashleigh couldn't seem to take her eyes off.

After the woman handed Austin the diamond ring, he took hold of Ashleigh's hand to place it on her finger. He looked stunned when she jerked her hand away. "What's wrong?"

Looking horrified, she backed away from the counter. "I can't try that on. It's much too expensive for me to even dream about owning."

Austin chuckled inwardly. "Just try it on for size, Ash. You'll be sorry if you don't. It doesn't cost anything to try it on."

"He's right, young lady," the saleswoman urged. "Don't you want to see how it looks on your lovely hand? Women and men alike try on rings in here all the time."

Reluctantly, Ashleigh held out her hand to Austin. Smiling, he slipped the ring on her slender finger. Gaping at its beauty, she wondered how some people could afford such an obscenely expensive trinket when others didn't have enough money to buy food.

Grinning, Austin held her hand up. "It looks beautiful on your finger, Ashleigh. Look how it sparkles. But I'm afraid it's no match for the brilliant facets of light in your lovely eyes."

Ashleigh blushed. "Like a million stars, more than beautiful, Austin. It's fit for royalty."

He kissed her softly on the mouth. "Yes. It is, isn't it? That makes it perfect for you."

Not wanting to get attached to the ring, Ashleigh quickly removed it and handed it back to the saleswoman. "Thank you for allowing me to try it on. I'll never forget how it felt on my finger. It was easy to imagine myself as a fairy-tale princess." She looked at Austin with longing. *With you as my charming prince.*

Austin's heart melted at her expression of yearning. "You are a fairy-tale princess. Let me get you out of this store before you break down and cry. I know what you must be thinking."

He had easily guessed her feelings when he noticed the tears fringing her lashes. "Come here, sweetheart. Don't cry. Knowing the challenges you're about to face with Haven House, I understand why the cost of that ring would upset you so. It isn't fair, is it?"

She shook her head as he pulled her toward his chest. "Some have so much, while others don't have enough to obtain bare essentials. No, it isn't fair at all."

Austin smoothed her hair back. "Sometimes life isn't fair. I wish it were, so that disappointments could be kept at a minimum. Have you ever been seriously disappointed in something or someone?" If she was his precious Sariah, he already knew the answer. He couldn't stop entertaining the idea that she might have amnesia. Nothing else made any sense.

It didn't necessarily have to be amnesia. She could've simply blocked out all the horrendous pain she'd probably suffered over the years, along with all the people whom she held responsible. That could include him since he failed to keep his promise to her back then.

"No." Lacking the courage to tell him how disappointed she'd been in him and his family for sending her away from the only place she'd ever considered home, she'd lied to him. No explanation from them was what had hurt the most. As they sat on the bench they'd vacated earlier, she suddenly fell headlong back into the pain of her past. . . .

A wilting sadness had replaced the beautiful smile normally covering her budding lips as she was led from the Carrington's ranch-style home. Wanting to scream out loud, but fearing she wouldn't be heard, twelve-year-old Sariah had remained deathly silent, wallowing in her unyielding grief.

"It will be okay, Sariah," Miss Townsend, the children services worker, said soothingly. "Your new foster home is going to be better than all the ones you've been in before. You just wait and see. The Macks will love you!"

Exercising her right to remain silent, as though she were being hauled off to jail, Sariah stared helplessly at the house she'd come to know as home over the past four years. No one had said a word about her pending departure—and none of the Carringtons seemed to be rushing to her rescue. In fact, there wasn't a single soul in sight.

Only minutes before, she recalled, she had been sitting on the front stoop talking to one of the sixteen-year-old Carrington triplets who had just promised to take care of her forever. Had Austin known this was going to happen when he'd made his seemingly sincere promise?

As the car sped away from the curb, Sariah turned and looked out the back window. While pressing her small hands against the sun-heated glass, she had released the tears brimming uncontrollably in her luminous topaz eyes.

"Why," she recalled whispering against the window, "why are you doing this to me? You said you loved me. You even promised to start adoption proceedings."

It hadn't taken long before the four-door late-model sedan had pulled up in front of a small cinder-block house painted an awful shade of lime green. The house was pitiful looking, especially in comparison to the sprawling ranch house she'd just been snatched away from. The dead brown grass was much too long. Discarded beer bottles and trash were strewn recklessly around the drab property.

Hadn't Miss Townsend said that this was the best home yet? Sariah had wondered if Miss Townsend was legally blind, or perhaps just an outright liar.

When a short, balding man and a dumpy woman emerged from the house, looking as unkempt as the property, Sariah remembered letting out a painful wail, which she quickly cut short when she sank her teeth hard into her lower lip. Having drawn blood, she quickly sucked the oozing red liquid into her mouth before Miss Townsend could notice the self-inflicted injury.

Six more years of this, she had told herself, choking back the sobs strangling her uneven breathing. Six more years, then I'll be eighteen. I'll never again have to be shoved from place to place. Ashleigh's twelve-year-old tender mind had grown far too mature and hardened from far too much pain and suffering at the hands of the adults who were supposed to take care of her.

Only six more years . . .

Austin's warm hands on her waist awakened her from the past. "Where did you go?"

To hell and back. "I was deeply contemplating your question. I must admit I never allow myself to get that close to anyone, nor do I let anyone get too close to me. If I don't expect anything from anyone, I don't have to worry about the disappointment."

Austin's heart turned cold from the arctic chill in her voice, yet it wasn't the coldness that concerned him. The pain in her eyes nearly brought him to his knees. Her words stuck in his craw like a jagged fish bone.

He tilted her chin upward. "I thought we were getting close, Ash. As friends, of course. Nonetheless, close."

She looked from his intense gaze to focus on the water. "Friendship is something totally different than what's going on between us, Austin. Let's face it. What we're starting to feel for each other goes deeper than friendship. It seems that neither of us is in a position to do an in-depth exploration of those feelings. Since we've already visited this subject . . . and have decided not to think about us beyond this cruise, let's promise not to revisit this subject again."

He turned her face back to him, hating the sadness he saw in her eyes. While he hoped that she was his precious Sariah, he knew there was still the slightest chance that she might not be. That meant that he had to be careful with his probing questions. Amnesia still hadn't been completely ruled out by him simply because it was the only thing that would explain her behavior.

Ashleigh got up from the bench and stretched her hand out to him. "Let's hit a few more of these shops. I need to get a few souvenirs. I'd also like to get a magnetic travel board since I hope my travels are just beginning. This is my first trip out of Texas."

Austin reached out and pulled her down on his lap. He then touched his lips to her ear. She giggled as she tried to worm out of his tender grasp.

"Wait, Ash. I want to know if you'll accompany me to a special team function this evening. Invitation only. It's a private gig."

"That depends on what's going to go on at this private gig."

"Texas two-step, cotton-eyed-Joe, to name a couple of events. We're going to have an old-fashioned hoedown aboard the ship. We're going to rock the boat CW-style. By the way, Texas girl, can you two-step?" His smile was riveting, causing Ashleigh's inner thighs to sweat.

Ashleigh threw her head back as she laughed out loud. "I'm going to make you wait and see. I accept your invitation and I just happen to have the perfect outfit with me. Thanks for the invite." She grew silent for a moment, looking perplexed. "What about my girl Lanier?"

Austin ruffled her hair. "She'll probably receive an invite from everyone in my crew. She's very popular with all the fellows. But we'll invite her along to be sure."

Ashleigh kissed his cheek. "Thanks again."

As Ashleigh pulled herself up from his lap, Austin placed her hat back on her head. "If you don't keep this on, you're going to live to regret it. This sun is a lot hotter than it feels. Let's go get this shopping finished so we can get back in time to relax before dinner."

Ashleigh and Austin took delight in flitting in and out of one shop after another. Ashleigh purchased a magnetic board, a St. Thomas magnet, several colorful T-shirts, and an assortment of postcards for the travel book her travel agent had presented to her as a gift. She also bought a couple of boxes of imported chocolates for Mr. Early, a chocoholic.

When Austin picked out a hand-painted silk scarf for his mother, Ashleigh had to fight hard to keep from bursting into tears as the gentle face of Angelica Carrington came to mind.

The dimly lit, spacious club reserved for the country-western festivities had been decorated with artificial bales of hay and other Western-theme decor. The blaring country music could be heard throughout the room. Several couples had already taken to the dance floor where they participated in an old-fashioned square dance. Hoots and hollers were as much a part of the dance as the actual steps. Practically every head in the club wore a Stetson.

Although this was a private party, the ship's activities itinerary had listed country-western music as one of the nightly themes, which was the actual reason Ashleigh and Lanier had chosen to pack their Western gear.

Dressed in skin-tight black denim jeans, the belt loops laced with a silver-studded belt boasting a large silver buckle, a fabulous black-and-silver Western shirt, and gray leather cowboy boots, Ashleigh looked the part of a true Texan. Completely obscuring her copper curls, a gray, fetchingly feminine Stetson sat atop her head. It completed her totally Western look.

Austin's attire, very similar to Ashleigh's, only the male version, was fashioned in dark blue denim. It fit his athletic physique like a body glove. His camel-brown cowboy boots had been designed from genuine snakeskin. The camel-brown Stetson he wore was much larger than Ashleigh's feminine version. The hat made him look even taller than six-foot-three. Although he looked ruggedly handsome, he appeared somewhat formidable.

Ashleigh looked around for Lanier, wondering why she hadn't made an appearance yet. They had left the cabin at the same time, but when Lanier had stopped by the purser's desk to have her postcards stamped and mailed, Ashleigh had gone on to meet Austin at the piano lounge. Austin whirled her into his arms before she could tell him she was going to go and see what was keeping Lanier.

The words to "Looking For Love In All The Wrong Places" described her life exactly as it had been—still was. Nothing said could be truer. Especially if Austin was still emotionally attached to his fiancée—ex, or otherwise.

Austin smiled down at her. "Are we looking for love in all the wrong places?"

"Are we looking for love, period, Austin?" Her eyes burned into his.

Without answering her question, he whirled her around the floor, spinning her one way, then quickly reversing the spin. Ashleigh surprised him when she was able to keep up with him effortlessly. Her feet stayed in step with his fast, impromptu whirls and turns.

When she spun away from him to show him all the latest CW moves she knew, Austin looked on with appreciation for her talent. As her curvaceous hips moved seductively to the bumping CW rhythms, Austin grinned widely. The girl sure knew how to work him.

As Ashleigh initiated the steps to the Electric Slide, CW-style, several lines formed. Everyone fell into step, joining her in the popular line dance. Austin positioned himself behind her. Putting his hands on each side of her waist, he easily followed her animated steps. The rhythm in their moves came with a mixture of funk and soul. Unwittingly, they stole the show.

As the line dance ended, a slow song wended into the room, allowing pulse rates to cool down. Austin pulled Ashleigh against his throbbing sexuality. "You keep surprising me, sweetheart. A lot of people are amazed when they find out that black people enjoy country-western activities—and that there are black cowboys and cowgirls. You've shown yourself to be a real Texan, Ash. Your moves are dangerously sexy, Texas girl. But can you rope a cow?"

Ashleigh kissed the side of his neck. "Your moves aren't

all that bad, either, Mr. C. As for roping, I guess that's something you'll never find out since there aren't any cruising cows."

Smiling mischievously, he looked around the room. "We could debate that statement, but I'm not going to go there."

She smiled gently. "It would be very insensitive for you to do so. Since I know you're a sensitive man, we'll steer clear of that subject. But I hope you understand that everyone wasn't born to be a size four. I hear that after a woman has children it can become an uphill battle the rest of the way."

"Thank you, but I was referring to the guys. Look at all the beefed-up jocks in this room." He led her over to an unoccupied table in back of the club. After pulling out her chair, he took the one that faced her. He covered her hand with his. "Children? Do you want children someday, Ash?"

Ashleigh didn't know quite how to answer that question. Of course she wanted children, but not without adequate finances. She'd never think of bringing a child into the world that she couldn't afford to take care of, nor would she ever consider having a child before marriage.

She shrugged. "I can't say that I've given it much thought. The only children I'm concerning myself with, at the moment, are the kids whom nobody seems to want." Austin's bare wrist caught her eye. "Where's that expensive Rolex I've seen you wearing? You look rather undressed without it."

Wondering how she knew it was a Rolex, Austin eyed her intently. "I don't know. I can't seem to find it. I must have misplaced it, but I'm sure it's somewhere in my cabin. If I don't find it in the morning, I'll panic then. There's no way it could've slipped off my wrist."

"I've heard that there are serious pickpockets in popular resorts. Do you think that's a possibility?"

Austin laughed. "They'd have to be damn good. To get that watch off my wrist without my knowing it would take a thief with major skills. Let's not worry about it tonight.

I'll do some serious cabin searching in the morning. Want to help me?"

"How early in the morning are you talking about?"

"Just before sunrise. We can watch the sun come up from the balcony off my cabin. The sunsets over the ocean are magnificent. I'm sure they're only rivaled by the sunrises."

"You're right. I've been on deck practically every morning when the sun's come up."

Austin looked surprised. "I've been out there with you a couple of times, but I wouldn't have thought you'd be a habitual early bird. I rather imagined you were so beautiful because you get plenty of beauty sleep. Any other secrets you'd like to share with me?"

"None that I can think of." She stood. "I'm going to run out and see if I can round up Lanier. I'll be right back."

"Sariah!" Ashleigh had just barely moved away from the table. Without thinking, Austin had called out to her using the name she'd left behind with the past.

Ashleigh's steps grew burdensome, her heart froze inside her chest, and tears welled in her eyes. She moved on through the crowd like she hadn't heard him. But she had, loud and clear. Whether him calling her by that name had been intentional or not, she was now sure that Austin at least suspected her of being Sariah. *What a mess,* she moaned inwardly, hurrying to the exit.

Austin stroked the sexy, shadowed growth of hair on his handsome face. His eyes followed Ashleigh out of the club. Becoming more and more of an enigma to him, it appeared that Ashleigh hadn't faltered a step or flinched a muscle as he'd called out the name. More perplexed than ever before, he shook his head.

Ashleigh presented him with a real challenge. He had fallen in love with a woman he didn't quite know what to make of. He had so many questions for her but no courage to ask them in case they might bring her pain. Somehow, some way, he had to find out everything he wanted to know about Ashleigh Ayers—and time was quickly running out on them. By the end of the cruise, he would know for sure if Ashleigh was actually his forbidden fantasy of long ago. Either way, he had fallen sea deep in love with the most intriguing woman aboard the ship. . . .

SIX

The Carrington men seemed to be in an uproar when Ashleigh and Lanier reached the outside table that they'd chosen to eat breakfast at. Their faces looked grim. Their voices sounded loud with something akin to anger.

Ashleigh grabbed Lanier's hand and turned her in the other direction. "I think we'd better pass on eating with them for now. Something major is going on between them and I don't think we should get in the middle of it. They seem to be having a big disagreement of sort. I hope it's not about me."

Lanier's brow creased in a frown. "Why would they be in an uproar over you? Dallas and Houston seem to like you very much."

"They may not like the fact that Austin and I seemed to be getting too close. They might be really fond of his fiancée and may have hopes of them getting back together. That is, if they've really broken off their engagement."

"I guess."

When they reached the buffet line, Ashleigh removed two trays from the stack and handed one to Lanier. After retrieving two sets of silverware, she laid one set on Lanier's tray. Once they'd filled their plates, Ashleigh and Lanier started toward the outside seating area, on the opposite side of the ship from where the Carrington brothers were seated.

Lanier turned around when she heard her name called.

She saw Dallas summoning them over to their table. Lanier gave Ashleigh a questioning look. "What do you think, Ash?"

Ashleigh looked directly at Austin. When he smiled, she smiled back. Glad that she wasn't their problem, she sighed with relief. "It's seems to be okay with Austin for us to join them. I guess their conflict doesn't have anything to do with me."

"I never thought it did. You've got to lose the paranoia, friend," Lanier chided gently. "We just partied in Dallas's cabin last night, after the CW gig. All the guys were perfect hosts."

Ashleigh clicked her tongue. "Okay. I see your point."

The triplets stood when the two women reached their table. Dallas pulled up a chair next to his for Lanier. Austin slid out the chair right beside his for Ashleigh.

"Good morning, ladies" came their simultaneous greeting. Lanier and Ashleigh laughed at their unison response. The women sat down after placing their trays on the table.

Lanier placed the white linen napkin in her lap. "You guys seem to be in a better mood than you were a few minutes ago. You all looked really upset when we first came up," Lanier mentioned nonchalantly.

Dallas shot his two brothers an amusing glance. "You noticed, huh? Sorry about that, but we were in a discussion about politics. We can get really riled up on that subject. Austin and I are Democrats. We're trying to talk some sense into our younger brother. He's thinking about voting Republican in the next major election."

Lanier looked shocked. "I can see why that would whip up quite a storm."

"I think our younger brother is missing a screw or two. Becoming a Republican isn't the smartest thing for a black man to do," Dallas said.

"Guys, you're the ones that are missing something. The Republicans are going to take over, so I'd rather be on the side of the party with the most money," Houston remarked.

"And the most crooks," Dallas countered.

Austin turned to Ashleigh. Pursing his lips, he twisted them to the side. "Since everyone is speaking of something missing, I thought you were coming to my cabin to help me search for my missing watch. I waited for you. Why didn't you show up?"

The suspicious look in Austin's eyes made Ashleigh feel terribly uncomfortable. She put her fork down when her hands started to shake. "I overslept. I was really tired from all the dancing we did earlier in the evening. Also from the lively time we had in Dallas's cabin."

Austin frowned when he caught the perplexed look Lanier gave Ashleigh. "I see." Austin eyed Ashleigh curiously. "We shouldn't have upset you girls with our petty arguments. With that said, let's get off this anger-stirring subject. Houston will come to his senses before the next election. If he doesn't, he'd better not let Beaumont Carrington know how he voted. Dad would lose his mind over it. Are you two ladies getting off the ship when we make port in Barbados?"

Lanier handed Austin a colorful brochure that she'd removed from her bag. "We're going to explore Harrison's Cave first. We've decided to hire a private taxi or van to take us on a tour of the island. It's cheaper than taking the ship's tour. I hear the caves are truly awesome."

Austin scowled. "I don't think it's such a good idea for two women to go off alone with a stranger. It's too risky. I suggest that we all go as a group and tour the island together. It'll be much safer that way, don't you think?"

"I agree," Houston and Dallas chimed in at the same time.

Austin looked at his wrist, forgetting his watch wasn't there. "What time is it?"

"Seven-thirty," Houston responded. "The morning is getting away in a hurry."

"Shall we all meet at the disembarkation ramp at eight-fifteen?" Austin queried.

Ashleigh pushed her chair back from the table. "That's fine. Lanier, I'd like for you to come back to the cabin with me. I need to change my sandals for something sturdier to accommodate all the walking we're probably going to do."

Lanier grabbed her bag from under the table as she got to her feet. "We'll meet you guys at the ramp. Let's go, Ashleigh."

Before Ashleigh could take one step forward, Austin brought her to him. "You owe me a sunrise, friend. I plan on making you pay up." He kissed her directly on the mouth. "I'll be eagerly awaiting your arrival at the designated place."

Ashleigh wished the floor would open up and swallow her whole. Austin's display of wantonness in front of his brothers still embarrassed her, yet it made her feel good all over.

Once Ashleigh entered the cabin, Lanier closed the door. Looking upset, she pushed Ashleigh down in a chair. "What's going on with you? Why did you tell that bald-faced lie to Austin? You know darn well you were awake and out of the cabin before the sun came up."

Ashleigh rolled her gold bracelet around on her wrist. "Should I have told him I chickened out at the last minute? Do you really think I could've told him how much I wanted him? I knew if I went into his cabin, I would've begged him to make love to me. I watched the sunrise all right, but I didn't dare watch it with Austin from the balcony of his cabin."

A fat tear rolled down Ashleigh's cheek. "Lanier Watson, have you actually forgotten how much I love that man and what I would give to be in his arms and in his bed forever? You couldn't possibly have forgotten, but we both know that's not an option open to me right now."

Lanier pushed her hair back from her face as she blew out a stream of air. "Oh, Ash, I'm sorry. I should've known you had a good reason for lying to Austin. I know you're not used to being dishonest, but I wish you would just tell him who you are and get it over with. What have you got to lose? What's the worse-case scenario?"

"I'm scared to tell him. I've missed too many opportunities already. If I tell him now, he'll come to hate me. He called me Sariah last night and I almost stopped breathing. I wanted to fling myself into his arms and openly confess my love for him, but the fear of getting my heart broken is so much bigger than I am. What if he can't feel about me the way I want him to? He may go back to seeing me as nothing more than his little sister. I think I've fantasized about Austin so often that I've actually made myself believe the fairy-tale outcome I've created in my mind. I thought I'd faced all of my fear of yesteryears, but I was dead wrong. I just don't know how I'd face the truth if Austin were to tell me he can only love me like a sister."

Lanier pulled a pair of comfortable shoes from the floor of the closet. "I hate to ask you this, but I have to. It's been on my mind since Austin mentioned his watch. Ash, are you responsible for the missing watch? Have you somehow decided you need to exact revenge on Austin for whatever happened to you when you lived with them?"

Ashleigh dropped from the bed to the floor as though she'd been shot down by a shotgun blast. The look she gave Lanier was nothing less than contemptuous. Ashleigh glanced away, looking as though she'd been stabbed in the heart with a serrated dagger.

Swallowing the bad taste in her mouth, Ashleigh looked back at Lanier. "I could answer your question, but then I'd have to kill you."

Lanier was thoroughly shaken by the hostile look she saw in Ashleigh's eyes. "What was that? I didn't hear you."

Ashleigh slowly pulled herself up from the floor. Without uttering another word, she changed into walking shoes, grabbed her tote bag, and walked out the cabin door. When Lanier bolted out the door after her, Ashleigh turned around and held up her hand for her to stop. Although Ashleigh didn't speak a single word, her eyes warned Lanier to back off.

Ashleigh's legs carried her swiftly to the lower deck where the disembarkation ramp was located. Instead of waiting for Austin to arrive, as was planned, she showed her passport and sign-and-sail card to the security officer and proceeded toward the exit. When the ship's photographer asked her to stop for him to take her picture, she totally ignored him.

Even in her turbulent emotional state, Ashleigh took heed of Austin's sound advice by accepting the invitation made to her by a group of passengers who asked her to fill the last van seat for the tour to Flower Forest, Harrison's Cave, and a few other popular island attractions. Ashleigh quickly withdrew her money from her tote and handed it to the group's leader. The tour rates came cheap when shared by so many, Ashleigh noted.

When the entire group was out of the van, Pierre, the driver, pointed to the entrance of Flower Forest. "Forty-five minutes will only allow you to cover a bit of the fifty-acre forest. If you are to see all the sites that you desire, we must limit our time at each attraction. The cruise ships are known to sail promptly. Although we would take very good care of you, we would not want to see anyone left behind, especially if the bulk of your money is in the care of the purser's office." Pierre joked with ease, making everyone laugh.

Ashleigh hung on to Pierre's every word, loving the melodious sound of his rich accent.

Fifteen minutes into the tour, Ashleigh cursed herself for not bringing along a hat. The whispering trade winds were blowing extremely hot air and the early-morning sun was already a scorcher. She hated to even guess at what the heat might feel like by noon.

Another fifteen minutes had passed when Ashleigh decided she needed to take a rest. Learning that the group would be coming back the same way, she took a seat on a gazebo bench, situated in the middle of the forest. It felt a lot cooler here in this spot. She fanned herself with several tourism brochures she'd placed together as a makeshift fan.

In Ashleigh's opinion, the forest offered a cross between a botanical garden and a nature trail. A profusion of tropical blossoms trekked freely over the beautifully manicured lawns. The description given in the brochure spoke of Flower Forest as Paradise, tucked away on a hillside in the picturesque Scotland District. From what she'd seen, she wholeheartedly agreed with the very accurate assessment of the magnificent forest.

As it turned out, the forest was located close to Harrison's Cave, which was the next spot on the route. When the van rolled up to the parking area and stopped, everyone filed out in a flurry of excitement. Ashleigh's enthusiasm was short-lived. Austin, looking mad as a wet rooster, took hold of her hand and squeezed it hard enough to make her wince.

"Ouch!" She jerked her hand from his grasp. "That hurt."

He again imprisoned her small hand within his much-larger one. "I didn't mean for it to tickle. You've stood me up twice, lady, and I want an explanation. If you don't start talking, your hand isn't the only thing I'm going to squeeze hard."

Before Ashleigh could utter a word, an attendant shoved a yellow hard hat into her hand. As she looked around her, she saw that everyone waiting in line was handed the same yellow headgear. Then the tour guide explained that the hats were needed because the stalactites that they'd encounter on the tour often dripped water from the roof of the cave.

Ashleigh looked over the long lines for Lanier, Dallas, and Houston, but her cursory glance proved futile.

"They're not here." Austin took the hat from her and placed it on her head at a silly angle. "I can see that you didn't bring along your own hat to protect you from the sun. Girl, I don't know about you sometimes. You're the most defiant woman I've ever met. You need to show your precious head a little more respect."

She bit down on her lower lip, hating that he'd read her

so effortlessly. "I don't know what you're talking about."
She reached up with both hands and straightened the hat.

Austin helped Ashleigh into the mining car that would
take them down deep into the cave. "Yes, you do. I don't
know why you ran off and left us all waiting for you, but
I just happened to get a glimpse of you when the van you'd
gotten into pulled off. I thought you might end up here
eventually. Looks like I played my hunch right. Now what's
going on between you and Lanier? She burst into tears when
I asked her where you were."

Ashleigh decided to take a tight-lipped approach to
Austin's seemingly investigative probe. In response to his
question, she simply shrugged her shoulders. As far as she
was concerned, what had occurred between her and Lanier
was none of his business. She didn't even want to think
about the seriousness of what had happened with Lanier.
That alone made it a certainty that she wasn't going to discuss it with Austin.

His eyes buried themselves within hers. "I see that failing
to wear a hat isn't the only act of defiance you're capable
of. Would you mind telling me why you won't talk to me?
Am I guilty of something you've decided not to tell me
about? Have I done something to hurt you?"

The tour guide speaking loudly into the microphone
saved Ashleigh from having to respond to Austin's heart-
wrenching questions. It also gave her the time she needed
to pull her emotions together. She wasn't far away from
bursting into tears as he'd said Lanier had done. In fact, all
she wanted to do was slip her head against Austin's chest
and bawl like a hungry baby wearing a waterlogged diaper.

Even in the darkness, as the tram descended below the
earth's surface, Austin saw the glistening tears pooled behind Ashleigh's pupils. He figured that something serious
had happened between the two friends, but Lanier hadn't
wanted to talk about it any more than Ashleigh did. In fact,
Lanier had become so upset, that Dallas stayed behind to
offer her support. Houston had gone off with the group of

female social workers after he realized that things weren't going as planned.

To offer Ashleigh his love and support, Austin slipped his arm around her shoulder and pulled her head against his chest. "I'm here for you as your friend and I'd like to be here for you as your lover. We're not fooling anyone but ourselves when we try to pretend there's nothing between us. I'm really very much into you, Ashleigh. It's time for us to lay all our cards on the table, sweetheart. I want you." Lifting her chin up, he kissed her hard on the mouth.

He buried his lips against the soft flesh of her neck. "I want us long after this cruise has ended. You're the only woman that can give me what I need. You're the only woman I want. I feel as though I've known you for a long, long time—and I want to know you for even a longer time than that. I've got some serious issues to deal with . . . and I suspect that you do, too. Do you think we can deal with them together?"

Ashleigh couldn't breathe, let alone speak. Austin had taken her breath away. He had said everything she'd imagined him saying in her dreams, but this wasn't one of her fantasies. What had just occurred, by far, exceeded her wildest fantasy about Austin Carrington. Yet the reality of it all frightened her in ways she'd never be able to make him understand. She knew they couldn't take their relationship to the level he'd suggested because of all the lies between them. But she needed to have Austin fulfill her physical desires for him, if only for one night. By satisfying her physical desires, Austin would also be satisfying her emotional needs. Just one night of Austin buried so deep inside of her core of life would make him forever a part of her heart and soul, forever her dream come true, forever her forbidden fantasy.

As her mouth opened fully against his, she slowly curved her tongue around his. Her hands ached to wrap around his maleness and stroke him to completion. That would have to wait until they were in private.

While she didn't give him a verbal response, he enjoyed

the way her lips talked so sweetly to his. The beauty of the cave was unrivaled by anything they'd seen so far, but Ashleigh and Austin had things even more beautiful than the cave on their minds. The moment the tram resurfaced and it was safe to get off, Austin guided Ashleigh out into the light of day. Ashleigh told the group leader she wasn't going to finish the rest of the tour. She then thanked the group for inviting her along. She also said her farewell to Pierre.

Austin immediately hailed a cab to take them back to the ship. Once there, he would go forward in his desire to come together with Ashleigh in a way that spoke to much more than just the heat of their passion.

Stretched out on a lounger, on the balcony of Austin's cabin, Ashleigh and Austin held each other in a tight embrace. While their desire for lovemaking had not been extinguished, neither of them wanted to go forward in a heated rush. As his hands slowly but eagerly made the acquaintance of her firm, velvet-soft flesh, his mouth searched hers with deep, obtrusively delectable kisses.

Ashleigh slipped her delicate hand under his shirt, catching his taut nipple between her thumb and forefinger. As she bent her head and massaged the nipple with her moist mouth, she felt his flesh grow even tauter with excitement. When his hands inched their way up her dress, to the top of her thighs, she placed her hands on both sides of his face to deepen their kiss. Gasping with wantonness, Austin brought her tongue into his mouth.

Austin pulled back from Ashleigh and looked into her eyes. "Do you want to discuss where we're headed?"

Desperate for his warmth, Ashleigh took his hand and placed it over her right breast. "I think we both know where we're headed. Discussing it is only going to further delay us from getting where we've both wanted to go from the very beginning." To show him how much she needed for them to come together as one, she undid the top button on his navy shorts. Feeling freer than she'd ever felt in her life, she lowered his zipper.

Through his briefs she slowly moved her palm against his rigid sex. Sensing strongly that their time had finally come, Austin stood up and held his hand out to her.

Inside the cabin, he drew her down on the bed. The low cut of her sundress gave Austin a perfect view of her swelling breasts straining against the soft material. As Austin's fingers blazed a heated trail from her neck to her tantalizing cleavage, Ashleigh closed her eyes, gripping his upper arms tightly.

Wanting to taste her sweetly scented skin, Austin dipped his fingers in the glass of water resting on the stand beside the bed. Sprinkling the cool liquid between her heavily heaving breasts, he lowered his head. After circling the tiny beads of moisture with his tongue, he lapped it greedily from her skin.

One button after another on Ashleigh's sundress popped open at the command of Austin's steady fingers. He stopped after undoing the one located just below her navel. Austin now had a full view of her splendid sun-bronzed stomach vying for his heated caress. Instead of dipping his tongue into her navel, as was his desire, his mouth went back to her stiffly puckered, ready-to-be-kissed breasts.

As his tongue laved one breast, then the other, his fingers worked feverishly to undo the remaining button on her dress. Seconds later, with her dress fully open, Ashleigh began to feel somewhat conscious about lying on Austin's bed. Though exposed all the way down to the wisp of black lace hiding her molten treasures, she in no way wanted the journey to end. It was only natural for her to feel some degree of embarrassment. After all, Austin had only touched her like this during her wildest fantasies.

The sudden loud pounding on the cabin door startled Ashleigh into an upright position. Austin grasped her hand. Sighing with impatience, he pushed his hands through his hair. "Be still, my love. I'm sure they'll go away in a second or two."

Ashleigh softly grazed his chin with her thumb. "It sounds like it could be important. Maybe you should go and see who's there."

Irritated with whomever was at the door, Austin looked around the room for his bathrobe. Spotting it on one end of the sofa, he quickly retrieved it and came back to Ashleigh. Pulling her to her feet, he wrapped the velour material around her nudity. She gave him a questioning look.

"I don't want anyone to see us like this. It's one thing for people to know we're intensely attracted to one another, but they don't need to know any more than that. There's probably enough speculation about us going on already. As I've said before, what we do in private is nobody's business but ours. Besides that, this beautiful body is for my eyes only."

He kissed her gently on the mouth. When the pounding grew louder, he pulled away. "I'd better get that now."

As Austin started for the door, Ashleigh rapidly dashed out to the balcony, wanting to give him his privacy. Looking out at the sea, which appeared calm, she thought of how close she and Austin had come to their destination. The delay annoyed her, but it also gave her time to think things over with a little more objectivity. Still, she wanted him desperately. Unexpectedly, the breeze kicked up, and she pulled the hood of the robe up over her head.

Austin was taking a lot longer than she'd expected, but Ashleigh decided to wait until he came back to her. Going inside might cause them further embarrassment.

Austin finally returned, but Ashleigh noticed that he seemed to keep himself at a distance from her. Instead of taking her in his arms, as she'd hoped, he shoved his hands into the pockets of the pair of pants he'd slipped into before answering the door.

She started toward him, but something in his eyes told her not to come closer. "Is there something wrong, Austin? You look very troubled."

He held out his watch for her to see. "Why, Ashleigh?

Why did you take this from my cabin? That was a security officer at the door. He said my watch was found in your laundry."

She would've died on the spot if she'd been guilty as accused, but she wasn't. For Austin to even think her capable of something so underhanded made her seriously ill. "I beg your pardon?"

His gaze turned steely. "You'd better get dressed. Security is waiting for me to bring you to them for questioning." When she pushed past him, he spun her around to face him. "Wait a minute, you. Don't you think I have a right to ask the question that I did? I don't know if it will make you feel any better since I've insulted you terribly, but if you tell me you didn't take my watch, I'll believe you. However, I need you to be perfectly honest with me."

How she'd managed to keep the tears from welling in her eyes, she didn't know, but she was grateful she hadn't yet showed the excruciating pain his question had caused. Deciding she wasn't going to answer his question—that she'd only speak to Security about the charge—she turned her back on him. After gathering her clothes, she slipped into the bathroom to dress.

Austin was dressed and waiting for her when she came out. As she leveled him with a look of pure disgust, the same type of look she'd given Lanier earlier, he found himself at a loss for words.

She held out her wrists. "Did they leave you with handcuffs so that you could take me into custody? If not, get out of my way so that I can remove myself from your presence."

He moved closer to her. She took several steps backward, causing him to halt his forward progress. "Can't we at least talk about this before you decide you hate my guts? I'm sorry if I wasn't as sensitive as I should've been in my questioning. Let's sit down and talk this over before this maddening situation goes any further."

"I have no intention of discussing anything with you. As far as I'm concerned, you can go straight to hell, Austin

Carrington." She was happy that their intimate rendezvous hadn't gotten any further along than it had. Before he could even make a move to stop her angry flight, she was out the door, slamming it hard behind her.

Outside in the corridor, her tears having spilled out, Ashleigh ran as fast as her legs would carry her back to her cabin. As she inserted the key into the door, she hoped Lanier was out somewhere. To face her already-estranged friend, after what had just occurred with Austin, would be unbearable. Especially with Lanier also suspicious of her being involved in criminal activity. But what she couldn't understand was how anybody could think she was a thief, of all things. Somebody must have set her up. But who, and why?

She now realized it wasn't only Austin that someone was targeting. For whatever reason, she was also the target of someone's sick ill will. Or could it have been the other two brothers who'd set her up? But why would Houston or Dallas do something that? To make her look like the guilty party? Were they trying to get Austin to see that he was making a big mistake in his personal life?

SEVEN

With her hands folded in her lap, looking contrary but sad, Ashleigh sat in an uncomfortable wooden chair inside the security office. This was the first time she'd ever been interrogated by an officer of the law. She felt rather intimidated by it. She hated it even more.

Seated behind his metal desk, the burly security officer, Tio Webster, studied Ashleigh closely. "I know this is extremely hard on you, Miss Ayers. But if you'll fully cooperate with me, I'll make this as quick and easy as I can."

Managing a weak smile, Ashleigh nodded.

Leaning forward in his chair, he rested his entwined hands on his desk. "I understand that you're an acquaintance of our distinguished guest, Mr. Austin Carrington." Ashleigh simply nodded again. "As he's already informed you, his missing watch was found in your laundry. Do you know why his valuables would be in your dirty laundry bag?"

Ashleigh blew out an unsteady breath. "No, I honestly don't. But I can assure you that I'm not the thief. I've never stolen anything in my life, except for some bubble gum when I was seven years old. Because I was so severely punished for it, I'd vowed to never steal anything ever again." The memory of that horrendous beating made Ashleigh cringe in her chair.

Tio laughed. "Who hasn't five-fingered a piece of bubble

gum or two in their youth? However, here on the ship, we deem stealing from guests, or otherwise, a very serious offense. We have no proof that you actually took the watch. Because it ended up in your laundry, we had no choice but to see that you were questioned. Did you first meet Mr. Carrington aboard this ship?"

Ashleigh pondered his question. Should she tell the truth? Lying wasn't going to help her position, but she didn't see how the truth of when she met Austin was relevant.

"I've become acquainted with Mr. Carrington aboard this ship. However, I knew of him. I know that he's the quarterback for the Texas Wranglers. I've been a fan of his for years, as I also live in Texas." Instead of admitting how she first came to know Austin, she'd simply hoped that her response would fly with the burly officer.

"So you already knew of him before the cruise?" Ashleigh stuck to nodding. "Would you say that you and Mr. Carrington have become more than close friends?"

"We are friends, period. Mr. Carrington and I have practically spent all of our time together since the first night we came aboard the ship. May I ask you a question?" Tio gestured his approval. "Does Mr. Carrington believe that I stole the watch from him?"

"I'm not really sure, but I don't think so. First off, he appeared stunned by what he'd learned. He did say that there was no way that that could be true. He promised that he'd see to it that you'd talked with me, assured me that you'd have no problem doing so. That was the extent of our conversation. And here we are."

Ashleigh looked relieved. "I'm glad to hear that. What happens now?"

"Since we don't have any actual proof, or even an eyewitness to the alleged crime, I can't charge you with anything, nor would I want to have to do that. You don't seem at all like the kind of person who would take something that didn't belong to you. I'm sorry I had to put you through this. Please forgive the unpleasant intrusion on your holiday time."

Ashleigh got to her feet. "Your apology is accepted. I do hope you find the person responsible, but it's not me. I would never do anything to hurt Austin Carrington." She started for the door but turned around.

"Do you think it could have been taken from somewhere other than his cabin?" she asked.

He looked nonplussed. "I don't think so. The watch had to be taken from the cabin, unless Mr. Carrington took it off outside the cabin and laid it down somewhere. I rather doubt that. I don't think he'd be that careless with an expensive watch like that."

"I see your point. Thank you for the faith you've shown in me, Mr. Webster. I'll keep my ears and eyes open. I'll make myself available to you should you need to talk with me again."

"You do that, Miss Ayers. Enjoy the rest of the cruise."

As she closed the office door behind her, all Ashleigh could do to keep from crying was smile. She'd expected the interrogation to be a much worse ordeal than it was. Mr. Webster had been more than fair with her . . . and she was glad to know that Austin didn't think she had taken his watch. She could also see how someone would suspect her since it was found in her laundry. Austin had asked the question he'd asked because it didn't seem as if he'd had any choice in the matter. Still, she was mad as hell at him for the way he'd asked. Even though he'd apologized for being less than sensitive in his questioning, she was going to have a hard time being around him again. It hurt that he might have believed her to be a thief even for a second.

Forgiving him may come hard for her, but there was no doubt in her mind that she eventually would do so. If she'd been able to forgive the Macks and all the other people who'd hurt her terribly, she could certainly find forgiveness in her heart for Austin. He had treated her so well when she'd lived at the Carrington home. But it was a matter of ego right now. Her feathers had been ruffled. Until they could be preened back into place, he'd just have to give her the space she needed to get over the hurt that the false accusations had brought on.

Watery-eyed and still very much anguished over her personal problems with Ashleigh, Lanier lay in bed quietly. When she heard the key inserted into the lock of the cabin door, she looked up. Unsmiling, Ashleigh entered the cabin. Without even looking in Lanier's direction, she dropped down on the bed with her back turned to her friend.

Lanier got out of bed and came over to Ashleigh. Kneeling in front of her, Lanier took Ashleigh's hand in hers. Lanier's watery, puffy eyes made Ashleigh feel guilty about the reason they looked that way. Lifting herself up, Ashleigh leaned over and rested her chin on Lanier's shoulder.

Lanier's tears rolled down her cheek. "I'm so sorry about everything, Ash. I should've never asked you the questions I did. I know you couldn't do anything like that. Please forgive me for hurting you the way I did."

Without moving her head, Ashleigh soothingly rubbed Lanier's back. "It's okay. I fully understand why you felt compelled to ask me what you did. I can see how you would think that. I'm the only person with any sort of motive, but I'm not guilty. I felt utterly betrayed by you, but I know better now. Friends should be able to ask one another anything. I just hope that you can forgive me for turning my back on you, for walking away without giving us the opportunity to discuss the matter and clear the air."

"You haven't done anything wrong, Ash." Lanier sobbed, relieved that permanent damage hadn't occurred. "I probably would've felt betrayed, too. I'm just glad it's all over, but I promise never to be that insensitive again. I don't know what I was thinking." Lanier wanted to ask what had happened with Austin but quickly decided against it. Ashleigh had had enough gloom and doom for one day.

Ashleigh laid her head back on the pillow as Lanier returned to her own bed. "Are you going out to any of the shipboard events this evening?"

"Probably later. I'm going to read this romance novel for a minute. It's really good. I've been having a hard time putting it down."

"*Ice Under Fire*," Ashleigh read aloud from the colorful cover. "Sounds hot."

"It *is* hot! You can read it when I finish."

"Thanks. I'd love to read it." Ashleigh got out of bed. "Right now I'm going to get ready for a night of fun. I really feel the need to let my hair down, all the way down. This has been a rough day." Smiling, Ashleigh pulled a black red-hot two-piece ensemble from her garment bag. "Now this one is going to set the decks on fire!"

Lanier's eyes bulged. "Wow, Miss Ash, you're full of surprises! That is some slinky knit camisole top and wrap skirt. That right side slit looks pretty high up. When you decide to be daring, you go all the way. Are you sure it's going to cover everything?" Lanier joked.

"As much as that black dress of yours covered. Check out the shoes I'm wearing with it."

Lanier gasped. "Oh, those are too cute." Done in a light pewter color, curved with two-inch lacquer heels, the strappy beaded slides were a perfect complement to the outfit.

"Thanks, Lanier. I'm going to slip my clothes on and be out of here. I've never been as ready for anything as I am for this night. It's time for me to move on. In fact, it's past time!"

Ignoring Austin shouting out to her, Ashleigh stared straight ahead. She had no intention of talking to him. He may not think of her as a thief, but for the moment there wasn't anything for them to talk about. Her ego wasn't about to be tranquilized so easily.

Austin caught up to her. Positioning himself in front of her, he blocked her path. With him being much too big for her to move out of the way, she turned around to go in the opposite direction. But he just darted in front of her.

He grabbed hold of her hand. "This has got to stop. You've been ignoring me long enough now. I've had it with the cold shoulder, sister. Ash, we've shared so much for us not to be able to at least talk this through."

She glared at him. "If I were violent, I'd knock you to kingdom come. Austin, we've done enough talking. When you even considered that I might be a thief, I decided you weren't deserving of me. That's that!"

He spun her around before she could walk away. "No, it isn't. I never said I considered you a thief. I simply asked you to explain why my watch was found in your laundry."

Her glare intensified, chilling him to the bone. "I told you that I had no idea, that I didn't take your watch. The problem for me is that you shouldn't have had to ask at all. And you wouldn't have if you didn't think me capable of such a criminal act."

Filling his jaws with air, frustrated, he blew it out in an uneven stream. "Okay, okay, so you don't want to talk to me. But could you please just take a few minutes to listen?"

"Not one second! Excuse me. I have a date."

"With whom?" Jealousy was written all over his face.

"The last time I checked, your name was not on my birth certificate." Knowing she wasn't going to change her mind, he watched in exasperation as she stormed off into a nearby club where Latin music could be heard rocking the ship.

A few minutes later Austin entered the same club as Ashleigh had, just as the beginning of "Rhythm Divine" filtered through the room. Everyone began moving to the sultry salsa beat, even those still seated. In a matter of seconds a large crowd had gathered on the dance floor. Almost immediately, a circle formed around something Austin couldn't see. Growing closer to where the shouting, cheering, and clapping took place, he finally managed to see what everyone was carrying on about.

His color began to rise. There, in the middle of the dance floor, sexy and beautiful Ashleigh was the main attraction.

Caressing her captivating figure, the knit camisole and skirt wrapped her up in a silhouette of sensuality. Moving in perfect harmony with the funky beat of "Rhythm Divine," Ashleigh's hips wildly undulated in a flirtatious manner. With her hair moving as freely as her hips, her swaying hands appeared to make sweet music of their own.

Ashleigh backed up into her partner, throwing her arms backward until they enclosed around his neck. Austin felt like strangling her with his bare hands. As the guy's hands closed possessively around Ashleigh's waist, Austin sucked in a deep breath. Knowing he had to get a grip on his raging anger, he momentarily turned away from the blood-boiling scene.

Unaware of Austin's presence, Ashleigh suddenly felt horrible for the way she was presenting herself. Shamelessly flirting with her dance partner was outrageous behavior for her. She'd never been this brazen in her life. This was not like her at all. Just as she was about to escape from the cheering crowd, Austin stepped in and swung her away from her partner.

Practically dragging her off the dance floor, he marched her straight out the club door. Despite her protests, he didn't stop moving until they reached the outside deck. The wind instantly raced through Ashleigh's hair, whipping it around her lovely face.

Helpless against her dangerous allure, Austin pushed her hair away from her face. "Do you have any idea of what you were doing in there? I'll tell you. You were acting like a brazen slut, Ashleigh. We both know that's not who you are . . ."

"Do we know that?" she interjected. "Maybe that's exactly what I am. Perhaps I've simply fooled you into thinking otherwise."

Instead of shaking some sense into her like he wanted to do, he shook his head. "Not a chance! But if you keep trying to be something you aren't, you might get into serious trouble. Your dance partner had more in mind than just a few twist and turns. By the look on his face, I'd say he was sure that he was going to have you as his nightcap!" Ashleigh couldn't take Austin's look of utter annoyance. Snorting under her breath, she looked away from him.

Putting two fingers under her chin, he turned her face back to him. "Looking disinterested in what I'm saying isn't going to shut me up. You made a spectacle of yourself on the dance floor. Can you tell me why? It's not like you to act that way. Are you trying to pay me back for hurting your feelings?"

Eyeing him thoughtfully, she pursed her lips. "This is just too rich! Let me get this straight. Stealing a watch is not as immoral as acting like a slut, as you put it? I'm not a thief or a slut. And you don't have the right to interfere in my life this way. No right at all. What I am or what I'm not is no concern of yours."

"Wrong, sister," Austin shot back. "Maybe I have no legal right, but what I feel for you gives me rights that go far beyond any damn legalities."

Wondering what he was really saying, she moaned inwardly. Did she dare ask what he meant? No, not at this point. She was better off not knowing anything else about the irresistible Wrangler quarterback. It could only hurt her more than she was already hurting. As much as she wanted him, she just wasn't the right woman for him or his opulent lifestyle.

"The look on your face tells me you're wondering about what I said. Wonder no more, Ashleigh. I'm so in love with you. That alone validates my rights where you're concerned."

Feeling the sweat forming between her breasts, Ashleigh gulped down the sweet rush of adrenaline his confession had caused. He'd actually said that he loved her, she cried inwardly. She was never more aware of how much she loved him than she was right now. Amazed by his confession, dazed by the way he looked at her, she had the urge to throw her arms around him, to confess her love for him, too. Sure they couldn't have a future together, she willed herself into remaining silent. The unspoken lies between them seemed insurmountable.

Austin saw the look of love for him there in her eyes, but he knew she wouldn't openly confess it. Not now, anyway. At the moment Ashleigh was operating on pride, standing on principle. But that would change in time. It had to change. He would stop at nothing to regain her trust, to recapture her respect, to win her love, and for them to share one heart.

Fighting an inner battle, a losing battle, Ashleigh ran away from Austin. Fleeing toward their favorite deck, she didn't stop running until she reached the uppermost part of the ship. Standing at the railing, breathless, her breasts heaving, she was grateful for the wind blowing her tears out to sea. The time she'd spent with him was great, but she'd have to leave that all behind.

"I love you, too, Austin. More than you'll ever know."

His hands came forward, meeting in the center of her abdomen. His lips pressing into her hair, caressing her bare shoulders made her shiver with pleasure. Leaving her shoulders, his lips pressed into each side of her neck. Unable to resist his amorous advances, Ashleigh tilted her head back against his chest, nearly breathless from the heat enveloping her. As his hands moved up from her waist to her breasts, she trembled, desiring his fiery touch to go on forever.

As if the DJ had somehow heard her desire, the song, "Could I Have This Kiss Forever," danced seductively on the sea breeze.

"Please forgive me, Ashleigh," he whispered. "I need to see your smile again. I need to feel the sunshine in your smile on my face. Turn around and let me kiss you like you've never been kissed before. Let me gently forge a place for myself inside your soul, Ash."

Slowly, as if she moved on a cloud, Ashleigh turned to face the man she loved. Magnetically, drawing his eyes to hers, she opened her mouth against his, without ever taking her gaze away. While their eyes and mouths locked in a riveting rendezvous, Ashleigh's fingers entwined in his hair.

As his hips undulated against hers, she found it next to impossible to keep her own still. The allure of his saluting manhood mixed with the heat from her trembling body nearly incinerated her steaming flesh.

As the love song played, they heard the music of their singing hearts. Their lips still meshed together, Ashleigh and Austin began to slow dance. His fingers threaded through her hair as his palms gently held the back of her head steady. Coming up for a brief snatch of air, Ashleigh pressed her lips into Austin's throat.

He ached to take her right there on the deck as her tongue teased his lips. Just the thought of them making love atop the deck, beneath the star-studded night, caused his desire to throb with sweet agony.

As though she'd read his thoughts, Ashleigh pulled him into the darkened corner where he'd first kissed her. There, in the darkness of midnight, she directed Austin's hands to all the intimate places aching for his touch. While this wasn't how she'd fantasized him taking her, nor was it the exact place, her romantic, adventurous nature saw it as the perfect place to physically unite with the man she'd often dreamed of being with forever.

If he had any doubt about what she actually wanted from him, her next move completely eradicated it. With her hands inside his zipper, stroking him with fingers of fire, Austin blocked out the niggling thoughts of not having protection. But only seconds later, he again thought of her safety. That wasn't something he should've even considered compromising. Still, that didn't mean he couldn't satisfy her. Half out of his mind from his own need, he made a silent oath to take care of her every want, her every burning desire.

Touching Ashleigh in ways that made her tender flesh crave for more and more of his agile caresses, Austin reveled in her soft moans and gurgling purrs of desperation. With his hands giving her untold pleasures, she joined in the melee of intimate frenzies. Her sweetly tortuous hands made him wish they were in one of the cabins, fully disrobed, melded together in a supine position.

Unable to take any more without exploding like a volcano, Austin took hold of Ashleigh's hands, holding them prisoner with his own. "Baby, I'm nearly out of control here. I want you like crazy, but I have nothing to protect you with. Will you come back to my cabin with me? Please don't say no, Ash." He moaned kisses against her lips.

Thoughts of what happened in his cabin the last time they were there caused the beginning downward spiral of the fever burning within her. "I swore I'd never enter your cabin again. That way, no one can falsely accuse me of stealing from you."

Not wanting the fire between them to smolder and die, he pulled her back into his arms. His lips silenced her while his fingers went back to work on her delicate flesh. A short time later, when he felt her burning need for sweet release, he kissed her deeply. Slowing the frantic movements of his hands to a snaillike, easy pace, he brought forth her spasmodic eruption.

Ashleigh's thighs trembled so hard against his, that he picked her up and carried her over to one of the loungers. After lowering her, he lay down alongside her. As he brought her full against him, she actually felt the arousing vibration of his manhood.

"Austin," she whispered, "show me how to satisfy you in the same way you've fulfilled me. Please don't say no."

Finding it impossible to resist her softly voiced plea, closing his eyes, Austin directed her hand down to where his need could no longer be denied. Glad for the handkerchief he always carried with him, he guided her hands through the most thrilling heated journey he'd ever taken. He was sure that Ashleigh had no idea of what she did to him, what she made him feel, what she truly meant to him. The slightest touch of her mouth against his made him want their kiss to last forever, the same way as in the song.

His eyes swept her blushing face. "Something tells me we belong together, something undeniably strong, Ashleigh. If you don't feel it, too, then I've got much work to do. You can fight me on this if you want, but I can guarantee you a resounding defeat. When Austin Carrington enters the field of play, he always plays to win. He may lose from time to time, but he never gives up, even when it looks hopeless. Up until the last second of the game ticks off the clock, I'm still in it to win it."

Emotionally injured, she pushed him back from her. "Is that what this is to you, a game?"

He shook his head. "Just a poor selection of words, Ash. If this is a game, then my very life is on the line here. In other words, I'm depending on you to save me from a fate that's worse than death. It's a no-brainer, Ashleigh. I'm lost without you. It's too late now, anyway. The transplant has already taken place."

She looked puzzled. "What are you talking about?"

"A heart transplant, Ashleigh." Gently, he pressed his index finger against her heart. "My heart is already beating inside your chest. If we don't stay together, my life is over."

She couldn't keep from smiling. "You are so charming, Austin. That is one hell of a forward pass that you've thrown me. I don't know whether to catch it, run with it, or fumble." For sure, she didn't want an interception to occur.

"Most all of the aforementioned works for me. If you decide to catch it, bring it in close to your body, hold it near and dear to your heart so a fumble won't occur. If you run with it, don't look back—just run for glory. When you step safely into the end zone, fall on your knees in celebration. Whatever you do, be careful not to give another the opportunity to intercept that which is only intended for you."

In awe of his mesmerizing speech, Ashleigh fought the urge to give way to tears. He was certainly on the mark regarding the interception. Though she wasn't sure how she was supposed to receive his pass, with so many unsolved issues between them, she definitely did not want another woman to intercept it.

"Austin, if I didn't know it was an impossible feat, I'd believe you can read my mind." Vulnerability seized her, aggressively so. "I'm frightened of what we're doing. So frightened . . ."

Silencing her with a finger to her lips, he pulled her close. "Don't be. I promise to take care of you. I even promise to keep that promise."

Ashleigh's heart nearly froze inside her chest. The same words again, the same exact words he'd spoken to her so long ago. "Let's not make promises that we might not remember to keep," she whispered. Her voice became hoarse with anguish, threadbare with desire.

He looked down into her eyes. "I made this same promise to someone a long time ago. Circumstances that were not within my control stopped me from keeping it. My death is the only thing that would cause me to break it this time. Fear is something I'll do all in my power to keep you from feeling." He kissed her lips. "Contrary to popular beliefs, promises were not made to be broken. I won't break my promise to you."

His comments stirred up something warm and loving inside of her. It seemed as if he had tried to keep his promise. Then why was she sent away in the first place? Logic was telling her that Austin was only sixteen at the time he made the promise to her. How could she hold him liable for things he'd said at such a young age? *Tell him who you are,* her heart encouraged. But Ashleigh somehow got the feeling that he knew exactly who she was, that she didn't need to tell him the truth about something he may already be aware of. Knowing she was dodging the real issues, she turned her thoughts off, silenced her fervent desire to get things out in the open.

"The midnight buffet is calling my name."

"Hungry, huh?" She nodded.

Sure he'd gotten his point across regarding the promise he'd once made, Austin decided not to probe any deeper into her psyche. Almost certain that she was Sariah, he made the decision to take things as they came. He'd continue to call her Ashleigh Ayers, for now.

He lifted her from the lounger and stood her on her feet.

"Let's go get cleaned up before we eat. I'll walk you to your cabin. To save on time, mind if I come in and wash up a bit?"

"I don't mind at all."

Ashleigh couldn't decide what she wanted to eat. There were so many choices, all of them delicious looking. Deciding on dessert wouldn't be as difficult. The thick slices of cheesecake made her mouth water. She loved to eat the creamy pastry with fresh strawberries on top. To keep from overdoing it on the calories, since she was definitely having her favorite dessert, she piled her plate with lean pieces of shaved turkey, a scoop of chicken salad, and a variety of fresh, uncooked vegetables. It was hard to pass up the freshly baked rolls but she managed to do so. A tall glass of raspberry tea, with lots of ice, was the last thing she placed on her tray.

Having a taste for Mexican food, Austin had piled his plate with fresh taco fixings: three lightly toasted taco shells, shredded lettuce and cheese, spicy hamburger meat, and minced tomatoes. After drizzling salsa over the Spanish rice, he topped it off with a dollop of sour cream and a spoon full of sliced black olives. A couple of cheese enchiladas were placed alongside the other spicy foods. Unable to resist the refried beans, though they didn't always agree with his stomach, he limited himself to two spoonfuls.

"Let me have your tray." He reached for it.

"I can carry it. It's not as heavy as yours."

"Sure you got a good grip on it?" Ashleigh nodded. "Good, now let's go grab that table right over there in the corner. It's too chilly for us to sit outside."

Several people strolled up and down the outside decks despite the chilly night air. Before settling down, Ashleigh looked around for Lanier, hoping she'd decided to at least show up for the late-night buffet. Though it wasn't good for them, they both loved to eat late at night. She couldn't remember how many pizzas they'd ordered well after midnight, though that occurred mostly on the weekends.

Houston and Dallas were no-shows as well, Ashleigh noted with disappointment. Thinking of how Austin had washed her face and hands with a wet towel replaced the disillusion in her eyes with a smile. He'd been so gentle with her, making her feel like a little kid again. But she couldn't remember anyone washing her so tenderly, as if her delicate skin might scar if they scrubbed too hard. Angelica came to mind, reminding Ashleigh that her foster mother had also been as tender with her as Austin was.

Austin didn't like the awkward silence that had somehow forced its way between them. Was Ashleigh regretting the intimate way in which she'd allowed him to touch her? It bothered him that he couldn't read her expression, but he had to admit that she didn't look the least bit unhappy. In fact, the blushing smile in her eyes was as sweet as the one she normally wore on her luscious lips.

Ashleigh had no regrets whatsoever. She simply couldn't stop thinking of the way he'd touched her; the bold way in which she'd touched him. Her inner secrets desired to have him fill her up with the same wondrous pleasures all over again. More than that, she couldn't stop imagining him deep inside of her, deeply immersed in the sea of their ecstasy. The desire to make love to Austin until she was too weak to move a single muscle caused a rush of heat to settle between her thighs.

Her thoughts were intruded upon when Lanier and the other two Carringtons appeared at the table. As Lanier and Dallas laughed and clowned around with one another, Ashleigh saw that her friend was holding Dallas's hand. That surprised her. She was even more astonished when Lanier kissed him on the mouth. Austin and Ashleigh exchanged curious glances.

"You guys didn't wait for us to eat," Dallas drawled.

"Didn't you think we were coming to the buffet?" Lanier asked.

"I looked for you, but when I didn't see you I thought

you'd decided to stay in the cabin and finish that hot book you were reading."

Houston grinned. "That was her plan until Dallas dragged her out of there kicking and screaming. I told him to leave her be. As you can see, he didn't take my advice." Houston laughed. "However, he did let her go back inside and change out of her sleepwear before he dragged her up here on deck."

Smiling brightly, Lanier pushed at Dallas's chest with both palms. "Dallas hasn't yet learned the meaning of no. The boy wants me! What can I say?"

"A big yes will do. You want me, too, but you're too stubborn to admit it. By the time I leave this floating party, girl, you're going to be begging me to take you home with me."

Lanier gave him the evil eye. "You wish!"

Trapping Lanier in his big, strong arms, he kissed her gently on the mouth. The smile she gave him told everyone how much she'd enjoyed his affection despite her attempt to hide her pleasure. Dallas must have seen it, too, because he kissed her again, only with more passion.

"Come on, girl. Let's get something to eat. You look as hungry as I do," Dallas flirted.

"If you don't stop acting like Kenneth Maxwell Jr., I'm going to find myself falling deeply in love with you."

"Who the hell is Kenneth Maxwell Jr.?" Dallas demanded with envy.

Lanier giggled. "The hero in the romance novel I'm reading. This man is so good to his woman—the same kind of man I've been looking for. Almost too good to be true."

Dallas took Lanier by the hand. "Tell me more about this hero of yours. If he's what you've been looking for, I want to know everything about him. But first let's go and fix a plate. I'm a starving man . . . and I'm dangerous as hell when hungry."

While laughing their heads off, Dallas, Lanier, and Houston went off toward the buffet line. Ashleigh's gaze followed after them in disbelief.

Austin smiled. "What was that all about?"

"Your guess is as good as mine. I think something special is beginning to happen between your brother and my friend. Something special indeed!"

"That's what it looks like to me, too. Dallas has been saying that Lanier is just trying to play hard to get. He feels confident that he'll win her heart before his departure. He and Houston have to get back to work."

"Is that what he has set out to do?"

"I think he just let his intentions be known, loud and clear. He definitely wants her."

"How do you know that for sure?"

"Texas darling, I know my brothers as well as I know myself. Perhaps even better."

"Yeah, but do you really know his heart?"

Austin circled his heart with his forefinger. "As well as I know the one that's now missing from my chest." Austin leaned across the table and kissed Ashleigh on the nose and forehead. "The heart that you've already stolen from me . . ."

Houston reappeared at the table. "Big brother, can I get a word with you in private?"

Austin looked a tad annoyed by the interruption, but he got to his feet. "Hold all your thoughts, Ash. I'll only be gone a minute." Ashleigh watched as Houston steered Austin a short distance away.

"You seem anxious all of a sudden, Houston. What's up?" Austin looked perplexed.

"You're not going to believe what I found out this evening. It's about your watch."

Austin listened with intense interest as Houston unfolded a scenario that he had a hard time swallowing. His heart ached as he looked over at the woman he loved. Ashleigh had known so much pain—and now there was even more to be added to the heavy weight she already carried. Still, he had to confront her with the truth.

Austin's emotions nearly shifted out of control when he heard the rest of the story, but Houston pulled him back and made him listen to the voice of reason. "You're too angry right now to get into a confrontation about this. Calm down first, big brother. Get a grip."

"You're right. I'm okay now. I have to be alone for a few minutes. Tell Ashleigh that I had to go to my cabin. I promise not to leave you holding the bag. I'll be back shortly."

EIGHT

The Valentine's Day dance was in full swing. The massive ballroom looked beautiful, decorated in bold reds, and blushing pinks, offset by subtle whites. Hundreds of red and pink heart-shaped helium balloons floated atop the ceiling. The crystal centerpieces held freshly cut red, pink, and white roses. It appeared that everyone aboard the *Forever Fantasy* was attending the special celebration.

Moving in her seat to the calypso music bellowing from the speakers, Ashleigh watched as Lanier and Dallas danced around the ballroom with a long line of other people. A smiling Houston was busy charming the group of social workers. None of the women appeared to mind him dividing his attention among the lot of them. Ashleigh could see that he had his hands full.

Houston seemed to be the only Carrington brother that hadn't latched on to one particular female. Austin had told her that Houston wasn't in any hurry to settle down. All of the brothers did a lot of traveling with their respective teams, but Houston didn't think it was fair for him to enter into a serious relationship since he was away from home so much. Austin didn't think it was much of a problem if each person was strongly committed and dedicated to the relationship.

Austin held his hand out to Ashleigh. "Let's go outside

for a minute. I'm in need of some fresh air." Ashleigh arose from her seat and placed her hand in his.

He loved the daringly sexy red dress she wore. The seductively plunging neckline and intriguing low-cut back made her look even more tempting, if that were possible. He liked the red dress sandals she wore, taking special note of the clear polish on her toenails. He liked that, too, disliking brightly colored nail polishes. Completing her sexy appearance, the slender golden lariat necklace sparkled against her golden bronzed chest.

He ran the back of his hand up and down her cheek. "What are you daydreaming about amidst all the noise around you?"

Wrinkling her nose, she smiled. "I was just thinking about swimming in the true-blue water. It's still very clear, even way out here. I bet it's really beautiful down there. I can see why scuba and snorkeling are such popular sports. Discovering the mysteries of the deep must be an awesome experience."

"We can take a lesson or two in both if you'd like. It shouldn't be that difficult to learn. I've never been that interested in it myself. But doing it with you is what would make it an awesome experience." Blushing was becoming a habit that Ashleigh wasn't too crazy about.

"As much as I'd like to try it, I think I'll just stick to swimming. I got to see quite a bit of the sea life when they lowered the glass bottom on the calypso boat tour."

Austin grinned. "You're not chicken, are you?"

"Chicken? I don't think so, mister. If I were a chicken, I wouldn't be hanging out with you. It takes a lot of guts to hang out with the superstar Carrington brothers!"

"Get off it, girl. The Carrington brothers are merely ordinary citizens. We just happen to take a few more risks at getting our necks broken than the average Joe." He kissed her earlobe.

"What about you getting a little risqué with me after the dance is over?"

Ashleigh blushed again. "You're as big a flirt as Dallas. Behave yourself."

"I might behave myself after we have another sensuous rendezvous like the last one. Interested?"

Baby, that's all I've been able to think about since you first touched me. But I have a little more in mind than any rendezvous. I want to experience the real thing with you.

Feeling the heat of sexual longing creeping into her skin, Ashleigh got up and walked across the deck. Leaning over the railing, she gulped in the sea air. Thinking about making love to Austin always left her breathless.

Following right behind, he pressed himself against her, his hands latching on to the railing on each side of her. Imprisoned between his granite body and the railing, taking a deep breath, Ashleigh tuned down her fear of tight spaces. Tucked between his arms she was secure. At least for the moment. The feel of his hard body against her was too thrilling to have it end.

"I guess I got you all hot and bothered, huh? Don't think you're by yourself in that, lady. I can't get out of my mind what happened between us a few nights ago. I don't want to ever lose the memory. But I want more than just physical contact with you. I want you long after the candlelight is snuffed out, far beyond the wilting of the roses. Still, I'll desire you even when the champagne loses its fizz." His lips rested on her right lobe as his tongue darted out to taste the fleshy part.

Enjoying the thrilling sensations, she closed her eyes. "Can you really offer all that, Austin? Or are you just talking to hear yourself talk? Not so long ago you couldn't promise anything beyond this cruise."

His chin came to rest on her shoulder. "That was then. This is now. I expect you to be somewhat wary of me . . . and what you probably think of as nothing more than a romantic holiday interlude. Believe me, girl, it's not like that. Not at all. You and I have been drawn together by something even more powerful than fate. Relax and let go.

Should you and I awaken tomorrow, we can continue to claim these wonderful blessings, together."

"What about your fiancée, Austin? What about the woman you have asked to become your wife?" As her question had come totally out of the blue, she was mortified by it. Even more terrified of his response, she feared that he'd walk away from her since she had dared to reveal his very own secret.

Noticing that she'd gone pale kept him from responding. He also needed time to figure out an adequate response. After taking Ashleigh by the hand, he led her to the deck that they'd claimed as their own. Silence prevailed as they made their way to the far corner. After situating himself comfortably on the lounge chair, he drew her down next to him.

He kept her hand tucked inside his. "How do you know about my fiancée?"

Disliking his seemingly admission of truth, her stomach grew queasy at his comment. "I read the story of your engagement in the *Houston Chronicle.*"

"So you've known that I was engaged from the beginning?" She nodded. He eyed her curiously. "Do you make it a habit of getting involved with guys that you know are already taken? Guys whom you know are about to be married?"

Though offended by his inquiry, she somehow felt that she deserved his impertinence. She saw that he was angry. "I guess that was a fair enough question. The answer is no."

"And?"

"And what?"

"You don't have anything else to say?"

"Should I? If I'm not mistaken, I think I asked the first question, which you still have yet to answer."

"I'm not engaged anymore. Is that what you wanted to hear, Ash?"

"I just want the truth."

"You've been given the honest-to-God truth. And I'm not going to say any more about it."

He got to his feet. The arousal of his lower physical endowment was outlined in painstaking detail, causing her to look away. She wanted to reach out and stroke him in the same way she'd done before. Not trusting herself, or her strong desires, she trapped both of her hands under her thighs.

It surprised her when he sat back down. Ashleigh choked back a sob. That he was no longer engaged brought her little solace since it seemed that he was terribly hurt by it. Had his fiancée been the one to break it off between them? Had Sabrina left him with a broken heart? God, why had she asked that question? Why had she spoiled things between them? The hurt he'd suffered was easy enough to see. How she deeply regretted bringing him even a moment's more of pain. Afraid to look at Austin for fear of seeing his pain, she got up and walked back toward the railing.

He stayed behind, debating whether or not he should tell her the whole story about his broken engagement. Sure that she'd think that he was just on the rebound caused him to abandon the idea altogether. They both had a hell of a lot more to tell, a lot more to get out in the open.

Coming up behind her, Austin wrapped her up in his arms. With her back against his chest, he gripped her waist with both hands. Feeling a sense of peace wash over her, she relaxed against him. Without the slightest hesitation, her arms went up behind her, entwining around his neck. The contact made her tremble.

"Just relax, sweetheart. I'll keep you safe and secure."

Safe and secure was just how she felt with him, the same as how she'd felt with him as a child. He'd been her hero back then. Still was. But was he ever going to be more than just a hero to her, more than just a fantasy? All she could do was hope like crazy.

His nose nudged at her right ear. "I know there's still a lot we have to learn about one another, Ash. For some unknown reason, we both seem reluctant to tell all. But I feel confident that we'll soon be able to talk about anything and everything that's worth discussing. I no longer have a fiancée, I have no wife, no ex-wife, no children, no felonies—and I'm not gay or bisexual. Believe me, there are no other skeletons in my past or present. There's nothing I need to hide from you." He tilted her head back and looked into her eyes. "Can you say the same?"

Immediately, her body grew tense. No, she couldn't say the same. But the only thing in her past that she couldn't share, or hadn't shared with him was about him. Other than the fact that she hadn't fully revealed her true identity, and the horrific life she'd been dealt, she had been clean with him. No big deal. Just a few colossal, unforgivable indiscretions.

Now facing Austin, Ashleigh pressed her lips to his, kissing him deeply. "I promised myself that I was going to tell you everything about me the next time we were alone, but I never did." She'd do just about anything to change the subject; anything to dodge the fatal bullet aimed straight at her heart.

Losing himself in her kiss, his hands reached down to touch her intimately. Bringing her in close to him, he squeezed her buttocks, running his hands up and down her bare back. Indulging herself in a few moments of delicious insanity, she touched his manhood, allowing the heels of her palms to caress the rigid flesh through his pants.

Tilting her head back, she directed Austin's mouth to the base of her throat, where he kissed and nipped until he was sure she never wanted him to cease his limited seduction of her. A thorough inveiglement was what he had in mind for later. Later, when and where there weren't any probing eyes to distract them from getting right to the heart of their desires.

The sexual tension between them began to flare out of control. With no way to bring their desires to fulfillment, not on a ship in front of a crowd of people, Austin had to pull himself away from her to cool things off.

He drew Ashleigh's head back against his chest. Unable to take his eyes off her, he stroked her hair with gentle hands. "I don't want you to think I'm on the rebound, Ash. I'm not. My fiancée and I just weren't right for each other. There's nothing more to our breakup than that. Compatibility is a must when entering into the sanctity of marriage. I ignored the incompatible issues for far too long. I was convinced of that when I overheard her tell her girlfriend that she'd leave me if I got injured and could no longer play the game. She loved the idea of being married to a quarterback. It sounded to me like any quarterback would do."

Ashleigh winced. "Ouch! That must've really hurt."

"My position as the quarterback was more important to her than our relationship. That incredibly selfish statement ended things for us. However, the price of divorce would've been much higher for all concerned. Had we gotten married, I'm in no doubt that it would've ended in divorce. What about you, Ashleigh? Is someone waiting at home for you?"

Ashleigh frowned. "You may not want to talk about these very personal things, but if we're going to move on into the future together, we need to first find out if we're both free to have a future. I am free, Ashleigh. Emotionally, mentally, physically, and legally."

Ashleigh lifted her head and looked up at him. She couldn't help smiling. Once again, he'd said what she'd longed to hear. He was free, really free, in every way. "There's no one waiting for me at home, Austin. No one at all. I'm also totally free. As for us having a future, we'll have to wait and see. You may not want a future with me after you learn all my secrets. . . ."

"Secrets? I believe I know all of your secrets, Sariah."

Agonized over his remarks, her heart stopped beating. Then it restarted with a bone-jiggling jolt. "You've known for a long time, haven't you? I'm sorry for not telling you from the start. I was so afraid to say anything since I failed to do it when we first met."

"None of that matters now. All that matters is that I've

found you. We're together again, the way it was meant to be. Once I tell you why you were removed from our home, I want it to be the end of our dwelling on the past. Okay?" Completely bewildered, she nodded. "Do you remember our next-door neighbor Barry Atkins?" She nodded again. "He's the one responsible for the agency taking you away from us."

"How's that?"

Austin's expression was painful. "It seems that he told his mother that I was thinking of molesting you. . . ." Ashleigh gasped in dismay. "She, in turn, called the agency and told them what her son had told her. My parents didn't find out until much later why you were taken away. They never found out who had made the false allegations. All I ever told Barry was that I couldn't wait until you got much older. You were completely off-limits to me until then—that the four-year difference in our ages wasn't going to matter a few years down the line. Barry purposely took those remarks totally out of context."

"How do you know it was Barry's mother that called the agency?"

"Sometimes, when people get drunk, they say all sorts of things. Apparently Barry guessed that you were Sariah not too long after he laid eyes on you. Your eyes were the dead giveaway. In a drunken stupor, he told one of our old teammates about what happened way back then. The story was then passed on to Houston. That's how it got back to me. During one of the team's late-evening visits to my cabin, he also took the watch and later put it in your laundry."

"But why would he do those things? Houston told you all of this?"

"Barry has been in competition with me since we were small kids. When he got hurt, and lost his position to me, Barry never got over the fact that the coach kept me on as the starting quarterback after he came off the injured reserve list."

"I clearly remember the day you came home and told

everyone you were kept on as the starting QB. But it still doesn't make any sense for him to do this after all these years."

"He obviously wanted to cause us trouble. That's what Houston pulled me aside for at the midnight buffet. I wanted to ring Barry's neck right then, but my brother rationalized things out for me. I needed time to cool off. That's why I went off to the cabin for a short time."

"When I said our relationship was getting complicated, I had no idea all of this would come out of it." She looked abashed. "Aren't you angry with me for not telling you the truth about myself from the start? I'm guilty of serious duplicities."

"We've both indulged in a little duplicity. Eventually, both my brothers and I were sure you were Sariah. But I wanted to see what your agenda was. I even thought you might have amnesia. Now that everything is out in the open, we can move forward. My parents are going to be ecstatic when they hear that I've found you. They were both brokenhearted when you were taken away."

"You're not the only one who was concerned about my agenda. Lanier thought I might have taken the watch to get revenge on you and your brothers for something or other. We had a confrontation about it. That's why she burst into tears that day. I never really told her all of what had happened back then, but I think she guessed that something had gone awry. Otherwise there would be no reason for me not to reveal my true identity."

"I figured something bad had happened between you two. Why did you change your name from Sariah Reed to Ashleigh Ayers?"

"Ashleigh Ayers is the legal name given to me at birth. Sariah is actually my middle name. The nuns at the orphanage called me Sariah because they liked the name so much."

"Thanks for clearing that up."

"You're welcome. Now what?"

He looked deeply into her eyes. "This Valentine's Day can be the first day of many celebrations that we'll have as a couple. You'll never again have to go through any sort of hell, not when heaven is right here beside you. Heaven is what you'll always find in my arms. Paradise doesn't have to end with this cruise."

"I don't want it to end, Austin. I never want *us* to end."

"Then it doesn't have to. All grown up now, you're no longer my forbidden fantasy. I'm deeply in love with you, Ashleigh Ayers. Will you please be my forever valentine?"

"I love you, too. I've always been in love with you, Austin Carrington. I'd love to be your forever valentine . . ."

Dear Readers:

I sincerely hope that you enjoyed reading FORBIDDEN FANTASY from beginning to end. I'm interested in hearing your comments and thoughts on the story of Ashleigh Ayers and her love interest, Austin Carrington. Without the reader there is no me as an author.

Please enclose a self-addressed, stamped envelope (SASE) with all your correspondence and mail to:

Linda Hudson-Smith
2026C North Riverside Avenue
Box 109
Rialto, CA 92377

You can also e-mail your comments to:
LHS4romance@yahoo.com

Web site: http://romantictales.com/linda/index.html

ABOUT THE AUTHOR

Born in Canonsburg, PA, and raised in the town of Washington, PA, Linda Hudson-Smith has traveled the world as an enthusiastic witness to other cultures and lifestyles. Her husband's military career gave her the opportunity to live in Japan, Germany, and many cities across the United States. Linda's extensive travel experience helps her craft stories set in a variety of beautiful and romantic locations. It was after illness forced her to leave her marketing and public relations administration career that she turned to writing.

Romance in Color chose Linda as Rising Star for the month of January 2000. ICE UNDER FIRE, her debut Arabesque novel, has received rave reviews. Voted as Best New Author, A.A.O.W.G. presented her with the 2000 Gold Pen Award. She has also won two Shades of Romance awards in the category of Multi-cultural New Romance Author of the Year and Multi-cultural New Fiction Author of the Year 2001. SOULFUL SERENADE, released in August 2000, was selected by *Romance in Color* readers as the Best Cover for August 2000. She was also nominated as the Best New Romance Author by the Romance Slam Jam 2001. Linda's novels' covers have been featured in such major publications as *Publisher's Weekly, USA Today,* and *Essence* magazine.

Linda Hudson-Smith is a member of Romance Writers of America and the Black Writer's Alliance. Though novel writing remains her first love, she is currently cultivating her screenwriting skills. She has also been contracted to pen several other novels for BET.

Dedicated to inspiring readers to overcome adversity against all odds, Linda has accepted the challenge of becoming National Spokesperson for the Lupus Foundation of America. In making Lupus awareness one of her top priorities, she travels around the country delivering inspirational messages of hope. She is also a supporter of the NAACP and the American Cancer Society. She enjoys poetry, entertaining, traveling, and attending sports events. The mother of two sons, Linda and her husband share residences in both California and Texas.

TEACHER'S PET

Janice Sims

Sincerest thanks to Deborah K. Calhoun, my Connecticut connection, for providing me with info only a native could be privy to. I hope I was able to depict her state in the manner in which it deserves.

Like the susurrant breeze on a warm
summer night, you wash over me.
Enticing, engaging my senses,
producing in my soul a jubilee.

Together, we are invincible. Much
passion, much power hour by hour.
Our love grows exponentially,
gaining strength as it continues to flower.

Ever shall the griots tell the tale of
how a black prince refused the glory.
And, instead, transformed a shy maiden
into the heroine of the story.

—The Book of Counted Joys

ONE

"Hey, man, slow down. There's somebody out there," Gabriel Merrick said to his friend Colin Armstrong. Peering through the windshield, Gabriel tried to more clearly see the person walking along Interstate 95. Colin slowed the pickup, his pride and joy. Emblazoned on the driver's side door was his company's logo, an illustration of a man's bulging biceps over the boldly printed words, ARMSTRONG JANITORIAL SERVICES.

"I don't recall seeing an abandoned car," Colin said. "Do you?" The only reason he and Gabriel were on the road at three in the morning was because they were returning from an impromptu bachelor party in Stamford. He was going to marry his high school sweetheart next Saturday. He was twenty-two. Frankly, he was surprised Nadine had stayed with him long enough for him to get his cleaning business established. She was very ambitious. She was not the sort of woman who could be put off for too long, and had insisted on a June wedding. What Nadine wanted, Nadine got. He was already henpecked, as Gabriel jokingly called him whenever his friend jumped to do Nadine's bidding.

"No," Gabriel answered. "Besides, that's a girl in a prom dress."

"How do you know it's a prom dress?" Colin asked as he pulled the truck onto the grassy slope of the shoulder and let the motor idle.

The tall, slender girl was standing about ten yards away, alternately looking at the truck then in the opposite direction, perhaps trying to figure out if she could outrun the occupants of the truck should they be up to no good.

"It's June. It's either a prom dress or a bridesmaid dress," Gabriel guessed. "Put two and two together. She ain't out here taking a leisurely stroll."

"Some horny kid abandoned her when she wouldn't give it up?" Colin surmised.

Gabriel hated it when men treated women like this! And on prom night—a night that was supposed to be one of the most memorable in a woman's life.

Colin's hand was on the door's handle. "I'll get out and see if I can convince her to let us take her home."

"She's gonna be jumpy," Gabriel warned. He stayed put. Seeing two men, both over six feet tall and muscular, could throw her into a panic.

Seventeen-year-old Bethany Porter's breath caught in her throat when she saw the tall, broad-shouldered man step down from the cab of the pickup. She wondered if she should ditch the high-heeled sandals now or try to sprint in them. She definitely wasn't going to be a statistic: PROM QUEEN FOUND STRANGLED ALONG I-95. Brad Johnston would pay dearly for making her get out and walk, just because she refused to have sex with him. She'd had over two hours to dream up ways of exacting revenge. And *nobody* was going to get in the way of it, not even this big guy walking toward her.

"You need a ride?" he shouted, sounding gruff in spite of the kindness behind the offer.

"Thank you, but no!" she called back defensively. She didn't know him from Adam.

"Don't worry. You'll be perfectly safe," he said, his tone placating. "I'm going to Bridgeport. You're heading in that direction, so I guess you are, too. Come on. Your parents must be out of their minds with worry."

"My parents told me never to accept rides from strangers," Bethany told him. Actually, she was tempted. She was hot, tired, and the shoes that had been impossible to resist in the department store's display window were killing her feet.

In the truck, Gabriel's ears perked up. That voice sounded familiar.

He quickly got out of the pickup and moved around to stand in the headlight's beams. "Bethany, is that you?"

Bethany's long, thick black hair was in disarray and several strands obscured her face. Gabriel couldn't discern her features from this distance.

Bethany turned in his direction. "Gabriel? Gabriel *Merrick?*"

Walking swiftly toward her, Gabriel laughed. "Girl, get over here!"

Bethany's tension-filled body instantly relaxed. She let out a strangled sob as she ran into Gabriel's open arms. Nervous tears sat in her eyes when she looked up at him. "Gabriel. Thank God. I was scared to death he was some kind of highway killer."

Laughing even harder, Gabriel said, "Him? He's big, but harmless."

Colin joined them. "Can we move this reunion to the truck? I'm tired and I need my beauty sleep. Unlike some college bums who don't have to work for a living."

"Does he ever!" Gabriel joked as he escorted Bethany to the pickup. Then he remembered his manners. "Bethany Porter, meet Colin Armstrong."

"Hello," Bethany said, looking up at Colin and sniffing. She felt like a wuss for crying.

"Miss Porter," Colin said coolly. She was probably one of those rich, spoiled brats Gabriel associated with up at Baylor College. Tall, too thin; a long, slender neck, large dark eyes, pert little nose, perfect lips. One day she'd be a real looker. But now she resembled a colt, all eyes and legs.

Colin mentally chided himself. She'd taken a gander at him and assumed he was there to harm her, and here he was judging her solely on *her* appearance. He knew better. Hadn't he lived all his life under the burden of the stigma some people attached to being foreign-born? His parents were Jamaicans. They came to the United States when he was six. The other kids in school teased him relentlessly because of his thick accent. Today his accent was barely noticeable. However he still knew how it felt to be singled out and ridiculed simply for being yourself.

Bethany squeezed in between Colin and Gabriel. "My parents are probably getting ready to call the police." She blew her nose into a tissue she'd gotten from her purse. "I was supposed to be home by midnight."

"I'm sure they'll understand once you tell them what happened," Gabriel said.

Colin put the truck in gear and pulled back onto the highway. "What *did* happen?" he asked, momentarily glancing at her out of the corner of his eye before returning his attention to his driving.

In the close confines of the truck, Bethany could smell stale beer on them. She assumed they'd been partying. Gabriel had a reputation for being on the wild side, which was why she'd had a crush on him since she was twelve. She'd aspired to be just like him. Her opinion of him had only improved over the years.

Growing up as the only child of a college president and a chemistry professor, she sometimes thought she'd die of ennui. Daydreams saved her. Gabriel Merrick had been the star of most of them until she started high school and discovered boys her own age who were not as nerdy as the boys in eighth grade had been.

"You can guess what happened. But I don't want my parents to know. If my father finds out, he'll never allow Brad to enter Baylor in the fall. He has a four-year football scholarship," Bethany said, surprising both men.

"He should have thought about that before leaving you stranded," Colin said dryly. "How long have you two been dating?"

"Nearly seven months," Bethany said wearily. She looked at Gabriel, then at Colin. "I haven't heard any promises from either of you. Are you going to keep quiet, or not?"

"You're a kid," Colin said bluntly. "If Johnston molested you in any way—"

"He didn't," Bethany said, cutting him off. "He just lifted me out of the car and left me on the side of the road."

"Why?" Colin asked, still not sure he should be making promises to a teen who obviously wasn't mature enough to make sound judgments. Otherwise, she wouldn't have been dating a guy like Brad Johnston.

"What happened between me and Brad stays between me and Brad. I don't want to ruin his future. I only want to see him suffer a little."

"And you're going to accomplish this by . . . ?" Colin asked, curious.

"I'm going to have one of my friends lure him to a secluded spot. Then we're going to hold him at gunpoint—don't worry it isn't a real gun—and make him strip naked. We're going to leave him out there. Once we're back in town, I'll call the police and tell them I saw a naked man exposing himself on I-95."

Colin and Gabriel laughed.

"Remind me not to get on your bad side," Colin said. "What if something goes wrong? A football player, and three dainty girls? He could overpower all of you."

"Nothing's going to go wrong. I have two very dependable girlfriends. We're all strong women. We can handle Brad. And I'll plan it down to the last detail before actually going through with it."

"Nah," Colin said, shaking his head. "There's only one way I'd agree to this."

"We'd have to be your backup," Gabriel answered for his friend.

Bethany immediately warmed to the suggestion. "Cool!"

Bethany's parents, Dr. Rafael Porter and Dr. Corrine Collier-Porter, were downstairs in the kitchen drinking decaffeinated coffee, the house silent around them, when they heard the key in the lock. Rafe, though twenty years older than his wife, was the first one in the foyer to greet their bedraggled daughter.

"Beth, dear God, where have you been!" He pulled Bethany into his arms, almost lifting her off the floor. His face was drawn.

"Brad's parents said Brad hadn't gotten home, either. We went to the school gym to see if the festivities had been extended, and the place was already shut down for the night."

Bethany wondered what time they'd phoned Brad's parents, but asking would only make them suspicious. What was important was that they didn't know Brad had left her on the side of I-95. She hated deceiving her parents, whom she loved more than anything in the world, but she dearly wanted revenge.

"Brad's car broke down, Daddy," she lied. "Two hours later, Gabriel and a friend of his happened by and, while Gabriel's friend stayed with Brad to repair the car, Gabriel brought me home. He's on the way back out there now to get Brad's car going again or, if that's not possible, to take Brad home."

Corrine pulled Bethany from her husband's arms to give her a warm embrace. After hugging Bethany, she looked her over from head to feet. "You look absolutely exhausted, sweetheart. Come on, it's to bed with you."

Rafe scratched his head. Something didn't sound kosher, but he followed Corrine and Bethany up the stairs of the Colonial-style mansion that had been the designated home of the president of Baylor College since the school was founded in 1937.

At Bethany's bedroom door, Corrine turned to her husband. "I'll tuck Beth in and come on to bed, honey."

Rafe briefly kissed Bethany's forehead. "Sleep well, baby. I'm sorry you had such a miserable night." The sorrowful look in his gaze gave Bethany pangs of guilt.

"Oh, Daddy, the prom was wonderful! It was the drive back that was miserable," Bethany assured him with a genuine smile. Her father loved her unconditionally, and she didn't want him to needlessly worry about her.

He returned her smile, his dark brown eyes sparkling behind his glasses. "That's my girl. Always resilient!"

"Let it roll off you like water off a duck's back," Bethany said, quoting her father's favorite saying when faced with irritating but not life-threatening setbacks.

Rafe bent to kiss her cheek, pleased she'd remembered the admonition. "You're safe and sound. That's all that counts."

"How dare you hand your father and me a load of *bull* like that!" Corrine said when she and Bethany were alone in Bethany's bedroom. She was busy undoing the zipper on the gown Bethany had bought with saved money she'd earned while working as a waitress at a local restaurant after school hours for the past six months. "The car broke down, indeed! Your shoes look like you've logged ten miles on them tonight."

"I'd guess only seven," Bethany responded with a weary sigh.

She turned to face her mother who was three inches shorter than she was and ten pounds lighter. Corrine wore her natural hair in a two-inch Afro that framed her pretty, smooth dark brown face nicely. Her light brown eyes were narrowed.

"You mean that boy left you alone in the dark?" she asked, incredulous. Her expression was determined and calculating. "Let me guess, he told you to either fight or foot it."

"Mama!" Bethany cried with a slow smile. "Does Daddy know you talk like that?"

"Don't smile at me as if you suddenly know my worst secret, child. Did he . . . ?"

"No, Mama, he didn't get my clothes off. We struggled until he gave up."

"And left you to foot it," Corrine said. "Something's got to be done about that boy." She began pacing and silently deliberating. After several minutes of this, she turned and looked at Bethany. "You were right not to tell your father. He would have stormed over to the Johnstons' house tonight, and demanded satisfaction. I don't want to frighten you, sweetheart, but I don't think his heart can take that kind of excitement. He *will* have to be told eventually though."

"Mama, this is what I want to do. . . ." Bethany began.

"Beth." Brad's hot breath was in Bethany's ear. "You won't regret this. I promise."

Bethany was so repulsed by his touch, she hoped her stomach wouldn't roil under all his sweet lies. Brad's left hand cupped her bottom, and his right was insistently trying to unbutton her blouse. "You know I'd never hurt you, baby. I only want what's best for us both. I want to take care of you. I'm gonna be a pro one day, and you're going to be my lady. We'll live in style. What do you need with a college degree? Support your man now. Take care of him, and he'll take care of you when the time comes."

Marvin Gaye's *Sexual Healing* was playing on the radio. Bethany kept glancing at the luminous dial of the clock on the dashboard. Her back was pushed against the passenger door. Brad was becoming more aggressive. He was going at her blouse with both hands now.

She clasped his hands and smiled coyly. "Let me. I don't want you to rip my blouse. That would be hard to explain."

Brad grinned. Bethany's eyes had grown accustomed to the dark, and she could see the lascivious gleam in his green-brown eyes. His eyes had been one reason why she'd become mesmerized by him in the first place. In a school full of brown-eyed boys, he had stood out. As he well knew. Brad was an expert at using his looks to snare girls.

In retrospect, she wondered why he'd ever pursued her. He didn't think her father, being the president of Baylor College, had anything to do with his receiving a football scholarship there, did he? It was his prowess on the field that had gotten him the scholarship, and it would be his performance in school and as an athlete that would keep him there. If he had anyone to thank for his getting into Baylor it was the football coach, Charlie Jones; and Coach Jones had been led by a compulsion to win, not by some altruistic notion of every black kid deserving a college education. *So, where,* Bethany wondered, *do I fit in the equation?*

"Tell me why you chose me, Brad," Bethany whispered, her voice rife with passion.

"Because you're pretty," Brad said, kissing her mouth lightly. "Because you're from a good family. You'd never embarrass me in public by behaving like a ghetto rat."

Hearing Brad's reasons for wanting her made Bethany realize one thing: In the many months they'd been dating, she'd learned nothing about him. *Ghetto rat.* Brad's family was not well-off. His father was a mechanic, and his mother worked in an office. Bethany's parents had come from humble beginnings, too. They had worked hard to educate themselves, putting education before social status and wealth.

They certainly had never taught her that she was better than anyone else. No worse, but no better. She was equal to the task, if she applied herself.

Brad's hands were adeptly unfastening the clasps on Bethany's bra when someone began pounding on the passenger side window with such force it rocked the car.

"It's the police!" Bethany cried frantically, pulling her blouse down and hastily slipping her feet back into her flats. "If my parents find out, I'll be grounded for life."

Bam!

Again, someone hit the passenger side window. "Break it up, and come out of there!" a man with a deep, authoritative voice ordered.

Looking at Brad with a horrified expression on her face, Bethany said, "I told you it was the cops. We'd better cooperate." Her hand was on the door's handle.

"No! What if it isn't the police?" Brad cautioned her.

As soon as Bethany released the lock, the door was jerked the rest of the way open by a huge guy dressed in black, a ski mask over his head. Bethany fell out of the car onto the ground. The man pulled her, none too gently, to her feet. "What have we got here? Pretty little thing, ain't she?"

To Bethany's utter shock, Brad had started the car and was attempting to put it in gear. However, another hulk in a ski mask acted quickly, clambered onto the front seat of the Pontiac GTO, and wrested the car keys from Brad's grasp. "Out!" he growled at the quaking eighteen-year-old.

Brad, seeing Bethany cowering before the man who had picked her up from the ground, tried to show a bit of bravura. "Take the car," he told them. "But don't touch her. If you do, I swear I'll hunt you down like the dogs you are."

The man standing closest to him pulled a length of rope from his jacket pocket. "Don't worry, kid, we ain't gonna hurt her. We're here for you."

Brad gulped, immediately losing the brave pose. "W-what does that mean?"

"Strip," the man told him.

"Take off my c-clothes?" Brad stammered. He was conditioned from weight lifting, running and football practice. What if he tried to take the guy nearest to him? They didn't appear to have any weapons. He could possibly get the upper hand in the situation.

That thought was squelched when the man holding on to Bethany's arm reached behind him and removed a gun that had been concealed in the waistband of his jeans.

"Don't be foolish," the man warned. "Do what my partner says and you might get out of this without any broken bones."

"All of my clothes?" Brad whined pitifully.

"Yeah, all of 'em!" the man with the gun told him.

"I don't want to see him naked!" Bethany spoke up. She wrenched her arm free of her captor's hold and went to kick Brad in the shin. "You were going to leave me out here with these maniacs!"

"I was going for help!" he denied, hopping on his good leg.

"You were running home to your mommy," Bethany accused him.

"Okay, enough of that," the tallest of the two men, the one with the gun, said, as he grabbed Bethany by the arm and pulled her away from Brad. Pointing the gun at Brad's feet, he said, "Hurry up, we ain't got all night. Keep the underwear on, per the lady's request."

Down to a pair of black briefs, Brad stood, rubbing his sore shin with his foot. Looking at Bethany, he said beseechingly, "Forgive me, Beth. I'm sorry I left you the other night. I lost my head."

The guy with the rope went and tied Bethany's hands behind her back. He tossed Brad's keys to the guy with the gun. "I'll meet you later," he said. "Don't waste too much time on the kid, we have a schedule to keep."

With that, he led Bethany to a darkened vehicle parked several yards behind Brad's GTO. The guy with the gun gestured for Brad to start walking. "You know the way home, dude. Get to steppin'."

When Brad started walking, the guy paused to pick up Brad's clothes and toss them onto the backseat of the GTO. This done, he got behind the wheel of the car, started it, and drove off.

A mile or so down the road, he met up with his partner who'd left earlier with the girl.

The two men pulled off their ski masks and laughed until tears formed in their eyes. The girl was likewise afflicted by a laughing virus.

"Did you see how scared he was?" she asked when she was in control of her speech. "I thought he was going to pee in his pants."

They went on in that vein until Gabriel spied Brad, still about a hundred yards away, via a pair of binoculars he'd scavenged from his dad's office.

Bethany went into action, quickly hugging Gabriel. "Thank you, Avenger #1!"

Then she tiptoed and hugged Colin, who beamed at her. "So, I'm Avenger #2?"

"You'll always be number one with me, Collie!"

"Collie? I hate that nickname." He scowled at her.

"Then Collie, it is," she responded, grinning.

Giving him a serious perusal, she said, "Tomorrow's the big day, huh?"

"Yeah. Me, Nadine, and the Preacher Man."

"Well, I wish you the best, Collie. See you around?"

"Nah, you won't see *him* around," Gabriel spoke up, coming to stand next to Colin. "This dude let Nadine convince him he had to be in New York City in order to be a success. They're moving there right after the wedding."

"That's great!" Bethany said enthusiastically.

"Spoken like a teen who's raring to blow her hometown," Gabriel grumbled, walking toward Colin's pickup. "I'll see you on campus, Beth. I can't believe your mom went along with this. You Porter women are something else."

"He thinks that because I'm getting married we won't be friends anymore," Colin said.

"I'll look out for him for you," Bethany promised.

Colin placed Brad's car keys in the palm of her hand. "You do that, string bean. And try to stay out of trouble."

He opened the car door for her and handed her in. "You should have let him walk all the way home. Remember, lock the doors, and tell him it was a fraternity prank."

"I've got it," Bethany assured him. "Have a happy life, Collie. The next time I see you, you'll be rich, fat, and have five children!"

"I don't know about being fat and having five children, but I *am* going to be rich!" Colin called back before climbing into the truck and starting the engine.

Bethany kneeled on the car seat with her head out of the window, waving good-bye. She believed him. After all, he was a man of his word.

TWO

"If you go to Baylor, I'll get you that horse you've been wanting," Colin bribed his seventeen year-old daughter, Sabrina. He ate a mouthful of the oat cereal their housekeeper, Mrs. Bryant, was intent on feeding him to keep his cholesterol down, and peered at his obstinate offspring. Lord, why did she have to inherit her mother's stubbornness? She'd gotten his height, and Nadine's cunning.

Sabrina chewed on her cantaloupe, considering his offer. "Where would I keep it? I don't want to board it someplace. You never know how he'll be treated when I'm not there. Plus, I'd want him to be close enough so I could exercise him regularly."

Colin knew his daughter well enough to know when she was edging up on something. She was simply taking her time getting there. He glanced down at his watch. He had forty-three minutes before he had to be in midtown Manhattan for a meeting with his lawyer and Justin Trainor of Citywide Janitorial Services. Trainor was hoping to buy him out, and Colin was thinking of selling. His life was changing. With Nadine in Miami with her doctor husband, living la vida loca, and Sabrina soon to be heading off to college, he felt in need of a change, too. He was forty-two. Could he be going through a midlife crisis? All he knew was, he felt something in the air, some stirring in his soul that he had to answer. If only he knew what that "something" was.

"What have I always taught you, Brina? If you have a point to make, make it. Don't waste time beating around the bush."

Sabrina's mouth turned up at the corners in a smile. She looked into dark chocolate eyes that were the same hue as her own. "Okay, here it is: If you sell the business, what are you going to do with yourself? Sit around the house all day watching *The Jerry Springer Show?*" She pursed her lips. "If you sell the business, I think you ought to take the extra time you'll have and get that college degree you've been threatening to get all these years. That's the one thing you regret, you said."

"And?" Colin coaxed her, knowing that was not everything she had on her mind.

"Here's the deal." Sabrina spelled it out for him. "I'll go to Baylor if *you* go to Baylor. You could major in business administration, or finance or something! I'm going to be pre-Law. We could buy a house on the outskirts of Bridgeport, a house with a barn, and I could have my horse, live at home, saving money on dormitory fees, and we could drive to Baylor together every morning. It would be perfect!"

"You've got it all figured out," Colin said with a shake of his curly-maned head. He was not surprised. Ever since Nadine left him—well, she left both of them actually, because she'd given him custody of Sabrina without so much as a protest—Sabrina had taken it upon herself to take care of him the best she could. Now, he supposed, with her going away to school soon, she was worried he was going to be a sad, lonely man without her there to pester him.

"Honey, when I said I regretted not getting my college degree, I said it nostalgically, you know, like I do when I talk about my football days in high school."

Sabrina seemed to have to ruminate on his comment a while. She sat there twisting the end of a long auburn braid, looking at him. "Do I detect fear in your voice, Daddy?"

Colin frowned and leaned back in his chair. This kid was spooky. How could she know he doubted his ability to apply himself at school? In high school he'd relied on his physical strength more often than not. He made C's in most of his courses. On the football field, he'd been a star. He had no interest in algebra or American history. Would he ever *use* that knowledge? However, auto repair and woodshop he could profit from. His first after-school job was at a garage. Another time he worked as a furniture maker's apprentice. These skills put money in his pocket. He was a practical man. That's how he'd made Armstrong Janitorial Services a success—with hard work, common sense, and dependability. His word was his bond. Nobody could ever say Colin Armstrong didn't complete a job satisfactorily, and be telling the truth.

But going to *college?* That wasn't for him. Hadn't he already proven he could make it without a sheepskin? He had to his way of thinking.

"I'm too old to go to college," he said.

Sabrina laughed. "You are *old.* I'll give you that. But answer me this: Which would you rather be four years from now, forty-six years old without a college degree, or forty-six years old *with* one and possibly a whole new outlook on life? You're middle-aged, Daddy. What are you going to do with the second half of your life? Because, I'm telling you now, if you run through all of your money before you're eighty, don't come looking to me for a handout 'cuz I'll just put you in an old folks' home and go party."

"You're a heartless child," Colin said, smiling at her with his love for her evident in his gaze. He'd finished his cereal. Rising, he bent and kissed Sabrina on the top of her head. "I'll give it some thought. Now, I've got to go see a man about a horse."

Sabrina rose and threw her arms around him. "I'll cook dinner tonight." She then straightened his tie. "Go get 'em, Daddy!"

* * *

A few days later in Bridgeport, Connecticut, another daughter was saying good-bye to her father in an entirely different manner.

"These were one of Rafe's favorites," Corrine said as she lovingly filled the puff pastry with chunky apricot filling. She quickly folded the crust over and pinched it closed. Her hands moved knowledgeably, as if by a will of their own, while her mind fast-forwarded through the life she'd shared with her husband whom they'd lost only three days earlier.

Bethany felt tears prick at the backs of her eyes. Alone with her mother in the big kitchen of the family home, she knew she was at liberty to shed all the tears she wished, but she felt it imperative to be strong for her mother.

She'd driven over here an hour ago, after returning from the funeral parlor where she'd made arrangements for her father's memorial service, to find her mother in the kitchen preparing her father's favorite dishes. She'd washed her hands, rolled up her sleeves, donned an apron, and joined in. Both women were alchemists in the kitchen.

The service would be held in the college chapel. Every past president of Baylor College had been honored in this way. Hundreds would turn out. Her father had been retired for more than ten years, but he was well loved and fondly remembered by students and college personnel alike. To Baylor he had been a mainstay, the ballast with which the school held itself steady for many years. To Bethany, though, he had been much, much more.

"Next to your apple tarts, these are my favorites, too," Bethany said quietly.

Corrine's hair was solid white. She still wore it in a short afro, and her weight hadn't fluctuated much over the years. A healthy, young-looking sixty-eight, she was head of the science department at Baylor and had no plans to retire soon.

She smiled at her daughter. "You two had very similar tastes. Always did. They say the daughter takes after the father, you know, and the son takes after the mother. That was true in your case."

Corrine picked up the two filled baking sheets and transferred the apricot turnovers to the preheated oven. Closing the oven door and straightening up, she regarded Bethany. "May. I never thought Rafe would succumb in May. It was his favorite month. We met in May. We got married in May. You were born in May." She paused. "Oh, Beth, I hope you won't associate this month with your father's death from now on. Rafe wouldn't like that at all. To cause you pain."

"Then why did he have to die!" Bethany cried, and the tears finally began to flow.

Corrine, though several inches shorter than her daughter, held her firmly in her arms. "He was eighty-seven years old, baby, and he was tired. So tired."

Bethany's body shook with her sobs. She knew her father had been fifty when she was born, but she'd never thought of him as old. He'd always told her she was his reward from God. Like Abraham was rewarded with a child through Sarah in his dotage.

With a father who thought of her as a special gift, why would she ever disappoint him? But she had. After graduating from Baylor with a bachelor's degree in English, she chose to move away from home to pursue her master's degree and doctorate elsewhere. Grants from Tulane University in New Orleans were a big help. Still, she had to work in order to pay for meals, clothes, any extras she required while in school. Not wanting to ask her parents for anything due to the fact that she'd declared her independence, she lived a frugal existence. Whenever either of them phoned to ask how she was doing she'd always answer, "Fine!" Even when she could have been hungry, or about to be evicted.

Then there was Adam. Professor Adam Malveaux.

At age twenty-three, only a year from earning her doctorate in record time, she lost herself in him. Literally. She had never loved a man as completely, as unselfishly as she loved Adam. She met him right in the middle of writing her dissertation. At every turn her professors were telling her that her chosen subject, African-American literature, was not scholarly enough. She blanched at their advice. Stubborn and willful, she continued her research, writing with conviction and fervor.

After dating Adam for two months she allowed him to read what she'd written so far. He was bowled over, and told her so. She showed her appreciation by bestowing on him an almost worshipful adoration. Making love was a ritual of boundless pleasure for them. Bethany lived in a world that consisted of her dissertation and Adam. They became her two great passions.

She worked feverishly when she wasn't with Adam. And when he came by her apartment, she concentrated on him as intensely. When she completed her dissertation and the detractors who'd said it wasn't scholarly enough, preferring a topic more Eurocentric, now touted it as an example of great American exposition, Bethany was ecstatic. She'd earned her doctorate. Later, it would be published as a book and used as a reference in American Literature courses across the country.

The elation she felt upon completion of the work would be short-lived, however. Because Adam chose that time to confess he was estranged from his wife, not divorced, as he'd formerly told Bethany.

Bethany blamed herself. How could she not recognize the fact that for the past seven months she'd been making love to a married man? She'd previously prided herself on her ability to spot a married man at a hundred paces. Her mother explained that she'd been blindsided by Adam. Focused only on the work, and letting Adam in her life for snippets of pleasure, she had not been cognizant of anything else.

Adam went back to his wife and, armed with a doctorate degree in African-American literature, Bethany returned to Baylor College and the bosom of her family.

That was thirteen years ago. Today, at thirty-seven, she was a tenured professor known for her scholarship and a propensity to inspire her students to new heights of academic achievement.

Bethany raised her head from her mother's shoulder, took a step back, and grasped both her hands. "How do you stay so strong? You were together for more than forty years."

"And they were the best years of my life," Corrine told her. "But Rafe made me promise I wouldn't mourn him with tears, but with laughter." She smiled warmly. "He was ready to go home, Bethany. I know that's hard for you to accept. A child never wants to lose a parent." She gently squeezed Bethany's hands. "I'm going to tell you something he told me about you the day before he passed. He said the years you spent away from us were the hardest he'd ever had. But they were for a purpose. They made you stronger. Therefore, how could he fault you for going away? All he ever wanted was your happiness."

"Did you ever tell him about Adam?"

"Of course. We talked about everything."

Fresh tears appeared in Bethany's eyes. "What did he think of that? Of me?"

"Because Adam was a married man?" Corrine smiled slowly. "Darling, he hurt for you because you were hurt by Adam. And he wanted to run Adam through with his Italian rapier." Her father collected antique swords. His collection was in the study. He'd left them to her in his will because he'd given her fencing lessons as a child, and she had excelled at the sport.

"I thought of that a time or two myself," Bethany admitted, wiping her cheeks with the back of her hand.

The doorbell rang and startled them both. They'd become used to the silence when, after a deluge of visitors the first couple of days, it began to trickle off.

Bethany went and grabbed a paper towel to wipe her face. "I'll get it."

It was half past three on a Wednesday afternoon. The memorial service was scheduled for eleven A.M. tomorrow. Bethany passed a profusion of flowers as she hurried down the hall to the front door. They'd gotten so many flowers, they had begun lining the bouquets along the hallway walls. Every surface in the living room was covered with flowers. Corrine had arranged for most of the arrangements to be taken to a local nursing home and given to the patients.

Bethany opened the door and found Gabriel Merrick standing there with his pregnant wife, Kiana, and their five-year-old niece, Courtney.

Bethany was delighted to see them and ushered them inside. Gabriel hugged her, then moved aside so Kiana could embrace her, as well. "How are you, sweetie?" Kiana asked. Bethany loved Kiana as much as she loved Gabriel. She never thought it would be possible to love a woman who'd married a man whom she'd had a crush on for most of her formative years, but Kiana had proved her wrong.

There was very little guile in Kiana. The face she showed the world was who she was. Which could be a frightening thing if you ever harmed someone she cared for because Kiana protected those she loved with the ferocity of a mother lion.

They parted and Bethany said, "I'm holding up." She looked at them all in turn. "Come on back to the kitchen. We just put a batch of apricot turnovers in the oven."

"Girl, you've got my number," Kiana said.

Corrine met them at the entrance. She immediately went to Courtney and held out her arms. Courtney went into them, and they hugged fiercely. Corrine adored children. It was sometimes painful for Bethany to watch her mother with small children because it reminded her how much Corrine wanted a grandchild, and she'd been unable to give her one. Bethany sighed now, looking at them together. She wanted children. She just hadn't been lucky in that respect.

What worried her was the fact that she'd recently begun telling herself that maybe she was not meant to have children, and should be satisfied with her fate instead of harping on it. However, she still had a three-year window of opportunity if she considered forty to be the cutoff age to safely conceive and deliver a child.

"You all will be heading to Florida soon, won't you?" Corrine asked.

"In about a week," Gabriel replied. He hugged Corrine. "You know I loved and respected Rafe, Corrine."

Corrine smiled her pleasure. "The feelings were mutual," she told him. "Especially after graduate school when you decided to settle down a bit and stopped giving us all prematurely gray hair."

"Was I so bad?" Gabriel asked, his dark brows drawing together in feigned hurt.

"Yes!" Corrine answered, not giving him a break. She turned to Kiana. "I'll never forget the time he painted the statue of our benefactor, Aaron Baylor, a proud white Yankee, black!"

Bethany went to the table and began pulling out chairs for their guests. "We should get comfortable. This could take a while, as our Gabriel has a particularly l . . . o . . . n . . . g history of mischievous behavior to relate, and Mama has a memory like an elephant."

The next day, after the memorial service, a hundred or so personal friends and family gathered at the Porter home. By that time, the bulk of the flowers had been transferred to a nursing home and Gabriel plus several of the Baylor College football team members had moved the living room furniture to the upstairs bedrooms. Therefore there was enough standing room, though nowhere to sit. Tables were laden with the food Corrine and Bethany had cooked, along with catered fare and the requisite cakes, pies, hams, fried chicken, potato salad, and gelatin molds that caring friends brought over. Visitors helped themselves to the food, and Bethany had enlisted Daniel and Deborah Anderson's sixteen-year-old daughter, Evangelista, called Angel, to serve the coffee and the soft drinks to those who came up to her table to request them.

Bethany drifted around the room thanking everyone for coming. She was amazed by the sentiments some of the people expressed. One woman, not a close friend but someone who worked at Baylor in an administrative position, pulled Bethany aside to say, "I thought he'd never die. He just kept on and on."

Bethany knew, logically, that the woman was referring to her father's advanced age, but the way she'd put it it sounded like she was relieved he was finally dead.

Yet, the faux pas obviously hadn't registered in the woman's brain because she stood there with her mouth full of potato salad, expecting a response from Bethany. "Yes, my father was a strong man" was all Bethany could come up with. "Please, excuse me."

Someone clasped her upper arm and she was grateful for the interruption. Turning, she looked up into the face of a stranger. He was very tall, about six inches taller than her five feet seven inches. Tall, and attractive in a rugged, utterly masculine way.

For a moment, they simply looked into each other's faces, smiling. He had a nice smile. Full lips that peeled back from lovely white teeth. High cheekbones in a dark brown, clean-shaven face. Rich, dark eyes.

She knew all the instructors at Baylor and he wasn't one of them. Though he could have been. The dark summer suit hung gracefully on his well-proportioned body.

"Hello, string bean," he said, his voice deep and resonant.

Bethany cocked her head to the side, her mouth open. She clamped it shut. Then she laughed suddenly and threw her arms around the big stranger's neck.

He chuckled and bent to receive her hug. After a fair amount of squeezing, and a few groans of pleasure thrown in for good measure, Bethany reluctantly let go of him.

They parted and regarded one another again.

"I'm sorry for your loss," Colin said.

"Thank you, Collie," Bethany said with a wan smile. "And thank you for coming. How long has it been?"

"Twenty years," Colin answered.

Bethany took his arm and began leading him toward the back of the house. She was determined to find a secluded spot so they could talk in private. Maybe the kitchen was empty. However, as she was leading him away, it occurred to her that he might not have come alone. Maybe—what was her name?—*Nadine* had come with him.

She paused and gazed up at him. "I'm sorry. Here I am leading you off somewhere private and you may not be alone."

"I'm not. I came with someone."

Bethany removed her hands from his arm. "Oh."

Colin grinned down at her. "My daughter, Sabrina. She's seventeen and thinking of coming to Baylor in the fall."

This time, tears appeared in Bethany's eyes. Why had that piece of information come as such a monumental relief to her?

Colin went into his jacket pocket, produced a linen handkerchief, and offered it to her. Bethany took it and wiped her eyes. "I'm sorry. I'm a little emotional."

"Of course you are," Colin gently said.

Bethany glanced at the handkerchief. A man who carried real handkerchiefs in this day and age! She peered up at him and reached for his hand again. "Okay. I guess your daughter won't mind if I steal you for a few minutes in order to catch up on the last twenty years."

Across the room, Lourdes LeDoux, a history instructor at Baylor was watching Bethany lead Colin through the swinging doors of the kitchen. "Look at her. Milking the moment for every bit of sympathy she can get," she commented to her cohort, Gayle Henderson. Gayle was not only Lourdes's partner in spreading ill will, she was also her administrative assistant which, undoubtedly, was the source of her loyalty because when Lourdes's back was turned, Gayle was known to make disgusted faces at most of her employer's observations, as she did now when Lourdes's attention was directed at Gabriel and Kiana Merrick who had just entered the room.

"Dear *God!* She looks fatter every time I see her. What does he *see* in her?" Lourdes said derisively. Her eyes were riveted on the attractive couple.

"I think she's pregnant," Gayle said conspiratorially.

"What?" Lourdes said much too loudly.

Other guests standing nearby turned to give her quizzical looks.

"Are you certain that isn't plain old fat?" Lourdes asked hopefully, her voice at a more acceptable level. She took a large sip of her cold drink as if the news had suddenly caused her mouth to go dry. "That little county bumpkin is pregnant already? They've been married only a few months!"

"Southern girls work fast," Gayle said snidely. She hailed from Georgia herself, but Lourdes would never deign to find out anything personal about her lowly assistant. Gayle enjoyed inciting Lourdes whenever they were in a social setting and the Merricks put in an appearance. Gayle knew Lourdes regretted botching up her engagement to Gabriel Merrick. Off she went to France ostensibly on vacation with a girlfriend, (whom *that* was, Gayle didn't know because she'd never seen Lourdes with a female friend and suspected she didn't have any) met a French artist, Guy LeDoux, married him, and came back to Baylor flaunting him as if he were a trophy. She still wore his name, but had divorced him more than a year ago.

Gayle believed Lourdes's bitterness was caused by embarrassment. Baylor was a tight community of scholars and she'd made a fool of herself over a French con artist. Not that anyone would remind her of her folly. They were too polite for that. Lourdes didn't allow exchanges to get that far, though. At the first sign of censure, she cut them off with her sharp, poisonous tongue. They'd learned to give her a wide berth.

Gayle sighed as she observed Lourdes frowning at the Merricks. *Which is why she makes a beeline for me whenever we both attend social functions,* she thought. *I can't tell her where to get off, without losing my job.*

Bethany and Colin finally found some peace and quiet on the back porch. The day was warm and bright. Bethany gestured to a round patio table with a glass top and an umbrella to keep the sun off. There were three such tables on the large porch.

"Physically, you haven't changed much at all," Bethany said as they sat down. "It's truly amazing." Why was it that some men seemed to get better with age?

"I didn't get fat," Colin said. His gaze swept over her face. "And I don't have five children." He smiled at her, wondering if she'd remember to what he was referring.

"You remembered what I said back then?" She sighed regretfully. "I was such a smart aleck. I didn't mean that in a derogatory way, Collie."

"I know you didn't. You were just young and exuberant," he told her. "You haven't changed much, physically, either."

In her short navy blue sleeveless sheath, she looked cool and elegant. She wore her wavy hair long, and pulled back in a chignon at the base of her slender neck. *She's grown into her eyes,* he observed. Still large, they were absorbingly deep brown, thickly fringed, and sad. Or maybe that aspect was due to the occasion. The bow mouth she'd had as a seventeen-year-old had matured, too. It was now full-lipped and sensual. His eyes lingered there a moment longer than was necessary.

Bethany smiled at his expression. How odd to be sitting here with Avenger #2 after all these years. "New York isn't that far away. Why haven't we met before now?" She enjoyed the play of emotions that crept across his strong face as he formed a reply.

"Gabriel would give me occasional updates on you," Colin said. He met her eyes. "I know, for example, you were in Louisiana for a while."

"That's right, at Tulane. I got my master's degree and my doctorate there."

"Wow," Colin murmured, putting his elbow on the table-top, his chin in his palm, and staring at her. "Dr. String Bean?"

She leaned toward him, an intimate smile on her lips. "Don't look at me like that."

"Like what?" Thick brows arched ever so slightly in an askance pose.

"Like I've suddenly grown a third eye in the middle of my forehead. Deep down, I'm still that scared, insecure girl you met late one night twenty years ago. I don't admit that to just anybody. But I know I can trust you."

Again his brows went upward. "We haven't seen one another in twenty years. You didn't know me then. I just happened to drive by with a friend of yours. How can you be sure you can trust me?"

"You're here now. That's why. What sort of man comes to express sympathy over the passing of a strange woman's father? Admit it, Collie. I've meant something to you over the years. Just as I've always thought of *you* fondly."

There was a speculative expression in his gaze. "Have you, really?"

"Yes, really," she answered, and placed her hand atop his.

Clasping her hand, he said, "It's true. I have wondered what kind of trouble you were getting into that I wasn't there to get you out of."

Bethany laughed softly. "For the most part, I've kept my nose clean. There have been some hairy moments, but none I haven't been able to get myself out of."

Colin drew his bottom lip between his teeth as if considering his next words, "I noticed you're not wearing a ring. There is no *Mr.,* Dr. String Bean?"

Bethany's cheeks grew warm. Warmer than they already were in the lovely summer day. Marriage, like children, had somehow eluded her. After Adam. God! Why did she always think of her love life as consisting of vignettes "after Adam?" Little episodes that lasted only moments in time. She often wondered if she was afraid to trust another man after being bamboozled by Adam, whom she'd trusted implicitly. Until he dropped the bomb, that is.

"I guess I've been unlucky in love," she said with a sad smile. It was difficult to hide the pain in her eyes when she looked directly into his. "I mean, I've come close to the altar a couple of times. But one, or both, of us always got cold feet before the ceremony. And you? You're not wearing a wedding band, either."

Colin's eyes narrowed. "Do you really want to hear my sob story today? Why don't we save it for next time?"

Bethany sat up straighter on her chair. "Oh? There's going to be a next time?"

"Most definitely," he answered. "I'm in the market for a house in the area. Sabrina wants a place with a barn so she can buy a horse, finally. We've been bandying about the subject ever since she was nine. Now she's going to make me stick to my promise. You see, I offered her a horse if she'd come to school here in the fall."

Bethany was observing the way his eyes lit up when he talked about his daughter. She could tell he truly adored her. Seeing that love mirrored in his eyes made her even sadder over her father's passing. They wouldn't enjoy the animated exchanges they'd had in the past. They would never share another embrace. Her father used to kiss her low on the forehead, right between her brows. The scent of his aftershave would waft over her, and a feeling of security would envelop her.

Colin hadn't missed the pensive mood Bethany had slipped into. "Whatever happened to the kid who left you stranded that night?" he asked, hoping to snap her out of it.

Bethany laughed. "You mean you haven't heard of Brad 'the Madman' Johnston? He's one of the top draws in professional wrestling!"

Colin guffawed. "You're kidding. *That's* your Brad? He's all over the place. He just starred in some teen action-adventure movie. I can't think of the name of it, but I'm sure Sabrina knows what it's called."

He regarded Bethany with a feigned solemnity. "Imagine. You could have been Mrs. Brad 'the Madman' Johnston!"

Bethany's face crumpled in laughter. "Oh, God, no! That would have been a total disaster. I would have been ex-wife number one by now. Last count, Brad had gone through four wives."

"So this is where you got to!" a feminine voice said from the direction of the kitchen entrance. Bethany turned in her chair to smile up at a tall, slender young woman with auburn braids down her back. She wore a very hip dark blue double-breasted pantsuit, and high-heeled chunky black boots that were all the rage with teens nowadays.

Colin rose. "Sabrina, come here. I'd like you to meet an old friend of mine."

Sabrina smiled warmly at Bethany, who had also risen.

The two women clasped hands. Sabrina was five-ten. It was apparent she'd gotten her father's height. Her flawless mocha-colored skin was a bit lighter than her dad's but she had his dark brown eyes.

"Sabrina, this is Dr. Bethany Porter. She teaches literature at Baylor College."

Sabrina pumped Bethany's hand. "Really? I was just having a conversation with a guy who took your class last semester and he says you're *very* good!"

Bethany laughed shortly. "Hello, Sabrina. It's wonderful to meet you. It's also nice you met one of the students I actually passed."

Sabrina laughed, too. They allowed their hands to fall to their sides. Glancing at her father, Sabrina said, "Uncle Gabriel *said* you'd probably be somewhere chatting with Dr. Porter." She regarded Bethany again. "Dr. Porter, will you be teaching any freshman courses in the fall?"

"Introduction to African-American Literature," Bethany told her. "We start with Zora Neale Hurston and work our way up to Toni Morrison. Have you ever read anything by either of them?"

Sabrina's interest was now fully engaged. "I read *Mules and Men* and *Their Eyes Were Watching God* by Ms. Hurston, and I read *Beloved* and *The Bluest Eye* by Ms. Morrison. I enjoyed all of them. But I really didn't get the symbolism in *The Bluest Eye*. It was way over my head."

"It was way over mine, too, the first time I read it," Bethany readily admitted. "Ms. Morrison is the type of writer you have to sneak up on. You can read her work over and over again and find something new and surprising in it each time."

"This is great!" Sabrina said animatedly. "I know I'm going to enjoy your class." She turned to her father. "Daddy, did you tell Dr. Porter that you'll be attending Baylor in the fall, too?"

Bethany's heartbeat accelerated at the news. She looked expectantly at Colin.

Colin cleared his throat. "Well——"

Bethany couldn't contain her excitement. "But that's wonderful, Colin!"

Colin noted, with some satisfaction, that she referred to him as Collie only when they were alone. Perhaps he had misjudged this education thing. It might prove to be elucidating, after all. How hard could a beginning class in African-American literature be? Plus, he'd have the added bonus of seeing Bethany Porter practically every day. That, by itself, would make it worth his time and trouble.

"You don't think I'm too old to return to school?" He didn't want to appear too eager.

"Too old?" Bethany laughed at the idea. "Colin, you're never too old to learn."

She hugged him in spite of his daughter's presence.

Sabrina stood to the side, smiling at them. Her father was coming to life again.

THREE

"Who is that Beth just came into the room with?" Deborah Stephens-Anderson asked Kiana before biting into a chicken wing. Kiana balanced a full plate in one hand and a drink in the other. Her dark gray dress fell smoothly over her protruding stomach, its hem falling a couple of inches above her knees.

"That's Colin Armstrong. He and Gabriel were childhood friends. He's been away a long time, but he's going to be moving back home."

"Wonderful. We could use a transfusion of new blood around here. Is he married?"

Kiana smiled at her shorter friend. Deborah was in her early forties. Her skin tone reminded Kiana of her late sister, Dionne's. It was a rich golden brown with reddish undertones. Very healthy-looking. Deborah wore her short black hair in a curly cap, and tapered at the nape of her neck. Her light brown eyes were nearly the same color as her skin, but they had dark brown striations which made everyone looking into her eyes for the first time look twice—they were so unusual. She'd been married to Daniel Anderson, professor of physics at Baylor, and Gabriel's best buddy nowadays, for more than twenty years. She and Kiana had become fast friends last year when Gabriel had married Kiana and brought her here to live. Deborah, Kiana, and Bethany made a fierce threesome. They always had each other's best interests at heart.

"They know each other?" Deborah asked of Bethany and Colin.

Kiana told Deborah the story of the night Bethany and Colin had met. Then she said, "I believe there could be something there. I'd like to see what blossoms. But as you know, we're getting ready to go to Florida for the summer. You're going to have to keep an eye on them by yourself until I return in September."

Deborah watched the couple across the room. They were laughing at something, their heads close together, their foreheads nearly touching. Yes, there could definitely be something worth keeping an eye on there.

"What is it with married women?" she joked. "We can't stand to see one of our girlfriends unattached."

"Those of us who're happily paired off know how good it is to have a man in our beds every night," Kiana said honestly.

Deborah laughed, showing rather large white teeth in her pretty face. "Ain't that the truth? Having a man in your bed isn't the half of it, though. Having a *good* man in your bed. Now that's what *I'm* talking about!"

"Amen!" Kiana heartily concurred.

Deborah glanced at Bethany and Colin again. "Okay, Chief, what is my assignment in your absence?"

"All you need to do is ask Bethany about Colin from time to time. Don't be obvious about it. Colin told us he's buying a house in the area, and his daughter, Sabrina, is going to be starting school at Baylor in the fall. A lot can happen between June and September. I think if we can keep Colin in her thoughts, Bethany will do the rest. Look at our girlfriend. She can't keep her hands off him."

Across the room, Bethany was straightening Colin's tie. *If that's not a come-on, I don't know what is,* Kiana thought.

Bethany didn't teach classes at Baylor during the summer session. The summer was devoted to unwinding and taking short excursions around the state. Longer jaunts took her to Barbados, or the Seychelles, her two favorite destinations, both for their beaches. This year, due to her father's prolonged illness and subsequent death, she hadn't planned any trips whatsoever. She was not in the right frame of mind to go anywhere. With her father gone, she felt she'd be showing disrespect by frolicking on a beach somewhere. So it came as a surprise when, three weeks after her father's death, her mother announced she was going to Israel. They were having dinner at Bethany's Cape Cod in the same upscale neighborhood where the Merricks and the Andersons lived. The neighborhood was only a fifteen-minute commute from Baylor, and a sizable population of the college's instructors and support staff lived there.

Bethany put down her fork with Chicken Dijon still on it. *"Israel?"*

"I've been wanting to go for a long time. But I didn't want to go without your father. With his weakened heart, he was advised not to take extensive trips," Corrine calmly explained. "Rafe wanted me to go alone, but I couldn't do that without worrying how he was every second I was away. We would lie in bed at night and talk about it. He wanted to go, too. Therefore, now, I'm going for the both of us."

Corrine met her daughter's eyes across the table. "Why don't you come with me?"

Bethany's first reaction was to go in order to make certain her mother would be safe halfway around the world. Though Corrine was in excellent health she was still a sexagenarian, and prone to the attendant ills advanced age brought with it.

"Maybe I *should* go," Bethany began hesitantly.

Corrine smiled slowly. "If you think I need you with me as a chaperone, a nurse, or a baby-sitter, you can forget it!"

"I didn't think that," Bethany denied unconvincingly.

"You thought it," Corrine maintained. She took a sip of her chardonnay and then turned sharp eyes on Bethany. "Unless I'm senile, infirm, or both, you will not assume responsibility for me, Bethany. I am a capable woman. I'd traveled to six countries before I ever met your father, and I know my way around."

"I can't help feeling responsible for you, Mama. You're all I have left."

"That's part of the problem," Corrine said, her tone low and regretful.

"What problem?" This was turning into an altercation, and Bethany wasn't quite sure why. What had gotten into her mother? "I don't see a problem."

Corrine sighed. "After the incident with Adam, you came back home and never left again. You made a nice safe haven for yourself, and have been in your cocoon ever since. You didn't come back home to please your father, you came back because your experience with Adam had made you timid and unsure of your own instincts."

"That's not true. I came back home because I was sorry for hurting Daddy."

"Think about it, Bethany. You wanted to prove you didn't have to rely on your father to make a life for yourself. No one at Baylor could say you'd ridden on your daddy's coattails in order to earn your doctorate. You did it by yourself. You had nothing left to prove by coming back to Baylor. Believe me, your father would have been proud of you no matter where you chose to teach."

"I wanted to carry on the family tradition."

"You wanted to return to a place and time where you felt safe and secure," her mother contradicted her. "Admit it, Bethany. Admit it, and start living your life before you turn into a scared, dried-up old lady. And, by God, I won't allow that to happen even if I have to get you thrown out of Baylor myself!"

Bethany sat there with tears pooling in her eyes. She wanted to scream. She wanted to yell at her mother, "You're wrong! You're dead wrong!"

But she knew her mother was right.

"I could be selfish. As a matter of fact, I *have* been selfish these past thirteen years. I let your father talk me out of telling you how I felt back then. We both enjoyed having you nearby. What parents don't want their children close at hand? I'm not saying you should leave Baylor, if that's where you truly want to be. I'm saying that it's time you stopped playing it safe. You're not living your life fully, darling. Not by a long shot. Not when you're avoiding the very things you want most."

"In your opinion, what would those things be?" Bethany asked petulantly, her feelings hurt in spite of the fact that she knew her mother was speaking the truth. Let her mother have her pound of flesh.

"Don't think I haven't noticed how you look at Kiana and Gabriel. You're envious of what they have, Bethany," Corrine told her. She would not back off. She would not be a good mother if she didn't help her daughter face up to her shortcomings.

"Why shouldn't you have that kind of love in your life, too?" Corrine continued. "You're every bit as accomplished and attractive as Kiana is. The only difference between you two is, Kiana isn't afraid to risk her heart, and you are. You loved once, Bethany, and it blew up in your face. Now you're too scared to try again."

"Same old, same old, huh, Mama?" Bethany asked, rising. "Have I become a cliché?"

She paced the dining room. The lights had been dimmed, and the French doors stood open to the backyard. The roses she'd planted last spring were in bloom. The heady fragrance served to quell the unreasonable anger inside her. It wasn't easy having your life laid out before you. Not when you were in denial. She thought she was relatively happy. Of course *happy* might be too strong a word to describe her life. Most days she was perfectly capable of convincing herself she was accomplishing something lasting. Something that would matter after she was dead and gone. Other days she felt crippled by her existence. Boxed in. Like nothing would ever truly excite her again.

Corrine remained seated. Her limbs were weak. It had taken a lot of energy to speak so bluntly to Bethany. She didn't want to hurt her little girl. Not for anything in the world. She didn't want to see Bethany continue on her present course, either.

Losing Rafe had taught her one thing: *You have to live your life to the fullest right now, because it can be taken from you in an instant.*

Bethany stopped walking. Her back was to her mother. "You're right," she said, her voice low. "I'm living by rote. A continuous script goes through my mind on a daily basis and I follow it like an automaton. I've shut off my desires, my ambitions. I've already accomplished the pinnacle of success, haven't I? What more is there left for me to do?" She faced her mother. The hardwood floor felt cool on the bottoms of her bare feet. She wore a pair of button-fly jeans and a plain black short-sleeved T-shirt, the lower half of which was rolled up to reveal her midriff. Her body was fit from alternating swimming and running five days a week. It was a body that had not known a man's touch in more than three years. She was somewhat resentful of that fact after putting in all that time keeping it in shape. Logically she knew the reason she stayed in shape was for her overall health. But heck, where were the fringe benefits?

Corrine rose slowly. "You have every right to be angry with me. I was shooting from the hip, and I know it." Her light brown eyes met Bethany's. "I love you so much, I'm willing to alienate you if that's what it takes to help you."

Bethany quickly crossed the room and bent to hug her mother. "I needed that kick in the butt, Mama." She held her at arm's length. "I'm so entrenched in my cubbyhole that, three weeks ago, when Colin Armstrong came back into my life and I found myself overwhelmingly attracted to him, I convinced myself it was only my emotions, still raw after losing Daddy, making me feel that way, and I really wasn't drawn to him."

"Oh, child, *please!*" Corrine said, smiling broadly. "Anyone observing you two that day could see the sparks flying off you."

* * *

Funny how things always seem to work out for the best, Colin thought as he drove his SUV along the drive leading up to his new home on the outskirts of Bridgeport. The house sat on ten acres. It had been farmland until the family who owned it decided the property was much more valuable to them as real estate. They kept fifty acres for family and sold the other eighty in ten-acre parcels. The house Colin had bought had been built by an actor who was extremely successful on the New York stage, but had recently broken into films. He was now based in L.A., which meant he no longer needed the Connecticut house. Colin got a good deal on the four-bedroom, three-and-a-half-bath, Tudor-style home. Nestled among indigenous trees, and gently rolling hills, the house was bordered by a white picket fence and was beautifully landscaped. What's more, there was a barn out back. Not a large one but big enough should the Armstrong family need to board a couple of horses.

The thing Colin was thinking had worked out for the best was him and Bethany. Or, rather, the lack of communication between the two of them. He'd happily given her his home number, his cell phone number, his fax number, his beeper number and his E-mail address. She hadn't seen fit to use any of those means of communication. Therefore he was convinced she wasn't interested enough in him to make an effort. He'd obviously imagined the looks that had passed between them. Had dreamed up the intimate body language he'd witnessed and actually felt when she'd impulsively hugged him several times. Not once, not twice, but *three* times!

Maybe he'd gone overboard with the numbers. He should have just given her his home number, and if she couldn't get him, she could have left a message. At least then he wouldn't have seemed like such a lonely, desperate leftover, as he thought of himself lately. The only attachment he had was Sabrina. He was naturally not good at dating. When you got to be his age, and desired women around your own age, those relationships came with certain expectations. Let's face it, some over-thirty-five women were unfairly pressured by well-meaning friends and family to "find" Mr. Right. And quickly! Therefore, when you approached them they immediately wanted to know your intentions. Did they have the time to waste on you was their ever-present question? Colin was raised to respect women. He didn't believe in jumping in the sack on the first date, which had been expected of him on at least a couple of occasions. He'd beat a hasty retreat both times. He was a red-blooded American male. He was strong, healthy and virile. However, with all the STDs out there, he'd be a fool to behave so irresponsibly. Besides, a woman would have to be more than good in bed to satisfy him. God knows he wanted to be more than that to her!

He'd learned to watch a woman for a while before approaching her.

He didn't know what he expected when he'd walked into the Porter home that day over a month ago. To see Bethany again was all he'd set out to do. She was right when she'd told him she'd meant something to him over the years. He'd never been able to get her innocence out of his mind. Nor her feistiness. Getting revenge for a wrong done her, no matter what it took. Okay, revenge was not always advised, or sweet. In Brad Johnston's case, though, it was well deserved. He was glad to have played a part in it.

That girl had lived in his memory for twenty years. He couldn't help wondering what had become of her. Gabriel dropped tidbits about her from time to time. But Colin had not asked after her because Gabriel was a terrible ribber. If Colin had shown the slightest interest in Bethany, Gabriel would have accused him of lusting after her in his heart, à la Jimmy Carter, and would never have let him live it down.

What he found that day in May was an entirely prepossessing woman. Gabriel pointed her out to him, otherwise he would not have recognized Bethany. Gone were the coltish figure, and the eyes that were too large for her face. She had a fit, but lush body, with gams that could make a leg man drool. He didn't know how any male student she taught heard a thing she said because her beauty was way too distracting.

And I'm thinking of taking her class? he thought as he pulled the Expedition behind the moving van that was parked on the circular drive of the new house and got out. *I must love to suffer.*

"Call him, Bethany, you coward!" Sweat ran down the bridge of Bethany's nose. For the middle of July it felt like August, ninety in the shade. She was kneeling on her garden pad pulling weeds from the rhododendron bed. It was a young shrub with lovely pink flowers. Not much of a fragrance, but Bethany loved the shiny, leathery leaves on it, and the bush gave her garden a burst of color when the roses weren't in bloom since it was an evergreen, and bloomed practically year-round.

"What would I say to him after more than a month?" She'd begun talking to herself in her mother's absence. Corrine had left for Israel the previous week. Now, the only close friends she had left in town were Deborah and Daniel Anderson. And she was sure they were getting tired of seeing her face day after day. She and Deborah ran together two times a week. Deborah wasn't fond of swimming—she had a thing about getting her hair wet—so she didn't join Bethany for her swims.

Bethany rarely popped in on the Andersons without phoning first. They had two teenagers, a girl and a boy, and were kept busy in the summer by all the activities the kids were involved in.

Bethany yanked a particularly stubborn weed out of the soil, sat back on her legs, and drew the back of her hand across her sweaty brow. She tipped her old wide-brimmed straw hat off her head. It hung by a string about her neck. After wiping her hands on her khaki shorts, she reached for the cell phone sitting inside the wicker basket she used as a conveyance for her garden tools.

She'd looked at Colin's home number so often lately, she

knew it by heart. The phone rang, and then she heard a click. The call was being transferred to another number. This time she got an answering machine. "Hello," Colin's deep voice said, "you've reached the Armstrong residence. Sabrina is grounded and can't receive any phone calls . . ."

"Aw, Daddy," Sabrina's voice whined.

"And I'm unavailable at the moment. Please leave a message and we'll get back to you as soon as possible. Thank you, and God bless."

Beep.

"Collie, it's me, Bethany. Forgive me for not calling sooner. But you could have phoned *me,* you know!" She laughed. "At any rate, I'm going out on a limb here by asking you to come to dinner at my house one night soon. Too intimate for a first date? Wait a minute, I think I should back up. Neither of us have said we're dating, have we? That's why I hate leaving messages on somebody's machine. I always end up sounding like a fool! Just dinner, all right? Forget I mentioned the 'D' word, okay? Erase this message as soon as you listen to it. I don't want evidence of my stupidity lying around. Bye!"

Bethany got to her feet, closed the cell phone, picked up her basket of gardening tools, and walked to the garden shed a few feet away. She placed the basket on a shelf inside the shed, locked the door then went into the kitchen via the French doors that opened onto the patio. She put the phone down on a table.

She'd made the first move. Now the smart thing to do was not wait around for his call back. Locking the French doors behind her, she began unbuttoning her damp white sleeveless cotton blouse. It was a little past two on a Saturday afternoon. She would shower and dress and maybe take in a matinee. But matinees were usually packed with kids on a Saturday afternoon. No, she would do some window-shopping at the mall. The mall was air-conditioned, and if she impulsively bought a new outfit, just in case Colin did come to dinner one night soon, so be it. She couldn't be held accountable for an itchy credit card finger.

An hour later, she was strolling past brightly lit and decorated stores, nearly as brightly decorated herself. Feeling buoyant, she'd grabbed the most colorful summer dress in her closet, a sleeveless electric-orange linen dress that fell three inches above her knees and revealed a bit more cleavage than she was used to showing. Not exactly plunging, but daring for her. Her accessories were beige low-heeled strappy sandals and a beige straw shopping bag. She'd even painted her nails beige. Her long, curly black hair was combed and pinned up in a carefree, funky style.

If any of her colleagues from Baylor saw her in this getup, they wouldn't recognize her. Her mother, however, would applaud her choice in dress as a step in the right direction. *Okay, Mama, I'm stepping out.*

Two hours into her stroll in the mall, Bethany had successfully resisted buying anything over ten bucks in value. For a late lunch she'd eaten her way through the food court: a pretzel, a paper cup of hand-squeezed lemonade, and an egg roll from the Chinese Hut. She got downwind of the food court after consuming the egg roll, fearing she'd be waddling before the day was over if she didn't. She was positive it was the aromas that pulled you in like a magnet. A cinnamon roll was stashed in her shopping bag in case she couldn't make it across the huge parking lot without sustenance.

"Bethany!"

Bethany, who was peering at the display in a jewelry store window, looked in the direction of the masculine voice. Lee Chase. He taught mathematics at Baylor: algebra, calculus, geometry, and trigonometry.

Lee was the product of a mixed marriage: an African-American father and a Vietnamese mother. The result was a very handsome man with dusky skin, curly black hair, and warm brown eyes. Lee was so comfortable in his own skin, that he had the ability to transfer that grace to anyone who came in contact with him. He was high on life and his personality reflected it.

Five-ten, he was nicely built due to an interest in climbing. He'd even persuaded Bethany to join him at his gym where they'd constructed a wall that simulated rock climbing. Smiling at him now, Bethany had to admit Lee's thighs were in great shape from all that wall climbing.

"Hello, Lee. How are you?"

They hugged briefly. Lee grinned as he released her. "What are you doing, getting ready for a hot date tonight?" he asked hopefully.

Bethany knew he was seeing someone special. Like her, he'd never been married. But unlike her, he'd wanted to. His fiancée, Linda, had been killed in a hang-gliding accident nearly two years ago. Lee had had a hard time of it. Bethany sometimes believed his positive outlook on life was a pose behind which he hid the sadness.

Bethany understood sadness. Therefore she empathized with Lee, and liked him a great deal. There had never been anything romantic between them. Lee felt comfortable confiding in her about the women he dated because he trusted her judgment. And she bounced things off him occasionally, too.

To Bethany, his asking her for advice on love was like the blind leading the blind. What did she know about lasting relationships? She'd never had one!

"Big *date?*" she asked, laughing. "At this point, I'd settle for a little date."

"Dry spell, huh?" Lee sympathized.

"Bone-dry," Bethany told him confidentially.

They started walking. It was obvious Lee was just shooting the breeze, with no set itinerary or destination, either. "I asked Julie to marry me," he said quietly.

Bethany was delighted to hear it and told him so.

"There's a problem, though. Her parents don't like me."

Frowning, Bethany turned to look him in the eyes. "Did they tell you why?"

"It's not me, actually, that they don't like. It's the part of me that's black they can't abide. Julie has no problem with my being black but her parents, who are traditional Vietnamese, believe in keeping the line pure."

"You're in a difficult position, Lee. We could cry racism all we want, but when an idea is ingrained in a people, it's difficult to change their minds." Bethany was never less than honest about her feelings with Lee.

Lee's head was bowed. Bethany could tell the situation pained him greatly.

He looked her in the eyes. "I've been walking all afternoon, trying to figure out what to do about it. Julie says she loves me, and would marry me even if her parents refused to give their blessing. But how can I do that to her, Beth? I know how close she is to her family. To her, separation from them would be like dying. And I've already had one woman die on me."

Bethany placed a reassuring hand on his arm. "It's never easy to love anyone, is it?"

"It's painful," Lee said.

"Talk to her, Lee, really talk to her. Sometimes hardened hearts are softened by example. I hope that will be the case with Julie's parents."

Lee hugged Bethany again, and as her chin rested on his left shoulder, she peered across the way into Colin's eyes. He was purposefully moving toward them, a shopping bag held in his right hand.

Bethany managed to extricate herself from Lee's embrace. "I hope everything works out, Lee," she said, her voice sounding hoarse. She was shocked to see Colin less than ten feet away.

Colin was upon them now. "Hello, Bethany. How have you been?"

He sounded as though he ran into her in the mall everyday. Pleasant, cheerful even. It irked Bethany just a little that he wasn't as nonplussed as she was. Her heart was beating in her throat, her palms had grown moist in the few seconds her gaze had locked with his, and she felt an urge to explain to him her proximity to another attractive man. Silly, all of it, but that's how she felt.

She composed herself enough to introduce Colin to Lee.

Colin extended his hand to Lee after the introduction. "Good to meet you, Dr. Chase."

"Oh, call me Lee. Any friend of Bethany's . . ." Lee's voice trailed off. He briefly gave Bethany a questioning look. Bethany quickly raised her brows. Lee smiled knowingly. After that, he hastily excused himself saying he had an appointment he didn't want to be late for.

"Nice to have met you, Colin," he said. "Bethany, thank you for the advice."

"Anytime," Bethany said.

That was just like Lee to give her an out in case Colin regarded her as more than a friend. His thanking her for advice put their relationship on a personal level, but nothing more intimate than friendship. At least she hoped that's how Colin would see it because she was definitely interested in taking *their* relationship past the friendship stage. She could hardly draw her eyes away from his face.

He was watching her as intently. A smile played on his lips. "I got your message."

Bethany wanted the floor to open up and swallow her. She blushed down to her toes. "And you're actually speaking to me after that horrible display of ineptitude?"

Colin laughed shortly. "I've never been asked out so sweetly before, Professor. I accept, of course. In fact, I'm looking forward to it."

FOUR

"You did say you liked fish?" Bethany asked after she and Colin had finished putting dinner on the table. They sat down across from one another in her dining room. The lights were turned low. Candles sat in the center of the table, and an India Arie CD played softly in the background.

She'd prepared trout amandine, garnished with lemon slices and parsley, a garden salad, stir-fried string beans, baked potatoes, and homemade yeast rolls. A double-chocolate cake was waiting in the fridge for dessert. She'd bowed to her drug of choice, chocolate. It would help her remain calm later tonight after dinner was over, and she would be compelled to make first-date small talk when she'd rather the talk be intimate.

Colin marveled at how put together Bethany looked after preparing such a feast. To be honest, he would have settled for hot dogs on the grill. It wasn't the food he was interested in, after all. It was the woman.

"I love fish," he told her. "I'm Jamaican. It was a main staple in our household when I was growing up. We had it at least three times a week."

"I love Jamaican food," Bethany said. "Have you ever been to Avery's Little Kitchen in South Norwalk? They're so popular, the lines to get in are out to the parking lot."

"You know it?" Colin said, surprised. When he smiled,

crinkles appeared at the corners of his eyes. Bethany thought they gave his dark, handsome face more character.

"They have great jerk chicken and ox tails. One night we ought to get some takeout from there and have a moonlit picnic by the pool. You swim, don't you?"

"You have a pool?" Bethany asked, cutting a piece of fish with the edge of her fork.

"It's not Olympic-size, but yeah. The house came with it," Colin answered. He took a bite of the trout amandine, savoring the delicate flavor. "Mmm, very nice."

Bethany shyly lowered her eyes. "I'm glad you like it. And, yes, I swim."

The air was charged with sexual energy. Bethany felt it. Colin was emboldened by it. "You certainly did fill out nicely, string bean." His tone was a caress.

Silence ensued.

Then Bethany placed her fork on her plate. Colin followed suit. Their eyes sought one another's and, in silent consensus, they leaned forward and gently kissed. No parting of lips, simply a coming together of mouths, the enticing sensation of sweet, warm breath up their nostrils, and the promise of more to come.

To Bethany there was something extremely sensual about a man who could kiss you without putting his tongue in your mouth and *still* make your toes curl with anticipation. Colin was one of those men.

His kiss ended with his taking her lower lip between his, tasting and lingering for a moment. Until that second, Bethany had no idea her lower lip was an erogenous zone. He'd lit a fire in her with just that minute action.

Still gazing into each other's eyes, they sat back in their chairs.

"Eat before your food gets cold," Bethany said, her voice thick.

Colin picked up his fork, but before digging in, he said, "What happened to you that made you so careful about your actions, Bethany?"

"I grew up," Bethany answered.

"Okay," Colin said, not wanting to press her. He turned his attention to his food.

Bethany sat eating and watching *him* eat. Tonight, he'd worn a short-sleeved body shirt that revealed the muscles in his upper body and arms. His biceps bulged in his arm every time he brought the fork to his mouth.

Bethany knew now whom he reminded her of: Taye Diggs. Although he was taller than the actor and, in her opinion, more attractive. Colin wore his wavy dark brown hair shorn close to his head and he had smooth squared-tipped sideburns.

They ate in silence. Bethany was grateful for the chance to gather her thoughts. It was obvious to her that Colin was going to want to know everything about her. The question was, could she tell him everything? She had intuited, from his comments about his ex-wife, Nadine, that their parting had not been amicable. What if Nadine had left him for another man? How, then, could she tell him she had once had a married man for a lover? Would he stick around long enough to hear her explanation? Or would he put her in the same category as his ex-wife, and break off their relationship in fear of getting hurt again?

To lie, or not to lie?

"My last year at Tulane, I was involved with a married man. I didn't know he was married until seven months after we'd been together," she blurted. "So, if you think that's awful of me, and you don't want to see me anymore, I'll understand. But that's it. That's my deep, dark secret. I don't have any skeletons in the closet. No children I gave up at birth. No ex-husbands who'll come out of the woodwork wanting to 'try again.' Basically, I've led a very boring life except for that one huge mistake I made when I was young, gullible, and blinded by first love. Besides, I broke it off as soon as I found out. It's not as if I kept seeing him, for God's sake. If I hadn't been writing my dissertation, I *know* he never would have been able to pull the wool over my eyes."

Colin reached over and clasped her hand. "Bethany, will you slow down?"

Bethany took a deep breath and gradually released it. She wore a pained expression.

Colin rose and, bending, kissed her on the forehead between her brows. Sitting down, he drew her hand, which he had been holding for the past few minutes, to his heart. Meeting her eyes, he said, "I knew you'd been hurt. But not how deeply you'd been hurt. It wasn't your fault, Bethany. You bear no blame, so stop carrying the guilt in your heart. He wasn't worth it. And I know, from experience, that no matter what you do, some people aren't going to live up to your expectations of them. He took pleasure where he could find it. With no compunction. With no thought of how his behavior would affect you, his wife, or their children, or, God forbid, any children he might have had with you if you'd gotten pregnant. These people are a breed apart, Bethany. Don't try to understand them because you'll get a brain hemorrhage in the attempt."

Bethany's heart broke for him. "Oh, no, Collie. She left *you* for another man?"

Colin actually smiled. He'd learned to laugh about it. Finding the humor in the situation had saved his sanity. "While I was working my behind off, she was having an affair with her gynecologist. I guess he saw something he liked."

Bethany burst out laughing. "She's a fool! Doesn't she know that wet response some women get when on the examination table is caused by self-preservation, and not sexual attraction for one's doctor?"

Colin cocked his head to the side, looking at her. "Self-preservation?"

"Yeah, you don't want to scream in pain when that cold speculum goes in."

Shaking his head, Colin laughed, "Girl, you're crazy."

"I thought you knew that twenty years ago, Collie."

* * *

"I want to come home, Daddy." Sabrina's voice sounded so forlorn over the phone that Colin was tempted to tell her to hire a cab, go to Miami International Airport, and he'd have a ticket home waiting for her by the time she arrived. However, he refused to spoil his child. He knew the temper she was displaying was because of her own stubbornness. She'd never forgiven her mother for leaving him. He'd tried to explain that Nadine's leaving didn't have anything to do with her, but she remained combative toward her mother. No amount of concessions on Nadine's part had softened her teenage daughter's heart toward her. Over the years Colin had observed that women were often harder on other women because they expected better behavior from females. Sabrina had put her mother on a pedestal; now she was discovering her mother was only human, subject to the same foibles as anybody else.

"It's only been two weeks, Brina. You promised to stay a full month. Does your mother know you're phoning me with this?"

"No. You're not going to rat me out, are you?"

Colin sighed. "Listen to me, Sabrina. Nadine is your mother, and you're not going to get another one, so you'd just as well accept her as she is. You don't have to agree with everything she does, but you *will* respect her."

"How can you say that after what she did to you?" Sabrina asked, hurt by his stance.

"I'm over it, baby girl. I've moved on. I've forgiven her. Why don't you try forgiving her, too?" Colin said gently.

Sabrina sniffed on the other end. "You're over her?"

"You've had my back from the beginning. I appreciate your loyalty. But this has got to end. I can't stand the drama every time I send you down there. If you're not calling about an argument you've had with your mother, your mother is phoning. I'd like to, someday, get married again myself. Am I to expect you to behave in this manner toward the woman I marry?"

"Behave in *what* way?"

"Proprietary, Sabrina. As if you have to defend me at

every turn. I'm a grown man. I can take care of myself. If you're hanging on to animosity toward your mother because of me, then you can let it go. But if you have a personal grievance against your mother, you should get it out in the open. Because, believe me, somewhere down the line you're going to need a mother. And like I said . . ."

"She's the only one I've got!" Sabrina finished his sentence. There was a long pause. "So, you're not going to let me come home?" She was pleading again.

Exasperated, Colin said, "Exactly. I'm going to hang up now. Daddy loves you."

He closed the cell phone, thereby severing the connection.

It was a warm afternoon in late August, and he and Bethany were by the pool about to have a meal of jerk chicken from Avery's Little Kitchen when the phone rang. Bethany wore a sheer white cover-up over a royal blue two-piece swimsuit. She was sitting with her legs crossed, eyes shielded by shades and her long hair, which she had in a single braid down her back, covered with a big, floppy wide-brimmed straw hat.

"You're a good dad," she complimented him. "I probably would have caved in if my daughter were pleading with me to come home."

"I can't stand to hear her whine, and she knows it," Colin said with a short laugh. "Plus, when Nadine left, Sabrina became an expert in playing one parent against the other. I'm not falling for that any longer. She'll be in college in the fall; she has to learn that adversity builds strength. It'll do her good to solve a problem or two without my help."

He gave her a sensual perusal. "That hat becomes you."

"I can detect your accent better now since we've been spending more time together. It's very sexy," Bethany returned. She moistened her plump lips and removed the dark glasses to peer at him with an amused aspect in her eyes. She loved it when he looked at her as if she were something good to eat. His ravenous gaze would sweep over her body, leaving her shivering with pent-up desire in its wake.

It had been three weeks since their first date. In the interim they'd talked about anything and everything. He knew her preference was to wait at least three months before even *thinking* about consummating a relationship. He thought it a reasonable length of time. However, holding themselves to it was becoming increasingly difficult.

"Ice water!" Colin suddenly announced, rising to hurry toward the kitchen entrance.

Bethany laughed and rose to follow him. She cut him off before he could go through the doorway and sidled up to him. It was instantly evident to her why he was in such a rush to get out of her presence.

Grinning down at her, Colin wrapped his arms around her waist. "I thought we agreed that if either of us yelled, 'Ice water,' the other would be advised that the conversation, touching, or whatever, was getting too intense. Have you changed your mind about waiting?"

He kissed her lightly on the mouth. Raising his head, he seemed to be considering his next move. Then he kissed her again, harder. Bethany's hat fell off and the breeze blew it across the flagstone patio. She didn't care. Colin's tongue had parted her lips and she was falling into a swirling pool of desire.

Good news, her brain transmitted to her pleasure points. *We have contact!*

Colin had the fortitude to break off the kiss. Bethany kissed his throat, his chin, his bare chest. She was working her way down to his washboard stomach when Colin drew her up short. "Bethany, with your sense of right and wrong, you're going to feel very guilty in the morning if this goes any further."

Bethany sighed and fell against his chest. He held her in the circle of his strong arms.

"Three months isn't so long to wait. I've been waiting for you to grow up much longer than that."

* * *

"What is this?" Corrine asked, pointing at the calendar on Bethany's kitchen wall.

Corrine had returned full of her adventure in Israel. The tour had sailed the Mediterranean Sea, docking in Jerusalem. From there, the group had made its way in Land Rovers down to Masada where Corrine waded in the Dead Sea, then up to Hebron, past Tel Aviv and the Plain of Sharon to their destination, Nazareth. All the while their guides warned them to stick close to the caravan because even though they did everything within their power to keep tourists safe, Israel and the PLO were still not in bed together and anything could occur, at any time.

Danger aside, Corrine had a wonderful time and came back referring to the country by its Hebrew name, *Yisra'el*.

"What are you counting down to?" Corrine repeated when Bethany continued chopping onions on the cutting board.

"Nothing in particular. The days until school starts?"

Corrine laughed. She'd gotten lots of sun in Israel, and in spite of copious amounts of sunscreen, had come back home a shade darker than she'd been when she'd left. Bethany thought she looked beautiful. Beautiful and happy. "You've never counted down the days before," Corrine said, unconvinced.

Bethany put down the knife and turned to face her mother. "Okay, it's about Colin and me. I'm counting the days before . . . you know."

"You've set an appointed time to make love?" Corrine had never heard anything so ridiculous. "What if one of you dies today, or tomorrow?"

Bethany's eyes stretched in shock. "That's a terrible thing to say!"

"Considering that I just lost your father, it is," Corrine told her. "But isn't it excessively cautious of you to put time constraints on how you feel about Colin? How *do* you feel about him, Bethany?"

Bethany didn't have to ponder her feelings for Colin. She adored him. There weren't enough superlatives in the English language to describe him. She wished she'd met him again ten years ago. But he was with Nadine then. And she despised men who cheated on their wives. She would not have given Colin the time of day. Now was their time. It had taken them two decades to find each other again, and she didn't want to ruin it.

"I love everything about him," she told her mother while she scraped the chopped onions off the board and into a freezer container. She used onions in a lot of her recipes and had found if she chopped several and put them in the freezer, it saved her a lot of preparation time later on. All she had to do was use a fork to separate the frozen onion pieces and add them to recipes accordingly.

"Then what are you waiting on?"

Bethany faced her mother. "I'm slowly coming out, Mama. But I'm not going to rush things with Colin. We'll know when the time is right."

Colin was poring over a prospectus for a new business he was considering investing in when the phone in his home office rang. Hoping it was Bethany, but figuring it was Sabrina calling from Brooklyn where she was spending the weekend with a girlfriend and hitting the stores for a bit of preschool shopping, he picked up right away.

"Colin Armstrong."

"I got my classes' preregistration roster in the mail today. It gives me an idea of how many students I'll have in my classes for the new school term. I didn't know you had registered for my Introduction to African-American Literature class. I'll also have Sabrina in one of my intro classes. This is so cool!"

"You won't feel that way when I fail," Colin joked.

"Failure is not an option, Mr. Armstrong," Bethany said, and then giggled, which spoiled the effect of quiet authority her tone had implied. "Anyway, I've uploaded the course requirements and the list of books we'll be reading this fall.

They're on the college's Web site now if you want to download them."

"Savvy students already will have purchased their books and read half of them by the time the term begins, huh?"

"That's what the smart ones do," Bethany confirmed. "It pays to be informed. What have you decided to major in, Collie?"

"Finance. I'm taking your course and two others. Starting slowly. The old brain hasn't been used in years. I don't want to throw it into shock."

Bethany laughed. "Well, congratulations. I'm glad you decided to give us a try."

"Hey, Professor?"

"Mmm?"

"Are there any rules against a professor dating a student?"

Bethany honestly hadn't thought about that. Now she realized that there were. They were designed to protect both the student and the teacher. However, the rules had been relaxed on campus for many years. Students were getting older. Nearly half of the student population were twenty-one or older. It was difficult to govern the behavior of adults. No one had brought charges of impropriety against a professor since Bethany began teaching at Baylor 13 years ago.

"I think the question of ethics comes into play here," Bethany said after considering his question. "Can I remain objective about your course work? Or will I be swayed by that sexy smile of yours, and be tempted to give you a good grade because of it?"

"If my work stinks, I have faith that you'll tell me it stinks and advise me to get a tutor," Colin said with laughter evident in his tone. "At any rate, I don't plan on taking any more of your courses, Professor. This one is going to be hard enough to get through with you as a distraction every day."

"I assure you, Collie, you won't even recognize me when I walk into the classroom."

* * *

Colin sat four rows deep in the auditorium-size class-room. The concert of voices made him think of the hum of an engine. He noted, with satisfaction, that he was not the oldest student in the class. There was a white-haired gentleman sitting several seats to his right, an Asian woman who could be someone's grandmother was walking through the door at this moment, and two attractive African-American women who appeared to be in their early fifties had their heads together in conversation in the front row. The majority of the hundred or so students were of African descent, but there were also a smattering of whites, Hispanics and Asians present, as well.

They carried their belongings in backpacks, large canvas bags and, in some instances, briefcases. He'd brought the first book on the reading list, Ernest J. Gaines's *A Lesson Before Dying,* and a college-rule notebook. These he carried in his hand. He supposed he needed to get with the program and purchase something in which to carry his books more easily.

He picked up *A Lesson Before Dying.* He'd read it in one sitting. If all of the books Bethany had chosen were as engrossing, this class would be a cinch. He might even excel at learning. The book was written in first person, and while reading it he'd felt like the protagonist himself. He was in the middle of the action every time anything happened to the hero, teacher Grant Wiggins.

Suddenly, the voices went silent.

Colin looked up to see a tall woman in a gray pinstripe skirt-suit, carrying a black briefcase, walk through the side door and, with purpose in her steps, approach the podium. She wore black conservative two-inch-heel pumps that still couldn't disguise the curve of a gorgeous pair of legs. Her black, wavy hair was pulled back in a severe bun, and a pair of glasses sat on the bridge of her nose.

"I think I'm going to like this class," a kid with fuzz on his chin said behind Colin.

"Yeah, man, she's hot!" said the boy next to him.

Colin turned and glared at them.

"Good afternoon, ladies and gentleman, I'm Professor Bethany Porter. You're in Introduction to African-American Literature. If that's not where you're supposed to be, I suggest you leave now." She paused. As she suspected, a couple of people rose, gathered their belongings and left the auditorium. It never failed; someone always wound up getting their classes mixed up.

"All right," Bethany continued, "I suppose the rest of you are here on purpose. Although, toward the end of the course, you might wish you'd joined those who got out while the getting was good." She didn't crack a smile.

Some laughed nervously and looked around to see if anyone was taking the professor seriously.

The laughter petered out.

"I will not be taking roll call. I realize some of you are fresh out of high school and the practice is familiar to you, but this is college and you're an adult now. It's your responsibility to be in class every day. I don't do reviews, so I suggest you make friends with your neighbor in case you miss something and would like to copy their notes. I hope to get to know your names and faces eventually, but this is a large class and I doubt I'll learn all of them. Once again, it's a question of your ability to take responsibility for your performance in this class."

A petite female student was walking down the aisles passing out papers. "My assistant, Miss Sandoval, is distributing the course requirements plus the list of books you'll be reading the next three months." She actually smiled. "I noticed some of you brought the first book we'll be reading, *A Lesson Before Dying,* with you. I commend you because we will be discussing the book in class today."

Groans.

Bethany's smile got broader.

"Stop. You're breaking my heart," she quipped. "All right. Everyone should have a copy of the course requirements by now. If you'll look toward the bottom of the page you'll see that you'll be asked to write a total of ten papers. The grades you receive for those papers count for fifty percent of your grade in this class. The other fifty percent will be equally divided between written tests and an oral exam toward the end of the course. Yes, you will get up here and speak to your fellow classmates. Don't worry. I don't grade on performance, but on content. You can blunder through the speech and still earn the full twenty-five percent. You may recite a poem you've written, or an essay. Maximum of five hundred words. Piece of cake, right?"

Another collective groan.

Bethany smiled. She loved this group already. They were exactly as she liked them to be in the beginning: lazy, apathetic and bored. All of which would soon change.

The Merricks were back from spending their summer months in Florida with Kiana's extended family. Bethany couldn't have been more pleased. She, Kiana, and Deborah drifted right back into their old routine of morning jogs together. Although, with Kiana eight months pregnant, the speed of their run had been reduced to a crawl. Bethany and Deborah didn't care. The object of their morning exercise was to catch up on each other's lives anyway.

This morning, Kiana was regaling them with tales from their stay in her hometown of Damascus, Florida, the highlight of which was a murder in the sleepy town, and then the wedding of Kiana's sister, Kerry, to the FBI agent who'd helped solve the case.

"Oh, ladies, talk about a match made in heaven. They had an affair over ten years ago, broke up over some foolishness or other, and were brought back together by chance—I say Providence—and now they're on their honeymoon. Can you believe it?" Kiana's golden brown skin had a healthy glow to it. She wore her long, thick black hair in braids. She spoke with her hands, so at the times she was especially excited by the story she was telling, she gesticulated wildly. She had Bethany and Deborah in stitches when she told them about how Kerry had run down the aisle to her waiting husband-to-be instead of strolling down the aisle in a dignified manner.

"But that's our Kerry," Kiana said now, her eyes bright. "Mac is just as crazy. After the minister pronounced them husband and wife, he swept Kerry up into his arms and carried her out of the church, down the steps to a waiting limousine. We were two hours into the reception before they put in an appearance."

"They had better things to do," Deborah said, laughing, remembering *her* wedding day. She and Daniel had made love in a closet of her parents' home while nearly two hundred guests were enjoying a repast in the garden downstairs.

"Life is never boring in Damascus, is it?" Bethany said, smiling warmly at Kiana. "How can you bear to come back to old, cold Bridgeport after being wrapped in your family's loving arms all summer?"

"That's easy," Kiana answered. "This is where my man thrives. He loves teaching at Baylor. And I've made good friends. So has Courtney. What's more, I think I'm making a difference at Fair Haven. I miss the colleagues and the patients I worked with at Green Meadows but, as care facilities go, Fair Haven is one of the best places I've ever worked."

"With your master's degree you could be *teaching* nursing," Bethany reminded her for the nth time. Bethany was determined to get Kiana on the staff at Baylor.

Kiana stopped suddenly and reached back to adjust the seat of her leggings. "These things ride up like crazy."

Bethany and Deborah laughed at her. "Could it be that huge stomach out front pulling the fabric too taut in the back?" Deborah asked knowingly.

"Oh, quit it," Kiana said. She glanced at Bethany as she continued walking. "I want to hear what's going on with you and Colin. Deborah's been keeping me posted."

"Before she left for Florida, she made me promise I'd spy on you two," Deborah said in her defense.

Smiling, Bethany could only shake her head at her friends' nosiness. They were almost as bad as her mother, and Corrine stuck her nose in her business all the time. "We're enjoying spending time together" was all she'd give them.

Kiana chewed on her bottom lip before saying, "Just answer this question: On a scale of one to ten how much does your temperature rise when he looks at you from across a crowded room? And I'm not talking about touching, just a look."

"Girl, it's off the scale!" Bethany couldn't resist crowing.

You would have thought one of them had just won the lottery, or something equally exciting, there was so much whooping and hollering going on on that quiet tree-lined street. They wound up in a group hug.

"You know what we've got to do now, before the weather gets too cold," Deborah happily suggested. Her eyes were misty.

"Backyard barbecue!" Bethany and Kiana said in unison.

FIVE

It was *the* day.

That morning, Bethany had to run back into the house twice for something she'd forgotten because she couldn't focus on anything else with any degree of success. Her morning classes were a blur. By afternoon, when she knew she would see Colin, after anticipating the moment all morning, she was sure she wouldn't be able to conduct the class with her usual finesse, and would conclude early because of it.

What happened, however, was even more disturbing to her equilibrium.

They were discussing Dorothy West's, *The Living Is Easy*. A male student commented that the book was old-fashioned and pedantic. The manner in which Ms. West wrote, he said, was unnecessarily scholarly. It was as if she were shoving her education down the throats of her readers who, he figured, didn't understand half the words she used because many of them probably had very little education themselves.

Colin spoke up. "You assume too much," he told his younger classmate. "The book is set in Boston, Ms. West's hometown. It's quite possibly semiautobiographical. She was also one of the Harlem Renaissance writers, and writers who were a part of that era were trying to prove they were as good or better than their white counterparts. How do you suppose she *should* have written the book, in Negro dialect? Perhaps if the story had been set in the South, as many of Zora Neale Hurston's stories were, she might have used dialect; but her story was set among the black elite of Boston. I didn't have any trouble understanding her style of writing and, in fact, enjoyed it very much. I could relate to her main character's scheming to maintain her position in society. My parents were penniless when they came to this country and had to claw their way to middle-class status while their children, inspired by their example, have done a lot better. I don't want a writer to write down to me. If anything, I want them to challenge me to keep up with them."

The entire assemblage applauded, including the kid who'd just been publicly upbraided.

Bethany experienced the strangest sensation as she stood there watching Colin deliver his oration. Her face grew warm, as did her insides. She felt tingly all over.

Colin had turned her on with his passion for books.

She cleared her throat. "Well said, Mr. Armstrong." She hastily turned to another, hopefully less volatile, subject. "Cleo's relationship with her daughter, Judy. Would anyone like to give their opinion?"

There was another heated discussion; however, Bethany barely heard a word of it. As the students filed out of the classroom, she gathered her books and papers, preparing to hurry across campus for a meeting with the head of her department. Dr. Jamison was retiring and Bethany, as a tenured professor, was being considered as his replacement. Bethany didn't know if she wanted the added responsibility. Lately, she'd had to rethink a lot of things. One of them, whether she wanted to continue teaching at all. Perhaps she would finally get up the nerve and pursue a full-time writing career. It was what made her truly happy, after all. That, and cooking.

What would they all think if she quit teaching and opened an eatery? That she'd lost her mind? What would they think if she shirked her responsibilities and moved to an island to write?

"You're beautiful." His voice, though low, seemed to echo in the cavernous room.

Bethany looked up into Colin's mellow brown eyes. She'd been under the impression everyone else had left. Her mouth formed an O in surprise. She sucked in air and slowly exhaled. She and Colin had agreed that, while on campus, they would treat each other formally. Therefore she was taken aback when he possessively pulled her to him and, peering deeply into her eyes, said, "It took the self-control of a priest, a saint, and a minor god to resist coming down here and kissing you. Tell me you felt it, too."

"W-what?" She regretted it the moment the word was out of her mouth.

The hurt reflected in his eyes was her judge and executioner. She had not *wanted* to hurt him. If she weren't afraid of being caught, she would have thrown him down on the podium and ravished him then and there. But she had to maintain a sense of decorum.

Colin laughed shortly. "I guess it's been too long for me, because I've been turned on by you the entire session. I had to touch you at least once." Remembering where they were, he relinquished his hold on her. "You must have someplace to be. If I hurry I'll miss only about five minutes of my accounting class."

He went to turn away and Bethany grabbed one of his big hands in both of hers. "Yes," she whispered desperately, her eyes meeting his. "Yes. I felt it, too!"

She stood on tiptoe and gently kissed his lips. Flat on her heels again, she said, "I want you, Collie. I've thought of little else all day." She wiped her lipstick from his mouth with the pad of her thumb.

Colin leaned in and kissed her. This time her lipstick was smeared all over his generous mouth. Perturbed, Bethany went to wipe the lipstick off with her index finger. Colin stayed her hand. "If you've got another minute to spare, put it to good use and kiss me again. I've got a handkerchief for lipstick removal."

Bethany laughed shortly, and did just that. "Wait until I get you alone tonight."

By the time they parted, they were both obliged to exit the classroom, separately of course, on slightly wobbly legs.

Later that day, when he was heading to student parking to go home, Colin was waylaid by Lourdes LeDoux. He was in a very good mood. It was a beautiful fall day in New England. The leaves were beginning to change colors, and there was a nice breeze. Plus, if his surroundings weren't enough of a mood elevator, he was in love.

Not even Lourdes LeDoux could say or do anything to alter that.

"Colin," she said, her beautiful lips parting to reveal an orthodontist's masterpiece of modern dentistry. "Long time, no see. What are you doing on our fair campus? Visiting Gabriel?"

Not waiting for an invitation, she fell right in step beside Colin as he continued walking. "Yes, it has been a long time," he allowed. "But not long enough. Now if you'll excuse me, I have an important appointment."

"You don't have to be rude," Lourdes cried, offended. She drew her five feet five inches into a proud posture. Her light brown skin was as smooth as porcelain.

Because she was so fair-skinned, the strawberry-blond color she'd recently dyed her short tresses actually complemented her. Green eyes looked accusingly up at Colin.

"I see you've been listening to rumors about me. Gabriel will never forgive me for dumping him. But it's unfair of him to spread lies about me."

Colin blew air between his lips and paused in his steps. His eyes were narrowed when he said with an exasperated sigh, "No one had to tell me anything about you, Lourdes. You treated one of my best friends badly. That's enough for me."

Lourdes pursed her lips and screwed up her face in a frown, considering her next move. "Gabriel had a part in our breakup, too, you know. I would not have been susceptible to the charms of my ex-husband if Gabriel had been warmer toward me. All I wanted was a little human kindness."

"Maybe Gabriel would have taken it better if you'd paused long enough in your rush to marry LeDoux to break off the engagement with *him* first!"

"Ever the loyal friend, aren't you, Colin?" Lourdes said. "Let's see how long you stand by the side of your other 'friend' when she's thrown out on her ear for improper behavior with a student. I saw that *passionate* kiss you shared this afternoon. I knew, if I waited long enough, I'd be rewarded. Now I have the goods I need to bring down that smug, thinks-her-stuff-don't-stank, phony!"

Colin took a threatening step toward Lourdes. Her eyes stretched, and she went pale beneath her make-up. Colin's hands were poised at her lovely throat, but he thought better of it and let them fall to his sides. His nostrils flared in anger. "You must be a very unhappy woman, Lourdes, to always think the worst of everybody. To always want to make others suffer." He met her eyes dead-on. "I can't imagine why you'd want to hurt Bethany. She's never said a mean word about you in my presence. But whatever your reasons are, know this: I will fight you to the bitter end. If you go through with your threat I will not rest until you pay. And I'm a very rich man, Lourdes. I have the funds with which to destroy you, if I want to. Think about that before you go off half-cocked."

He turned and walked away from her then.

"I'm going to destroy her!" Lourdes taunted him.

"Then I'm going to destroy you" were Colin's final words to her.

Bethany fairly floated through her house, preparing for Colin's arrival. The shrimp étouffée was simmering. Though

Jamaican food was Colin's favorite, he was also fond of Cajun cooking. The recipe for the étouffée was extremely easy. She'd chopped all the vegetables before leaving for work that morning. All she had to do was sauté onions, green onions, minced garlic (light on it tonight for obvious reasons), and chopped celery. When the vegetables were tender, she added a couple pinches of plain flour and stirred the mixture until it was browned. This made the roux, which was the basis for practically all Cajun stews and soups. To that she added water and tomato paste, various spices, including a generous amount of hot sauce. Let it cook for half an hour. Finally, the last ingredient to go in the pot was a pound of peeled, deveined jumbo shrimp. Cook for another fifteen minutes, and serve over rice.

She'd taken a long, hot bath and dressed in a gray lightweight V-neck sweater, which she'd probably roll the sleeves up on before long. She loved the comfort of sweaters, but long sleeves were cumbersome. Slim, white leggings completed her casual outfit. She'd given herself a manicure and a pedicure, painting her nails a shell pink, and a black bandeau held her hair away from her face. Tonight, she was going for simplicity. She planned to enjoy her man without any pretense, without anything to stand in the way of real intimacy.

When the doorbell rang, she had to suppress the urge to sprint to the door. She swung the door open and Colin stood there all in winter white. He wore a raw silk shirt that buttoned up the front, and pleated slacks. He smelled so good, her body followed her nose into his embrace. They smiled into each other's soulful eyes. He kissed the tip of her nose. His breath was warm and fresh, and she wanted his mouth on hers so badly, she reached up, grasped his face between her hands, and planted a kiss on his waiting mouth. "God, I've missed you!"

Colin moaned deep in his throat and kissed her once more. Then he set her away from him and turned to walk back through the door. "I brought a few things for us."

He returned with a large white box tied with a red ribbon,

a dozen white roses, and a bottle of chilled wine. He handed the box and the roses to Bethany and held on to the wine. "Open it," he said, his smile so sweet all she wanted to do was stare at him.

However, unused to receiving gifts from men, she tore into the box with the excitement of an avaricious child on Christmas morning. Inside was the most beautiful white lace negligee she'd ever seen. Taking it out of the box, she held it up. You could see right through it. She looked at Colin. He raised an eyebrow suggestively. "I *did* say they were for *us*."

"That, you did," Bethany said, coming to nibble on his earlobe. "Mmm, I'm famished. How about you?"

She placed the negligee and the roses on the foyer table so she would have both hands free with which to explore Colin. Colin grinned at her as he backed up enough to close and lock the door, which he'd forgotten to do after retrieving the gifts from the front porch. All the while Bethany was playfully nibbling here, suckling there, kissing everywhere.

Colin couldn't have been more delighted by her eagerness, but there was something he had to get off his chest first.

He kissed her lips and said, "Why is Lourdes LeDoux out to get you?"

Bethany stopped in midkiss. Frowning, she met Colin's eyes. "She came on to you?"

"No, no, she didn't," Colin replied, brows knit in concern. "She saw us kissing this afternoon. She told me she'd been waiting a long time to get something good on you. And she threatened to accuse you of improper behavior with a student."

Bethany held her bottom lip between her teeth, thinking. It was true she'd never gotten along with Lourdes. Especially not after Lourdes jilted Gabriel. She might have even been able to stomach the woman after that if Lourdes hadn't launched a hate campaign against Kiana once Gabriel brought her to Bridgeport as his bride.

She took Colin by the hand and led him over to the couch

where Colin sat down. Bethany made herself comfortable next to him on the arm of the big overstuffed couch.

"I think Lourdes resented me, in the beginning, because she felt I had an undeserved advantage when it came to earning my doctorate *and* becoming a tenured professor."

"Because of your parents," Colin deduced.

Bethany nodded. "Mostly my father. You see, I thought by going away to get my master's degree and my doctorate I'd be able to prevent some of the criticism about my credentials. Sometimes I think I should never have bothered worrying about what others think. But then you have people like Lourdes who are always looking for some dirt on you. Always wanting to pull you down to their level. I'm actually amazed by her attitude. Black women are very much underrepresented in higher education. We should be displaying a generosity of spirit and helping other sisters make it over. Earn their doctorates. A lot of us *do* give back. But some feel they have to compete with their sisters. Lourdes is that type. She's jealous and spiteful and, for the life of me, I don't know why."

Colin had to agree on that point. "At first glance she seems to have it all together. I met her nearly four years ago when she and Gabriel were engaged. I thought he'd struck gold. I was shocked to learn she'd dropped him."

"We all were," said Bethany. "I'm not saying Gabriel didn't have a part in it. No one knows what goes on behind closed doors."

"She says he didn't express enough human kindness," Colin provided.

"Can't say I agree with that. Have you ever known Gabriel to turn his back on anyone who needed help?"

"No," Colin said at once. "But I'll tell you what. After that relationship broke up, she had him *believing* he'd done something wrong."

Bethany peered into his upturned face. "What do you mean?"

"He phoned me to tell me how much he'd always appreciated our friendship. He said he wanted me to know that, in case he'd never mentioned it before. Made me think he was thinking of checking out or something." He laughed. "But no. Apparently after Lourdes returned from France married to Guy LeDoux, he'd confronted her and she'd told him it was his fault she'd turned to someone else. Because he was distant."

"Manipulative, that's what she is," Bethany said with vehemence. She brightened. "Well, all's well that ends well. He met Kiana."

"A happy beginning," Colin said. He smiled at her. "Back to the reason why Lourdes dislikes *you*. We could be here all night trying to analyze *her*."

"That's true," Bethany admitted. "Okay. Besides the fact that she resents my meteoric rise in the ranks," she joked, "I embarrassed her in front of her cohorts."

"Now we're getting somewhere."

"It was at a faculty soiree thrown by President Alden to welcome everyone back for the fall term. Gabriel was there with Kiana. They were newly married. I hadn't met her because I had returned from a trip that very day. Anyway, I went to the powder room. While I was in a stall, Lourdes came in with her usual two or three poisonous cronies. They started talking about how Gabriel was showing off his new wife, proud as a peacock, when she was no prize. Lourdes commented on Kiana's mounds of hair. She ought to either cut it off or hire somebody to shoot it and put it out of its misery, she said, alluding that Kiana's hair looked like a wild animal sitting atop of her head, no doubt. The witches were cackling up something!

"I came out of my stall then, and they went silent. Lourdes knew Gabriel and I were good friends. While they were standing there dumbstruck by my presence, Kiana walked out of another stall. She went to the sink and washed her hands. Went into her purse to get a tube of lipstick and applied it. After that, she checked her hair, which was beautiful, by the way. I was at the sink ostensibly washing my hands, but really watching every movement of this outsider.

When she was satisfied her hair was as she wanted it, she turned and faced Lourdes.

" 'You must be Lourdes,' she said with a warm smile. She grabbed Lourdes's hand in hers and vigorously shook it. 'I want to thank you for not marrying Gabriel,' she said. 'Because of your actions I'm the happiest woman alive!' "

"With that, she actually hugged Lourdes.

"Lourdes was in a state of semishock," Bethany continued. "That's the only way I can explain the fact that she didn't say a word the entire time Kiana was in her face."

Colin laughed.

"After Kiana let go of Lourdes, I went to her and introduced myself. 'Anybody who can render Lourdes mute is someone I'd like to get to know,' I told her. We left the ladies' room together, I walked back to her table with her and we've been friends ever since."

"Therefore, you're in the enemy camp because you aligned yourself with Kiana."

"Exactly," Bethany said, sliding off the arm of the couch into his arms. "Let her do her worst." She kissed Colin's strong, freshly shaved chin. He smelled like soap and water, and shampoo.

Colin reclined on the couch and Bethany lay on top of him. They were cheek to cheek. "Feeling good?" Bethany whispered. She pressed the lower half of her body into his and gyrated. His member was already swelling and pressing into her abdomen.

"Mmm-hmm," Colin murmured. He placed both big hands on her nicely rounded bottom. "Very good, indeed." Her fragrance surrounded him. The taste of her was in his mouth. Only a bit of fabric separated their naked bodies. . . .

Bethany suddenly raised her head and sniffed the air. "Oh, my God!"

She quickly climbed off him and ran to the kitchen. Colin got up to follow her through the house. When he got to the kitchen, Bethany was standing at the stove with the lid to a Dutch oven in hand. She looked at him accusingly. "I've never burned anything before in my life. It's your fault for distracting me."

She'd already turned off the stove. Now she put the lid back on the pot and lifted it by both handles and carried it to the stainless-steel sink. Perching it on the edge of the counter, just a moment, she put the stopper in the sink, ran water in it, and then lowered the pot into it.

Colin, who was no cook, did not find anything out of the ordinary. The air was not smoke filled. The aroma from the pot was mouthwatering. He didn't know why she'd gone running into the kitchen.

"I don't smell a thing," he told her.

"It's scorched. The bottom of the pot will be black. I can't save it."

"I love blackened fish," Colin offered.

"It's not the same," Bethany said. "You can't eat blackened shrimp étouffée."

Bethany sadly looked at the ruined pot. "I cooked it for you, Collie. I put a lot of love in that stew."

"I love étouffée . . ." Colin said regrettably. ". . . But not nearly as much as I love you," Colin finished his sentence.

Bethany slowly turned to stare at him. "What did you say?" she said, her voice cracking. If he'd said what she thought he'd said she'd gladly cook another pot of stew.

Colin was at her side in a heartbeat. "I said I love you," he told her again as he wrapped his arms around her waist and lovingly gazed into her eyes.

Bethany grinned so wide, her jaws hurt. Throwing her arms around his neck, she cried, "Collie, I love you, too!" Tears sprang up, spilled forth. She was a melodramatic idiot, but she couldn't help it. From the night they'd met, she'd known Colin Armstrong was a man of his word; and if he said he loved you, he meant it. There was no taking it back with him. There would be no revelations of another woman somewhere down the line. He was as true as any knight in any fairy tale except he would not cease to exist once you closed the pages of the book and turned out the lights.

She kissed his face repeatedly while Colin laughed. "Oh, Collie, why'd you have to stay away for twenty years?"

"Don't complain, sweetness, because our love was right on time," Colin told her as he bent his head to kiss her until the tips of her ears were hot, and her female center was singing like a siren.

"Bedroom, now, hurry," she breathlessly said.

Colin picked her up, placed her over his shoulder fireman-style, and did her bidding. Bouncing on his shoulder, Bethany giggled all the way.

Some say time is a river, ever flowing, ever changing, transforming everything in its path as surely as water reshapes the surface of the earth. That's how Bethany felt as she slowly unbuttoned Colin's shirt and ran her hands over his hairy chest. Time had brought Colin to her. Time had molded him into the man he was today.

After she'd removed his shirt, she took it and placed it on the bench that sat at the foot of her queen-size bed. Then she did a striptease for him, pulling off her sweater to reveal a lacy beige bra, and rolling the waistband of the leggings past her hips until the matching panties came into view.

The sweater and leggings joined the shirt on the bench.

Standing before him in her underwear, Bethany's eyes locked with his across the room. She knew she didn't have a perfect body. But she'd long since stopped trying to achieve physical perfection, and had come to cherish what God had given her.

Colin swallowed hard. He didn't think he could speak at that moment. Nor, it seemed, could he command his body not to respond to the stimuli his eyes were sending his brain. He'd seen her in a swimsuit, so he knew she was in good shape. But the sight of her nipples beneath the fabric of her bra, and the dark thatch of hair, seen through her panties, at the V where her thighs came together, made him swell inside his pants. He'd imagined this moment many times before. His imagination had been sorely lacking.

His hand went to his washboard stomach, and it occurred to his feverish brain that he was still wearing slacks. With his eyes trained on Bethany, he quickly undid the top button, gingerly unzipped the slacks, and pulled them down. He wore a pair of black stretch jockey shorts that hugged his muscular thighs and did nothing to disguise the bulge in front. He was suddenly struck by how vulnerable Bethany appeared. He went and pulled her into his arms. "You're so beautiful, you take my breath away."

She smiled, let out a peaceful sigh and relaxed in his arms. But as suddenly as the tension flowed out of her, passion seemed to fill up the spaces. As he held her, her hands were busy working their way inside his briefs, and grasping hands full of his gluteus maximus. The more she squeezed from behind, the harder he grew in front.

Bethany didn't want to blink; she might miss something. Colin's face was so dear to her. In the throes of arousal he was gazing at her with such love, such need that she nearly climaxed in her panties. *Get some control, girl,* she thought with an inward laugh. *You've got a good man. Show him you know what to do with him.*

She completed her task of pulling down his briefs. Colin stepped out of them. Bethany stepped forward, clasped his engorged penis in her right hand, not taking her eyes from his, and smiled at him. Her thumb and index finger could barely close around him, and the thought of him inside of her made her tremble with anticipation.

Colin had successfully gotten the hooks on her bra undone. Bethany took it and threw it above her head. Glancing up, she saw it hanging from the ceiling fan which, thankfully, wasn't on. She laughed briefly, and the laugh turned into a moan because Colin was running his tongue across her left nipple with devoted precision. Bethany was so wet she was sure there would be a wet spot in her panties once he got them off, which he was working on doing right now.

"What is that scent you're wearing?" he asked, his voice thick with passion.

"It's a mixture of tropical flowers. I had it made when I

was in Barbados last year. It's called Erotica," Bethany told him.

"It's aptly named," he said, and pulled down her panties, going down, too, in order to kiss her belly. The smell of her body, coupled with Erotica, wreaked havoc on his senses. It wasn't his desire that they come in a heated rush. He wanted tonight to be a slow dance, one that would elicit wicked grins when remembered years from now.

Bethany ran her fingers through his thick, soft hair as his tongue left a trail around her navel; lower, still lower. Bethany suddenly clutched both sides of his head and looked into his upturned face, a look of panic in her eyes. "I don't do that."

Okay, now he would find out what a prude she was. But with other men, she had not felt safe enough to allow that kind of intimacy.

Colin was instantly concerned. In the time of AIDS you had to ask the hard questions. *Please, God, don't let her be . . .* He caught himself. Just ask. "You're not *ill?*"

Bethany's face fell. "No!" She'd been tested. What smart sexually active woman didn't get tested just to be sure? She was also adamant about using condoms. Occasionally two of them if her partner was especially vigorous in lovemaking. She was healthy. She met his eyes. "I'm fine, Collie."

Colin rose to pull her into his arms. "Good. Girl, you nearly gave me a heart attack." He peered down at her. "I was tested, too, after finding out about Nadine's affair. As a married couple we didn't use condoms. She was on the Pill. She says she did, however, use them with her lover. He was a doctor. You'd think he'd have the sense to use them." He sighed. "Okay, we're both healthy. What's the problem?"

Bethany rolled her eyes. "I'm worried about odor and how I'll, you know, taste to you." She said this in a whisper as though it was something to be ashamed of.

Colin laughed. "You're a virgin."

"I'm not a virgin. I've made love to three, count 'em, *three,* men in my lifetime!"

"You've allowed them to make love to you, but you've never been made love to," Colin begged to differ. "How often did you achieve orgasm?"

Bethany paused entirely too long to make her reply anything but suspect to Colin's way of thinking. Finally, she said, "Okay, I didn't have an orgasm every time. But does that make me a freak of nature?"

Colin couldn't stop laughing. "Absolutely not. Some women can achieve orgasm in the good, old-fashioned missionary position. But as for that soul-deep, bone-shattering, explosive type of orgasm, many women say they don't achieve it until their clitorises are manually or"—he ran his tongue over his top lip—"orally manipulated."

Bethany had to admit he had her curiosity up. Just hearing him talk about it had brought her back to a state of arousal after having it interrupted by her earlier outburst.

"Of course," Colin went on, "you would have to fully trust your partner. Believe that he is only interested in your pleasure and would never cause you any pain or discomfort."

"I know *that's* right," Bethany said. "A woman is in a very vulnerable position during the act."

"Mmm," said Colin, lips pursed, nodding as if he'd suddenly been given insight into her psyche. "That's it. It's control. You are afraid of giving up control. Because in this act you must implicitly trust your partner."

"I trust you," Bethany said softly. Her big brown eyes were downcast.

Colin tipped her chin up with a finger. "Let me be perfectly clear. I don't want you to do anything you're not comfortable with. Ever, Bethany." He bent and kissed her high on the cheek. "Your pleasure is my pleasure. I would have to be a masochist to enjoy doing something to you that you weren't deriving the utmost pleasure from. The same goes for me. I don't want you doing an act on me that you don't get pleasure from. Now, since that's out of the way . . ."

"I don't want you to think I have hang-ups, Collie. . . ."

Colin silenced her with a deep kiss. His tongue was sweet and insistent. Bethany felt an instant reaction in her clitoris. She knew it must have been all that talk about oral sex. Honestly, could she lie there and allow Colin to put his tongue where no man had gone before? And actually *enjoy* it?

By the time they parted, Bethany was dreamy-eyed. "Maybe we could try it. If I could take another shower first."

Colin was game. "I'll wash your back."

Bethany had no problem with that.

In the shower, Colin ran the soapy washcloth along her glistening golden brown limbs. Bethany let him wash every inch of her then she did the same for him. Enjoying running her hands over his chest, arms, buttocks, and thighs.

After drying off with warm, fluffy towels, Bethany preceded Colin back into the bedroom. She was amazed by his patience. Another man might have told her to forget it, after all of the starts and stops they'd gone through tonight. But Colin just laughed and assured her he understood.

She sat on the bed. She was nervous.

Colin sat beside her. "You look like a virgin bride on her wedding night. Well, a virgin bride who has been told sex is bad." He smiled warmly and traced her jaw with a finger. "Just lie back and relax, my dear, and holler if something doesn't feel good to you."

Bethany lay back on the bed and scooted farther up on it, making certain there would be room for Colin to join her. She had her knees up. Colin knelt before her raised knees and put his hands on either side of her legs. "Relax, Bethany." She had her knees tightly together.

Gritting her teeth, Bethany opened her legs.

Colin laughed. "Look, don't clamp your thighs back together without warning me. You might decapitate me."

Bethany laughed and relaxed further.

Colin positioned himself above her and began by kissing her inner thighs.

Bethany was in a giggling mood. The feel of Colin's lips

on her inner thighs cracked her up. Colin let her laugh while
he continued his journey to her center. Slowly and methodi-
cally, he moved upward.

Bethany stopped laughing when his tongue parted the
lips of her vagina and laved her clitoris with maddening
delicacy. She wanted him to press harder. Just a bit. She
went still, and her thighs widened of their own accord. *Yes!*

She whimpered. She sighed, and practically melted into
the bed. She reached for him.

Colin paused long enough to ask, with fake concern,
"I'm not hurting you, am I?" He knew he was driving her
to distraction. "Because if I'm hurting you, I can stop."

"No, no!" Bethany breathed. She arched upward on the
bed. "It's—" She didn't want to seem overly eager. "Interesting." In the meanwhile, she was panting.

Colin smiled, reached down with both hands, and parted
the lips of her vagina. He ran his tongue along the pink
insides of the labia. Bethany groaned. His tongue went deep
and he was rewarded with a sudden attack of trembling
thighs on Bethany's part. He sensed she was on the verge
of one hell of an orgasm.

Bethany screamed when the orgasm seized her. Colin did
not let up; he stayed with her until she stopped convulsing,
and then he kissed her inner thighs, close to her female
center, because he knew that would bring on even more
tiny spasms of pleasure.

Her reaction had been all that he could have hoped for.

Bethany sighed as she got up on her elbows to peer at
him. "Are you sure you can't get arrested for that? 'Cuz it
feels too good not to be illegal."

Colin rose and went to retrieve his slacks from the bench
at the foot of the bed. He dug in the pocket and came out
with a foil-wrapped condom. "We're just getting started,"
he said. Going to the bed, he handed Bethany the condom,
which he'd already removed from its wrapper.

Bethany got up on her knees and slowly rolled the condom onto him. She was already throbbing again, ready for
him. Finished, she spread her legs and pulled him down on

top of her. Colin kissed her mouth. Bethany tasted herself on his tongue, which was a strange, though not unpleasant, experience. Raising his head, Colin smiled at her.

"For the record, you taste good to me."

With that, he slid into her slowly until all of him was inside. Bethany couldn't believe it. She could feel him expanding. Colin began rhythmic thrusts. Bethany was tight around him and he had to concentrate in order not to come too fast. He thought of the ocean and the tide coming in to wash clean the shore. Cool. Cool things.

Bethany met him thrust for thrust. She thought she might yell out when he changed the rhythm and almost pulled out of her entirely. He was only heightening the sensations for her, though. Each time he pulled out and went back in, he massaged her clitoris with his hardened member. Bethany's center was quivering with the want of release. Oh, but it was sweet torture.

Colin's eyes were narrowed. He looked at her through slits, for if he gazed fully into the rapture plainly mirrored on her beautiful face he would surely lose it, and he wanted to extend their joining as long as possible.

It was difficult enough for him, because Bethany was so vocal. Her moans and sighs, and outright screams excited him, thrilled him, made him believe in the power of forever once more. Because he had forgotten how good it felt to make your woman scream. He had forgotten what bodies washed down in sweat, writhing in passion, butt naked and joyous felt like.

"Oh, Collie, I can't hold on any longer!"

"Come on then, girl. Come on, I've got you."

Bethany moaned loudly. Colin felt her body convulse in an orgasm. Her vagina clenched and released, clenched and released around him. He came. "Oh, *God.*"

He blew air between his lips, and thrust urgently until his swollen member stopped throbbing. Bethany was also making a "whoosh" sound with her lips as she raised her hips to meet him.

Spent, they lay facing each other a long while, satisfied smiles on their faces.

Bethany broke the silence with "I'm starved."

Colin grinned. "Come to think of it, so am I."

They got up and hastily put in a call to the local pizza place.

An hour later, they were back in the bedroom working it off.

SIX

SIX

"There's a step-off between the Sigmas and the Dogs on the set!" a young male student yelled to one of his friends several yards away. Bethany was hurrying across campus to join Sabrina at the main cafeteria. Sabrina had pulled Bethany aside after her first period African-American Literature class to ask her to lunch. Bethany figured it was time for Sabrina to ask what her intentions were toward her father. She and Colin had already discussed the possibility that Sabrina might become concerned about the direction their relationship was taking, especially since she was her father's self-appointed protector.

Bethany loved October in New England. The leaves had changed to their fall colors, and the air was cool and bracing. She could walk for hours on a day like this. As she walked across manicured lawns of the stately campus she was greeted by several past and present students. The students were who kept her at Baylor, more than anything else. She enjoyed helping them expand their minds, and learn to think independently.

To her surprise, Bethany spotted Sabrina coming toward her. In honor of her transition from schoolgirl to college woman, Sabrina had cut off her long hair and now sported a short, natural style. She was attired in the latest trendy hip-hop togs.

Sabrina was smiling broadly as she approached Bethany.

"Is it true, the fraternities are going to step? I've never seen it done before and I don't want to miss it."

"That's the word," Bethany said. Today, she was wearing a navy blue pantsuit, navy leather boots, and a lined blue suede jacket. "You're in for a treat," she said. "The Q's and the Sigmas have a running feud on this campus; it's bound to be exciting. We can grab a hot dog and a Coke from the cafeteria and head on over to the set."

"Okay!" Sabrina readily agreed.

The two women turned around and began walking in the direction Sabrina had come.

"My dad told me he's in love with you," Sabrina said suddenly.

Bethany's practiced composure stood her in good stead this afternoon. Her facial expression didn't change one iota, though her heart had begun racing. *Colin told his daughter he loves me.* That was a huge step. One she and Colin hadn't discussed. But, she supposed, they could not be in sync all the time.

Bethany chose the middle ground. Acknowledgment, but no declarations of intent.

"Your dad's a wonderful man."

Sabrina, however, didn't want to beat around the bush. "Does that mean you love him, too? I've got to know, Bethany. You don't know what I've been through with my parents. I was fourteen when Mom left. I'd never heard my father cry before that. I've never seen him cry, because he only did it late at night when he thought I was asleep. But I now know that he can be hurt. Before that, I imagined he was superhuman, you know? Nothing could beat my daddy down. Yet one little philandering woman did."

Bethany's expression must have shown her surprise at Sabrina's reference to her mother because Sabrina laughed. "I was mad at her for a long time."

"I'm sure you were," Bethany said sympathetically. The two were standing facing each other, Bethany with concern written all over her face, her cool pose forgotten.

"I've observed you with your mother, at your father's

memorial service and at the barbecue," Sabrina stated, her voice flat. "You've probably never been truly disappointed in her, have you?"

Bethany shook her head in the negative. She realized this seventeen-year-old had had to grow up fast because of her parents' divorce. She'd had to learn to rely on her own instincts. She'd been forced to form her own idea of what kind of woman she wanted to become when her mother had proved to be an unreliable role model.

"Daddy thinks I was mad at her for leaving us," Sabrina went on. "That was only part of it. The other was the fact that she was the one who set the example I would follow when deciding how to behave as a *woman* in this world. Will I ever have a lasting relationship after my mother broke her marriage vows and, because of that, tore our family apart? It took me years to come to the conclusion that I don't have to follow in her footsteps just because I have her genes. Daddy tried to drum that into my head, but I had to come to the realization on my own."

"You're mature beyond your years," Bethany said with a note of awe in her voice.

She'd fancied herself advanced for her age when she was seventeen, but Sabrina surpassed her in so many ways. She realized, now, that her parents had provided a buffer between her and the world. Her first truly rude awakening had been Adam Malveaux.

Sabrina began walking again, and Bethany fell into step beside her. "I'm fine now," Sabrina said with a happy sigh. "All the acrimony where my mom is concerned is out of my system. Which brings us back to Daddy. He's my major concern these days. Will he be all right once I'm gone?"

Bethany grasped Sabrina by the arm. Sabrina paused and turned to face her. "The answer is yes, Sabrina. I do love your father, and I would never do anything to intentionally hurt him."

Bethany was astonished when tears appeared in Sabrina's eyes. She had to abruptly drop her briefcase to the sidewalk when Sabrina impulsively threw her arms around her neck and hugged her tightly.

Letting go of her, Sabrina said, "You don't know how relieved I am to hear you return his feelings. I'd hate to see my old man look like a chump!"

They both laughed at that.

"You're worrying unnecessarily, Sabrina. Your father is one of the most capable men I've ever known."

Sabrina sniffed and they continued their trek across campus. "I know he's got it going on upstairs, but that doesn't stop me from worrying about him. We've been through a lot together, and until I see him happily married, which I think is his preferred state, I'll keep worrying. He's an absolute loser when it comes to dating. I could tell you horror stories about his early attempts at dating after Mom left."

Colin had already told Bethany about some of the embarrassing episodes. She'd shared her dating mishaps with him, too. "We both have horror stories," she told Sabrina.

"See?" Sabrina cried. "You two are a perfect match."

Bethany laughed. She truly liked Colin's daughter.

As they neared the "set," which was what the student body had designated the area in front of the main cafeteria, they became a part of the crowd that had gathered at short notice when the news spread across campus that the frats were getting ready to step. Students, instructors, and support personnel alike bundled themselves in jackets and coats and spilled out of their respective buildings to witness the time-honored tradition of a challenge being accepted and summarily dealt with.

The crowd formed a circle around the two sets of opponents. Phi Beta Sigma's—The Sigmas—colors were royal blue and white. The six young men who represented them were of various heights and weights and wore royal blue T-shirts with their Greek letters printed in white on the front. Omega Psi Phi's—the Q-Doggs—colors were purple and gold. They were also displaying their colors. *All* the fellas stepping wore either black or blue jeans and black combat boots. Hence the sound of their stomping was formidable.

No one truly knows where stepping originated, but most agree it had its origins in the Motherland. It had evolved over the decades from dance routines reminiscent of those of the boy groups like the Temptations to something more sophisticated.

Bethany saw step-offs as a combination of chants, taunts, rapping, dancing, and stomping with the purpose of putting the competition to shame. The beat of the music, along with the precision of the young men's bodies were a sight to behold. No wonder so many females stood on the sidelines gawking at them as if they were hip-hop stars.

Music blasted from hastily set-up speakers. Each group had their own prerecorded musical score to which they chanted, while simultaneously going through an energetic, rhythmic dance routine. Their rap was usually about how much better they were than the other group.

The noise level was so high, Bethany had to lean close to Sabrina's ear to say, "I'll go get the hot dogs and Cokes. You stay and enjoy the show."

Sabrina nodded her thanks and turned her eyes, once again, on the Q at the end of his line. He was tall and fine and had the most gorgeous brown eyes she'd ever seen.

Bethany *would* have the misfortune to run into John Alden, president of Baylor, when she went to the register to pay for the hot dogs and drinks. John was there paying for a cup of coffee. John had been one of her father's best friends, and since his death had let Bethany know that he considered it his sacred duty to watch out for his friend's only child. Of average height, rotund, and bespectacled, John resembled a black Santa Claus with his beard and penchant for wearing suspenders, which only emphasized his girth. In private, he called Bethany, Beth. However when in the presence of others he referred to her as Dr. Porter.

"Dr. Porter! How advantageous to bump into you like this. There's something you and I need to talk about." He paid for his coffee and stepped aside while Bethany paid for her foodstuffs and tried to balance it all in her right hand while holding on to her briefcase with her left. John reached for the cardboard drink caddy that had four spaces for drinks. "Here, let me take that." He placed his coffee in one of the spaces for drinks and he and Bethany exited the cafeteria, which was busy, as usual, this time of day.

As they walked down the front steps, with the set directly ahead of them, John said, "Something interesting came across my desk recently. In fact, I believe my staff must have postponed giving it to me because today's date and the date on the letter are three weeks apart. My staff likes you, Bethany. Whereas they're not particularly fond of the complainant."

When he said that, Bethany knew Lourdes had made good on her threat. Once they had descended the steps leading from the cafeteria, Bethany turned to John. "What exactly did the complainant have to say?"

The creases in John's forehead wrinkled more as he considered his reply. "It states that you're romantically involved with a student, Bethany. Now, knowing you, I know it isn't true—"

"But it is, John," Bethany interrupted him. She nodded in the direction of the step competition. Sabrina was where she'd left her although, in Bethany's absence, she'd been joined by her father. "The man I'm involved with is standing right over there. Come meet him."

She knew John would not refuse her request since he probably thought it his place, as her father's crony, to check out whomever she was dating. "I'd be happy to," John told her cautiously. He'd been thrown a bit when she'd so easily admitted the charges against her were true, if not wholly well-founded. He'd have to wait and see.

"Here you are, Sabrina," Bethany said, handing Sabrina a hot dog while John held out the drink caddy from which Sabrina could choose a Coke. "Have you met our president, Dr. John Alden?"

Sabrina smiled warmly at John. "Yes, we met at the freshman mixer. Good to see you again, sir." She motioned to her father with a tip of her head. "This is my father, Colin Armstrong. He's a student here, too."

Colin shook John's hand. "I missed the freshman mixer," he joked. "I didn't want to cramp my daughter's style."

John laughed. "Indeed. I have a granddaughter Sabrina's age, so I know what you mean. She once asked me if they had cars when I was a child or if everyone rode horses."

"Did they?" Sabrina asked, all innocence.

John threw back his white head and roared with laughter. "Actually, I had a roan I was quite fond of when I was a boy. But yes, cars had been invented. Although my family didn't buy one until I was in my first year of school here."

"Oh, well, now you've got her started," Colin warned lightly.

Sabrina and John began a lively discussion on horses.

Bethany took the opportunity to pull Colin aside. Her hand was on his arm. "John told me Lourdes has formally lodged a complaint against me."

Colin frowned deeply. "Obviously, my threat didn't work."

"What threat?" Bethany asked, leaning in so she could hear him better over the roar of the music and the step-off in the background.

"I told her if she tried to ruin you, I would see that she went down, too."

With her head tilted upward, Bethany smiled lovingly at him. "I don't care if I lose my job, as long as I have you."

Colin was preparing to say something when they heard a man clear his throat loudly. John stepped around Colin. "I lost her when a young Omega asked her what her name was," he said of Sabrina.

Colin looked around for Sabrina and spotted her laughing delightedly at something a tall boy in a pair of low-slung jeans had said. Didn't the Q's have reputations as ladies' men? Gabriel was one, so the rumors were probably true!

John grasped his arm. "Don't worry, I know the young man. He's a gentleman." When Colin turned to face him, John continued. "I couldn't help overhearing your conversation. It's true then, you and Dr. Porter have . . . an understanding?"

"I love her very much," Colin was not shy about proclaiming.

"Then marry her," John suggested, as though it were the next logical step.

"John!" Bethany hotly protested.

John raised a hand to silence her. "Now, listen to me, Bethany. You're in an untenable situation. You should not be involved with one of your students." He glanced up at Colin. "Young man, I don't mean to be rude, but you look older than the teacher."

"By five years," Colin said.

John shook his head. "Yes, yes. All right. Bethany, this looks bad from an ethical point of view. There is nothing improper about you two dating. The problem comes in whether or not you can judge his work with the same clarity and discrimination as you do the rest of your students. I believe you can, but if this goes any further, I will not be on the tribunal that will determine your fate at this school." He looked up at Colin. "What grade are you earning in Bethany's literature class?"

"So far I have ninety-six percent out of the possible one-hundred percentage points."

"I assure you, he earned them, John," Bethany spoke up.

John ignored Bethany's comments for the time being. He was thinking. "And what sort of grades are you making in your other classes?"

"I have A's in those classes too, sir," Colin respectfully said. He'd burned the midnight oil, challenging himself to eclipse his own expectations. Could a spiteful woman reduce his efforts to ashes? He wouldn't let her!

"That's excellent," John told them. His brown face lit up in a smile when he regarded Bethany. "I knew you weren't guilty of anything, Bethany. We all know Lourdes has been acting out lately. But she's a part of the family and, as you know, you can't have all sane, loving family members. There have to be a few nuts in the bunch. I will have a nice, long chat with Lourdes. I hope she'll see reason. If not, I may have to pull out the file full of complaints staff members have filed against *her*. What I'll do about this is sweep it under the rug for the time being much like my staff tried, but failed, to do. In the meantime, I hope to be invited to your and Colin's wedding in the near future. You know I'm an ordained minister. I could marry you here in the chapel. Your father would have liked that. What do you say?"

Bethany nor Colin didn't "say" anything. Bethany stepped forward and gratefully kissed John on the cheek, and Colin pumped the poor man's hand until John thought it might fall off.

Thursday, February 14, 2002.

"Now you see why most people get married in the spring," Corrine commented as she adeptly fastened the cloth-covered buttons that ran the length of the back of Bethany's wedding dress. They were in the dressing room of a little church in the woods. Outside, the world was covered in a snowy mantle.

Corrine was nervous. More so than her supremely together daughter. Bethany thanked her mother for buttoning her dress and moved away to go stand in front of the full-length mirror. She was not wearing a veil. Her hair was up on her head in a simple French twist, and she had a sprig of baby's breath behind her right ear. Pearl stud earrings were in her ears and she'd kept her make-up to a minimum. The dress was champagne-colored and made of a matte satin. It had a scoop neck and its hem fell an inch above her knees. Satin pumps in the same shade completed her ensemble. She looked cool, calm, collected, and sophisticated.

The door opened and Kiana and Deborah strode in. Both women wore simple short dresses, Kiana in a pale blue and Deborah in a pale green. Sabrina was serving as the third

bridesmaid in the intimate wedding. Bethany had spied
Marcus Jackson, the Que Sabrina had taken a liking to earlier when she was entering the chapel, and figured Sabrina
was somewhere with him. Kiana had not lost all of the baby
weight after giving birth to Kevin three months prior. A
few extra pounds were not going to stop her from being a
part of Bethany and Colin's big day, though!

She went to Bethany and pressed her face against hers.
"I always knew you'd make a lovely bride."

"Thank you, sweetie," Bethany said. "Who has Kevin?"

"Oh, Mrs. Rutland came to the house to sit with him."

Bethany's eyes sparkled at the mention of Kevin. She
loved holding him to her chest, and inhaling the fragrant
newness of his skin. He was like a miniature Gabriel. His
skin was his mother's golden brown but you could tell by
the tips of his ears that he would eventually be as dark-
skinned as his father. "I admit it," Bethany said to Kiana,
"I envy you."

"Well, like I told you," Kiana cracked, "you're welcome
to baby-sit the little rugrat anytime the mood hits. But don't
come running to me when he fills his diaper with something
you would swear is toxic waste."

"Besides," Deborah put in, "your belly is going to be
round as a basketball soon, and we'll be dragging *you* down
the street on our morning walks laughing at you while you
pull the seat of your leggings out of the crack in your butt."

"Don't get vulgar," Corrine admonished, chuckling herself.

"Mama," Bethany said, "remember the night I met
Colin?"

Corrine laughed. She'd used much worse language that
night. Leave it to your children to make note or store in
their memory, and remind you of your foibles in your old
age.

She went to Bethany and kissed her cheek. "My job is
done here. I'm going out to schmooze with the guests until
it's time to walk you down the aisle." In her father's absence, her mother was going to do the honors.

Later, as her mother escorted her down the aisle during the candlelit ceremony, Bethany looked into the faces of all the people she loved. They had braved inclement weather to be there, and there was not a sourpuss in the building. Their love shone in their eyes, and she was struck by how blessed she truly was to have such people in her life.

Then she arrived at the spot where Colin was waiting, and everything else receded in the background. Colin was beautiful in a black tux, a white rosebud as his boutonniere. Their eyes met and she was crying at once. John Alden started talking quickly, afraid the bride would dissolve into tears before he could pronounce them man and wife. Colin held on to her hand the whole while.

When the minister got to the part where he asked if anyone present had an objection to this union, it was so silent in the church, you could hear a pin drop. Everyone turned to look at Lourdes, sitting in the back. "I certainly don't have any objections," she said. To which the assemblage laughed.

John cleared his throat and finished the ceremony: "Do you, Bethany Porter, take this man, Colin Armstrong, to be your lawfully wedded husband? Do you promise to honor, love and cherish only him as long as you both shall live?"

"I do!" Bethany emphatically said.

"Do you, Colin Armstrong, take this woman, Bethany Porter, to be your lawfully wedded wife? Do you promise to honor, love, and cherish only her for as long as you both shall live?"

"I do!" Colin cried.

"Then with the power invested in me by the sovereign state of Connecticut and by God above, I now pronounce you husband and wife. You may kiss the bride."

Whoops of joy rose to the rafters as the guests got to their feet and cheered Colin and Bethany on as they kissed beneath an arch of white roses.

Dear Readers:

Thank you for choosing to read TEACHER'S PET. I hope you enjoyed it.

My next story for BET/Arabesque will be FOR YOUR LOVE. It's Solange and Rupert's tale. The setting will be Ethiopia and it will debut in July 2002.

For those of you who wrote to inquire about Rupert's mysterious background, the answer is yes. His home country, Guyana, will be mentioned in the storyline.

Until next time, keep turning those pages!
Janice

E-mail: Jani569432@aol.com
Web site: http://romantictales.com/janicesims.html